GHOST TOWN

"Is your name Fergus Grimm?" Cole asked.

"I think you know it is," I said.

"I might," Cole said, "but I'm still asking."

The policeman waited patiently. While we waited, more cops came in through the door, and a couple more stood on the porch. That was a lot of cops for Grafton. I finally nodded.

"We're going to take you in as soon as these guys are finished, Mr. Grimm," Cole said. "You don't give anyone a reason not to, and we'll treat you fair. Sound like a deal?"

I nodded again and looked over at Mrs. Cooper. Bile rose in my throat at the acrid scent of gunpowder, at the sight of splintered white bone fragments scattered over the carpet, at the dark blood splattered over the back of the couch.

That person had once served me pancakes.

I looked back at Cole and tightened my jaw. "Did Mrs. Cooper get the same deal?"

A corner of the man's lips curled, slightly. "From what I've seen, no one in this town gets anything but what they have coming for them."

BOOKS BY CHRIS J. CRANFORD

GHOST TOWN

A Grimm Story

CHRIS J. CRANFORD

Forged Iron Press

Acknowledgments:

Evil wins sometimes. From an early age I've seen it, through my life I've watched it, and every now and then I've been beaten by it.

In times like those I've had incredible people around me. Family. Friends. The ride or die types. All of them have kept me standing, when I needed it. Hopefully, at times, I've done the same for them.

Ultimately, that is what this book is about.

Evil wins sometimes. It's up to us to keep the fight going. To stand alone when we must, to help others when we can, and to get back up, always. Evil does win, but good *endures*.

So, with great acknowledgement and love, I want to thank my family and friends. Thanks to my mother, who showed me what it meant to live life selflessly. My dad, who has always given us a place to call home. My brothers and my sisters, who all were there when I needed them. To my close friends, the Fantastic Four of Shakin' Aiken, who have helped me back up time and again.

You have all showed me in life, as in writing, the fight must always go on.

This book would be much different, without you.

CHAPTER ONE

I see ghosts. It's something I've been able to do for a while. Most of the time I have to use an ethereal sense to really see them, but sometimes a spirit is strong enough or has a powerful enough message that it'll come to me.

Like right now.

It was dark out, the kind of night where the moon buried its head deep under a gray blanket of billowing clouds. The kind of night where the only sound was the low thrum of an air-conditioning unit hanging loosely in the window next to me. The kind of night most people found a well-lit place to ride out the gloom.

The hollow moan of an autumn wind wandered around and stirred up flutters of paper. Empty brown bags danced across the parking lot in front of me. A bleak yellow glow hung from a lone streetlight, and slumbering cars hid along the edge of its illumination.

The cold evening air burrowed under my army jacket, the icy chill raised the hair along my arms. The canvas was better at keeping out the rain than keeping in the heat, but I tugged the dark green flaps tighter around me anyway. My breath came out as a light mist, and the air tasted like fresh snow. Winter was too far away for it to be this cold, but tonight the season seemed closer, somehow.

I stood outside an aging motel, at the bottom of a concrete stairwell that led to a second level of rent-by-the-hour units. Above me, a transparent silver-and-blue figure posted itself outside the door to my motel room. A bright glow emanated from the spirit that strangely lit nothing else in the night. I rolled my eyes at the spirit's warning. *Great.*

The ghost had appeared the night before, an old man with the twisted face of someone fighting an ulcer. Tonight, he stood at the railing right before my room, wrapped in a ghostly secondhand suit coat, eyes wide-open. His mouth opened and closed around silent words. I knew he had died right outside the door to my room years ago, the same room he had stayed in decades before, and from then on he had been forever lost in a motel in the middle of nowhere. Nowhere to go, nowhere to be, a silent spirit on the edge of immortality.

Most ghosts helped me with warnings or silent messages. There was some connection we shared I didn't understand because I didn't know why I could see them. Some spirits would warn me away from a place, tell me about a local werewolf on the hunt, or tell me not to eat the fish. I never knew why or when they would talk to me. But when I stopped somewhere, I made it a point to choose a place haunted by a spirit.

One thing about a friendly ghost, it makes a hell of a watchdog.

And tonight the ghost of the traveling salesman had a purpose. A message. I wasn't the greatest lip-reader, but I swore his mouth carefully formed the words *Get out.*

My instinct to run kicked in, a finely honed talent I counted on to keep me alive. I had a fast car, fast legs, and I was willing to use both. Running has saved my life more times than I want to count, and I like to stick to what works.

Something cold touched the base of my neck, like the breath of a corpse, and goosebumps rippled down my arms. That was all I needed to turn toward my car. There was no doubt about it: it was time to go.

My car had company, though. A figure leaned up against the hood of my '68 Camaro, jean jacket open, hands tucked into his front pockets. His smile told me he knew what I was thinking, and his pointed incisors let me know he could keep up with me anywhere I was going to run. Flight was not going to be an option. On the positive side, it looked like whoever was in my room at least wanted me alive. If they had wanted me dead, they wouldn't have set up the trap. Or so I told myself.

I grabbed the cold iron railing and headed up the stairs, navigating old paper cups, broken bottles, and faded scratch-off tickets. The old motel complex must have been built back in the seventies. The light on the wall in front of my room cast a weak yellow halo that fell just short of my door, spotlighting a few fresh cigarette stumps before the threshold. Which told me who I would be dealing with. I looked down longingly at my car, and the guy next to it waved back, still grinning.

The air was eerily empty of the usual nightly sounds and I bowed with the feeling of an ominous pressure, like an invisible hand pushed down on me from the sky. I was sure that air weighed pretty much the same wherever, but tonight it carried a weight.

I pulled out my .38 Smith & Wesson and finger-spun the cylinder, listening to the light ticking of the metal action, checking the rounds before dropping it back into my jacket. It was hammerless, easy to conceal, and easy to use; I could fire it from my pocket if I needed and didn't mind ruining my jacket. Which in a life-or-death situation, I didn't. I was pretty sure whoever was in there knew I was out here. I was also reasonably sure that person would come out here if I didn't go on in.

I've run from a lot of things in my life. It's how I survive. My general rule is to put everything in the rearview mirror and let time sort it all out. Sometimes, though, even the fastest dogs get cornered.

I took a deep breath, then quickly unlocked the door and swung it open. Of course it creaked, a long squeal that stopped only after the door thumped against the wall. My blood pressure skyrocketed, and my blood pounded in my ears. I found my hand in my jacket pocket, squeezing the handle of my gun.

I stepped in.

A man stood inside the door, one of those hulking guard types that are in front of neon clubs. His skin was slabbed and edged in planes that made me think of boulders and golems. Veins ran down his skin like thick, muddy tributaries. His eyes narrowed on me with the watchful attention of a guard dog. He was big enough for me to worry about, but for now, he radiated the measured patience of a hound on a leash.

The room itself was unremarkable. Twin beds with a cheap nightstand between them, a chair and table near the window, an old tube television on a dresser in front of the beds. The bed I'd slept in was still unmade. A standard floral wallpaper matched the faded bedspreads. An old air conditioner rattled underneath the window by the door, and musty air mixed with the smell of a lit cigarette.

Another man sat in the hard square chair next to the beds, wearing a white suit with black pinstripes, a dark black shirt underneath. He was smaller than the muscled man but no less menacing. He rolled a cigarette back and forth in one hand and watched the smoke trail bob from side to side. When I stepped in, the man stopped playing with his cigarette and focused his attention on me.

"Azazel." I kept my hand in my pocket, tight on the handle of the gun. There are plenty of reasons why I'm on the run, but right now Azazel occupied what I called *Problemo Numero Uno*. I kept my face emotionless, but inside my heart rhythmically pumped out an SOS signal.

I would have to focus to make it out of here alive.

"Grimm." The man nodded, bringing his cigarette to his lips for one long draw. The cigarette now perched between his ring finger and his pinky, and smoke leaked from the corners of his mouth. He had short, dark hair that in the right light looked dark red, and he had a square face with a well-manicured Vandyke. "I thought we might chat for a minute."

"That would be a change of pace for us." Azazel had long wanted something I had. I was unwilling to hand that thing over, and that had defined our relationship for the past four years.

Azazel smiled. "Maybe I'm trying something new."

"Yeah, maybe." I raised my eyebrows. "Let's chat about all the things we have in common."

Azazel took another long puff from the cigarette and slowly let out a deliberate stream of smoke. The smell of hot tar flooded the room. "You might be surprised. We have more in common than you'd think."

"It's hard for me to believe I have a lot in common with the devil's top enforcer." I slid slightly inside the room, forming a tight triangle with the bouncer and Azazel. It would be harder to get out of the room, but I didn't like standing in the doorway with Hulk Number Two behind me in the car. I wiggled my free hand back and forth in the air. "You like eating the souls of innocents, I like a hamburger medium, medium-well done. Not sure how that relates."

"There are links, Grimm, in every chain, between each and every being on earth, which bind us all together." Azazel took another puff. His dark eyes glittered behind the smoke. "Do you know, do you have any idea, how long it took me to get Native Americans to grow tobacco? It took me centuries of work. Hundreds upon hundreds of years."

"Is that what we've got in common?" I looked back at the bouncer; he watched me out of tiny hardened eyes, black pebbles of malice. Muscles bulged out of him as if he had flexed his whole body in place from the moment I looked at him. Maybe he was showing me the benefits of isometric exercise, but I doubted it.

"Indians were a tough nut to crack. Just wouldn't smoke tobacco, even though it grew all over the place. Like they knew better. Then I started working on shamans, medicine men, chiefs. I started by calling up a ghost here, a specter there, figures with a few feathers in a headband or two, each time I lit up a pipe." Azazel's arms swung open, dark eyes glistening, face lit up in an eerie fascination. "*Then* the tribes started smoking this weed with a real zest. You have to appreciate the angle. They wouldn't smoke this shit, Grimm. It was all around, and they wouldn't smoke it. Hundreds of years of working on them, and then finally I got them. In the end, man, they ate that shit up." He grinned then, a smile with too many teeth.

"Great." My nerves were taut and vibrating, as though the very fibers could feel a fight coming on. A tremor started in my fingers, bleeding off excess energy. "I'm glad you could pass some history on to me. Maybe next time save yourself the trip and just call."

"My boy," the demon said, brandishing his pearly whites from the abyss of his mouth. Tiny wisps of smoke slithered out from between his teeth. "I'm trying to tell you, when you watch me smoke a cigarette, you watch me appreciate the years of hard work I had to put in, of hundreds of years subverting an entire culture with an addictive poison that is now one of the most successful killers in the world." He took another deep breath of the cigarette and blew all of the smoke back out. The room got a little hazy. "It's an appreciation most don't get when they light a Marlboro. They lack my ... perspective, the *appreciation* of scope, the history of a thing."

The demon went quiet, looking at the smoky threads hanging in the hazy air. His words reminded me of the particular evils Azazel was capable of. The man sipping whiskey in a three-piece suit in front of me could easily be found sauntering out of a trailer park, carrying the corpse of a baby like a briefcase, or whispering to a guy with a rifle in a room above a concert. I shivered and tried to hide it. He was a major demon, one of the highest of the high, and he had had thousands of years to fuck with the human race. This tobacco story was something Azazel likely had done on a whim and likely was the least of the evils the demon had committed on earth.

And what I carried would help him commit evils much greater at a much faster pace across the earth. I steeled myself, knowing what was next. "So now we're to the Key."

Azazel laughed. The demon worked hard to look the part of a human. He grabbed the glass of whiskey and poured it down his throat. His eyes closed for a minute as he pretended to feel the burn, then opened again to focus on me. His other hand bobbed the cigarette and wrote a smoky trail in the air. For a moment I had seen something in his eyes, some blend of malice and glee, something he quickly covered up by intensely focusing on me. The demon's voice thickened. "Yeah. We're at the Key."

CHAPTER TWO

The bouncer moved, growing larger as he started toward me, as if whatever had held him back had been unleashed. Large veins bulged along his arms, and his black shirt stretched until it ripped. The room darkened like the man had blotted out the light.

I pulled out my gun and pointed it at the guard. Azazel grinned and blew another smoke trail out of his mouth. The bouncer halted midstep. The seconds ticked slower and slower in my mind, and the gun weighed a hundred pounds in my hand.

"You ever get tired of running, Grimm?" Azazel held both hands out, gestured at the room. "Look at this dump. It's just like the last hundred places you stayed in. You eat when you can, you stop for a night here or there. ... How many times have you slept in your car? That piece of shit?"

"Hey, now," I said. I was driving one pristine beat-up '68 Camaro with actual working hideaway headlights. "It's a classic."

"I can't really change my pitch to you," Azazel said as he leaned forward. "You know where the two of us stand. I can tell you that this kind of life is hard. It wears on you, and it'll keep wearing on you. You'll get more and more tired, you'll cut more and more corners, and one day, maybe ten years from now, maybe thirty, you'll get tired of it and just give up."

"So the answer is to give you the Key now, and then you let me walk?" I asked. As I understood it, there was one rule to the Key: all a demon needed was to have a human hand it to him. "Are we in the movies now? Is that guy your cameraman?"

"I won't try to convince you," Azazel said. "But I've seen this before. Do you think this is the first time I've chased the Key? The first time I've come within inches of having it in my grasp? I've been on this chase for thousands of years. I usually end up killing the Keeper just to see if the next one is easier." The demon rolled his eyes. "Each one of you always wears down. Each of you always *has* to stop somewhere. You *have* to have an escape. Maybe sleep in a good bed and have a good meal for a night, maybe talk sports at a bar. Feel human for one moment of your life. Grimm, think about it, did you really need to stop in this rat's nest for *two* nights?"

A cold stone sank in my stomach. It scared me because Azazel was right. I had been tired, tired of sleeping in the car, tired of shitty meals, tired of driving, and driving without stopping anywhere. Last night, I had stopped at this place and had had such a damn good burger that I had decided to stay one more night, to treat myself to that burger one more time. Suddenly I realized how even a mistake that minor might be the end for me. Just one burger, cooked perfectly, cheese melting down the sides, covered with fresh onions, tomatoes, and sweet relish, sizzling and fresh off the grill.

"So, Grimm, how many years do you have left before you make that one fatal mistake?" He sipped his whiskey again and looked through me, relaxed, one finger tapping the edge of his glass. His dark irises grew larger, hypnotic. "Or have you already made it?"

My arm was getting tired. I straightened it and kept my gun pointed at the guard. "If we're going to do this, Az, then let's get started." The bouncer sneered at the little .38. I shrugged. It wasn't a Colt Peacemaker, but it got the job done.

"What's the rush?" One corner of Azazel's mouth crept up in a crooked smile, like he was placing the final nail in my coffin. "I was just getting to the interesting part. You ever lie awake and wonder who you are, Grimm? You ever lie in bed at night and wonder why you can do what you do?"

I couldn't help it, I pulled my finger away from the trigger and cocked my head at the demon. He had me balanced between starting a fight and wanting to learn more. I knew nothing about myself. One day I had been an orphan, living in an old man's house with other orphans. We grew together as all castaways would. Maybe as close as a real family, we had hung everywhere together, played ball. Then I had seen my first ghost. And then everything changed, and I had run away.

I had been running ever since. Across the earth. And though not many ghosts speak to me, I had discovered there are plenty of terrifying reasons not to listen, when they do. No ghost had a happy tale. And nothing undead had been able to tell me anything about myself. Why I could do what I could do, who my parents were, why I was alone—I knew none of that.

But Azazel apparently did.

I was a loner for a reason—anyone I cared about could get hurt by what followed me. Of course I wanted to know why I could see ghosts. And certainly tonight, trapped in this motel room, I wondered why I carried the Key. If anything could change my focus, it was the idea of knowing for certain of all the people on earth, why me?

Tonight the demon felt ... different. He had held his best pitch for the end, but I struggled to see the point of it. Did I want to know what he knew? Absolutely. Was that enough for me to hand Azazel the Key?

I put my finger back on the trigger of the .38. Not tonight.

I was in a bad spot for a fight. Azazel had picked a good location, somewhere isolated where I wouldn't have full use of my abilities. Among my assets were a single ghost and my gun. Plus my wits, which Azazel had proved were in short supply.

Azazel flicked his cigarette and winked. He felt he had hooked me. His hand held the cigarette like a paintbrush, the smoke trail hanging in the air as the demon drew until I recognized a stick figure of myself. If I squinted, I could see where tiny blobs of smoke made it look like my feet were running.

A concrete block of a fist collided with my chest. The force of the blow tossed me back into the room until I tumbled backward over the far bed. The earth golem had moved.

I scrambled to my knees. My hands were empty. I had lost my gun. Pain clawed out from my chest as I tried to draw a deep breath. The golem plodded in.

I ran a lot, but when it came to a fight, I was all in. There was some-thing in the *it's him or me* in a fight that energized me. If this room was going to be the end for me, I was going to make it cost.

I stumbled up from my knees, swaying a bit. I took a long, deep breath, ignoring the pain in my chest. A warm liquid ran down the side of my head, and I made myself believe it was sweat. The golem stepped forward, boulder fists in front of his body, looking back at Azazel and nodding. Just once, I wanted to meet someone with a bodyguard the size of a ten-year-old Girl Scout.

Reaching out, I grabbed some ghost.

That was what I called what I did, grabbing ghost. Ghosts were part of an ethereal plane of energy, and I could tap into that energy through the ghost. What I siphoned through them made me stronger, quicker. The energy mended broken skin and hardened bones. I drank in raw, unworldly force and grinned at the bouncer. He was about to check into whatever kind of hospital they had in hell.

Little trails of blue and white wisps hung in the air between the ghostly salesman and me. The specter faded as I pulled more energy from it. Time around me slowed down. The bouncer began to swing another fist, moving like the golem was deep underwater, his hand slowing as it descended through the air.

I ducked under the arm, grabbed his wrist, and twisted with newfound strength. A deafening pop, like a shotgun blast, filled the room and his arm suddenly dangled from its socket. The golem screamed, a rumbling roar, and I shot the palm of my hand up his chest and struck his chin. There was a considerable crack and a squirt of brown blood as his jaw snapped shut on his tongue. The golem's head swung back, and the colossus fell away from me with a loud thump. The motel room shud-dered briefly, as though a young elephant had fallen down some stairs.

I took a breath. One down, one to—

Azazel slammed into me, driving me back into the wall with a crunch of old plaster. In slow motion, an unremarkable print of a bucolic land-scape teetered and then fell, the frame falling apart as it hit the wall.

The demon's forearm dug into my chest, and studs gave way and broke behind me. I pounded his arm, trying to get the demon to release me, but the arm pressed harder and harder against my chest. My ribs cracked, then healed with ethereal energy, then cracked again, a painful tug-of-war that lasted milliseconds but felt like a lifetime.

A clawed hand headed for my skull. I caught it at the last second. Dust flowed out from the smashed wall behind me, I shook my head to try to see through it. Azazel remained pressed against me, hand locked on to my arm, staring with eyes twisting wildly in their sockets. His nostrils flared wide with strain, though his hair remained perfectly in place.

I pulled more of the ghost, trying to throttle how much I used but still take enough to survive. My ribs healed one last time, and I could finally turn my chest enough to get Azazel's arm to slip past a little, still pinning me to the wall. I felt the ghost weaken through the tether. Some spirits seemed to be able to funnel more power than others, and this one was limited. So was my time.

"Azazel," I grunted, "we can keep this up and destroy some shit, but it's not going to get you any closer to the Key."

"Bullshit, Grimm," Azazel hissed. His mouth twisted. I could feel his hate, a heat radiating off his skin. He inhaled deeply right by my ear. "I can't see it, but I can sense it. I can smell it on you." His breath smelled of brimstone and burned oak. For a crazy moment, I wondered why demons needed to breathe. "Give me the Key and I'll let you live."

"That's a tough line for me to buy." I grunted and struggled to push his arm aside with one hand and tried to move his other arm at the same time. Stalemate.

"It would behoove you to give me what I want," Azazel rasped from deep in his throat. His eyes had stopped twisting and had settled to a slight vibration, side to side, over and over. Fucking demons and their weird-ass eyes.

I felt the old ghost I was pulling from start to shimmer, a kind of fade that let me know I had taken too much out of it too fast. It seemed Azazel could feel the ghost weaken as well. He turned his head slightly to look in that direction, though I wasn't sure he could see spirits at all. Or maybe he was sending for his second elephant of a bodyguard.

I was going to have to make a move soon or find something else around to pull from, and since there was no other spirit around, things were beginning to look grim. "You know how the saying goes, Az. I only behoove unto others as they would behoove unto me."

Azazel cracked his grin of perfectly packed teeth. "Funny, funny, funny, Grimm."

I took that moment to snap my head forward and split his nose with the crown of my skull. My head exploded with pain, but the crack stunned the demon, so I head-butted him again. He swore. A sharp headache split across my temple. His grip slipped down me, so I slammed my head forward one last time.

His grip loosened further, one hand reaching for his nose and the fountain of black demon blood that poured over us both. I pushed Azazel hard, and he tumbled backward over the bed while I fell to my knees on the floor. For once luck was with me, and my hand landed right on my gun. I grabbed it and, as Azazel pulled himself up, fired a few shots into his chest.

He recoiled with a piercing scream, a sound like hundreds of voices shrieking in his throat. Demons aren't hurt by regular bullets or even silver bullets, but dip some lead into holy water and now you're talking.

I emptied round after round into the demon and Azazel simply flipped over the other side of the twin bed as tufts of old feathers floated in the air. I took a deep breath, then got up from my knees. The golem moaned in front of me, so I gave him a hard rap to the temple with the handle of the Smith & Wesson. *Nighty-night, big man. Dream of big biceps and a new tongue.*

I wanted to take some more ghost to heal myself, but since the specter was fading I let him go. Letting go feels something like releasing the tension in a taut rubber band. Immediately pain swept over me, sharp pains, and burning aches that the ghostly energy had helped me to ignore during the fight. The fights had lasted for less than a minute, but I was bruised and battered and my heart still hammered. My fingers shook as I pulled a few rounds out of my jacket pocket to reload my gun with.

I needn't have bothered. Azazel was nowhere to be seen, leaving behind a burnt figurelike shape on the floor. I had seen it before and knew I had hurt him, but I also knew I'd see the demon again. This fight was just part of the dance.

I looked over at the spirit, still outside the door. It appeared washed out to me now, more transparent. I had no idea what pulling ethereal energy did to them. Even if I asked, they could never answer. Pulling their energy made me feel a little like a thief, and I wasn't sure how to go about apologizing. I figured viewing their memories was the price I had to pay for what I borrowed.

The specter stood still, rooted in his spot. One hand constantly rubbed the top of his belly. I looked back into the room. A strip of wallpaper faintly fluttered by a hole in the wall, and the earth golem remained on the floor. Beside me the charcoal outline of Azazel mocked me. I was sure I was forgetting something....

The vampire slammed into my back, driving me into the edge of the door. The two of us bounced back, and I quickly slid underneath the vamp's grasp and made sure my neck stayed away from his teeth. The two of us wrestled and stumbled out onto the passageway. I couldn't get a grip on him. He was all over me, and a couple of steps later we both fell over the railing.

A few seconds of empty air passed, and I hit the top of a car, punching the roof in with a metallic crunch. I grunted back a scream as the impact wrenched my shoulder from its socket. For the second time that night I lost my gun. It skittered across the pavement. I wondered if I should maybe slap some rope or glue or something on the pistol.

The vampire hit the pavement beside the car with a wet thwack and lay there, moving around slowly. My body felt stuck inside the dent of the car roof, and I was having trouble finding the energy to pull myself out. The vampire shook his head a bit and moved around on the ground, even while I struggled to move. Getting to our feet became a kind of slow-motion race. He got to his knees as I rolled off the roof, holding on to the car with my good arm. My other arm hung there, and for a moment I let the car hold me up.

The vampire's steps on the pavement warned me. I ducked. His fist burst through the car window instead of my skull. The slight rocking of the car knocked me on my ass. I looked up, past the bouncer, at what was left of the ghost, knowing I would have to pull more of the spirit to survive, and yet not wanting to live more of that guy's life.

The vampire kicked me a couple of times and peered down at me. A nasty grin split his face, sharp incisors nestled in grayish, rotted teeth. I looked away from the smile. What vampire didn't take care of his teeth?

There was really no choice. So I pulled.

The last faint traces of energy left the specter in long, glistening lines of blue and white. Time slowed, and the bouncer leisurely slid his arm from the splintered window. Bits of glass hung in the air, menacing multi-shaped stars sparkling in the faded motel light. The ghost disappeared as I felt the energy hit me, and for a second I lived him...

Then I was sitting on a stool. Well, not me-me, but him-me. A felt hat sat next to a whiskey on the bar in front of me. I knocked the drink back. It was a cheap, raw whiskey and burned all the way down. Something gave in my stomach, and a slow, fiery ache crept its way back up my throat. I motioned for another, and the bartender shook his head. He still kept pouring, though.

"Ready, baby?" An older woman spoke on my right. Her face was lined with the trails of a rough life, and her hair smelled like smoke, sex, and cheap hair spray. Her jacket was open enough for me to see a lace bra peeking out from between two white fleshy mounds. I nodded, knocked back the next whiskey, and followed her out of the motel bar. She carried a bottle in her hand, looking back like we had done this before. My hand kept reaching down to my stomach. The burning there kept getting worse and worse, and I kept thinking the next drink would quiet it down, bury the pain along with the thoughts of my family.

We walked up the stairs together. The woman's hips swayed in the timeless motion that women had, and I hurried behind her to my room. I was tired of the trip and lonely. My bed wasn't too far away. My family was.

Inside the room she undressed quickly, revealing pale, lumpy skin in too-tight panties and bra. I complained about my stomach, and she laughed and opened up my shirt and kissed it some. The burning hit the back of my throat, and with disgust, I felt myself stir when her hand reached my pants. I grew excited as she pressed her face against my zipper, one hand undoing my belt. Then the pain in my stomach got worse, and I pushed the woman away even as she laughed some more and tried to pull me back and ...

... then I saw my wife, sitting in the chair we had first bought together, reading one of her Little House on the Prairie books, a tiny light on behind her. I had seen her like this a hundred times, each time I got home. She looked up with the smile I had fallen in love with. The smile I traveled thousands of miles to provide for. The smile I had accepted worse and

worse commissions to provide for, the son and the medical bills, and the gas price hike, and here I was, hundreds of miles away and just wanting to be close to anyone if I couldn't be with the one I loved ...

... and the hooker yanked me back to the present, drawing my belt out and tugging my pants down, laughing the drunken laugh of someone who has no idea what is going on.

And then I burped, something loud and stale and smelling like old meat. And right after that, my heart gave out....

Back in the parking lot, I got to my knees, shaking my head to clear it. Trying to stop my hand from grabbing my own stomach. Trying to reverse an erection. Sometimes the visions overwhelmed me and I would have no idea where I was until long minutes had passed. I couldn't afford that time now.

I hated this shit.

But I was back in the real world, with power. My ribs fitted together again like a pencil broken in the middle. At the same time, my shoulder pulled into its socket with a booming crack.

Time sped up. The vampire finished pulling his hand from the window and pivoted back around. Bits of glass scattered over the parking lot with a tinkling sound.

I swung a fist into the side of his knee, felt the joint give. The vampire roared and fell to his remaining knee, which still put him a foot taller than me. I took another swing with my fist, amplified with what energy was left of the ghost, and I felt his skull give a little when I connected. I could feel my knuckles burst, one at a time, and immediately heal themselves in tiny pops of pain.

The vampire toppled to his side, blood running out of his ear onto the pavement. I kicked him a couple more times in the head with my steel-toed boots, which were really silver-toed. When he finally stopped moving, I gave him a final kick to make sure.

At that moment the last of the ghost's energy left me, and the pain flooded in again. I clenched my teeth as my right leg throbbed and bruises spotted my body. The pain was significant enough that for a moment the motel lights went hazy, and little colored lights danced in my vision.

I gingerly moved around. My shoulder was tender but together. My chest ached a little less, and nothing jabbed out from my rib cage. The knuckles of my left hand tightened with swelling. Feeling a little wobbly, I took a few steps back from the fight and looked at the car I had fallen on.

Of course … it had to be mine. I sighed. My Camaro now sported a man-sized dent in its roof and a shattered driver's window. I worked my keys out of my pocket, staggered around to the back of the car, and opened the trunk. I grabbed my duffel bag and pulled my shotgun out. It was a Benelli M3, black and short without its stock. A cross had been scratched into the dark metal above its trigger, from the gun's owner prior to me. I wasn't that big a believer.

While I was doing all that I kept glancing between the bouncer on the pavement and up at the open door of my room. A few faces poked behind curtains in other rooms, but nothing undead was moving, and the vampire was still sleeping the silver-toed sleep of the dead. Or maybe was dead.

The Benelli would even any odds if anyone felt like popping back up. I had the switch to pump-action, but I could select semi-auto and one-hand it if I needed to. I wasn't looking for accuracy, but for speed and widespread damage. It was good for both. The buckshot was silver and also dipped in holy water. It worked great against demons and vampires and undead alike. What it didn't kill, it sure as hell would hurt.

When I can, I like to use tools that vary in application.

I shut the trunk and leaned on the back of the car, and the old springs in the suspension gave a little with a rusty squeal. There wasn't any movement from inside the motel, but I tended to stay in places where people minded their own business. The night air still pressed down on me, and it was still too quiet. It was one of those calm-before-the-storm moments. There was a feeling of something going on that I hadn't quite figured out.

I didn't know where Azazel was, but I hoped he was in a lot of pain. I had never killed a demon, but I was okay with leaving them as burned outlines in carpets. I snorted and grabbed my ribs at a burst of pain. *That damn burger.* I couldn't afford to make a mistake like that again. If staying an extra day somewhere for a burger led to tonight, would I even be aware of my second mistake?

Azazel had mentioned killing other Keepers. I had been given the Key by a dying man. He hadn't had a lot of time to pass on any extra information, the history of the thing. But I had kept the Key because if anyone was made to run from a demon, it was me.

I pulled the Key out from where it hung next to a locket on a silver chain. The Key was a bronze disc that looked vaguely old Egyptian. It was weighty without being heavy, all metal and pounded flat edges. Three concentric circles surrounded a small hole in its center, with many cuneiform drawings carved around each ring. Each circular section of the disc could rotate in a way that the pictures inside each circle made patterns across the entire disc so that when all three circles were rotated into certain configurations a different figure would be revealed.

I believed the Key held seven such figures in its puzzle, each made up of 216 different lines that forming the smaller cuneiform drawings. An ancient Rubik's Cube, inscribed with seven names of powerful demons that were interred in limbo back in Solomon's day. Every jail cell had a key, and the best Solomon seemed to be able to do was lock his key behind a puzzle, scrambling the inscriptions to keep the demons from ever being called back onto earth.

I wondered who had made it. And why.

The Key was entrusted to me. It wasn't too long after being given the Key that Azazel appeared. Apparently a fringe benefit of finding an artifact of great power was that demons suddenly wanted to socialize. Azazel wanted his brothers-in-arms back so they could continue their ruination of souls on earth, and the Key was the first step in his plan. Keeping it away from him was mine.

I'm not the best-intentioned guy, or even that religious, but I could puzzle out what would happen to humans in a world ruled by demons. I would never give Azazel the Key. And it seemed like demons could sense me carrying it, the way a compass senses true north. Maybe bearing the Key was a test from Solomon. As long as I carried the Key, demons would sense it. If I set it down, someone else could find it and happily trade it for a favor from a demon. The only way to keep the Key safe was to take it with me, and run. It's what I did anyway. I ran, and on the occasions where Azazel caught up to me, well, things like tonight happened.

Part of him told the truth tonight, though, when he talked about the grind. I worried about how long I could keep this chase going. It was draining, and at some point, I would make another mistake. I was alone all the time, and I could see where I was starting to lose the edge I'd had at the beginning of all this.

I was tired. One look in the back of my car, where a blanket was twisted among fast-food wrappers and empty wax cups, revealed to anyone the kind of life I lived.

I took a deep breath and tried to clear the ringing from inside my head, a ringing that usually came from head-butting a demon one too many times. I carefully walked over and picked my pistol up from the parking lot, slipping the Key back inside my shirt as I walked, feeling the silver chain snug up against the back of my neck.

It dawned on me that the ringing I was hearing was an actual phone ringing. A pay phone sat crookedly in the back of the parking lot, near the road. The dirty plastic of the booth was lit by the faded yellow light of the old hotel sign, and from here I could see the receiver of the phone tremble as it rang. The booth with its halo of light seemed like something straight from a cheap horror flick. It was an old model you don't see anymore, blue-paneled with a sliding folded door.

The ringing of the phone pulled at me like a riptide from the beach. A wrong feeling hung in the air, and yet I still found myself walking toward the booth. I opened the door and got in, noticing the years and years of scrawled names and numbers.

The phone rang again. I still felt uneasy about answering it. Nothing good came from answering the phone on a night like tonight. But the riptide had caught me.

"Hell with it," I said aloud.

The ring cut off with the tick of an old plastic receiver being lifted from its cradle. I listened to the receiver, but the phone was silent. An ominous quiet vibrated against my ear as lines crossed over telephone poles and switchboards until a small *click* let me know the lines had connected.

"Hello," I said.

"Gus ..." Her voice was throaty, raspy. "I'm in trouble."

I knew the voice, even though I had last heard it ten years ago. A group of friends. A small town. The raw tone reached through all those wires across all that distance and latched deep into me. Something I had missed without knowing how bad I had missed it. I gripped the phone tighter in my hand. "Jen?"

"Gus, I need you."

My chest tightened. I found it difficult to breathe. Static broke in and out of the connection.

"Jen ... how are you calling me here?" I stared at the phone with disbelief, looked past the phone through the dirty plastic to the motel, the bouncer in the parking lot, the open door to my room. "I mean, Jen, I just—"

Static broke through the line and I thought I'd lost her. There were a few words I couldn't quite make out, and then Jen said, "Can you come?"

"I don't know what I could do."

It was an excuse, and she called me on it. "We both know what you can do."

The silence after that was telling. I had left Grafton the day I found out I could see ghosts, and I had never told Jen. When a person finds out something that changes his life, he can accept it, he can fight it, or he can run. I was still running.

After a long moment, Jen said, "Fergus, Sarah's missing."

Sarah was her little sister and part of our group back then. I let out a long sigh.

"Fergus. If you don't come, she won't make it."

"Jen, I don't know if I can." My mind warned me not to go, but my heart was already in the car. I was terrified of what had happened the day I left. I wasn't sure I could be the person she wanted.

"Gus ..." Jen's voice caught. "My mother ..."

"Jen." A warm feeling tugged free in my chest. A memory of going to the freshman dance together in high school, of seeing her in a dress for the first time. It had been sleek, red, off the shoulders, and seeing her wearing it was like seeing her for the first time. Her eyes had widened with delight when I opened the door and saw her standing there. She had smiled, and her smile, it made me stand a little taller.

But I had left Grafton because of a reason, and that reason was still there. Waiting for me. Maybe I could meet her in the next town, get her a bus ticket or something. "Look, I—"

"Fergus." Jen's voice grew firm, tense. "Stop the bullshit. I need you."

When the only girl you've ever loved tells you that, you start moving heaven, and you let earth know it's next in line. I let out a shaky breath. "I'm on my way."

"Good." Jen sighed, a my-life-depends-on-you kind of breathy, trembling exhalation. There was a sound, like car doors shutting, and Jen's voice grew urgent. "I've got to go."

Voices shouted, faint over the phone line and disappearing with distance. A *tap-tap-tapping* sound repeated from her side of the connection. I realized it was the rapping of the phone receiver against a wall, as if it had been dropped.

"Jen?" I pressed the receiver tight to my ear and listened. The voices grew louder. I could almost make out what they were saying. Static washed in and out of the connection, masking everything. Someone else spoke to another someone. A third came up. There was a shout and another shout after that one. Others in the distance.

The static swelled and all I could hear was shouting and none of the voices sounded like Jen's. Then the phone line burst with static, like a downed power line spitting sparks, and thunder boomed around me. The fresh smell of ozone, like chlorine, poured out of the phone, and I covered the mouthpiece a bit with my hand.

"Jen?" After the thunderous boom, my voice sounded small in the phone booth. Another round of thunder scattered through the night, so suddenly I almost dropped the phone, and the line went dead.

A moment later I was in the Camaro. I burned a little rubber on the way out of the parking lot and headed west. Thick grooved lines ran the length of the pavement and wove out into the night. As I drove the grooves tugged the tires of the car back and forth across the road, no matter how hard I gripped the wheel.

CHAPTER THREE

A classroom, two-thirds full. Middle school. Kids sitting in groups at wooden desks, spread out over the room, a large book open in front of most. Some kids were writing, some weren't. The tick-tack of chalk hitting the chalkboard, a teacher speaking in a monotone voice about something that had happened hundreds of years ago, as if we all knew the past could never affect the future.

Such a normal day, for a world to change.

Partway through the class, the door to the classroom opened. In front of the principal stood a new student. A girl, with straw-colored hair and the serious, studious face of a person searching specifically for one thing. She was tall, with a long blond braid stretching down her back.

Her eyes scanned the room. Then she flashed a bright smile and skipped over to an empty desk next to a young boy who sat by himself, his book closed. The teacher frowned and gave the "harrumph" all teachers do when a promising prospect connects with the prospectless probability.

Then the girl leaned over and whispered something to the boy, and the kid looked at her and grinned.

On the other side of the room, another kid frowned and ground his teeth. His eyes flashed as he stared at the new student, sitting next to one of those orphans. His foot tapped the back of the chair in front of him in a *steady rhythm, and the kid in that chair knew better than to say something.*

Such a normal day, and the world had changed.

I never thought I'd come back.

Those were my first thoughts as I eased the Camaro over a hill overlooking the withered town of Grafton. Tiny houses lay below me, spotted in grays and blacks that resembled old, mottled skin. Streets meandered through the town like varicose veins, swollen in spots, thin in others. Spots of neglect lay everywhere: overgrown grass, shingles hanging from rooftops, pools of trash lying over parts of streets.

Grafton had never been a big town, but it was a survivor. A tire factory and a train line had kept commerce going in an age of interstates and outsourcing. The factory brought employees in, and the rail line was cheap enough to keep the factory there. I'm sure fifty years ago the town was the picture of the American Dream, but now Grafton was a thin shadow of that dream.

The car coasted down the hill, and I felt much the same. I was exhausted; nothing starts a long drive off better than a life-or-death fight with a demon. I needed to rest, but even now my body leaned toward the town like I was a dowsing rod and the town was a large pool of water. The car seemed to slow, like it pushed against some kind of resistance. The pressure in my ears changed, like I was descending in an airplane from a great height.

The rumbling of my car became muffled. The resistance grew greater. I hammered my foot down on the gas and the Camaro lurched forward. Something in the air gave and swallowed me up. The resistance evaporated, like one bubble had absorbed another, and I no longer existed as myself anymore. I had merged with Grafton.

My foot stayed on the accelerator. The car sped down the highway. The town and I now existed in the same world, a fragile world surrounded by a weak, translucent wall. A wall that could burst open under the slightest pressure, releasing Grafton like maggots wriggling out from rancid meat. My stomach flopped uneasily like I leaned way too far over the edge of a cliff.

The tires tugged against little corrections on the road, and a cold brisk wind blew through the broken window of my car. The wind fluttered under the dented roof and generated a metallic thrumming sound. The air was clean and fresh and masked the grime of the town. It was cold for autumn, but the trees still held a few green leaves along the yellows and reds.

I passed the old motel, King's Lodge, at the top of Grafton. It looked abandoned. Windows and doors alongside the inn were boarded, and a darkened lobby hid behind broken plywood and jagged triangles of glass.

I kept the accelerator down. I still imagined the plastic cup of the receiver pressed against my ear.

Fergus. Stop the bullshit. I need you.

Jen knew those words would bring me back. No matter who I had become.

No other traffic passed along the road, no trucks or vans, or kids cruising the strip. I got to the bottom of the hill and drove along the edge of town. My car rocked as it ran over a bunch of pitted potholes in the road with a quick *thump-thump-thump.*

I slowed as the county road ran into Main Street. Houses cropped up to my left and right, turning into buildings and stores. One or two people moved furtively, quickly walking the sidewalks. The old water tower perched at the other end of town, a place I had climbed many times as a kid. The tower was white, with more rust than I remembered, the town's name circling it in big blocky black letters.

The neglect I had noticed on top of the hill was worse close up: paint peeling everywhere, faded signs, stores closed and boarded up, mailboxes with their mouths agape. The few people standing around watched me cautiously from behind windows or doors, and I had the feeling of being in some old western. One where the cowboy rides into town, slowly eyeing the people in the streets, one hand on his gun, not knowing who or what or where the outlaw was.

I let my car drift to a stop by the first intersection on Main Street. The engine idled underneath me and was the only sound for miles. To the left was the town's diner, to the right a gas station and garage, a closed fast-food place behind the garage. Where the teenagers had hung out, back when.

My fingers tightened around the steering wheel. I had seen places like this before from the places I had run through over the past ten years. I hadn't seen a whole town like Grafton, but I had seen a city block, a village, a suburb or two all suffer from the same infestation.

Vampires' nests. There were slight giveaways. No homeless around, not a lot of people walking in daylight. The ones that were out now stayed near the shadows of buildings, and were most likely thralls, people bitten by vampires. Vampire saliva was a rush in small doses, and some thralls would do more and more to get another bite.

The shut-down stores, lawns overgrown, peeling paint—thralls when teased with the gift of immortality immediately stop caring about mundane chores. And their vampires would care even less. Odd how they chose to spend their moments when they have all the time in the world.

The car rumbled low as I pulled past the diner and down Main Street. It had been a decade since I had been to Jen's house, yet I remembered the way like I had driven it yesterday. I made my last turn and saw the Coopers' home: a big white house, white fence, matched blue shutters and trim.

I shut off the car and flipped the sun visor down. Tucked into the band was an old picture of Jen and me. The picture had been folded and bent and was missing a corner. I looked at myself, the cocky smile, the confident set of my shoulders, and wondered where that guy had gone.

I got out of the car and swung the door shut softly. The *thunk* sounded loud on the quiet street. I looked inside the windows as I walked up to the house. The second stair leading up to the porch still squeaked when I stepped on it. I knocked on the door and called out for Mrs. Cooper, and then Jen.

There was no answer. The house had the empty feel of a model home, all decorations and no substance. I peered in the window and didn't see any lights on. The television in the corner of the living room was off. No one appeared, so I knocked harder. After a minute I tried turning the knob and jabbing the door with my shoulder, but the door was solid and the dead bolts were thick.

I left the porch and headed over to the side of the house, where an oak tree stood guard beside a second-story window. It was an old tree with large, gnarly limbs, like a hand burst up from the earth. Back in high school, I had often climbed the tree and dropped on the top of the porch, where I was a few quiet steps from Jen's window.

The oak tree was a little harder to climb now. Funny how things performed as a kid seem harder as you get older. Breathing heavier than I should, and brushing a few leaves from my hair, I dropped loudly on top of the roof. I waited, hearing nothing move around inside. I started to worry, and with that worry, I crept across the porch roof and tapped on Jen's window.

There was no answer. I took a quick look around. The neighborhood, like Jen's house, seemed abandoned. I didn't see any neighbors, no one watched me. Jen's window slid open on the first pull, and I quickly slipped into her room.

Inside, before I even shut the window, Jen's scent was the first thing to hit me. I'm not sure what perfume she wore, but it always reminded me of honeysuckle after a cool, fresh rain. Something sweet, invigorating, and utterly natural. The scent brought back a million moments of us: me leaning close to whisper something into her ear, her hair brushing my face; Jen pressed against me on the couch while we watched a movie; the two of us sitting together on the water tower, watching the town below. The time she had leaned close and kissed the side of my jaw, the feel of her soft lips warmly placed on my chin, how that had left an impression that I could feel for days.

As strong as the perfume was, Jen wasn't here. Her room felt empty. The house felt empty. I pulled the curtains closed. The room darkened, and I worked from memory as I carefully crossed Jen's room. My fingers found the wall switch. I clicked on the light and looked around the room.

A pale yellow quilt with blue edging was tucked carefully around her bed. Pictures hung on the wall instead of the boy-band posters of a teenage girl. Jen's desk sat across from the bed, and was neatly organized now, where I remembered heart-shaped erasers and colored pencils scattered across its surface. Her dresser sat next to her bed, with a framed mirror above it, a few framed photos sitting on its surface.

I pulled up a few of the pictures on her dresser, some older ones of the group of us as kids, a few of just Jen and me. Nothing anywhere told me where Jen was, or what trouble she was in. Neither of which I liked. I opened the door to the hallway and called out a hello, but the only thing that answered me was silence.

The doors upstairs were all shut. I opened them all. Sarah's room, Jen's mother's room, the bathroom. All the beds were made. Sarah's room was a mess of goth posters, vampire books, and CD cases. She had a guitar in the corner of the room, on a stand, a little acoustic thing. As I walked through the rooms, I felt much larger than I had when I was a kid, as if the entire house had shrunk around me.

I checked downstairs. Living room empty. Dining room empty, though there was a vase of white lilies on the table, wilted and drooping, maybe a day or two weeks past watering. The kitchen had a faint shine on the old tile floor. There was food in the fridge, some eggs and milk, butter, a big container of what might have been grape Kool-Aid.

I banged the counter with my fist. No Mrs. Cooper. No notes hanging on the fridge. No mail. No big red X on a map showing me where Jen was.

The door to the laundry room was ajar. I opened it fully. The washer was empty, but the dryer was full of towels. Out of desperation, I pulled one out, a bright blue towel with a large dark spot in its center.

I grabbed another towel. Then another. All different color towels, all stained with dark blotches. Maybe from cleaning something that wouldn't come out of the fabric as easy as it might come out of a person.

I shivered. It was colder in the house than it had to be. I took a deep breath and realized I could smell a scent in the house, faint, dusky, and coppery. I stuck my nose deep into the towels and took one big inhale.

Blood.

Immediately I blinked and put on my ethereal sight.

That was what I called it. I could use the same sixth sense I used to locate ghosts, but visually. I would close and open my eyes and see the ethereal world overlying ours with fuzzy blue and white edges. People would radiate in the same manner. I would see the person in the real world but also a shimmering white-and-blue shadow over the top of that person.

The ethereal world tied into ours, and I could see it most effectively around live people. Footsteps I could see everywhere, echoes of where a person had been. In high-activity places, I could see where someone's hand had been placed the day before, or sometimes even their reflection in a window, like a ghostly mirror of the day before.

If it was tied to the living, it would leave an echo in the ethereal world. If it was undead, it wouldn't leave a single print on the ethereal canvas. So while the extra sight didn't help me fight the undead, I could use the vision to see things in the ethereal world that didn't normally show up in mine.

After I blinked, the kitchen became a ghostly image of itself. The counter, cabinets, cutting board, most of the objects had a blue-white outline that resembled the shine of the spirits I could see. There were handprints on the counter, around the sink, and footsteps before it, like someone had recently done the dishes.

The ethereal world revealed some evidence of life, which gave me some hope, until I noticed tinges of red. Little spots spattered across the cabinets, like blood. Red in the ethereal world was usually the remnant of brutality in the real world. A vicious reverberation that lasted long after the deed had been done.

A lot of the spots were smeared as if someone had tried to wipe it all away. But where the blood had been cleaned in the real world, the violence had been left behind. And it was that violence dotting the cabinets and forming a large shimmering crimson pool that snaked its away across the same tile floor I was standing on.

Someone had died here and had died in such a panic that I could still see the evidence of it a day later. *My mother,* Jen had said over the phone. The window over the kitchen sink stood before me. Horrifyingly it revealed a ghostly reflection of Mrs. Cooper, aged past my memory, mouth open in a scream and hand reaching behind her for a person not visible to me.

Unbidden, a memory of a warm apple pie with vanilla ice cream floated across my mind. Jen and me sharing a spoon and eating the pie directly from the tin, with Jen's mom laughing and telling us to eat like proper ladies and gentlemen. My hand tightened until the knuckles hurt.

Delicate blue hand- and fingerprints lay everywhere, across the red pool, the cabinets, the towels in the dryer. So Jen had come home. She had either found her mother dead or found all this blood, and sometime soon after she had called me.

I glanced at the phone, hanging on the wall. The antenna was pushed all the way in, and there weren't any recent ethereal prints on the handset. Jen had not called from here.

I shivered. This house was empty. And cold. I couldn't get the violence of Mrs. Cooper's death out of my head. The only thing I knew for sure was that Jen had been here and now she wasn't, and now I had to figure out where she might be and find her before the violence got her too.

CHAPTER FOUR

I was hungry, but before I ate I wanted to check out a hideout we'd had as kids on the north side of town. As adults, we sometimes turn to the safe spaces we hid in as a child. I still felt safer when I was tucked underneath a thick blanket. The hideout might be a place Jen would run to if she needed someplace safe.

I didn't know where else to go that Jen might be. I got back in my car and fired it up. Soon I was back on the main road and followed it back the way I had come in. I passed the diner and the gas station, and before I got to King's Lodge I turned off a little side road and followed it for a half mile or so. I wasn't too far off from where I had originally entered the town, just a bit down the hill from it.

Grafton seemed somewhat the same, an old run-down town in the middle of nowhere, but something sinister lurked underneath. On the outside the town appeared dead, but inside an evil writhed like a parasite worming its way through the corpse of its host.

This town was very dangerous, and I kept feeling the weight of the Key against my chest. Even if Jen wasn't there, I could stash the Key there, at least for a day or two. I didn't think anyone else would find it, and it wasn't something I wanted to flash around in a town full of vampires and thralls.

I parked at a familiar spot and turned the car off, feeling the engine chug once or twice and idle for a long moment before giving in and shutting down. It had been a long night, and I felt much the same way as the Camaro. I had maybe one chug or two left myself.

I got out of the car and walked into the woods. An old trail there wove its way through the long grass and into the trees. Once, it had led to a hideaway we had called the Rock. There had been six of us then, Jen and me, her sister, Sarah, jokester Johnny, and Nick and Danny. Nick and Danny were both from the orphanage where I had lived.

Before that group, I had been a loner, a boy who had watched other orphans come and go, a boy no parent wanted. Until I had met the others I had only myself. Danny, Nick, Jen, Sarah, and Johnny, they had become my family. No matter what happened we always stuck together. The Wolverines, Johnny called us, a reference to some movie I don't remember.

Nick was the original founder of Partisan Rock, where a group of large boulders protruding from a hill formed a semicircle of stone. The boulders fit together in such a way that they almost looked like the entrance to a cave, and we had cleared the ground out underneath the slab roof to form a little hideout of sorts. In the middle of the forest, it had been our own little world.

The Rock didn't look much different now, although it had been a long time since anyone was here. Long tendrils and weeds and vines had overgrown the boulders and wrapped around the stones. Leaves had piled across the entrance of the den. I brushed the leaves aside with my shoe and ducked into the small cave.

It was cool and peaceful there. Enough light came in to see by. I reached into my shirt and grabbed the Key, feeling a tingling in the palm of my hand as my skin touched the cold metal, and pulled the chain over my head. As always whenever I took the Key off, something like relief washed over me.

I looked up. Our names had been chipped into the granite there, under a big, broad "Wolverines": Fergus Grimm, Jennifer Cooper, Nicholas Turgot, Sarah Cooper, Johnny Benoit, Danny Fleer. Nick had brought us up here the day he etched those names into the roof, and we'd been so happy.

Two lines had been scratched in the stone now, one through Danny's and one through mine. My fist clenched, and I took a hard breath. I knew why Danny's was crossed out. Wolverines didn't always make it.

The Key was heavy in my hand. I planned on storing it in what we had called the Vault, a place we had dug up and placed a flat rook over. A place we had always hidden our secret valuables in, like baseball cards or a pack of taffy.

The Vault was covered by a mass of mulch and dead leaves. It took some work to clear it away so I could pull out the flat stone and reveal the hole underneath. Spiderwebs crisscrossed the hole and thickened the empty space. I thought it was safe enough for the Key. I pulled a white gas station shopping bag out of my jacket, wrapped the Key in it, and tossed it into the Vault. Then stopped when it bounced off something soft in the back of the hole.

Curious, I got on my knees and reached past the Key, deeper into the Vault. Spiderwebs drifted across my skin, goose bumps popping up under their light, silky touch. I stretched my arm as far as I could and knew exactly what the Key had hit as I closed my fingers around it. Danny's baseball. Somehow it was still white, and the leather still felt new, the threads stitched perfectly.

The ball was a souvenir from a game where Danny had driven in a run. We had still lost, but Danny had gotten a hit, and we had celebrated. The whole group of us had walked back from the game singing and laughing. Danny had tossed the ball up and down and had grinned his big goofy grin; Johnny used to joke if I was Grimm, then Danny should be Smiles.

I dropped the ball back into the Vault. Quickly covered the hole with the rock, then moved the leaves and dirt back on top of it the best I could. A few minutes later I was back in the car, firing up the throaty chug of the engine, looking back down on Grafton. Not thinking about back then. Small towns are much the same. Whatever happens in a small town usually stays there, and Grafton was no different. It was easy enough to hide monsters here while the rest of the world passes on by.

CHAPTER FIVE

I was in the parking lot of the diner, and my stomach was rumbling. It had been a long time since I had eaten that burger in the motel, and back in the day I had always eaten a meal here. The old railcar-shaped restaurant had been a hangout for us orphans. The lady there had a soft spot for kids and always found a way to feed us. I had spent a lot of time here.

It had been cleaner then. The walls now were stained in large cauliflower-shaped blotches of dirt that grow only under years of neglect. Splotchy glass windows faced the parking lot. People were inside eating, so some humans still remained. Whether or not they were thralls and wanted something other than their master's blood, well, that would be a different question.

I got out of the car, and my eyes went directly to the pay phone on the side wall of the diner. The cord hung limply from the phone, and the handset lay on the ground past the diner. I picked up the receiver and walked over to where the phone hung. My feet crunched over the small pebbles of the lot.

The metal cord hung from the cradle, lifeless. Thick black marks spiderwebbed across the wall. I leaned forward and took a deep breath; the marks reeked of ozone. I remembered the static across the line, the thunder crashing around me in the phone booth, and I looked at each of the marks and how they traced outward from a center point.

Here, my mind told me. *Jen was here.*

And she must have been, last night. My fingers traced the marks on the wall. There had been a fight. Something could have happened to her, and I had been miles away. I hung the phone up in its cradle. The cut ends of the metal cord circled each other.

I looked to the west. The sun perched carefully on the horizon and was ready to slip over the edge into night. The gray of dusk settled around me, the smoky gray of a darkening sky. I turned around, seeing a few more people on the streets now that night was coming on. People with the slow walk of junkies, a staggering, limping motion of need. Hoping to find a vampire and get a quick fix.

I tugged my jacket around me and turned to my car. Someone crossed the street from the garage. The person wore in a hooded jacket, tightly hugging himself. Huddled in. The figure headed for the diner, walking straight past me until he looked up and saw me.

He froze.

I froze too.

Nick. He was taller than ten years ago, tall enough to look me in the eye. He was still a wiry guy, thin with a little muscle, straight brown hair, cut short. His face was all angles, sharp like he didn't eat enough and all that was left was bone. He still wore his glasses, black wire frames.

He glanced at the diner, then back to me. His face contorted into a million different emotions, but the last one was anger. Furious, maddening anger. The kind that makes you hate.

I held up my hands. "Nick. Wait a—"

He swung, and his fist connected under my chin, right below where the jaw hinges. I bit my tongue and my head snapped back. I fell against my car, knees weak, and I grabbed the side mirror to keep me upright.

Gravel crunched in short, quick steps as Nick ran away. His dark figure slipped away behind the diner. I took one step after him, but my legs felt like rubber, so I held onto the car.I needed a minute or two. I doubted I'd find Nick now. He had given me a good shot, and unfortunately, that was something I was used to.

"Hey," an old woman's voice crowed. "That you, Fergus?"

I half turned, my hand still lying on the scorch marks. An older woman stood at the corner of the diner, gray hair tied up in a thick bun, broad hips wrapped with an even grayer apron. She had been old when I was a kid, and she had gotten much older. Her face sagged now, and her eyes were dim, like a cloud overshadowed them.

"Miss Tammie," I said, "how are you?"

Tammie Dempsey smiled then, a real smile that firmed up her face. "Miss Tammie, I haven't been called that in years!" She nodded vigorously. "It is you, then. I thought so, I thought so. You don't much look the same, Fergus, but you don't much look different neither."

"Was that Nicholas you were talking to?" she asked.

My hand went to my jaw. "If you can call it talking."

Miss Tammie *tsk-tsked*. "Don't you say anything about Nicholas. He's had it hard lately."

"Yes, Miss Tammie." The words, once routine when I was a kid, came right out of me.

"There you go, then, Fergus, there you go." She smiled at me, and some of the age fell away. She had always taken care of us kids when we were younger, and we minded her like we would have minded a grandmother.

"Have you seen Jen, Miss Tammie?" I held out the phone in one hand, the cord dangling from the end.

She looked away before she answered me. "She's been around."

"Last night?"

Miss Tammie looked past me, toward the setting sun, and briskly rubbed the fat of her arms with her hands. "Why don't you come in and get yourself a quick bite to eat?"

It was the reason I was here. But I wanted to find out what had happened to Jen before I did anything else. I shook my head. "If you know something, Miss Tammie, I need to know it too."

She had been gazing at the sun, the fiery half circle sinking lower and lower, but when I answered she looked directly at me. All nervousness had gone. "Fergus, you done forgot who you are here. You been gone a long time. And I'm telling you to bring yourself in and get something to eat, and then maybe I'll tell you about Miss Cooper."

I had been gone ten years. Maybe she had something she could tell me if it was quick. I broke first. "A bite would be good. Maybe a quick cup of coffee, if I don't have to wash any dishes for it."

"Lord, I ain't had anyone wash something for me in a while, Fergus, Lord no, not in a while." Just like that, Miss Tammie flipped from being solemn to herself again. She chuckled a bit, reached out as if to push me away with her hand, then motioned me to follow her.

I followed her to the front of the restaurant, which was one large window, and the few patrons inside stared at me as I walked by. Most of them were older folk that had that Grafton look, something I connected with; I knew them without really knowing them.

The door had a little bell on its top, which jingled as we walked through. An older man who was leaving stood to the side. His face was lined, and the black-and-white clerical collar of a Catholic priest circled his neck. I hadn't been to church much when I lived here or since, but I remembered the man. Father Benjamin. Now in his eighties, straight-backed with deep furrows in his cheeks. Some smile lines around his mouth, tiny ones that had fallen into neglect like the rest of the town.

He cocked his head as he held the door for us, then nodded politely as he passed by. Tammie hurried to the back of the diner, and I watched him leave, wondering why or how he was still here. A town of vampires and thralls don't look kindly on faith. The priest gazed up at the darkening sky and moved a bit faster as he strode up Main Street.

The inside of the diner was cleaner than the outside. The tabletops were old and worn but wiped down, and the floor was swept if not recently mopped. Worn brown barstools lined a countertop in the back. A row of booths sat under the long front window of the restaurant. Square tables filled the remaining space. Chairs were placed meticulously. The few patrons there ate quietly.

I walked to the counter. Miss Tammie was already working the griddle. She had seemed much older outside, but here at the grill, in her element, she had the economy of movement one acquires after long years at a trade. That briskness made her appear a few years younger.

She grabbed a mug, filled it with some black liquid that vaguely resembled coffee, and set it on the counter before me.

"I figure you drink it black," she said. "Instead of all that cream and sugar you used to put in it." She never had children of her own, but for kids like me from the orphanage, she was our mom.

"I still like it with all the cream and sugar," I said. "But black is easier now."

Beads of sweat dotted Miss Tammie's face from the heat of the grill. Bits of bacon and grease stained her apron, and she dabbed her forehead with a faded towel. Except for more white hair and a few extra pounds I convinced myself Tammie didn't look much different than she had ten years ago.

"Tell me about Jen," I said. "Where can I find her?"

Miss Tammie snorted. "That girl, she's more trouble than you ever were, Fergus."

"Does she still live in the same place?" I asked. "Is she with her mom?"

A double snort. "That mother ain't much farther than her daughter." She leaned part of her bulk against the work surface. Her apron overlapped the counter's edge. "We all figured you was dead these past ten years, and you show up now and all you can ask about is that Jen Cooper?"

Her eyes picked out my disheveled appearance. I was still in my clothes from yesterday, with dried brown blotches of blood on my shirt and jacket. Miss Tammie was always good at letting kids be kids, without the need for the *whys* and the *wheres*. She had been a mother figure when I really hadn't had one, and she wasn't going to get to Jen without me giving her something first.

"Been in the army," I half explained.

"Sounds like you, that it does." She nodded and turned back to her griddle, mixing a few things together. The hot metal spat and sizzled in response. The smell of sausage grew thick in the air.

That was all I had to say to get Miss Tammie to open up. She just wanted to know I was okay, and that was enough for her. She talked while she cooked. "This town, Grimm. It's changed. Changed for the worse."

"I see that," I said.

"You seen the town?" she asked, still facing the canvas of the grill, painting me a meal.

"Yeah."

"You know what it means?"

"Yeah."

"Then you should know." Miss Tammie's shoulders moved up and down as her hands worked the griddle. "You shouldn't be in town, Grimm, not now, not anymore."

I stopped with the cup halfway to my lips. "I know." The bitter scent of coffee steamed up my nostrils. I blew across the top of the mug. "But Jen called and, well, you know me, Miss Tammie."

"Lord, kid, you did have the hardest head." Miss Tammie sighed, large and expansive like she was letting the world out. "Lord, Lord, Lord. You remember Raphael?"

"Yeah." A chill washed over me. I had seen him the day I left town.

"He's still here."

"Ah," I said over the top of the coffee cup. "That explains a lot."

Of course Raphael had to still be here. I had hoped he was long gone. He was a vampire, his father the head of a clan of vampires. As a kid Raphael always had the newest things: cars, clothes, friends, you name it. Part of me wondered why he wasn't living in Los Angeles or New York, buying sports cars and seducing younger women.

Tammie nodded a few times, still working the griddle. "It's his town now."

"His town?"

"It's Raphael's," she repeated. "He don't leave it."

Raphael's father was a Vampire Lord. A man wealthy beyond just money. The head of a clan of vampires. It didn't make sense that he would keep his son here in Grafton. Unless maybe that son had displeased him. I had the uneasy feeling that Raphael being here was somehow related to me, but I didn't know why.

"I'm not worried about Raphael, Miss Tammie," I said. "Just worried about Jen."

"You shouldn't be in this town." Miss Tammie ignored what I had said. "Ain't nothing happens in this town Raphael don't know about, and you being here, he's going to know about that, fast."

Sometimes I could still see Danny kneeling, looking at me. I could almost see him now, in the reflective white surface of the counter. Some things left scars that never healed. And some scars ached more than the wound that caused them.

"Miss Tammie," I said, "tell me about Jen. I was just at their house and no one was there."

"What do you want me to say, Fergus?" She pulled some stuff off the griddle, scooped it onto a plate. She set the plate next to me. It smelled heavenly. "She should have left too."

"She's in trouble, Miss Tammie. And she's not at her house. I need to find her." Miss Tammie wouldn't look at me, so I ducked my head down a bit to try to meet her eyes. "Can you tell me where to find her?"

Miss Tammie set her jaw. "Fergus, this town is trouble. And if you stay around here long enough, and stick your head into it, then that trouble will find you."

"What did she stick her head into, then?" I asked.

"Fergus, I been here too long to get in the middle of these things," Miss Tammie said. She took her rag and started polishing the counter.

"If this town is that kind of trouble," I said, "then what are you still doing here?" I surveyed the patrons. "What is anyone still doing here?"

The couple eating refused to meet my eyes, ducking closer to their plates. The guy by himself in the corner looked out the window. Another older fellow looked back at me like he had just seen me there, and I stared back at him a moment.

Miss Tammie was muttering something behind me. I turned, and she was furiously polishing the counter with her rag. It took me a moment to figure out what she was saying, the mutter was so low and fast, like a repeated mantra that had been said so many thousands of times all the words blurred together.

"Got to take care of the kids," Miss Tammie said, over and over. "The kids, the kids, the kids …"

I wondered what kids she was talking about. Then I looked down at my free plate of food and coffee and felt ashamed. The whole time I was here she had gone out of her way to provide food and a place to be for me, for Nick, for Danny and Johnny. For all of us orphans. Some people couldn't change who they were.

I leaned back and turned away, taking a slow breath, cursing myself. This diner had been a fun place for us as kids, and she had been its caretaker. And once you started taking care of someone, it was hard to turn away from it. I shook my head, grabbed my mug of coffee, then took a long gulp of the hot liquid, and grimaced at the bitterness.

Miss Tammie grabbed my arm. I swallowed the last of the coffee. "I'm sorry, Miss Tammie."

"No never mind, Fergus." The big woman leaned over the counter to put her face close to mine. "Young Miss Cooper was here on account of

Raphael, and what he has going on in this town. I think she aimed to figure it out."

I still couldn't believe Raphael still was in this town, and not in New York, or Los Angeles. Those places seemed more his style. "What was that?"

She shook her head. "That's all I know, Fergus, that's all. I don't go learning things that will get me in trouble."

I could understand that. Especially in a town full of thralls and vampires.

Just then Tammie's eyes flicked over my shoulder, then widened. She released my arm and leaned back, putting some distance between us.

I turned to where she looked. A police car had pulled into the lot, a shiny car that was a lot newer than the cruisers I remembered from long years ago. It sat in the lot, idling, red brake lights lit in the darkening evening light before the engine finally cut off. Both front doors opened, and the roof light revealed two patrolmen. They canvassed my car on foot, taking note of my license plate and peering through the broken window.

"Go sit in a booth for a minute, will you?" Miss Tammie whispered as the cops walked up to the door. She held my plate out to me.

"Miss Tammie?" The plate was loose in her hands as I grabbed it.

"Fergus." She looked at me, then back to the cops. Her eyes narrowed. "You know this town is dead. If you stay, you're going to die with it."

I wanted her to say more, but she was already moving away, quickly filling a couple of to-go containers. The cops were talking in the parking lot, so I found a booth where I could sit and watch everything. The diner was thrumming with the feel of a bomb about to explode.

CHAPTER SIX

The cops walked in, looking enough alike in the face and their builds to be cousins. I didn't recognize either. There had been an old sheriff back when I was in Grafton, and a deputy, but that was it. These two guys I didn't recall. They looked too hard for the Grafton I remembered.

They both were older, maybe early forties, one taller with grizzled gray and black hair, the other spiked red hair and big sideburns. Both moved competently, and their uniforms and badges were cleaned and pressed. Everything about them screamed outsider in this run-down Grafton, and their image didn't fit in with the town I remembered. To someone who had once served, the two had a distinct military feel.

"Your dinner will be ready in a moment, sirs," Miss Tammie called out, focusing on her grill.

The red-haired cop scanned the patrons. The first one had walked in looking at me. "Anyone know who drives that Camaro out there?"

I sighed. He was going to get right to it. "That's mine, Officer."

"You from around here?"

"Nope," I lied. Lying and running were two of my better traits. "Just passing through."

"Huh," the cop with the red hair said.

The first deputy eyed me, gaze staying on the dark spots of my jacket. "You know your window's busted. You get that here? Anything stolen?"

"No, sir." I answered. "That happened a town over. I was sleeping. Someone broke in."

"They didn't take anything?"

"No," I said. "My eight-track didn't tempt them."

Neither cop chuckled, but then the joke wasn't my best effort. I glanced at the other diners. Slightly, in ever so small a motion, they all had pulled back from the two deputies. The motion may have been subconscious, and maybe even unnoticeable, unless you watched it happen all at once.

The red-haired cop grunted. It seemed like he was a one-syllable guy. "Still got broken glass in the car."

"Along with a bunch of trash," the first cop said.

I lived fast, and fast wasn't clean. There hadn't been a whole lot of time to detail out a car while I had been running from a demon, but I wasn't going to tell these guys that.

"You a drifter?" Red Hair surprised me with a full sentence.

I held up my cup. "Do drifters pay for their food?"

"Food will be ready in a moment, sirs," Miss Tammie called out again. There was the slap-chop of a spatula hitting the griddle, some sizzling, and she began piling food into white boxes. The taller cop kept looking at me like there was something about me he didn't like or couldn't figure.

Then Tammie was handing the food over. No money changed hands. While a lot of places would give a free meal to the local law enforcement, this didn't have that type of feel. This had the feel of payment owed.

Both cops turned and headed out, and the taller one stopped right before the door and looked over again. As if something had just occurred to him. He nodded to my car. "You mind if we take a look inside?"

"My car?"

He nodded again. I could feel the rest of the diner staring at us, not directly, but glancing over while pretending to have a conversation.

"Don't take this personally," I said, "but I kind of do."

They both looked at each other, holding their containers. The taller cop paused, like he wanted to make it an issue, but then let it go. "Suits me."

"Yes, sir."

The red-haired guy had paused too, though. He glanced over my clothes, and I tried not to hide them. Dried blood and mud can look similar, especially when your jacket hasn't seen a washer in a long time.

"You from the military?" he asked. His name tag spelled Marks in big white letters.

"Army," I said.

"Where you headed?"

"Just came down from up north," I explained. I pulled a name out of a hat. "Ohio."

"Huh," Marks said. He was back to one-syllable words. Maybe it gave him a second to think. "You need a job, we're looking for guys like that."

"On the force?" I said. Weird enough that the town could afford these cops from the military, but odder still was offering me a job. "Here?"

Marks gave a little shrug. "You could do worse. Might make enough money, get that window fixed."

Both of them hit the door and left, the little bell tinkling. The whole diner seemed to let go of one large breath. Conversation resumed. I picked at my dinner. It was as good as I remembered, and enough to keep me eating, but my mind was elsewhere. There was a lot more going on to this town than a first glance would give it.

I leaned back and watched the cops. The taller one walked around my car again, said something into the walkie-talkie on his shoulder, then looked back at me for a long moment. I went back to eating and didn't look up again until the police car fired up.

Miss Tammie came over and refilled my mug. Her face was pursed, and she watched the police car back out of its spot with a flash of brake lights, then head out onto the street.

"This town has gotten strange," I said.

"Fergus, this town has always been strange." She set the coffeepot directly on the table. "I want you to listen to me now, you've got to get out. You need to get gone while you can."

"Miss Tammie, Jen's in trouble," I said.

"Boy, that girl's been in trouble the last few years." Miss Tammie wiped off her face with her rag. "She's made it so far. You just let her figure her stuff out, and you get on out of here."

"What happened to your pay phone?" I pulled out my wallet to pay, but Miss Tammie shook her head and put her hand over mine. I could feel her fingers trembling. "Was Jen here last night?"

"Fergus, you're not listening." She pushed my wallet away. "Whatever you feel you need to do here, you don't."

"But—"

"Fergus." She leaned closer. She seemed smaller than me now. Her voice dropped to almost a whisper. "If you can leave, you need to leave. Find someplace to go. When I see Jen I'll tell her to follow you."

"So she does stop by here?"

"Last night she was walking by. We're always a little empty at night, anymore," Miss Tammie said. "I seen her hurry, round to the side." She glanced out the window. "A minute or two later I heard a noise, something like thunder and lightning. A bad storm whipped up then, for a bit."

"And?"

"And?" Miss Tammie bit her lip. "And that's all. You don't go outside at night if you can help it, Fergus." Her eyes were somewhere else, wet and glistening. "You just don't."

I took a deep breath. Whatever was going on, it wouldn't be fair if I got her in trouble with whatever was going on in the town. She was here for the kids. I nodded. "I understand."

Tammie patted my hand and got up, eyes gazing a little into the distance. I leaned closer to her. "Miss Tammie?"

"Hmm?"

"You know, if there's something here that has you scared, you can tell me about it," I said. "Maybe I can help."

She smiled. It was a sad smile, full of regret, full of years gone by and choices made. "Oh, Fergus," she said. "I don't think anyone can help here."

Carefully she walked back to the kitchen, like she had never walked that way before. I finished my coffee, took a few bites of the eggs, sausage, and potato scramble on my plate. Nothing to say about it other than it was just good food. I finished the last bite, savored it for a minute, and felt my body feel warm up a bit, felt a little less achy, a little more like doing something. After that, I finished my coffee, got the plate, and walked it back over to the counter.

"It was good seeing you, Fergus," Tammie called out. I think she had decided I was leaving, and I wasn't going to disabuse her of the notion.

She grabbed the plate and the cup, moved to drop them into the sink with two watery plops. "I'll tell Parker you were here when I can."

"Yeah." Parker wasn't high on my list of people I wanted to see. He had been the father figure in our house. Parker might have known things that he could have told me. Things that might have saved Danny's life. I wasn't headed back there unless I could help it.

Tammie washed her hands nervously, smiled one last smile. It was more nervous than real this time. Her fingers twitched nervously in her rage. "Fergus, you be careful. Things happen after dark around here."

"I will, Miss Tammie." I could handle myself if it came to it. Seeing what I had seen at the Coopers' had shaken me, but I still needed to go out in Grafton and see what was going on, what had caused Jen to call me. Maybe that way I could find out where she went.

I tucked some cash underneath the saltshaker on the table and took a second to wash up in the restroom. I understood why Miss Tammie had made me come in for some food. Dark blotches hung under eyes, my face looked gaunt, my hair was pushed down on one side of my head and scattered on the other. I ran some water through my hair, but it didn't help. The dark strands were locked between a wave and a curl.

I walked back out with a wave at Miss Tammie. The bell on the door announced my departure, and I was back in the parking lot. It had gotten colder, and darker, while I was eating. Grafton was down in a valley, and cold air seemed to sink its way into the town.

People shouted from deeper into the town, horns blared, some faint music played. As soon as night had fallen, the thralls had come out, waiting on their sponsors. Activity was happening down Main Street. There was a liveliness in the air I had missed during the day.

Someone stood by my car. The customer from inside the diner, the one who had been staring at me. The guy was short and stocky and looked like he had made one too many trips to the diner and one too few to the gym. He still had his phone in his hand and was looking at it when I walked up.

"Can I help you?"

The man looked up from his phone. "Are you Fergus Grimm?"

"Do I know you?" Back in the diner, I had thought the man was a good deal older than me, but up close he just looked like he had a lot of wear and tear on him. Aged.

"You might," the man said. "I was in school with you back when, a year or two ahead, I think. We played ball together." He reached out the hand without the phone. "Grant Morris."

The name faintly rang a bell, but no memory came up to lock his face in. The man's handshake was limp and his flesh was flabby. Whatever he had been doing lately, it wasn't anything to do with sports.

Grant's phone beeped. He looked down at it and frowned. Then flicked the volume switch off. "Sorry about that," he said. "Friends are wanting to go out."

"Huh." I was curious where people went at night now. That spot would be a good place to get information. "Where do you go?"

"The Cauldron," Grant said, then at my blank stare: "It's the club in town. Can't miss it, there's a big neon sign of a goat in front."

I was thinking of a town of vampires and wondering about the mix of alcohol, humans, and vampires. I controlled a shudder. "There's a night-club in town?"

"It's great." Grant grinned. "Wish it had been around back when we were younger, right?"

We were definitely on different wavelengths.

Grant checked his phone again. It must have vibrated. "Anyway, man, I think I can help you."

"Help me with what?"

"I heard you asking about Jen Cooper in there," Grant said. "It kind of caught my ear because I saw her a bit ago."

"Tell me," I said.

"So you are Fergus Grimm." Grant grinned again like he had caught me out.

I rolled my eyes. "Just tell me."

"Oh. Okay," Grant said. "It wasn't much. She was in front of the club shouting at one of the guys bouncing there. They were getting ready to open, I think."

"So she's in the club?"

"No, man, no," Grant said. "She was yelling at him, but the guy wouldn't let her in, so she left and headed west from there."

West—toward her house. Maybe she was there now. Maybe I had just missed her when I left and hid the Key. My heart beat a little faster, and I was about to thank Grant and head to my car when I noticed the odd way

Grant looked at me. Expectantly. Like he was leading the witness. "I appreciate the info."

Grant winked. "Anything for an ex-teammate."

The wink and the line bothered me. And I had gotten pretty far on paying attention to those feelings. I didn't remember Grant at all, and our team just hadn't been that big. I paused. "Where'd you play again?"

"What?" he asked like he had been expecting me to say something else. "Oh, center. The center field."

I had played center field. So now I knew I didn't know the guy. And the way he answered told me he had never played baseball. I wasn't sure why Grant wanted me to go to Jen's house, but I had a feeling it wasn't because Jen was there.

"Thanks again." I reached out and shook his hand one more time. As soon as our hands clasped, I gripped his hard and didn't let go.

"Hey, now," he said, and tried to squirm away, tugging at his arm. I held on tight and rolled down his sleeve with my other hand, turning his arm to see the fleshy forearm. Thralls, like junkies, hid their habits well, but if you knew where to look the teeth marks were easy to find.

And there they were: a nice half circle of molars with two precision punctures where the incisors would be. The bite was healed a little, so Grant had been bitten in the past few days. Likely at the club we were just talking about. He was definitely a thrall.

And therefore doing someone else's bidding. Likely the person who had been texting him. I swiped the phone from his hand. The screen was locked, but the last message remained on the lock screen, from someone named BigPapi00.

BigPapi00: *You send him this way yet?*

"Where am I headed?" I asked Grant.

"What's wrong with you?" Grant ignored my question and pushed me. "A guy can't go get a thrill in this town? You prejudiced against thralls or something?"

I held his phone up. "Where's Big Papi want me to go?"

"It's just one of my crew, man." Grant started pulling again. His eyes were tearing. He was suddenly very scared, and his voice squeaked. "Just one of my boys."

Grant kept yanking, and I let him go. He stepped back, pulling his sleeve back down and rubbing his wrist. I held up his phone. "So, tell me more about being center fielder."

Grant stood there, alternating standing on one foot, then the other. I waited him out, and the phone buzzed in my hand while we waited. I looked at it, then back to Grant. "You need to think a little harder when I ask you something. Big Papi is a little upset I'm not there yet."

"Man, I didn't even want to do it," Grant said.

I smiled. Grant had just gotten a text from VampS33ker95, but I wasn't going to tell him that. "Stay there, Grant." I walked over to my car. I popped my trunk and pulled a few long black tie-straps from a bag there. And the heavy .357 revolver I had stored there.

"Come on, man," Grant said. "I just did it for the fix, man, just the fix. I didn't mean any harm."

I walked back and motioned for him to follow me. Reluctantly, with the slump of shoulders common to junkies who had learned how to endure, Grant followed me. I looked in the diner window as we passed. The few customers left were studiously not paying attention to what was going on in the parking lot. Miss Tammie had been serious about people being careful out at night.

Thralls are much like they're portrayed. They get addicted to getting bitten, much like addicts get addicted to the rush of a drug. The bite gives the thrall some supernatural abilities, mostly physical in nature. Greater strength, faster, longer lives. Things that allow the thrall to live longer as a source of food to the vampire. Repeated bites will link a vampire to a thrall, and they form somewhat of a symbiotic bond.

Some thralls go overboard. They need more. They become junkies. Much like any other drug, they can't handle it and forget about anything else but the need. They wither away, desperate for some vampire to bite them again. Willing to do anything for just a bite. At that point, most vampires steer clear from them. Unless there is some dirty work around.

I walked Grant behind the diner and had him sit down by the Dumpster. I strapped his legs together, and his hands behind his back.

"You don't need to do this," Grant said.

"I got to make sure you don't tell anyone I know it's a trap." I held his phone out to him. "If you want to be found sometime tonight, give me the code to your phone and I'll text VampS33ker95 for you."

Grant shook his head. "Man, you're messing with my fix."

"You and I both know that's the price you're paying tonight," I said. "Don't make the price go higher."

"Man," Grant said again, and I waited. Then I opened the top of the Dumpster bin.

"Okay!" Grant said. I paused. "Eleven, eleven, ninety-four."

I typed it in and the screen opened up.

"Let me call Seek," Grant said.

"You don't get to make the deals," I said. I flipped down the messages.

Grant: *Hey, aren't you guys looking for Fergus Grimm? He's here in the diner and looking for Jen Cooper.*

BigPapi00: *Hold on.*

A few minutes later: *Tell him to go to the Coopers'*

Grant: *How am I going to do that?*

BigPapi00: *Make some shit up. Tell him you saw her at the club arguing with me, and then she went west after that*

Grant: *I'm going to get bit for this, right?*

BigPapi00: *Sure. You get him to the house, you're set up*

Grant: *Okay. I'll catch him when he walks out*

BigPapi00: *You get him to the house, you're set. Remember that*

Then a few minutes later: *You send him this way yet?*

I flipped the messages to VampS33ker95. These, I didn't read, but I typed in the message *Hey, got something going on. See you tomorrow.* And then turned the phone off.

"Seek coming?"

"Sure," I said, tossing the phone in the Dumpster. "You're all set."

Then I took the handle of the revolver and rapped him hard on the back of the head. Grant's eyes rolled up in the back of his head and he tipped over sideways. I picked him up and tossed him into the Dumpster after his phone. I didn't want to take him with me. I traveled light and didn't like having to worry about whether or not a thrall would call out at the wrong time.

I went to my car. Before I took off I made sure my Smith & Wesson was loaded and resting comfortably in my jacket pocket. This was a setup, and someone wanted me to think Jen was back at her house. I could see who it was, and maybe that would get me one step closer to her.

I parked my car right outside the Coopers' house. This time the lights were on, in the living room and the kitchen, and even Jen's room upstairs. Before I parked I had circled the outer blocks a few times, but nothing looked out of the ordinary.

I took a quick look around the street as I strode to the door, not seeing anyone. No neighbors walking their dog, no mother calling her kids in, no delivery van parked on the corner. In fact, no other houses on the block had their lights on, which felt … eerie.

It was a trap, but I still couldn't stop a feeling of hope rise in me. I climbed the porch stairs and glanced through the windows for Jen. But no one was in the kitchen, and no one was in the living room, although the television was on and mumbling words I couldn't make out from outside the house.

Heart thumping, I rang the doorbell. And put one hand in my jacket pocket, resting it on the gun.

No one answered. A weird déjà vu feeling went through me. I knocked, and then I knocked again urgently. I had started to call out Jen's name when someone walked into the living room from the kitchen.

Mrs. Cooper.

She walked a little slow and looked around like she was confused. I knocked a few more times, and that sound triggered something in her. She headed toward the door as I knocked. Her face was pale, and her neck was wrapped in a scarf, and her eyes were blank.

I was worried. But I kept knocking. Somehow she had survived the vicious attack I had seen in the kitchen. Maybe Jen had gotten home in time to rescue her mother. Maybe Jen had somehow gotten her to a doctor. Mrs. Cooper walked like she was drugged, and when I stopped knocking, she stopped moving.

But finally she reached the door.

I tried the handle; it was open. I watched Mrs. Cooper through the tiny square windows in the door as I opened it. She seemed fascinated by the rotation of the doorknob.

The door swung out. Mrs. Cooper looked up from the doorknob and saw me standing there. She began to smile, and I reached out my hands to ask if she was okay.

Her mouth kept opening past the smile. And a hissing sound came out of her throat. It took a second, but I finally saw tiny incisors descending from her teeth.

They had turned Mrs. Cooper into a vampire. And not any vampire, but a leech—someone who had been turned into a vampire at the last second after they had lost all their blood, and their brain had stopped functioning. All leeches knew as a vampire was a terrible thirst. Their brain was dead, and they couldn't recognize anything but warm flesh and blood.

And I was caught with both my hands extended toward her.

Mrs. Cooper launched herself at me. I ducked and dove into the house. She swirled around, faster than she had ever looked walking toward the door, and jumped on me. I stumbled back, holding Mrs. Cooper away with both my hands and trying to find a way to throw her off. Her head snaked around my hands and she fought to bite deep into my neck, my scalp, anything she could put her mouth close to. I was losing the battle.

It was time to grab some ghost.

Mentally I looked for one. What I did reminded me of the old radar screens in a military movie. There would be a sweep of a green hand around the circular map around me, and as the hand passes it leaves behind a scattering of dots.

So I waited for some dots of ghosts to reveal themselves.

And waited.

And waited.

Oh, shit.

There were no ghosts within reach. Right then Mrs. Cooper snagged part of my hand in her mouth. I swore and punched her in the temple. Her mouth let go and she fell to the side. And got right back up.

I jumped back and grabbed my gun. Then hesitated. Even though she was dead, I couldn't bring myself to shoot her. The first act of me coming back to Grafton couldn't be killing Jen's undead mother. And thinking that slowed me.

Mrs. Cooper barreled into me again. We both fell over the couch and crashed into the coffee table. For a brief moment, her mouth rested hot and wet against my neck, and I jerked away and kicked her off.

She hissed louder and louder. Her scarf had fallen off and revealed a thick, jagged rip in the side of her neck. Some of the hissing came out of the gash.

Fuck it. I couldn't kill Mrs. Cooper, but I couldn't die either. So I shot out both of her knees.

Mrs. Cooper screamed and fell to the floor, writhing and grabbing her knees. I carefully stepped back and kept an eye on her, putting the couch between us. Here I was, in Jen's house, and I had shot her mother in both legs. Her dead mother, who once had welcomed me every Saturday for football and French toast.

I swallowed down some bile. I was sick to my stomach. Mrs. Cooper started pulling herself toward me on the floor, around the couch. Her head turned past me. A cop stood in the front door. He was huge, muscled, with an impeccably pressed uniform that stretched over his frame, and he had his gun out.

Thank heaven, I thought at first.

"Sir," the cop said. He had a gravelly voice that sounded like it was echoing up a deep well. "I'd appreciate it if you would just keep your hands where I can see them."

I paused long enough that the officer's finger snicked off the safety, then held my hands out.

"Now go ahead and drop the Smith & Wesson," the cop said. I looked back at Mrs. Cooper, who was still hissing and winding her way around the couch. When I looked back the cop's gun was out and pointed at me.

I dropped my gun. But stepped away from Mrs. Cooper when I did.

"I'm going to need you to get on the floor," the cop said. He rolled his eyes at Mrs. Cooper.

I looked back at Jen's mother. Her eyes were empty but locked on me, and she was pulling her way past the couch.

"For fuck's sake," the cop said.

I jumped as he fired once, then twice. Mrs. Cooper's head exploded like someone had tossed a rotten cantaloupe as hard as possible against the floor and red and pink insides had burst out of it.

The smell of gunpowder flooded the room. I looked back and the gun was pointed at me, a slight cigarette wisp curling up from the end of the barrel. The cop motioned with the gun for me to get on the floor, so I knelt with my hands on my head.

Some laughter came in from outside, on the porch. The big cop looked to his side and sneered a little to whoever was on the porch. "These little games aren't really my thing."

"It ain't your thing to worry about, Cole," Two guys came through the door, not cops, but guys I remembered: Jacob and Rand, old buddies of Raphael. Jacob was taller and more muscled and had a messy burn scar on the side of his neck. Rand was a good deal smaller and compensated for that by dressing nicer and slicking his hair back. My guess was one of these guys was BigPapi00.

Jacob smiled. "Hey, Grimm. Surprised?"

"Yeah, buddy," Rand echoed. His voice was smooth, and he was dressed like a ladies' man. Sharp jacket, half-buttoned shirt. "Surprised?"

"You guys didn't have to kill Jen's mom," I said.

"Oh, but we did," Rand said. He stepped close and squatted beside me so that he was staring at the side of my face. I kept looking at the big cop, who had his gun on me. "Your girlfriend was getting all up in Raphael's business."

"But make her a leech?" I shook my head. Mrs. Cooper deserved better than that.

Jacob swung then and cracked the side of my face with his fist. I glared up at him, and when he smiled I noticed the incisors there. Raphael had turned his cronies into vampires.

"Leech is a derogatory term, Grimm," Rand said softly. "We're a polite society now. You got to watch what you call people."

"She wouldn't have had to end up that way," Jacob said, "she hadn't fought so much."

I went to get up. Jacob threw another right and I fell back on my knees, looking back and locking eyes with Jacob. Rand put his hand on my shoulder, holding me down.

"Raph is thrilled you're back, by the way." Rand pulled some straps out of his pocket, thin black tie-straps like the ones I had used against Grant.

"Let my deputies do that," Cole, the big cop, said.

Rand and Jacob both looked at him.

The big cop's voice resonated through the room. "I'm still responsible for what happens in this town, right?"

"Whatever." Jacobs shrugged. He sized up the cop. The vampire was as tall as Cole but not as muscled.

Rand stood and held out his hands. "Sure, Cole, sure. Just get him to the jail for when Raphael gets there."

"I know what I'm doing," Cole told them. Jacobs and Rand left, but Jacobs leaned into the cop as he brushed by.

Cole grabbed something on his collar, a tiny microphone, and spoke into it. His voice was so deep even his whispers rumbled.

"Is your name Fergus Grimm?" Cole asked.

"I think you know it is," I said.

"I might," Cole said, "but I'm still asking."

The policeman waited patiently. While we waited, more cops came in through the door, and a couple more stood on the porch. That was a lot of cops for Grafton. I finally nodded.

"We're going to take you in as soon as these guys are finished, Mr. Grimm," Cole said. "You don't give anyone a reason not to, and we'll treat you fair. Sound like a deal?"

I nodded again and looked over at Mrs. Cooper. Bile rose in my throat at the acrid scent of gunpowder, at the splintered white bone fragments scattered over the carpet, at the dark blood splattered over the back of the couch.

That person had once served me pancakes.

I looked back at Cole and tightened my jaw. "Did Mrs. Cooper get the same deal?"

A corner of the man's lips curled, slightly. "From what I've seen, no one in this town gets anything but what they have coming for them."

A few cops came in around Cole. One of the cops coming in was a deputy I had known from my earlier days, Frank Herder. He had worked here with the old sheriff. His grizzled gorilla face said nothing. I wasn't sure if he remembered me. Both of the cops circled me.

"Now, Grimm, you going to do anything silly? Try to run maybe?" Cole leaned forward. "Or will you come along peaceably?"

I looked at Mrs. Cooper and swallowed again. I thought about the lack of ghosts around and wondered what that meant. And I remembered Saturday nights at the Coopers', with apple pie in the pan. Jen's mother deserved better, but I couldn't do anything about it, not right now. "Will someone at least cover her up?"

Cole grinned a big grin. "I'll take that as a yes."

Cold metal cuffs were slapped on my wrists with a ratcheting sound. I winced at the pinching feel as the cuffs tightened over my wrists. The deputy with Frank started reading my rights in a nasal tone like someone had broken his nose a long time ago. Out of the corner of my eye, I could still see Mrs. Cooper's body curled on the floor. No one still paid the slightest attention to her.

"Can someone please cover her up?" I asked. Nothing happened for a few moments, and then finally Frank grabbed something off the couch and put it over Mrs. Cooper.

More cops came in and started going through the house. Cole reached around my back and grabbed my cuffs, jerking me along outside. I caught the faint whiff of cigarette smoke in the air, and a few cigarette butts lay on the stairs.

Frank and the deputy with him followed us out. Cole handed me off to Frank and headed to one of the police cars. My stomach sank. If Raphael was in charge of the cops, that meant the town really was under his full control.

I turned back and saw Mrs. Cooper lying there, a muffled shape under a blanket, and I tugged away from Frank. I had known I was walking into a trap, but I thought by walking into it I would discover something pointing to where Jen might be. I didn't think I'd be the butt of some joke by two vampires who still thought like teenagers.

They could have just killed Jen's mom, but Jacob and Rand had taken it a step further and made her a monster, someone without thought or choice. Then, when the chance had come up, the two of them had let her loose in the house to spring on me and had laughed at the end. I kicked a column on the porch. Angry didn't begin to describe how I felt right then.

"Easy, Fergus." Frank pulled me back to him. I guess he did remember me. He had a slow way of talking, each word was carefully formed in his mouth before being selected to exit. His hair had thick, dark curls that had grayed some, and heavyset eyebrows that made me think of a gorilla.

Frank and his partner led me down the stairs and across to one of the police cars flashing their lights on the curb. It was dark out and a lot of the houses had lights on now. Like their inhabitants were waking up. The thought raised goose bumps up and down my arms.

The second cop, Marley, headed off to the driver's side. Frank carefully opened the back door of the car and tucked me into the seat. He buckled me up before shutting the door and getting up front in the passenger's seat.

"Frank, why Mrs. Cooper?" I struggled to sit up in the backseat, my arms tight behind me. I wanted to find out what Jen did that made Jacob and Rand kill her mother.

"You should have stayed out of town, Grimm," Frank said. "Coming back here is doing you no favors."

"Frank, what's going on?" I said.

Frank turned slowly to look at me. It was a motion that involved his whole upper torso. His neck looked like it didn't turn on its own.

"Now, what," he said slowly, "makes you think you got a right, that I should tell you anything like that?"

"Is Sheriff Dickson still here?" I asked, searching for answers. Where I was going. Who I might be able to talk to in order to let me go before Raphael found me.

Frank turned his body back around to face the front. Slowly. His partner glanced over at Frank and then back to the street.

I'm not sure if the silence got to him, or if Frank was in his heart not a bad person. His voice was small. "They closed the factory, is what happened here."

"What?"

"Closed the factory," Frank repeated, louder. Still staring forward. "Five, six years ago. What people could leave, left then."

"Why did anyone stay?" Closing the factory would have stopped all jobs in the town. There would have been nothing left to support it.

"That was the beginning," Frank continued. "All we got left now is this."

"What are you telling me?"

He slowly lifted one shoulder up, then let it sink back down. That was all I was going to get from him. Which was something. The only people that would close the factory would be the Antonados. But why? If the factory closed, the whole town would instantly become a living ghost town.

An empty town of vampires and thralls, and guarded by the police.

I got it.

I wondered if this had been what Miss Tammie was trying to warn me away from.

CHAPTER SEVEN

I had been in the station a few times in my younger days. In the lobby, a big wooden desk perched above a sterile, drab waiting room, with an older version of the cousins from the diner sitting behind it. A light blue floor ran up against sterile gray walls. Brown plastic chairs and benches lined the walls. Some dabs here and there of polished steel: doorknobs, chair legs, a chain holding a pen on the desk.

Frank and his partner brought me in, took off my cuffs, and got me fingerprinted by an old guy at the desk. Frank pulled off my jacket, and I watched him feel the weight of my gun in the jacket but didn't say anything; he just rolled the jacket up and put it in a big plastic box. It was followed by my wallet, belt, shoelaces. I had done a good thing keeping the Key out of Grafton. Who knows what they would have thought of that?

The guy at the desk opened up my wallet and checked the license. "Says here your name is Charles Wright."

Frank looked at me. "It's Fergus Grimm, sure enough."

I was quiet.

"Not going to look good, you being there." Frank kept up the slow tempo of his speech.

"Yeah," I said. Being in Grafton wasn't going to be good for me. And it was far worse here than I had thought, and not only had I not helped

Jen, but I couldn't find out where she was or what had happened to her. I wrenched my belt out of the belt loops and handed it to the desk sergeant.

"And in the Coopers' house."

"You going somewhere with this, Frank?" I was irritated, and I knew better than to antagonize the one cop who was somewhat kind to me, but I couldn't help myself.

"Nope." Frank had always been someone who got to where he was going on his own. "Let's get you to the cell."

The front doors swung open then, with Cole striding in, his footsteps echoing sharply on the tile. He nodded at Frank, grinned at me, and then went through a side door to the office area of the police station. I could finally see his face in the light. It was the square-jawed face of someone in complete control. His eyes were darkly intense here at the station, and it seemed for a second something flickered across the irises when his gaze met mine. It was only for a second, and then he grinned again as Frank grabbed my arm and pulled me to the other side of the station. Where the cells were.

In my past I'd occasionally found myself in a cell. They all had a common feel: a cold concrete floor, dark metal bars, a hard bench, and a shiny aluminum toilet. Sometimes the toilet wasn't so shiny. Most of the times cells held on to a chill that got into your bones. I was a little lucky here. In this cell, a scratchy gray wool blanket lay tossed on the bench.

Frank unlocked the bars and pushed me in. A sharp smell of bleached stone hit me. It was the middle of the night. Barred windows at the top of each cell formed squares of iron crosses under a black sky.

A quick check let me know there were no ghostly prisoners here. My radar came up empty. Again. And I hadn't sensed any around Mrs. Cooper's place. Somewhere over a hundred billion people had died on earth, and even if only a small percentage of them became ghosts, that still meant there should be plenty to go around. I should sense a spirit somewhere.

I could usually sense a ghost up to a mile or so away, but reaching out now, I didn't feel that comforting pull from a spirit anywhere. I had never encountered this before in a town, and not having my powers around terrified me in a way I hadn't been terrified before. A shudder ran through me. It's one thing to be trapped. It's another to be helpless. I had walked into Grafton so sure of myself, and now that I couldn't use my powers, my prospects of walking back out of this town had dwindled.

The picture of Raphael, Jen, and Sarah flipped into my mind, and I took a deep breath and tried to let it go. Why had the two sisters been around Raph? If Sarah and Raph were a thing, then where was Sarah now? And why would she let what happened to her mom happen? Those thoughts circled each other in my mind, and behind them, Raphael lurked, and a deep dread settled upon me. I'm not too sure how much time had passed before the bars rattled in front of me.

I looked up; Frank's gorilla face almost pressed against them. "They got your prints on file, Grimm. Says you were a Ranger once. Gus McNulty."

"Yeah." Hard times over there for a person who could see spirits. Late at night, under fire, when I didn't know if I was talking to friends or if their ghosts were talking to me.

"Says you're MIA," Frank said, spelling the letters out. "What's that mean?"

I sighed. "It means Missing In Action, Frank."

"That's not what I meant," Frank said. "I know what MIA means. What I meant was, what does it mean with you being here?"

"It doesn't have anything to do with me being here," I said. "I'm here, Frank, because Jen called me. Mrs. Cooper's daughter. Have you seen her, Frank? Do you know where she is?"

"Hey, Frank," Frank's partner called from the jail door. His mouth was twisted in an ugly, excited grin. "It says here we got a warrant for Fergus Grimm, from ten years back. From right here in Grafton."

My heart sank. That warrant could only be for one thing. That last day and Danny. It was a warrant that had probably just resided in this town, for just this purpose. My return. Frank moved off and the two cops conferred. Murphy remained excited and left the cell block. Frank studied me for a long moment after that before he followed.

The door to the cells shut. I sat down on the hard bench, feeling the cold of the metal bench through my jeans. I hadn't found Jen. Instead, I had found her dead mother, a town full of vampires, mysteries, and little else.

The fumes I had been running on finally ran out. Exhausted, I dropped my face into my hands. The cold concrete of the jail leached any heat from me, and I shivered. I stayed like that a long time, until the purring engine of an expensive car echoed from in front of the jail. It was the long, lean thrum of a car worth a lot of money. Raphael. Possibly with friends.

Car doors slammed in excitement. Wing tips tapped briskly along a sidewalk. Conversation out in the central station mumbled through concrete. Through it all I waited, both anxious and relieved. I was worried about what might happen. But on the other hand, I wanted to get whatever was going to happen over with.

The door to the lockup opened. Raphael headed down to stand in the door to the cells. He looked at me for a long moment, like he had found a long-lost favorite toy. He still looked like the linebacker he had played in high school, just taller. An expensive jacket, tailored perfectly, hung from his shoulders and tapered in at the waist. Black hair lay back in a long wave, not a hair out of place, cut even just past his neck. A goatee was expertly shaven below a short mustache. A tiny white scar traced down from the bottom corner of one eye along a chiseled cheekbone.

Raphael's lips were spread in a huge smile, tight white teeth almost glowing under a nice tan. Which I thought must have been bottled, him being part of the sun-averse crowd. His eyes contained a manic fury. The irises were too wide and vibrated a little, side to side. Like he was holding in an amount of energy that was moments from bursting.

We both stared like that for a long minute. Raphael excited, me exhausted. He broke the stare with a crisp walk down to my cell, shoes tapping the concrete floor. A group of cops, Cole included, followed Raph until he stopped and faced them. Something in his face caused them to all slowly back out. Cole last. Raphael kept looking until the door to the office shut silently.

I remained sitting. It had been a lifetime for both of us. A tiny flame of anger fluttered in me, but I was tired and fighting the cold chill of the jail, the death of Jen's mother, Jen missing.

"Welcome fucking back, Grimm," Raphael said. His voice was light, controlled, hiding a thrumming cord of tension inside it. He cocked his head a little, like a hawk looking at a rabbit. "How long's it been?"

"We both know how long, Raph," I said.

"Ten years," Raphael said, smiling. He punctuated each word by tapping the bars of the cell with his fist. "Ten, long, boring fucking years."

"For you," I muttered.

"For me," Raphael agreed. "But you made sure of that, didn't you?"

"What's that mean?" I said, and stood up. Stared right into his eyes.

"I'm sure you know." He kept the large grin on his face. "You knew what you were doing the moment you left."

"Knew what?"

"You playing with me?" Raphael waved his arms in a grandiose gesture. "About this. About my father's plan."

"Did I know about this?" I mimicked his hand gestures. "This jail? A bad game of charades? Why don't you skip the games and get whatever it is you want over with?"

Raphael slid the bars to my cell open in one smooth motion. I blinked, and he was through the door to my cell. He was fast, faster than I had ever been, and his anger stretched down into the taut tendons of his cheek and jaw. He pushed his face into mine, and spittle flew from his lips. "It will be a long time before we *just get it over with*, Grimm."

I stood chest-to-chest with Raphael, my back to the cell wall. My shoes felt funny, loose on my feet with no laces. Crap. I was in a cell with a vampire who hated me, likely wanted to kill me, with Jen's life in the balance, and no ghost around. And I still wanted to take a swing at him. "Okay, Raph. What are you asking me?"

"You fucking left, Grimm," Raphael said. "You fucking left, and you knew what would happen if you did."

"I didn't have a choice," I said. "You didn't give me a fucking choice."

"I didn't give you a choice?" Raphael punched the wall beside me. The concrete there cracked under his knuckles. "You're wrong, Grimm. I gave you one choice."

"That wasn't a choice." There was a seesaw of crazy between us, his anger and mine going up and down as we argued.

"It was the choice I gave you." He stared hard enough into my face that I looked away.

"Killing the retard wasn't example enough?"

Danny.

"*I told you,*" Raphael screamed, then stopped and took a deep breath. I smelled cigarette smoke on him and a sickly-sweet liquor smell, cinnamon-like. He took another breath. And then another. When he spoke next, his voice was low. "After you left, my dad banished me here. Jailed me in this fucking town."

"You mean your rich-ass father was upset with you? The head of the American clan? Was he surprised at how crazy his son turned out?" I rolled my eyes. "I can't see how that's my fault."

"Bullshit, Grimm." Raphael's voice stayed cold. "I told you who I was. I told you what you had to do. I told you to listen up and take orders from me. I even gave you an opportunity to make amends, and that you'd better fucking accept it. And what happened then?"

"Look—"

"What fucking happened?" Raphael screamed. Bits of spittle landed on my face, and his incisors had grown into two sharp canines.

"You killed Danny," I answered. "And you would have killed the rest in time."

Raphael stared right at back me. "You fucking *left*. And my father made this shithole my prison."

"It would never have worked, Raphael."

"It's not supposed to *work*." Raphael's lips twisted in a sneer. "We were never meant to *get along*."

The air grew still in the cell. A storm of emotion surrounded us, centered in Raphael. I could feel the seesaw rocking back and forth, faster and faster. I needed to slow it down, but Raphael and I had never worked that way, and so I opened my big fat mouth again.

"You know why I left?" I asked, nodding to the cops staring through the door to the cells. "I wasn't going to stay around and be your bitch." I looked straight into his vibrating irises. "I wasn't going to stay around you, whatever it cost *me*." And I pushed him away. "I'm here to find Jen, and then I'm out of this town again. You can stay here all you want. Whatever you or your father have going on, whatever you want to fucking blame me for, you can take care of that shit yourself."

The seesaw tottered, toppled. I could feel it in the snap of tension in the air.

"You want me to take care of things, Grimm?" Raphael said, voice flat, standing right where he had been like my push had meant nothing. "All you had to do was say so."

I swung first. I didn't see him duck, or the punch that followed. There was a blur in the cell and something smashed into my face. My knees gave out, and my legs danced backward on their own. I tried to blink away the dark spots in front of my eyes, and swung again, at anything, feeling my body spin around after the swing.

Air exploded from my lungs as a square of something dug deep into my gut. It felt like a cinder block. I'm sure it was just Raphael's fist. My back slammed against the stone wall, and my legs straight gave out. I'd like to say I slid down to the floor, but it was more of a collapse. I know because my head bounced off the concrete.

A hand grabbed my collar, dragged me back to the middle of the cell. A wing-tipped toe connected with my forehead; warm wetness rushed down my face. One eye stuck with blood, I was still trying to blink away stars in the other, and all my ears heard was a loud ringing.

I tried to get up, but my legs just flopped around a bit on the floor. Another foot caught me in my ribs, and something in my chest gave out. Another foot followed the first, and another, and I just tried to curl up as the wing tips drove into my arms, my back, and my sides.

It stopped sometime. I didn't know when or how long the beating took. All I felt was sharp pains and burning aches and warm blood soaking my skin. I could see. The spots in my one good eye had cleared. I wiped the blood out of the other one.

Raphael stood above me, breathing deep not with exertion but excitement. His head was tilted slightly down, toward me, and his eyes stared past me. I could see him muster himself together, a little bit more with each passing second. His chest swelled in and out, in and out, until Raphael finally took one long, shuddering breath.

He finally spoke. "Grimm, you've been warned." Raphael reached down and grabbed me. I screamed in pain as he tossed me on the bench. His hand pushed me against the wall, and his irises still trembled right and left as his eyes locked on to mine. "And I want you to know how serious I am right now."

"Sherioush?" I mumbled, blood leaking from the corner of my mouth. If I had the energy, I would have yelled at that guy to answer the phone that kept ringing.

Ralph nodded. "Serious. I could have killed you, *could* still kill you. And I've wanted to for a long, long time." He pushed my chest back. I bit back a scream, and he let me go when he saw I didn't slide back down to the floor. "So I am going to be as serious as I can be with you. And give you some instructions, instructions I want you to follow to the letter. My father's going to be coming to town, and I want you here to meet him."

"Jen," I said, my mouth full of mush.

"Jen," Raphael spat. "You're not listening. You're not here for Jen. You're here to meet my father." His face loomed larger. "You do whatever he tells you to, hear me? Everything. Like your life depended on it. Like Jen's life depended on it."

"Where is she?" It occurred to me that he must have her.

Raphael shook his head. "It doesn't matter where she is. You don't need to look for her. It only matters what will happen to her if you fail me. If that happens, if you leave, if you ignore my father, any of that, I will kill everyone you know. Everyone you've met. I will burn everything and everyone behind you until I catch you again."

He leaned close. "The only reason your friends are still alive today is I was hoping you'd come back again."

I huddled into myself. Raphael chuckled. A warm, liquid heat spread through my body where it had been beat upon. I was a loner for a reason. Early in my life people got hurt because of me. Now, in Grafton, Raphael had everyone I cared about within reach. Jen was here. Nick. Maybe others. If I didn't do what he said, or if I left, Raphael would kill them all.

"Grimm." Raphael's voice was calm. That scared me more than the beating. "I'm just going to ask you one more time, and then I'm going to move on. Do you understand?"

I turned my head to look at Raphael; I was embarrassed to find my eyes sliding away to the floor. Like a beaten dog. I looked everywhere but into his face. I couldn't leave now, but if I stayed, perhaps there was a chance I could get them out. Get all of us out. The idea solidified in my head. It sounded good, and it might be the only thing I could do. Watch, wait, learn, run.

"Yes," I said, feeling my jaw move a little funny, something popping in its hinge. "I understand."

"Good," Raphael said. I still couldn't look at him. His voice grew louder. "Bring the old man in."

Frank came in, and Parker followed. Parker looked like the same sturdy man I remembered, the same light brown skin, thick arms, and close-cropped gray-black hair. Nothing had changed about Parker except for his face. Thick scars ran vertically up and down his cheekbones, his jaw, his mouth, just missing his eyes. Some of them ran up his forehead and into his scalp. The gouges hadn't healed well. They were dark red, thick, and twisted.

"Boy," Parker said, his voice gruff. Just as I remembered.

I could see the glee Raphael felt, looking at Parker, and seeing me look at Parker like that.

"Parker is taking you back home, Grimm," Raphael said. "He's going to explain some things to you that he should have explained ten years ago."

Parker nodded at me once. I was having trouble breathing. "And then?"

"You just hang around, Grimm." Raphael squatted down in front of me, reached out, and grabbed my hair with one hand, forcing me to look right at him. I could feel him content with his power, and how he used it on me. I could feel him exude it over the others. "My father will be here soon enough. Relax, see the sights." He smiled. "Heal up a bit."

I tried to focus then. Something was happening I needed to pay attention to. Something I needed to figure out. Raphael had a plan, and I had been gone too long to know anything about what it could be. Maybe I could figure it out, if my head wasn't ringing so loudly. My voice cracked. "Why?"

Raphael waved his finger and made a *tsking* sound. "What I'm doing, and why, is none of your business. Your business is doing what you're told. Remember that."

I tried to take a breath, but a sob escaped instead. I hid my face in my hands. I hadn't known what I was getting into, coming here, but I had trusted that I could take care of it. I had a long history of taking care of things on my own. But I understood now the Grafton of my youth was gone, replaced by a town of vampires, ruled by a monster, and I had way overestimated my ability to take care of myself here.

CHAPTER EIGHT

I was in a ballpark. In the on-deck circle. Swinging my bat a bit, warming up. It was a cool spring day, one of those days when the breeze cooled you down and the sun warmed you up, and the smell of freshly mowed grass was everywhere. I could hear the crowd talking it up, and the batter at the plate took a huge swing and a miss. Strike one ...

There was some laughter. Danny pushed the top of his batter's helmet back from where it had slipped down and covered his eyes. It was too big for him, but I could say that about most things for Danny. He was small, and things had a way of not fitting him right. Especially in a house for orphans.

"Get the next one, Danny!" I shouted. He smiled, nodded a serious nod. Faced the pitcher who was winding up. One huge swing spun Danny a quarter of the way around. Zero to two. The crowd got louder, jeering, laughing. One of them called for the coach to replace Danny.

"Get the retard out of there!"

I turned around, looked over the crowd. Danny's brow furrowed a bit. I gave him a nod and a thumbs-up, and I could see him square up his shoulders and try to get tough.

I had told him not to listen to anyone else, that he and I would be fine on our own. All he had was a stuttering problem, but the kids and the parents here just took a problem and ran with it. Not a lot of people were nice to an orphan who stuttered, especially when he was nervous, and they all made him nervous.

"Swa, swa, swa, swing!" mocked another from the crowd.

I raised my bat, looked again into the little crowd section. They all blurred until it seemed like they were all the same person, the same jeer. I couldn't make out one face from another, and then it was everyone in Grafton, and then it was no one.

A smack of wood on canvas, and the ball popped up. Eyes followed it into the air as it quickly went foul. I pumped my fist. "Good job, Danny. Follow your eyes!"

I looked back, though, and saw Danny bent over the plate, being held on his knees by two of the crowd. I looked finally at the pitcher, saw Raphael winding up an elongated monstrous arm holding something black and big in his fist. One of the crowd kicked the batter's helmet off Danny's head.

"G-G-G-Grimmm," Danny said, trying to look up at me. The huge black rock headed for his head. I started toward Dan, but I was caught in that slow-motion dream movement that let me know I would never get there in time.

Hard G after hard G fell out of Danny's mouth, slowly pronounced syllables that seemed to tick each second off the clock. Raphael's arm finished its windup, and a rock the size of a basketball headed toward the plate. I ran and ran and ran, and the crowd held Danny down, with the dark blur streaking its way to Danny's head.

I woke in a start and bit off a scream of pain. Everything in my body ached. My pillow was stuck to my face, and I reached up and gently pulled it off, wincing as caked blood came off with the pillowcase. A few long moments later I still lay there, trying to take soft, long breaths, feeling a sharp pain each time my lungs brushed up against something. I'd have to reevaluate my calcium intake with the way my ribs kept breaking the past few days.

Raphael had Jen. I remember him telling me it didn't matter where she was, only what he would do to her. I hoped I wasn't too late to rescue her. I just had to find where she was and get her away. Wasn't much of a plan, but the steps were easy to follow, and right now finding out where Raphael might have Jen seemed about the limit of what I could do.

I slowly sat up in the bed and then slowly swiveled my legs to the floor. My lower back ached, and I hoped the pain wasn't telling me a kidney was failing. I gently fingered the top of my skull, wincing at the movement of my arm, feeling a bandage around my hairline. It would be nice to feel human again, so I reached out to see if I could locate a ghost. I wasn't surprised when none revealed themselves. The radar was clean. Another thing on the list of items I had to figure out. Another thing to worry about. It was like a big vacuum had come down and sucked Grafton clean of spirits.

I was in my old room, in a familiar bed that I had largely outgrown. Blue threadbare carpet lay against light tan walls. My dresser was wedged in one corner of the room, my closet door next to it. The door still had on old *Star Wars* poster tacked on it, with Luke Skywalker on the front, Darth Vader standing behind him. The years had faded the poster a bit, the corners around each tack curled.

For whatever reason Parker had kept my room the same. It brought back a feeling of comfort and protection that surprised me; I had been on the run for so long I had forgotten what having a place was like. Small childhood comforts have a way of making you feel safe, like a warm blanket on a cold night. I took a long moment to let the feeling just soak in.

I was still in my clothes from last night. Waking up in a clean bed helped me to realize how bad I smelled, but I didn't have anything else with me to wear. I grimaced and got up to check my closet and dresser, and ended up finding an old T-shirt that would work and some socks.

The upstairs bathroom was empty, so I took a quick shower. The water was hot and felt great, even if it stung a bit. It felt good to be clean. I checked myself in the mirror. If Miss Tammie thought I looked bad yesterday, she was in for a real treat today. I was covered in bruises and scrapes, had a good mouse going over one eye. It all hurt, but nothing was life-threatening unless a person scared easily.

The T-shirt was a little tight, and my pants hadn't been washed in so long they could almost stand on their own. I would have to go get my car today. Everything I owned was in there. And after yesterday, I felt like I could use the comfort of having my shotgun around.

My knuckles and fingers were swollen in places, which made rethreading my shoes a nightmare. After I had finished that grueling task I left my room, headed toward the stairs. On a quick whim, I stopped at what used to be Nick's room. I knocked and, hearing no answer, opened the door. It was barren, no bed, no dresser, nothing on the walls. Like he had never lived there.

I shut the door and struggled down the stairs and checked the kitchen. Signs of breakfast there, clean dishes in the dish rack, a drying towel over the faucet. An empty plastic gallon of milk rinsed out on the counter. A faint smell of bacon in the air. My stomach growled, but it also felt a little nauseated. I hoped my insides were in better condition than my outside.

To the right was the living room, and it was here I felt the strongest déjà vu hint of familiarity. The same tan couch still sat against the wall on the same worn beige carpet. Where Nick, Johnny, Danny, and I had watched cartoons together, sitting on the floor, backs against the couch, eating cereal. The same imitation paintings on the walls, the same books on the mantel. The same tube television, one of those big old ones in a wooden case and with huge black knobs, sat in the corner with a pair of folded rabbit ears on top.

I lingered there for a minute, looking into the living room. Remembering old laughs. Imagining Bugs Bunny and the Road Runner and the great cereal battles. Nick had launched cereal from his spoon, using the spoon as a catapult, which had obviously led to four catapults, until all of us were laughing and lying on the living room floor with milk-soggy cereal pieces all over us. And all over the house.

Something caught my eye out the front window, and I turned and saw Parker's hand on the edge of his rocking chair, moving ever so slightly back and forth. Past Parker the old rope swing, hanging from the front yard tree, moved gently in a breeze, twisting and turning on old, frayed strands.

I went back into the kitchen, got a glass, and filled it with tap water. I forced myself to take a couple of sips, and then a couple more. My stomach ached when the water hit it, but once I finished a second glass I started to feel better. I stood there and focused on the linoleum of the floor, seeing where the kitchen table had pressed round indented marks on the floor. There was a new microwave on the counter, something that hadn't been here ten years ago.

I walked out the front door, the screen door announcing me with a screeching swing. Parker watched me, rocking back and forth and saying nothing. I walked across the porch, the old wooden planks creaking a bit under my weight, and sat on the porch rail facing him. His scars looked a little better in sunlight. This morning they were just ugly. Last night they had been monstrous. In his hand, he held a tall glass of lemonade, big square ice cubes bobbing in the drink.

"You look like shit," Parker said, his face a mix of scowl and smile. I had gotten into a lot of scraps as a kid, and the words were familiar to us both. A pattern we both had followed.

"You should see the other guy."

"I saw him, right enough," Parker snorted. "Didn't look like he broke a sweat."

"Yeah." I let out a sigh, thought again to the night before. Raphael was much more terrifying than I had remembered. We had fought as kids, the way kids punched and rolled around. We had stood toe-to-toe with each other then. Last night he could have killed me.

"He's got Jen, Park," I said.

Parker shrugged and sipped his lemonade. "He likely does."

"I've got to find her," I said.

Parker looked past me, out to the field and the lone oak tree. The wind picked up a little, a fluttering wind that ebbed and died moments apart. "I'm sure you feel like you do."

That struck me as odd. Parker knew what Jen meant to me, or had known. It sounded like he thought there were more important things waiting for me, but he knew that I would put Jen before whatever else Raphael wanted to do. I wanted him to tell me more, but Parker would only tell things the way he wanted to. In the manner in which he wanted to get his points across. And in the time he wanted to tell them.

We both sat there for a bit. Him rocking, me leaning against the porch rail. Even in the shade of the porch, the scars stood out on his brown skin, twisted serpents of knotted tissue. He had been more of a father figure than anyone I'd known, but we had never really gotten along. It might have been my fault, maybe some of his, but all of it had been long ago. "What happened?"

Parker stared straight ahead for a bit. He set his jaw, in a way that meant he was thinking. The motion knotted his scars. "Your mother." Parker rocked to a slow, cradling creak. "She has a temper."

I sank back against the porch rail. I could have pulled a million reasons out of the hat for Parker's disfigurement and not come up with that one. Him telling me I had a mother wasn't as shocking as I thought it might be. It wasn't like a television show where a long-lost mother steps onto a stage to reunite with her kid, and some talk show host calls it a miracle. So I had a mother, but to me, I always had had one. Mothers to me were people like Miss Tammie or Mrs. Cooper.

My jaw tightened. That wasn't really true. People like Miss Tammie and Mrs. Cooper had taken care of me, and maybe they had taken the role of mother, but I think I had always felt like I hadn't deserved a mom. Part of me had always felt like some Frankenstein kid pieced together and put in an orphanage to bake into a person. I had felt alone from the very start, and it was the reason I had always been a loner, why I had always done things the way I wanted to do them. And that reason was why Parker and I never had gotten along.

So I had a mother, but apparently she didn't want me. My father either, if I was at Parker's. Why was I at an orphanage, when my so-called mother had come back and carved up Parker's face when I ran away? I sat opposite to where a rope swing hung lifelessly under the oak tree.

"I saw my first ghost there, on that swing," I said.

Parker's rocking stopped. "Was it a boy?"

"Yeah."

"He black?" Parker asked. "Young, a little chubby in the stomach? Big ears, missing his front teeth?"

It had been a long time ago, and I had seen many ghosts since, but I would always remember that one. The boy had swung on that swing in the twilight, much like Parker rocked in his chair now, and stared out over the fields, whistling a tune I couldn't hear. "Yeah."

"I figured," Parker said, and it was like something left him. His body shrank over a second, seemed smaller, deflated. The only thing left was his legs, rocking the chair over and over in the quiet of the day.

The kid had been maybe ten years old. I looked out to the swing I had seen him on, long ago. I remembered the moment clearly, remembered seeing a little boy shimmering with a white-blue haze, swinging back and forth on that old rope. Back and forth, back and forth, much like Parker's chair now.

"He was your son," I said, looking back at Parker. "Wasn't he?"

"All this time, I done what they wanted," Parker said, head down. "And now there ain't much left."

"I'm sorry, Park." The first ghost I had seen, it had been Parker's son.

"Not sure why you would be." Parker's head sank lower, and his elbows lay on his knees. His chair was tilted all the way forward, and the glass of lemonade hung loosely in one fist. "You didn't know what you was seeing. And it was me that was supposed to watch for it. Let her know."

"Watch for me to see ghosts?" I asked. "Why?"

"Had to make sure your power manifested," Parker said. "You were going to be a leash for Raphael's father. A way for him to control his kid without having to be around all the time."

"And I screwed that up." Growing up, I had only known Dominic Abandonado as Raphael's rich father. It was only later I had learned he was the head of the largest clan of vampires in the United States.

"Yep." Parker took a sip of the lemonade. "So Dominic told your mother to come here and remind me."

His job had been to babysit a kid who argued with him at every turn, had run away on weekends, had done anything and everything not to listen to him. And his reward for that had been gruesome.

"I'm sorry." It was the second time I had apologized to Parker in the past few minutes when I had never done it as a kid.

Parker shook his head. "I could never get you to listen, boy. You were always contrary. Whatever I told you, you'd go and do the opposite. I still remember taking you to Raphael's party, back when you were six or seven."

"I hated going there," I said. "His rich mansion, everything he had, everything his father gave him and how Raphael treated the rest of us."

"Yep," Parker said. "You weren't there five minutes and you were getting in a fight with him. You remember what I told you then?"

"Same thing you always told me," I said. "Don't pick fights you know you can't win."

"Exactly," Parker said. "But you kept picking them, didn't you? I could never get you to understand there were more things happening in this world than you not liking him."

"I was just a kid, Park," I said. As if that could fix what had happened to him.

"I was just a kid," Parker mimicked. "Keeping telling yourself that when Dominic and your mother get here. You should have stayed away, Fergus. You should have just kept on doing whatever it was you were doing."

We sat like that for a long time. Parker went back to rocking and sipping his lemonade. I thought of the Key, safe in the Vault, and of the last six years running, and wondered if my time would have been better spent here in Grafton. Could I have done something to change any of this had I stayed? It felt unfair—I had left because of Raphael, and everyone had been punished anyway.

I looked back to that empty swing and the ghost that used to be there. I wondered about Parker's past, what had happened to his son, why Parker was even here. There was a lot to figure out. And now Raphael's father was coming here and bringing my mother. Could my mother see and use ghosts like I could? Could Dominic control both of us, like Raphael could control me?

Is that what Parker meant, when he told me I was going to be Dominic's leash on Raphael. Was Dominic going to command me to obey his son, but report to Dominic? I didn't like where those thoughts were headed, and I shuddered. And I wondered what Dominic thought I could do, just with ghosts.

"You mentioned making sure my powers manifested," I said. "Does that mean my mother can see ghosts too? What did you mean by that?"

Parker snorted. The motion twisted his scars and turned his face ugly. "Boy, do I look like someone who's dying to give you all the answers?"

I passed some point with him, when I had run away. A point I wasn't coming back from. "No."

"Damn right," Parker said.

I looked away then, back to the swing. Remembered looking down at Parker's son, who was grinning and swinging higher and higher. The ten-year-old ghost looking at me as he swung, just for a moment, and then swinging on and on until he disappeared into the night. Behind me Parker had started rocking again, the chair creaking as it bent under his weight. We spent some time that way.

"Grimm, there's a lot I could have told you, had you stayed. Had you listened," Parker said finally, quietly. "That time's past now."

"I don't know what I would have done different," I said. "I don't know what to do now to fix any of it."

"That don't matter much now either." Parker's rocker was the slow movement of a ship at sea. The ice cubes in his lemonade tinkled gently against the glass. *Clink, clink.* "Not for either of us."

"That might be true," I said. "But I'm not giving up. Help me here, Park. Help me find Jen. Help me save her."

"What about Nick?" Parker asked, and his eyes glittered. "What about Johnny? They were your family too, right? Or you just going to run, like you did when Danny was killed?"

I couldn't say anything to that. I had run. And I still felt the shame.

"Time was, you was a scrapper, a fighter," he went on, angry. "We fought a lot, but at least I could respect that in you. You stood up for yourself, for your friends."

"You don't know the whole story," I returned. "What choice did I have?"

"Son. What choice is there for any of us?" His face twisted into a mask of angry scars and furrowed red lines. "*Look at me.* You think I wanted *this* town? *This* place? *This* job? *This* face?" He looked out over the field in front of the house, and the swing on the tree. "Everything in life takes something from you, boy, and you got to find a way to put that something back. That's how it goes. That's life." He looked like he wanted to spit again like something nasty and foul-tasting had worked its way into his mouth. But instead, after a long moment, he went back to rocking. Staring out over the yard. His lemonade glass sat forgotten beside him.

I had left to protect my friends, and I still thought that was true now. But maybe Parker had hit close to the mark, maybe I was more of a coward than I wanted to admit. Had I been telling myself a lie so long that now I believed it? Was I running not because it was the best thing to do, but because I was scared? There were bits and pieces of the truth in the pattern of my life: I had left my friends in Grafton, I had left people I had fought beside in the service. I was, even now, running from something. There was a reality behind Parker's words, and it hurt.

"I'll tell you one more thing," Parker spat. "One thing. Because I was told to."

I looked at the tree, and the swing, dangling there from an old oak limb and slightly struggling in the currents of air around it. Maybe lost a little in thoughts of a guy who had run for so long he didn't know who he was anymore.

"Raphael's father will be here soon, and your mother will be with him," Parker said. Each word echoed with finality, a piece of truth. "The moment they get here, Dominic's going to want to see you. And now that you're here, know there ain't no running from them, boy. There ain't far enough on this earth."

The swing swayed again in the breeze, back and forth, back and forth. Softly, gently, resisting the wind at the same time the current pushed at it. Parker mimicked the motion in his chair, back and forth, back and forth. The lemonade glass was in his hand again, and his face looked past me out into the yard. There was a symmetry here, the ebb and flow of choices made and opportunities lost. Forward and back, past and present. My life swung between both, and I could get away from neither.

CHAPTER NINE

It was early afternoon, so I decided to go get my car. I figured moving around would warm me up and stretch out all my bruises, and I would love to get some new clothes. Only so much that shower could do.

Walking through the bad side of Grafton brought back plenty of memories. The south side of town had always been run-down, but ten years later it appeared to be a long row of condemned lots: open doors, empty windows, here and there a roof collapsed with a broken spine. I had seen pictures of mining towns, and the south side of Grafton was a lot like those, copies of the same house on the same lot, square after square, row after row. All the houses were a mix of peeling off-white paint and gray boards underneath. Lawns were overgrown mixtures of weeds and grass.

Mailboxes gaped at me as I walked by, faded pieces of paper taped to their sides. One had a picture of a teenage girl under the washed-out words *Have you seen this girl?* The girl in the picture was dark-haired and plump. A few of her teeth were missing, but her smile was big and bright. She looked happy. I set my jaw and walked on. The girl was likely dead or gone now, as well as whoever had been looking for her.

The sidewalks were cracked in spidery webs, weeds pushing up and breaking apart the concrete. Potholes gaped on blacktopped streets. Not a single light was on in a house, nor cars in driveways. No sounds of kids playing in backyards, or a too-loud television. It was eerily quiet. I licked my lips, wishing for something to moisten them in the cool air.

I took familiar streets, heading north into town. I had walked this way many times with Nick and Johnny and Danny. Maybe going to school, maybe going to a game. Nick and I would be arguing who should win the Gold Glove, or the Cy Young. Johnny would take one side, then switch to the other and laugh.

At some point while I was walking I thought I heard someone tossing a baseball in the air and catching it, over and over. I stopped myself before I turned to look back for Danny. He wouldn't be there, but some ghosts I would always carry.

I smiled in memory, though. Danny had always walked with an earnestness, careful to not step on a single crack, for fear that he might break his mother's back. Like the old children's rhyme. Never mind that none of us had known our mothers.

The path I walked was the last place I wanted to go. But I had walked this way a thousand times growing up, and the path was hard to leave. Maybe Parker's conversation had steered me this way. Maybe I wanted to face something instead of always running. Whatever it was, my feet knew the way, and I headed directly to the place I had first run from.

Was that day, that moment, when I had changed into who I was now? Parker had brought up all the times I had fought with him, fought with Raphael. When Nick first got his glasses, I had been the guy to stop the other kids from making fun of him. When Johnny had maybe pulled a joke on a friend of Raphael's, it was me that helped Johnny settle that score after school.

I used to be the guy his friends could count on to defend them. But one day I had stopped fighting and starting running. Was Parker right, was that who I had become now? Could I change back into who I had been? Or was I an ill-tempered piece of steel, a brittle metal that would crack as soon as a weight was placed upon it?

I slowed down, and my steps grew heavier as I neared the liquor store. It sat on a corner, in the middle of Main Street. The store was still open. An alley ran behind it to a little closed area surrounded by an old wooden fence. A tiny parking lot for a couple of cars, and not much else.

I headed back that way, navigating old broken bottles of whiskey and tequila and vodka, and empty plastic versions of the same. Across from the back of the store lay a pile of glass, where someone apparently had thrown bottle after bottle against the wall. The sour smell of old beer in the sun and mildewing cardboard rose from the grimy lot.

I stood, transfixed, on a spot in the center of the lot. Surrounding me was the old brick wall of the store and the wooden fence, boards curving and bowing away from me. The question of who I was fell away and was replaced by the last memory I had of Danny. It was something I owed him.

It was the end of a school day, and I had just left Jen's house. Her mom had cooked us a nice dinner, and Jen and I had lain on the couch, guessing words on a game show before the last letter was turned up.

Walking home, I wondered if I was going to finish the homework I had to get done, or if I was just going to remember the press of Jen's side against mine, and her arm around my back. I kind of felt like it was going to be the latter.

It was dark out, with a duskiness to the air that was almost foglike in its grayness. A slight chill wove through the fog, and I thought about colored leaves and football and being out at the Rock with Jen this weekend.

I was a block away from Main Street before I heard the first bottles shatter, a sharp crack followed by the tinkling of glass across the pavement. Some laughter followed it and got louder and louder as I neared the liquor store. I had a good idea of who it was. Part of me wanted to hide, and part of me wanted to run, and I compromised by hunching over and walking faster.

A thump of a bat struck another bottle, followed by a bottle crinkling against a brick wall. In the corner of my eye, I saw the storekeeper look toward the back of his store, shake his head, and look back down at his counter. Something he didn't want to bother with, and I knew why. It was the same reason I didn't want to bother with it.

Then I heard Danny.

"L-l-l-let m-m-me g-g-go," he cried out. I froze, saw the storekeeper keep his face down, pretending not to hear anything. A cold sweat broke over me and I ran down the alley, anger flickering inside me, blossoming

into hate. I crunched my hands into fists—I knew who was down there, and I knew why they were down there.

Danny knelt at the end of the alley, in the parking lot, crying. He held his baseball in one hand. A group of boys surrounded him, some of the usual boys who hung with Raphael. I recognized a few of them: Jacob, Rand, and Darian. Broken bits of glass lay on Danny's head and around him, and Jake held a bat that was discolored where bottles had broken against it. They must have been making him kneel there, using him as a tee, knocking beer bottles off his head against the wall. I could see beer had run down Danny's face and neck, leaving huge damp puddles on his shirt.

Danny's eyes lit up when he saw me, and he struggled to his feet even as Rand pushed him back down. I ran straight at them, ducking as Jake swung the bat and landing a fist in his stomach. After that I swung at Rand, feeling my knuckles crack against his jaw. He reached out and grabbed me, and both of us tumbled to the ground, swinging away at each other. Rand was digging at my eyes. I pulled my head back just as something hard connected with my temple.

That was all it took. I fell off Rand and hit the ground.

"Well, now." Raphael's voice. His shoes stepped into my vision. I swallowed in an effort to keep my stomach's insides in. "Nice of you to show up, Grimm."

I mumbled something, and then Rand and Darian helped pull me up in front of Raphael. I bent over and threw up.

"Grimm." Raphael looked like he was grinning. His face was a little blurry in front of me. "These are new shoes."

"Raph." I spat and wiped the edge of my mouth with my arm.

"You having some trouble with standing, Grimm?" Raphael asked. "You look a little wobbly."

"What's your problem, Raph?" I blinked a few times, and Raphael got a little sharper. My stomach still rolled, much like a ship riding a huge wave. "Why are you always bothering Danny?"

"We were just waiting for you," Raphael said. "He just happened to come along. Got to pass the time some way, don't we?"

"Fine," I said, looking at Danny. Still kneeling, shivering a bit. "I'm here. Let him go."

"Or?"

"What do you mean, or?" I said.

"Or's a pretty simple thing," Raphael said, moving to put his face in front of mine. "Let me explain it to you. I'm asking you, Let the retard go … Or what'?"

I took a deep breath, my chest swelling a bit. Jake, Darian, and Rand all stood around me. Jake was holding the bat. The odds were good I was about to get a beating. All I wanted to do was get Danny free before it happened. "You want to beat on me, Raph, that's fine. Danny's got no part in it, though."

"I'm not sure you're in a position to say anything about that." Raphael wiggled his eyebrows up and down, and a couple of his boys snickered. "I tell you what, though." Raphael looked up like he had just had a thought. "Kneel, and I'll let him go."

"What?"

"Kneel." Raphael smiled and nodded behind me. Jacob swung the bat into the back of my knees. My legs gave out, and I fell to a kneeling position on the parking lot. I took a deep breath, trying to keep my stomach settled, and I was kneeling in my own puddle of puke. An acidic sourness hung in the back of my throat.

Raphael leaned over and whispered in my ear, "Feel like kneeling now?"

I grunted, then pushed up from the pavement, but both Rand and Darian held me in a kneeling position, and Jake stood by with the bat. I looked over at Danny, who knelt there wide-eyed. "Run," I mouthed to him.

"You know what yesterday was, Grimm?" Raphael had stood, looking into the air. Like he was waiting to receive something.

"Run," I mouthed again to Danny, motioning with my head to the alley. Danny looked to the alley, then back to me.

"Yesterday was my birthday," Raphael said, reaching into his pocket and pulling out a bottle of something. "Drink?"

"What are you doing, Raph?" The feeling that something was out of control was all around me. Raphael and I had fought a lot, but this was far beyond anything we had done before.

"I'm giving myself a present." Raphael put one knee next to me, not caring that he was kneeling in the puke. He leaned his face close to my ear. "A little birdie told me something about you, Grimm. Told me you were seeing ghosts." He cocked his head at me. "That true?"

I grew cold. I hadn't mentioned that to many people. It wasn't something I was sure I believed myself. "See ghosts?" I tried to snort. "Maybe in a movie."

"Sure, sure." Raphael smiled. Something wasn't right in his eyes, in his pupils. They were too large, and it frightened me. Something was wrong with his teeth too. They had grown larger, in the front. Sharper. "A movie, right? A movie about a boy on a swing?"

If I was cold before, everything inside me was frozen now. "Where'd you hear that?"

"What's it matter?" Raphael stood back up, and his friends dragged me up with him. He waggled his brows. "Want a drink, Grimm?"

I shook my head slowly. Danny did the same, a tiny, mimicking motion.

"Your loss." Raphael tossed the bottle away, and it shattered behind him. The sound was louder than it should have been. Every motion of Raphael's was exaggerated like he was taking special care to think of how he wanted to look as he walked around. Like he wanted to remember every moment. "You going to say happy birthday to me?"

"Probably not," I said.

Rand and Jake were holding me, so it was Darian who came around and poked my gut with the top of the bat. I whooshed out some air.

"It doesn't cost much, wishing someone happy birthday," Raphael said.

"You let Danny go," I said, "and I'll sing happy birthday to you."

"There's a thought." Raphael came closer. His voice took on a dark, commanding tone. "Or you could just say it."

"Happy birthday, Raphael." The words came unbidden from my mouth. I hadn't even thought to say them. It was like someone else had said them, right out of my body.

Danny's eyes opened in surprise. I tried to cover my mouth with my hands, but Jake and Rand still had a hold of each arm.

Raphael started laughing then, a wild, thin laugh. Something sharp, bordering on the edge of a knife. Rand and Jake and Darian all joined with him.

"Now sing it," Raphael demanded, his face wild and crazy and in my face. "Sing it!"

"Happy birthday to you, happy birthday to you," I sang. Jake and Rand laughed hard enough for me to free my arms, and I clapped both hands over my mouth, but I still couldn't control what I was saying. I muffled the rest from between my fingers. "Happy birfday, dear Rafal, happy birfday to youuuuu ..."

I took my hands off my mouth, shook them, shook my head. I didn't understand what was happening to me. Raphael gave a hoot and walked around in a circle, raising an arm into the air over and over. Danny's face was still wet with tears and old, spilled beer. "Danny, get out of here. Now."

Danny finally got up off his knees and started moving toward the alley, but Jake grabbed him. Danny tried to push him away, but Jake was large and just rag-dolled Danny to his knees. I lunged for Jake, but Darian and Rand wrestled me back down.

Raphael kept parading around in a circle, finally stopping in front of me. "Did you get me something for my birthday, Grimm?"

"I sang you a song," I said. "Let Danny go."

Raphael shook his head. "A song is just a song." His eyes were not even in the moment. They were looking somewhere far, far away. Recording everything. "It's not a gift at all. Everyone gets one. What else you got?"

"You're fucking crazy, Raph. Really fucking crazy," I said. I didn't have a word for how I felt, frightened or scared didn't seem to cover it. It was like I was on a roller coaster plummeting down the tracks of a huge hill, the bar of the cart holding me in tight, and a huge brick wall at the end of the tracks. All I could think of was trying to get me and Danny out of there. "You need to let us go."

"I do?" As he talked Raphael got more and more excited. It made his voice louder and louder. I think he realized it; he leaned over to me, put his lips next to my ear, and whispered, "I know about you and your ghosts, Grimm. I know a lot about them. I know more about you. But I'm betting you don't know that much about me."

Raphael was crazy, maniacal, and he and his friends had both Danny and me trapped in the back of an alley. I had no idea what he was talking *about, and no idea how to stop it. No idea how to jump off the roller coaster before it hit the wall.*

Raphael stood back up. "So my dad stopped by for my birthday. Tells me all about you. About your family and mine. About how you're going to be my enforcer. Even my assassin. And that I would need to keep you around, take special care of you."

I snorted. Even Jacob laughed.

Raphael grinned. "Yeah, I didn't think it was funny either. But then my dad explained that my family has a special power. That you, Grimm, are especially bound by it. And I thought to myself, That's something I got to try." He opened his arms like a showman. "After all, who gets a birthday present and doesn't play with it a bit?"

I didn't know what he was talking about. The rest of his group sat there, holding tight to Danny and me. Danny knelt there, afraid. I knelt next to him, terrified.

"Look at me, Grimm." Raphael grabbed Danny's hair and jerked his head toward me. Danny cried out and reached up to pull Raphael's hands off. I fought to grab Raphael's arms before Darian and Rand pulled me back. Raphael's eyes were too large, too open. "For my birthday, I want you to punch your friend in the face."

I stopped struggling with Rand and Darian, trying to freeze, trying to stop my arm. I could already feel my arm cocking back of its own accord. Danny stopped wriggling, and he shook his head at me in little motions, crying, one hand weakly pressed against Jacob's arms.

"You heard me." Raphael's voice broke, it was so tight. "Punch your friend in the face."

I fought the movement of my arm, willing my body to stop with every-thing inside me. I had always been stubborn. I didn't know anything or anyone more stubborn. I fought and fought, watching my hand tremble in the air, watching my arm shake as it was caught between my will and whatever force was trying to control it.

Raphael began to frown. I fought with everything I had. And right before I swung, I won. I took breath after breath, watching my arm hold still in the air like someone had nailed it to that spot. I could feel the force pushing me to swing, and I locked my muscles against it. Stalemate.

Raphael had watched every moment, his smile getting angrier and angrier with every passing moment until my arm had stopped. "I said fucking punch the retard, Grimm."

"No," I said quietly. My nerves were burning as electrical impulses fought to carry conflicting messages to my arm.

"Punch him," Raphael said again.

"I fucking said no." I looked at his eyes, his crazy wide-open eyes, and shook my head.

Raphael screamed, spit flying out of his mouth, and let go of Danny. The vampire's eyes were empty. Raphael had moved into some crazy dimension where nothing sane was left in him. Rand and Darian had let go of me, stepping back from Raphael. I was locked where I was, not able to move my arm, which still hung like it was nailed in midair.

"G-g-g-g-rimm," Danny whispered. He was shaking, his arms curled around like he was holding himself.

"It's okay, Danny," I said, voice low. "Just hang in there. It'll be okay." It was all I could say.

"Fuck, fuck, fuck, fuck, fuuuuck!" Raphael screamed over and over again. He stomped around and then came back to me, breathing heavy, lips pulled back over teeth. "You won't punch him?"

I shook my head. "You can't make me."

"Then what the fuck good are you?" Raphael took the bat from Jake, swung it at my head. I was still locked in position by my arm, and couldn't move out of the way. The bat swung through my arm and crashed into my head.

The next thing I could see was the side of the pavement. Something wet and warm crawled its way over my face and leaked onto the tarred surface, mixed with my bile. I couldn't move my arms or my legs, and I let out a low moan. I could see Danny kneeling there again, looking at me, frozen and not knowing what to do. He reached one hand out to me. As if he could help me. "Run." I tried to form the word, tried to mouth it to Danny, but my lips didn't move.

"You do what I tell you, Grimm." Raphael stared down at me.

I shook my head, and my cheek rubbed slightly against the blacktop. My head pulsed with a throbbing heartbeat rhythm where the bat had connected. I looked at Danny, who knelt there and reached back to me. There was no stopping Raphael now. The roller coaster had left the tracks.

"You do what I fucking tell you," Raphael repeated. His chest heaved in big breaths. He glared at me, then back to Danny, then back to me.

"Danny," I mumbled. I didn't know if what I was saying made sense. My mouth wasn't moving like I wanted it to. "You got to get out of here, Danny."

I pushed myself off the ground. My arms shook trying to hold me up. Blood ran down my temple and across my face, and I looked into Raphael's crazy eyes.

Raphael looked right back at me, tapping the bat in one hand and one corner of his mouth lifting in a curve. His irises shone bright and wobbled a little in their intensity and stayed locked on to mine. Then his mouth broke into a full grin and he swung back the bat one more time.

A baseball hit Raphael and bounced off his face. It broke his nose and blood splattered across the pavement. He took a couple of steps back and put a hand to his face. It came down streaming with blood.

Danny had stood up. His jaw was set. He wasn't big, but he faced Raphael with both feet on the ground, fingers wrapped tightly into fists. Behind Danny, Jacob had put his hand to his mouth, covering a look of surprise.

Raphael swung the bat as hard as he could.

I screamed and tried to push myself up. The bat cut the air and connected with a sickening, wet thump. Like a ripe melon popping open. Blood splattered my face, warm and wet, and then the thump of a body collapsing on the lot.

"Open your fucking eyes, Grimm!" Raphael's lips were next to my ear, and he was screaming. I could feel his hand grab my hair, shake my head violently, bouncing it up and down on the pavement. "Open your fucking eyes!"

I didn't want to. I felt like I was dreaming. A nightmare. Nothing felt real. Raphael gave my head one final shake and pushed my face down into a puddle of wetness, and I could smell a mix of ivory soap and warm copper.

I opened my eyes. Danny lay in front of me, facedown, with a large red area caved in on the back of his skull. Something pink and wriggly leaked out from a broken mesh of white bone and crimson blood.

"Holy shit, man." Jake grabbed Raphael and pulled him away. Darian and Rand ran with them.

"Open your eyes, Grimm!" Raphael shouted, fighting with Jake as the boy pulled him down the alley. "Open your fucking eyes!"

I could hear Raphael and his friends running out of the alley, onto the street, their footsteps a roller coaster clickety-clacking up a hill.

CHAPTER TEN

After a while I left the back of the parking lot, limping around to the front. Everything still hurt from last night's beating, but I looked almost normal walking down the street. I could place one foot after the other without wincing, at least.

I hadn't been the only person who had changed that day. The Raphael of last night had been much different than the spoiled kid I had fought, and even different than the boy who had killed Danny. We had been high school rivals. Now we were more, twisted by some sick geas. Raphael had taking the first step in becoming the monster he was now. I, one of many steps by running away. Danny had been a catalyst for the both of us.

I hit Main Street and glanced toward the other end of town, away from the diner. On the next block, Mingles was still open, the local pool hall with some tiny apartments above it. It was late afternoon, but I decided to head that way. I needed to find out more about this town, and the local bar was as good a place to start as any.

The bar was just like the town, worn-down. Old, dark wooden tables were sprinkled across the place, deep scars in the tabletops, chairs haphazardly placed here and there. Cigarette trays lay scattered, some full and some empty, the faint scent of stale smoke in the air. The bar was to my right, half-empty bottles sitting underneath a dusty mirror. On the far end were six pool tables, with a man and a woman playing at the farthest one.

Everything was lit by small-watt bulbs that weakly threw out tiny globes of yellow light, leaving shadows between them. Big sheets of plywood were nailed in the back of blacked-out windows. Customers sat in the shadows, in booths, at tables where the lights didn't quite shine. Not many customers, maybe four or five, plus the couple playing pool. I winced at the first crack of a pool cue against a ball.

The bartender had a good-size paunch and silver-white hair. While I approached he was quietly wiping down glasses, looking at me carefully as I slowly slid onto a barstool. I wasn't sure what I looked like, but I sure as hell felt like something that had been dragged around behind a horse for a week or so. I let out a deep breath. A few days ago I had only had to worry about staying ahead of a demon. Somehow, incredulously, my life had felt much simpler then.

I waved a couple of fingers at the guy behind the bar. He poured a double and slid it my way. Part of me was still back in that alley. I tossed the drink back, winced at the rough whiskey, and slid back the empty.

He grunted and poured another double into it. I tossed it back as well, and whatever it was burned maybe worse the second time. I coughed lightly into my fist, thumped my chest, and slid the glass back to him again. He smiled, maybe impressed by my dedication.

"Rough stuff," I said, a bit hoarse.

The bartender nodded. Talkative guy.

One of the customers in the bar had gotten up and now stood next to me. He signaled for a beer, which the bartender already started on. I took a look at the customer while he waited, and after several long moments, I recognized him. "Johnny?"

The man looked over. He had drunk enough that each of his motions was slightly exaggerated, but his smile was real. Johnny slapped my shoulder.

"Fergus Grimm," he said. "I heard Nick had put one on you, but man—"

"This wasn't Nick." I motioned to my face. "This was Raphael."

"Ahhhhh," Johnny said. "You saw him, did you? Any man hates you more would be hard to find."

"Yeah." I took another sip. The couple at the pool table had left.

Johnny looked at me out of the corner of his eyes and grinned. "Unless you do want to count Nick, now."

"Yeah." I shook my head. Nick and I had been close once. Almost brothers.

Johnny pulled up a stool and sat on it. "So, man, where you been?"

"Anywhere but here," I said. "Joined the army, been overseas. Afghanistan, the Middle East a bit."

"What are you doing here?"

"Jen called," I said. "She said she was in trouble. I got here yesterday and couldn't find her." I leaned closer and told him about what I had found at the Coopers', and what had happened later.

Johnny whistled, low. "Rough stuff. I feel for Mrs. Cooper. No one deserves that." He looked straight into my eyes.

"I think Raphael has her." My hand clenched into a fist, and my thumb rubbed back and forth over my forefinger.

"I remember," Johnny said. "Could never separate you two. Hell, could never really separate us." He shook his head. "Until Danny was killed."

I swallowed a lump in my throat. The memory was still fresh. Would always be fresh. "I'm sorry about that, Johnny."

"We all know who did it," Johnny said. His hand slapped my shoulder a couple of times, and I gritted my teeth when he found a bruise. "Even Nick. That wasn't your fault."

Parker had told me different. Had told me I just should have listened. If I hadn't picked those fights, Danny might still be alive. "I don't know, Johnny. I don't know. Parker and I had a talk. He said I always wanted to antagonize Raph. That things might be different if I had tried to get along."

He took a long drink from his glass. "Bullshit, Grimm. We both know Raphael hated Danny, and something would have happened at some time. You were someone Danny counted on and loved. You know that."

I wiped my eyes and looked away again. "I don't, Johnny. I don't. If Danny counted on me, then I failed him."

Johnny just shook his head. "You never failed Danny. Remember when he was on our baseball team? How he used to swing the bat like he was going to break open the world's largest piñata?"

I smiled a bit. Danny could have been blindfolded too, as often as he hit the ball.

"You used to stay late and just pitch softies to him, all the time," Johnny said. "Just hanging with him. And he loved every moment of it."

He laughed then, as a memory hit him, and tapped my arm several times with his fist. "Then remember he got that base hit? And danced on first base like he won the world series? You went out and danced with him. Man, that was hilarious. And we all laughed coming home from the game, all of us singing that baseball song, taking us out to the ball game."

"I remember," I almost whispered. Danny throwing the baseball high up in the air and catching it, singing, "Take me out to the ball game. Take me out with the crowd ..."

Johnny turned and looked me in the eye then. His were wet but happy. "He went and got that ball he had hit. He wanted you to have it, and you kept telling him he had earned it. That was you and him, brother. You remember that."

I looked away from Johnny, not trusting my voice to say anything. That was the same ball in the Vault. I was sure of it. But I didn't know why it was there.

Johnny ordered a round for the two of us. We got our beers, tapped glasses, and sat that way for a little bit, lost in thoughts of the past. A woman came out of the doorway that led to the apartments above Mingles. She walked over to stand next to Johnny and laid her arm around him.

"Hey there," Johnny said, in the kind of surprised way a person does when he sees someone he's looking forward to spending time with. She was a knockout brunette, with straight dark hair that shimmered in the dark of the bar. A slight girl, pale, slightly freckled. A knowing smile. A European feel. Her hair was tied back into a simple tail, loose but somehow conveying elegance. She was slim but proportioned correctly. There were some hints of Italian heritage in her face.

Johnny reached out and wrapped his arm around her waist, pulled her close. "Grimm, this is Gabrielle."

I nodded a hello. She smiled back; her incisors were ever so slightly pointed. Her head tilted a bit, as if she recognized me from somewhere.

"Gabrielle is the daughter of the Dumonts," Johnny explained.

The Dumonts were the head of a powerful European clan of vampires.

One that Dominic had been a part of before leaving a couple of hundred years ago for the United States. Her being here in Mingles, instead of staying with Raphael in his mansion, was curious.

I looked at Johnny, and he winked back. He was telling me he was a thrall and that there was no harm done, but my heart sank anyway. They seemed happy, but she was a vampire and Johnny a human. The movies always tell you there's only one way that ends.

"Gabrielle," I said, twisting a corner of my lips into a grin. "Pleasure to meet you."

She could sense what I was thinking. Her free hand involuntarily reached over and held on to Johnny's arm, protectively. "Fergus Grimm." Her voice was a little deeper than I expected, husky with a hint of sexy. "The pleasure is mine."

"The two of us will be headed to the Cauldron here in a bit," Johnny said. "You should come with us. If Raphael does have Jen, someone there might know."

"The club?"

"Yeah." Johnny looked me over. "You been there already?"

I shook my head.

"They got this drink they put out there, called Witch's Brew. It's like a little cinnamon schnapps mixed with liquid heroin, and it's addictive as hell," Johnny said. "Vampires come from other countries to get it, but Raphael won't let it leave Grafton. Any vampire caught taking it out of town gets staked out on the highway for the sun to come up. Stay away from it."

"So why do you go?" I asked.

Johnny and Gabrielle glanced at each other. She tilted her head in question, and he nodded.

She turned back to me. "This drink is a concern to the other clans."

"How much trouble could a drink cause?" I asked. Jake and Rand had hinted that Jen had been causing trouble, and I wondered if this was what she had been getting into.

"A lot, brother." Johnny looked at his beer, turning it in his hand. "This drink does something to vampires. Some weird mix of blood and chemistry and magic. They crave it uncontrollably. It ups their libido. They fight more, have sex more, everything more. And once they have it, they can't stop it."

"Raphael has started something here with this drink," Gabrielle added. "Vampires don't have natural cravings, and so they don't fight the addictions normal people fight. But this drink is starting to reach into other countries, and important people are getting addicted to it. And they are starting to worry what might happen, if Raphael continues to spread this drug."

"So you're here to what, learn about it?" I asked. "And then what?"

Gabrielle clamped her jaw shut—the edges cut fine lines on her face.

"Ah." I saw. "You want the formula for yourself."

Johnny shook his head and frowned at me. "Not Gabrielle."

Gabrielle looked at Johnny, and I missed the emotion that passed through the air between them. "Not I, Fergus Grimm," she said. "I believe the drug twists and abominates vampires, turns us into base creatures. We can be more." Her hand lay over Johnny's shoulder, and she squeezed him with it. "We should be more. But my family, I cannot control what they want."

"But you are here," I said.

She nodded. "I am here. Representing my family's interests. For now."

I considered her and Johnny. Wondered how much a person could trust a vampire. Johnny seemed the same to me. But I couldn't shake the feeling I got whenever I was around a thrall. Thralls were junkies, living a life where they pleased their masters for another bite. Grant had been a classic example.

Johnny sat relaxed before me. One arm slung around Gabrielle. She was a little formal but hung around him just as much. If I hadn't known, I would have guessed them a regular couple, happy to be with each other, out on a date.

Seeing Johnny again had been good for me. I felt better. Though I'm sure I didn't look it. It was nice to have an old friend around.

I polished off my drink. I needed to get my car. "The club later, right?"

Johnny nodded. "We'll see what we can find out. You know, I haven't heard anything about Jen in the past couple of days. I'd tell you if she'd been turned. Or ..." He motioned with his hands, not wanting to finish the sentence.

"I know," I said. Looking at Johnny but seeing Gabrielle standing a little behind him. Arms around each other. "See you guys there."

CHAPTER ELEVEN

I walked out of the bar hungry. I've heard there's a sandwich in every beer, but I'm not sure that includes the nutritional value needed by a growing adult. Or a healing adult. The diner being right down the street, I headed that way.

In daylight and on foot the town seemed more real, and yet less alive. Empty cups and broken bottles lay at the entrance to allies, and little bits of paper fluttered by on ghostly breezes. I could see, walking by the local co-op, where the plywood covering the windows had been broken into, repaired, and then broken into again.

Main Street was quiet. There was one stoplight in the center of town, and its lights changed from green to yellow to red. No traffic pulled through from any direction. In a few moments, the light flicked back to green, with the same results. Green to yellow to red to green, over and over. If I was the traffic light, I would have given up a long time ago.

It was edging toward evening, but still with plenty of light out. The sun smoked toward the horizon in an angry red burn. When I reached the diner, a tan sedan sat in the corner where I had parked the day before, dusty with out-of-state plates. I walked past the car and entered the diner to the familiar smell of sausage and potatoes. The same feeling as yesterday of déjà vu followed me in. Miss Tammie turned at the jingle of the door, shook her head when she saw me, and immediately went to fixing a plate. There was an old couple off to the right, just messing with the food on their plates. Nowhere to go, nothing to do perhaps, a ritual of the day ending and not willing to call it a night.

The booth to the left of the door, two booths down from where I had sat yesterday, held a couple of men. One of them I recognized. Father Benjamin. The priest nodded at me as I walked in.

The other man looked older. Worn. He sat slumped a little over his coffee. His face had seen a lot of sun and looked vaguely Middle Eastern, and he was fairly large. The leather jacket he wore stretched over his shoulders.

The priest and the man had been talking and had stopped as I walked by. I waved to Miss Tammie, who held up one finger and motioned for me to find a place to sit. I took the same booth as yesterday.

The old couple had finished their food and now just sat there. Not talking. Not getting up. Just looking outside, looking at their plates, looking at each other. The woman kept looking outside and back to the man. The man just sat there and stared at his empty plate. Behind them, the sky darkened.

I could sense the Key out there, out at the Rock, hidden from view. I was glad it was safe, out of this town of vampires and thralls and leeches. Or at least, I was pretty sure it was safe. I didn't think demons could sense the Key, at least I had never seen Azazel notice exactly where I had the Key when we met in the past. But that didn't mean a demon couldn't find it. Or stumble across it.

Part of me knew the Key was only safe for now, and even though Jen needed me, part of me wanted to get it and run. Before I brought more demons here. Before I brought more trouble here. And before a demon caught me.

A plate hit the table and startled me. The smell of sausage and potatoes accompanied it. A cup of coffee placed next to the plate. Miss Tammie slid her bulk into the booth on the other side of me, old face wrinkled with concern or sadness. On her, they looked a lot the same. I ate a few bites right away, wincing a bit at the soreness in my jaw.

"I heard," she said.

"About what?"

"Mrs. Cooper," she said. "Last night."

"Oh," I said.

"You okay?" Miss Tammie asked.

I nodded, savoring the food.

"You don't look okay," she said.

"I'll make it," I said, and winked at Miss Tammie to try to cheer her up. I even offered a grin, but she wasn't taking it. She wrung her hands for a bit and looked out the window while I worked on the plate.

"This town's like that now," Miss Tammie finally said. "People you've known all your lives, people you maybe just saw, they just turn up dead." She kept staring out the window, and her eyes watered.

"Miss Tammie," I said. Firmly. "I'll be okay."

She got up from the booth, wiping at her eyes. "You know the difference between being old and being young, Fergus?"

I discarded the obvious and shook my head.

"When you're younger you got more time to make up for the mistakes you make." Miss Tammie wiped her eyes again and headed back to the grill.

She strode back to the counter and took the spatula to the casserole, flipping large squares over, one after another. The food in my mouth didn't hold a lot of flavor anymore. I looked outside as the haze of dusk began to descend upon Grafton. Soon thralls and vampires would walk the streets. It was a dead town, but Miss Tammie was still here. I wondered if she was paying penance for some mistake earlier in her life.

The older couple had finally begun the process of getting up and leaving. Even then they took everything slowly, in bits and pieces, sliding the chairs out, fiddling with the plates, sliding the chairs back in. They delayed the inevitable as long as they could until the door gently rang them out.

I began to understand it all a little more, what the death of the town had done to the people still alive, still human, still here. I had left this place, but it was still home to some. A trap to others. And while it was home to me, it could trap me too.

Father Benjamin finished speaking to the stranger, got up. The priest placed his hand lightly on the man's shoulder. The man bowed his head for a long moment, and then the priest moved around the diner, stopping at each window and tracing something on the glass. As he walked by my booth he laid his hand on my shoulder, briefly. His hand was slightly warm, and I shrugged a little at the touch.

At the door to the diner, he stayed for longer, touching places around the frame, tracing something in the air, mouth open, and closing in silent prayer. When the priest was finished he picked up an empty plate from the booth with the outsider in it and brought it over to set it on the counter by Miss Tammie, nodding to her. She thanked him with a smile. As he turned around he tipped his head toward me in greeting, then walked out. *Jingle-jingle*.

There wasn't much Miss Tammie could do to keep herself from vampires, but having a priest come in and bless the area, smear a little holy water on the doors, might make it more trouble for the undead to enter than it was worth. Churches and holy grounds were places the undead could not go, but these constant wards and rituals of priests had served to create barricades to vampires and the like for thousands of years.

I was curious about those rituals, and Father Benjamin performing them. I also wondered about the blessing he had given the stranger. Grafton was a tangled mess of strands, and I needed to start pulling on loose ends to see what led where. My hope was that one of the strands would lead me to Jen.

I blinked on my ethereal vision and gasped.

Wards encircled the diners, on every plate of glass, on the door, even on tables and chairs. They were most dense where Father Benjamin had spent the most time, images laid one over the other year after year. Christian imagery, crosses and wreaths and swords, other symbols that looked more like hieroglyphics than anything else, all of these were in thick golden lines as if someone had taken a gold crayon and traced the same symbols over and over and over again.

The stranger in the booth was looking at me. A golden pool encircled his shoulder where Father Benjamin had laid his hand, slowly spreading over the man, fading at the edges of the glow. A tiny gold cross lay in the iris of each of the stranger's eyes.

I blinked, returning to the normal world of sight. The stranger caught my eye, and he motioned at the seat in front of him and waved me over. I forked a little more casserole into my mouth and swallowed. I didn't have any idea who this man was, or who Father Benjamin was, but it was a thread I was about to pull.

I grabbed my plate and headed over. The man grinned a bit and leaned back. He was younger than he looked, and had a few days of stubble on his chin. A thick black mustache. Both of us had black hair, but his was straight and speckled with gray. He looked about as worn-down as I felt, but seemed hard, capable. He moved as if he were in pain, and his jacket was covered in dust and grime.

"You enjoy the casserole, huh?" the guy asked. He had a thick accent like he was keeping his tongue from rolling his *r*'s. Middle Eastern, I thought. Pretty far from home. "I was surprised to see they do not serve burgers here."

It wasn't long ago that a burger had almost cost me my life. I was pretty happy with the casserole. "It's good enough for me." And it was. I ate more of it. "You want to tell me who you are?"

"Who I am?" The guy took a sip of his coffee. "I am called Greg."

"Sure."

"Does my name really matter?"

Up close we got the measure of each other. Just like I had recognized him as a hard man capable of doing tough things, he recognized a similar quality in me. We both had served in a military in the world, belonged to that brotherhood, and that service allowed each of us to acknowledge the other with a nod.

"It probably doesn't," I said. "But what you do does." I waved my arms at the windows. "What's up with the gold shimmer, the glow, the crosses, and the swords all over the place?"

"You can see those? Interesting." Greg squinted, and I could almost see his eyes shimmer. "You are not a brother, though."

"A brother of who?"

"The order I belong to." Greg took a small, seated bow. "The Knights Templar."

"Really?" I had heard of them, but I had heard of them in the way children hear of Santa Claus. Or how people chase rainbows for leprechauns. Though I had actually seen one or two of those creatures. They were never what you think.

"You look like you've seen better days, my friend." The guy took a sip of his coffee.

"I've been better," I said.

"You from around here?"

"Years ago," I said.

"You got friends here?"

"I wouldn't say I do." Though maybe Johnny still counted.

"So, why are you back?"

"You got anything better to do," I said, "other than to ask me pointless questions?"

"To serious talk, then?" Greg raised an eyebrow. "If I said the word *al-ʿidāda* to you, would that carry a special significance?"

I had never heard that word before. The manner in which he said the word carried a weight to it, and an age. Like it had come from another time and place. I shook my head. "Not that it matters."

He tried again. "Do you know *Hirdramabiff*?"

"Look, I play twenty questions as much as the next guy," I said. "And I've got no idea what you're asking about."

"Ah." Greg shrugged again, the jacket tightening around his shoulders. "I have been rude, then. Forgive me, I am not ..." He motioned around with his hands. "... local."

"Consider it forgotten." I went to get up, but the large man leaned forward and placed his hand on my arm. The tension at the table instantly ratcheted up. His grip was hard, the grip of a man used to getting things done.

Greg's Middle Eastern accent became more pronounced. "It was just that you had the look of someone being marked by an *Ifrit*."

I stopped. "The mark of what?"

"An *Ifrit*," Greg repeated. His eyes moved upward for a second, danced back and forth, as if they were looking for something inside his head. To explain what he was saying. "You have the look, such as when demons are after you."

My heart beat rapidly. My thought raced back to the Key. I had left Azazel behind as an outline of ash, but that would only buy me so much time. And nothing in Grafton was happening fast enough for me. Especially with Jen missing. With Raphael telling me he'd kill everyone I knew if I left, and Parker telling me my mother would hunt me down, and now this guy showed up and started throwing around demon words.

I needed to run. I reached into my jacket pocket and grabbed the handle of the .38. Greg noticed the motion and shook his head, and let go of my arm.

"Relax, my friend." He held both hands out, open. "Relax. We are all chased by our own demons, are we not?" He motioned with his hands, pointing to the blotches on my jacket, the bruises on my face. He opened his jacket slightly, revealing a long gash in his shirt and the white wrap of thick bandages underneath.

I let go of my .38. Took a couple of deep breaths and forced my heart to slow down. This guy felt like he was in the middle of a fight like mine. I wondered if he was maybe a Keeper too. Maybe chased by his own type of demon. "What is a Greg doing in Grafton? Is it a demon?"

"Not this time." Greg frowned. One hand disappeared under his jacket, where the bandages were. "Vampires. Making some kind of drug."

Funny that Johnny had just been telling me about this. About a drink so addictive vampires would risk getting staked trying to smuggle it out of Grafton. That Raphael was using the drink to grab more and more power from clans, getting the vampire elite and aristocrats hooked. And now the formula for the drug was something other clans wanted.

The undead didn't get hooked on anything, especially vampires. They only craved what their undead desires pointed them to. Vampires loved blood, zombies loved brains, wights, anything that moved. Cocaine or heroin had no effect on the undead, but Raphael had changed that.

"You understand, then." Greg had seen me working through it.

I didn't see any reason to hide it from him. "Sure." Then my hopes rose a bit. If Greg was here to fight vampires, I had an ally. Maybe he would help me with Raphael. Or Dominic, whenever he arrived. Maybe I had a chance to live through that meeting now. "Are you here to take the vampires out, then?"

"An entire town of the undead?" Greg barked out a laugh. "I'm just a soldier, not some vengeful angel, not some superhero."

"So it's just you?" One man seemed about a hundred too few against all the vampires I had seen so far, as well as the thralls. Plus Raphael and his father. And whatever waited at the club.

"I had a partner a few days ago." Greg turned his gaze away, out the window. His jaw set. "There's not enough of us around for this. We were maybe called to this town too late. Too many vampires here now. I hope, maybe, to find the source of the drug and destroy it."

And the idea of help floated away, just like that. Greg wouldn't likely be able to help me. I was still on my own against Raphael. "So, why did you call me over?"

"As I said, I am a soldier." Greg cocked his head. "And like recognizes like." His eyes had a permanent squint, and underneath the lids there did seem to be a type of shimmer. The irises focused on me, intent.

"So you're asking me for help," I said.

"Let us say I am gauging interest. You are not a brother, yet you seem like one. I am curious about a coincidence such as this."

"I can appreciate where you are coming from, Greg, but I got something I have to do." Namely find Jen, as fast as I could. Get her away from Raphael. Let him and his father and my mother settle their differences while I got the Key and ran. The Church was a big organization. Surely they had resources they could send. "You don't have an army of Templars somewhere you can call on?"

He barked out a laugh. His next words were resigned as if he had said them a thousand times. "A Templar isn't an attractive job opportunity. Recruitment isn't what it once was."

I felt for the man. Running to Grafton from another job. Having lost his partner there. Getting here and finding out the job was much larger than first thought. And here I was, someone who might be able to help him, and I was turning him down. I shook my head again. "Sorry, Greg. I got some things of my own to take care of."

"I see," Greg said.

"Maybe another time," I said.

Greg nodded as if he had heard that before, then stared back out the window. His coffee mug forgotten. "Another time, then."

I drank the last of my coffee, then set it down. Moved the cup around the plate a moment. Looked at Greg, who was staring past the darkening sky outside. The man took a large breath and let it all out, the window fogging a bit in front of him. Maybe thinking about his dead partner, or maybe thinking about the impossible task before him.

I looked down at my plate. The stained white surface stared back at me. I was struck by the similarities between us. And like Greg, I was also curious about coincidences, of Greg showing up at the same time as me. He was a brother of a sort, of a different order, but against the same enemy. I felt like I was abandoning him.

Night was coming, and the club would be opening soon. A place I needed to go to see if I could find out where Raphael had hidden Jen. And behind all that was the Key, something I always was aware of, what had driven my life that last six years, and what would continue to drive it for as long as I could carry it.

Greg turned back to me, settling back against the booth. His eyes were clear of worry, and he held an acceptance about himself. Not resignation, but a belief in purpose. Of a task needing to be performed and a person who could do it. He had accepted his fate and still ran from mine.

"Good luck, then." I got up, tucking a little cash under the plate.

Greg nodded in return and gave me a little wave. "To you as well, Grimm.

CHAPTER TWELVE

I left the diner, heading back to Jen's house like I had the night before, this time just to get my car. It was hard to believe that just a night ago I was headed in the same direction, hoping to find Jen and get out of town. Now I seemed mired in Grafton and sinking slowly into everything around me.

So the Knights Templar were in town. And they were going to try to destroy the drug. Or at least, one man was. I wondered if I should have told him others were looking for it as well, but I didn't think I could betray what little Johnny told me.

I didn't know much about the Knights Templar. What I'd learned about the supernatural world, I learned through experience. I hadn't had an old master lying around to train me, and I hadn't had the free time to do a lot of book learning. The rumors spoke about the Templars as highly trained guardians, or protectors, but here was one out on his own trying to eliminate a vampire threat. I assumed there was more to it than just the drug, or maybe what the drug represented was a greater threat than what I could figure.

I walked briskly toward the Coopers' house, noticing the dusk was still holding on before true night. I had made it a few blocks before a patrol car slid up to me, its engine a soft purr. The driver window rolled down to reveal the policeman with the shock of red hair. Marks motioned to me.

"Get in."

"Care to explain what I've done, Officer?" I looked into the car. The passenger was Mark's partner from the diner. Robinson.

Marks rolled his eyes. "Get in, or maybe I put one in your leg and drag you in."

"What happened to protect and to serve?"

"Get the fuck in," Marks said.

Robinson looked over, his face calm. He could have been talking about the weather. "Raphael wants to see you."

Already? I sighed, knowing this wasn't going to go anywhere but where these two wanted it. At best I could maybe run a few feet before Marks pulled his gun, and he looked the type to shoot first and ask questions later. I sighed, opened the back door to the police cruiser, and slid in.

The backseat was clean, new. Fresh. Smelled like new leather. I didn't buckle up, and they didn't remind me. Not very policelike. I leaned forward, looking between the metal grate separating the back and front seats. Mark slammed the shifter into drive and hammered on the gas. Robinson murmured something into the walkie-talkie on his shoulder. I couldn't hear the words distinctly until Robinson replied, "Ten-four, we're on our way now."

"Want to tell me where we're going?"

"Shut the fuck up," Marks said. "You being here is ruining a good thing for us."

"What the hell does that mean?"

"Figure it the fuck out," Marks said. "We're paid pretty good just to drive around and do nothing. Not a lot of *human* crime in this town, you know. Now you're here, and shit is getting stirred up."

Oh. Marks was unhappy because he had to actually do something, and not ride around and walk into diners to get free food. I leaned back against the seat and waited out the trip.

Marks turned sharply at the next stop, swinging the cruiser around to head northeast out of town. Back the way I had first come in the night before. Dusk was falling, night right behind it, and the streetlights in the town began to light up as we passed by. Shuffling figures were emerging from alleys and buildings, thralls in search of a fix.

We left the diner behind and passed the King's Lodge as the cruiser climbed out of the valley. The crooked letters still hung on the sign. It seemed like a lot had happened to me in the past twenty-four hours. Like someone had put a tape on of my life and fast-forwarded ten years into the past day.

There was still enough light in the air to see by. About two-thirds of the way up the hill a black Cadillac sat by the edge of a curve. We pulled up beside it. The Cadillac had mirrored windows, reflecting everything around it in shades of silver and black. As we rolled to a stop the driver's door opened and Raphael got out. Like the night before, he was well dressed. A black suit with red pinstripes, a crimson tie. Sharp, even if a little cliché. He leaned back against his car. Waiting.

"Get out," Marks said.

I opened the door and got out. The night was getting darker by the minute, and the cool night air smelled a little like a hayfield. Raphael watched me, giving the appearance of someone carefully composed, which freaked me out a little, after seeing him not hold anything back the night before.

Raphael nodded. "Grimm."

"Raph," I said. Wondering if he was going to kill me. Wondering if it was all going to end in the next few minutes, with Jen hanging in the wind.

"I want to show you something," he said. He pulled himself off his car, moving with a leopard's grace. His coat, jacket, hair, everything drifted around him. He flowed up the hill, a few steps past the car, and then put out his hands to the sides, palms outward. Expectantly.

"Here," he said, and looked back at me.

I struggled up the hill until I stood a short distance away from Raph. I looked up the hill, seeing nothing but a normal road running up a normal hill. Just a bit down from us was the trail that led to our group's old hide-out, where I had just been the day before. I didn't think Raphael knew anything about that place, and it struck me as odd that he would now. He was here for something else.

"Poke your hand out," Raphael said. "Slowly."

I looked at him, and he waited. His gaze was forceful but restrained. Calm. There was a tightness inside him, something coiled, something bottled up, but the exterior was a Raphael I hadn't known existed. Someone who thought beyond the current moment.

I poked my hand out.

As soon as I did I felt what Raphael wanted me to. A slight coolness on my hand, something I felt as a lifting of weight, a sensation of relief. It started at my fingertips, and as I moved my hand through whatever was in front of me the sensation traveled up my arm. It felt like I was pushing through the walls of a very cool, thick, peppermint bubble.

"I can sense everything inside this boundary." Raphael stepped back. "I know everyone, everybody, living and dead." He circled around, pointing to the tops of the hills of a valley. "This town is like a pool to me. I know when you're in, and I know when you're out."

"You knew the moment I came back."

"To the exact second." Raphael smiled, the kind of smile a person gets after taking a bite of a decadent and rich dessert. His voice lowered just a little in timbre. "Something I've looked forward to for a long time."

"Why tell me this?" I pointed to the wall. "Why tell me about that?"

"I wanted you to be aware that I meant what I told you, back in the cell. About knowing if you'd left, and what I would do to Jen."

"So you had your guys kidnap me and bring me up here for that?" I rolled my eyes. The beating he had given me had impressed me with what Raphael had meant. I was still going to find Jen and get her out of this town. And Raphael knew all that. Some things between us would never change. "Is that all?"

Raphael studied me, and I could sense the inner tightness loosen in him, like a tiger uncurling to pounce. Raphael swallowed once and set his jaw, and the tightness disappeared again. "I never liked you, Grimm, but that doesn't mean we can't help each other."

I just stared at him.

Raphael paused a moment, bit his lip. Mastering something inside him, again. "It's been suggested," he said, "that I was a bit rough last night. That I should try a different … *tact*."

"Tact," I said. I was sure I didn't look very believing.

"Yes." Raphael took a deep breath, let it out. "I laughed as well. But I've been encouraged to explain to you what I want. That you might see it in your best interest, and actually do it."

I wasn't sure he could convince me more than the bruises over my body had. The ribs, the jaw, the mouse over my eye. Raphael had tried a lot of things to get me to knuckle under him, but never the truth. So I didn't believe it now.

"I know." Raphael smiled like he had read my mind. "I know. But I thought, what the hell? Maybe you decide to do it. Might be easier for everyone involved."

Dealing with demons had been something I had become accustomed to. Azazel was evil incarnate, but I understood the demon to some degree. Azazel was evil with a purpose. He did things with a goal. Raphael was a loose cannon. He could flip a switch and kill anything for any reason. That kind of crazy was hard to deal with. It felt like a bomb with a short fuse, and I needed to buy time. So I took a breath and let it out. "What's the pitch?"

The vampire nodded. "Good." I got the feeling a lot was riding on this. "What I want doesn't change, but I need you to tell me you'll do it. Hang around in Grafton. Just until my father shows up. When he does show up, just do what he tells you to do."

"What's he going to tell me to do?"

"He's going to tell you to come get me."

I took a minute. Parker had told me much the same. I had to be here when Raphael's father and my mother came to Grafton. I didn't know why I had to be the lynchpin. "I don't understand why you have to tell me to do that."

"You have a tendency to do the opposite of what people tell you," Raphael said.

"I don't get why it's so important I do this."

"You don't have to get it," Raphael said, a little forcefully. His face shifted a little, became harder. He exhaled like he had too much breath in his body, like he had been holding it all inside him as energy, tight and coiled, and it was pushing to get out.

Memories of me and Danny in the alleyway, ten years ago, fluttered through my mind. Raphael screaming at me to punch Danny. Raphael screaming at me to look at him, *look at him.*

If someone had encouraged Raphael to try a different tack, the encouragement was barely holding on. But it did hold. When the vampire spoke next his voice was hard and brittle. "Look, Grimm. My father and I don't trust each other. I plan to kill him. He wants to control me. And at some point, we have to meet. And you're the only person we both trust."

"Trust?"

"Trust." Raphael's voice took on a deep tone, one that I recognized. "Be still."

I remained still. In fact, I could no longer even take a breath. And that became apparent when I started convulsing, trying to inhale air, but I was locked in place. It was like back with Danny, but much stronger now.

Raphael knew what he was doing now, and his smile was cold and knowing. My eyes widened fractionally as my chest started thumping for a breath. He knew exactly what he was doing, knew that he had that power over me, and chose now to exercise it.

And then he waited, for a long, long moment.

"Be free," Raphael said. As soon as he did I was able to take a deep, gasping breath. "Maybe you understand now. You might see why I trust you, and why my father can trust you. You were born to be a slave to both of us."

I did understand. I understood that I was an expendable messenger. Which told me if Raphael did have Jen, she was safe only as long as I was alive and doing what Raphael and his father wanted me to do. And I didn't know how long I could be either of those.

"So now you're thinking Jen is only alive as long as you are. And that you're expendable. So how could you trust me?" Raphael shrugged. "All your friends are still alive, still here. You've seen the town by now. You know that didn't have to happen. Especially when they have been a nuisance. I kept them alive to show you I could. So that right now you could trust me, that much."

Raphael could be lying. He could be telling the truth. It was hard for me to know. But it was plausible. But keeping my old friends alive only gave Raphael more leashes to tie to me. Still, I was buying time to find Jen. "So I'm to wait here. And when your father gets here, do what he says. Which is just to come get you."

"That's it," Raphael said.

"What do I get," I said, "if I do this?"

"Grimm." Raphael held out his fingers one at a time like he was counting points. "You get to stay alive. Jen gets to stay alive. Your friends get to keep living. And after you do what I ask you to, you can leave."

"That's a bit hard to believe." Everything I knew about Raphael told me I couldn't trust him, but it wasn't like he was asking me to hold up a bank, or rob an orphanage. What he wanted seemed easy. Too easy.

"Grimm, after my father comes here," Raphael said, still thumbing his chin like he was dwelling on some master plan, "you're honestly free to go. Provided you do go."

He smiled again. "I won't apologize for beating you to hell. I enjoyed it. I'd enjoy doing it again. But I don't *need* to do it."

Those words did have the spark of truth in them. Not something I was used to, coming from him. "If I don't do what your father asks?"

Raphael blinked a slow blink. As his eyelids rose, the sliver of crazy shone from them, the madness from the night before. It was frightening enough I took a half step back, even as his eyelids fluttered a bit and then firmly closed. His eyes still shut, Raphael swallowed once, tightened his jaw, and then open his eyes slowly. Normal.

"If you don't," Raphael said, simply, "I'll kill everyone. Jen, Nick, Johnny, Parker, everyone and anyone left in this town." He stared right at me, and his eyes seemed to vibrate a little. "And you know how much I *want* to do that. You *know* I'll do it. Then I'll come after you. I'll kill anyone in my way. I'll leave a swath of bodies until I find you. And then I'll show you Jen's head. I'll put her dead lips against yours, just so you'll know."

That sounded more like the Raph I knew. I was more comfortable dealing with that one, funny enough. That made my decision easier.

Raphael nodded to his Cadillac, and the back window rolled down silently, pausing halfway. I could see Sarah there, looking straight ahead. Too scared to look at me. Eyes wet.

"Sarah," I said, stepping toward the car. Raphael held his hand out to stop me. He gave me a look that said, *Be careful.*

I walked closer to the car. Sarah had grown. She was a little like her sister, blond hair, full lips, but her face was a little narrower, higher cheekbones, and she was slim, not as curvy. Fine lines of a tattooed symbol curved down from around the side of her neck and ran under the back of her shirt. But other than the tattoo, the resemblance to Jen was there. The picture of her and Raphael flashed through my mind, with her leaning on his arm. I wondered if they were still together. She had been happier then; she looked withdrawn now.

Someone sat next to her in the car, an older man I recognized from high school, back in the day. One of the teachers there maybe. I could see one of his hands on Sarah's arm, and the other hand inside something that looked like a doctor's white coat. And Cole filled out the passenger's seat. He turned and gave me a little smile and wave.

I got within a few feet of the car. Sarah stared straight ahead, past me.

"Sarah," I said. "Are you okay?"

"No," she said, her voice deep in her throat like she was holding back a sob.

"Your sister, she's looking for you," I said.

"Tell her not to," Sarah said. Her eyes brimmed with wetness, tears running freely down her cheeks. She was pale, way too pale. "Tell her to run when you find her, Grimm. Tell her to get somewhere safe."

"Sarah," I sighed. "We both know your sister. I don't know if I can get her to go without you."

I winced as I uttered those words. Sarah had been a close friend, just like Nick and Johnny. And I had just told her, if I could, I would leave her behind to save her sister. I would take Jen and run. Realizing that about myself made me feel small, and I clenched my fists.

Still, I leaned closer. "Do you know where she is, Sarah?"

Cole cocked his head. The doctor grabbed Sarah's arm, hard. For her part, Sarah didn't acknowledge either of them. "Not up the Hill, Grimm. Not up the Hill."

Not in Raphael's mansion, then.

"Have you seen her?"

Sarah shook her head. Another tear curved around the slight hollow in her cheek. Her mascara was smeared where she had wiped away others. Sarah knew I would rescue Jen, and she knew I would leave her behind, and she had accepted it long before rolling down the window. "Just take Jen away, Grimm. Take her before they do to her what they did to me."

The doctor place his hand on her arm. I didn't like how it looked. Sarah winced and tried to jerk her arm away from him. I watched it all as the mirrored window rolled up and cut the scene off. The last thing I saw of Sarah was her face staring ahead, and the grin of the old guy next to her.

I stared at myself in the window; a blank look gazed back. I didn't meet my own eyes. My image looked past me and out into the distance. I worked my jaw back and forth and took a deep breath. I should have told Sarah I'd find Jen, and that we'd both be coming for her. That we would save her too. But then the moment had passed. I looked away from the glass and its tattletale reflection.

Raphael walked up, one confident step after another, heels snapping sharply on the pavement.

I looked over at him, and I don't know what he saw, but it made him pause for just a moment.

"Grimm," he asked, "do we have a deal?" A monster confidently in control. Calm on the outside, terrifyingly mad on the inside.

It took me a long moment, but I could see no other way. I nodded.

"Good." Raphael smiled. "Good."

An uneasy feeling tugged at the back of my mind from his smile, like the light touch of a silken strand of a spider's web drifting across the back of my neck. A web that surrounded me and waited for the moment I made a mistake, when more and more of the strands would wrap me tighter in their embrace. And then the spider would pounce.

Raphael opened his car door. The car dinged, letting everyone know the door was open. He got in and smiled at me before shutting the door.

"If you need more incentive, Grimm." Raphael waved around at the invisible circle that ran around Grafton. "Just step outside the circle. Jen's here, alive and well. I'd be angry if you left town, but not for long."

He shut the door, pulled out onto the road. The Cadillac eased onto the pavement and glided in a circle, the engine smooth and strong as the car turned around and headed back into town. The headlights never came on.

I looked up the hill. Night had fallen while we talked. I could hear the crickets begin an endless chirping cry, sawing their legs back and forth. Back and forth. I looked at where the edge of the circle cut across the outskirts of Grafton, and I wondered about a great many things.

"Hey, dipshit," Marks called from where they were parked. "Get the fuck back in the car."

I sighed and headed that way, feeling invisible strands tighten ever harder around me.

CHAPTER THIRTEEN

I t was nice being back in my car. First thing I had done after getting dropped off was open the trunk and pull out a change of clothes. The second thing I did was change into them. I had a duffel bag full of shirts and pants and jackets I had picked up along the way because I never knew when I would need a new set.

A change of clothes brought about a change in perspective. I had been in town one day and a few things had been made clear to me. Vampires and humans both were flocking to Grafton for a drug Raphael had created. Multiple schemes were in play. Raphael and Parker both told me for different reasons that I needed to be in Grafton. Raphael had kept my friends alive all this time in order to keep me in line, even though they were nuisances. To become a nuisance they had to be looking into the drug.

So Raphael did have Jen somewhere. Maybe it was to hide her from me, and maybe it was because she had gotten too close to figuring out something about the drug. If I followed that same trail I could end up in the same place she was, or discovering where that might be. Especially if what Sarah said was true, and Jen wasn't at Raphael's mansion. All I had to do was find out more about the drug, like where they might be making it. And I had to figure that out before Dominic Antonado and my mother came into town. Easy peasy.

I fired up the Camaro, feeling the comforting rumble of the eight-cylinder engine shake the car. In a few minutes, I was back on Main Street. It was busier now, and I had to blend into a lane of other cars, all headed to the south end of town. Now that true night had fallen, the undead had begun to filter out onto the streets. It was eerie, how empty Grafton looked during the day, and how full it seemed at night.

The thrall earlier had mentioned the club was the old movie theater, and I could see the sign long before I got to it. Garish neon lights flashed over the theater in cursive script, declaring the place The Cauldron. Right underneath those lights were red tubes curved into what might be called a large pot with maybe a large ladle tucked into it, but it looked somewhat like a whiskey glass with a toothpick. Loud thumping music pulsed from the inside, and a line of vampires and thralls waited outside to get in.

I pulled past The Cauldron and parked on Main Street. Parking meters ran down the street, all of them listing no time remaining. I got out of my car, shrugged on my army jacket, and opened the trunk. I grabbed my hammerless .38 Special and made sure it was loaded, then tucked it deep inside one boot. It would only pass the laziest of searches, but I wasn't willing to go into a club of vampires without something. The idea was crazy enough as it was.

I walked down the street, seeing the line file down from the club. A few steps from the end, someone fell into step next to me, then two some-ones. I paused, feeling my heart speed up, until I recognized Johnny and Gabrielle. Then I let out a long exhale.

Johnny smiled. "Grimm." He had stopped next to me and had dressed up a bit, with a button-up shirt and jacket. Gabrielle artfully hung on his arm. She had dressed up as well, in a slick black dress that was tight in all the right places, her hair stylishly arranged, with one long curl dangling free over her cheek.

"Johnny." I relaxed, slightly. Nodded to Gabrielle.

"You ready?"

I moved my foot a little inside the boot, felt the .38 rub against my ankle. "Sure."

"Nice outfit," Johnny said.

I looked down at my grunge band T-shirt and camo jacket. I was never picky about cheap clothes. "It's what I got."

"Just kidding you, brother." Johnny slapped my shoulder, smiling. "You were never one for fashion."

He walked down the side of the line, Gabrielle leaning on his arm and staying in step with him, her hips sinking and lifting in one smooth motion. I got the feeling she was hanging on him to keep him from me. I followed. Some of the vampires waiting complained until Gabrielle looked back. Once they saw who she was, they shut up.

Johnny was dating a heavy hitter in the vampire world.

The music thumped louder the closer we got. The garish whiskey glass of a cauldron light flushed red over us. There was a bouncer at the front of the line, looking over everyone as they passed. He looked Gabrielle up and down, looked at Johnny, then looked back to Gabrielle and gave her a nod.

I started to go in with them. The bouncer raised his arm, barring my way.

"No humans," he said. "Members only."

"I'm going in," I told him.

"Hey, Jacob," the bouncer said, "this guy says he's going in."

I rolled my eyes. Raphael's cronies were everywhere. The tall vampire turned around from the front of the club with a cocky grin, sauntering down.

I set my jaw, remembering Mrs. Cooper. Remembering Danny.

"Well, well, well ..." Jacob looked me up and down. He had on a flannel shirt under his jacket, and he kept his incisors on full display as he grinned. "Fergus Grimm. You sure you're in the right place?"

I set my jaw, swallowed once. Twice. I tried to block the image of him standing behind Danny, the bat in his hand, Danny covered in broken dark glass and trails of beer. "Jacob. You letting me in?"

"Well, let's see." Jacob checked the list in the bouncer's hand. "You don't appear to be on the list today, my friend."

"I'm still going in. List or no list."

"You sure you're up for something like that? The way you look right now?"

I pushed the thrall's arm out of the way. Jacob's grinned and stepped down to me. My aches and pains and bruises washed away in the rush of adrenaline.

And then Gabrielle's arm separated us. I stopped. Jacob frowned.

"Jacob." Her voice was smooth, controlled. "Mr. Grimm is my guest tonight."

The vampire spat to the side. "Miss High and Mighty. You want someone on the list, you check with Raphael. Especially this guy."

"Such a lack of manners in this town." Gabrielle smiled. "Maybe I need to educate you on how to serve your betters."

Her gaze was a force. I took a step back from it. After a moment Jacob looked away too. Then waved me on, his confident smirk a little shaky.

I grinned, slapped Jacob on the arm, and walked past. "See you in there, champ."

"She won't be around forever, Grimm," Jacob said, his voice low.

I nodded to Gabrielle, and the three of us headed in. She took a moment to wrap herself back around Johnny's arm. Gabrielle seemed to really like him, and Johnny was relaxed with her. This was unlike any kind of thrall/vampire relationship that I had heard of.

Johnny opened the door for Gabrielle, laughing and talking into her ear. I lost the words in the music blasting from the doorway. The pounding music pulsed with every step, a deep rhythm with so much bass the hairs stood up on my arms.

I had a weird sense of déjà vu when I entered. The concession bar had been swapped for a real bar, spanning the length of the lobby and set between the two hallways. A huge mirror now sat back behind the bar. The floor of the lobby was full of plush chairs and oak tables, with little alcoved love seats rounding the edges of the walls and a tiny dance area in the middle. Vampires and thralls sat close together everywhere, drinking, kissing, rubbing each other. Aisles on both sides of the lobby led up and away, to where separate movie screens used to be, and each of the aisles had a couple of large vampires standing guard.

A strong musky scent, thick with cherry, floated in the room, something that triggered thoughts of sex in my mind as I looked around, looking at the skintight dresses, mouths pressed against necks, and the slow, pulsing motions of the crowd.

"You feel it?" Johnny asked. He had to lean closer and shout for me to hear him. Gabrielle had a hard hold of his arm as we worked our way through the crowd.

"Yeah," I shouted back.

"Something they pump through the ventilation," he said. "People get addicted to it." When he said addicted, Gabrielle set her jaw in distaste.

The windowed doors were covered up and blacked out. There was strange old art, mostly Greek or Roman, pictures or imitations, naked men and women performing all kinds of acts. Looking closer, I could see where some of the men and women were vampires and others humans. Kind of standard vampire trope, in my mind.

"We're going to find a place to sit," Johnny said.

"I'm looking around," I said.

"Be careful," Johnny said. "Don't go anywhere where you might be alone. Not the bathroom. Not some hallway you see. Things get crazy here quick if you're by yourself."

"I gotcha," I said.

"Grimm, I'm serious."

"I heard you," I said. "Still going to look around."

Johnny shook his head and took off with Gabrielle. They found a table. The lone vampire there got up at a glance from Gabrielle. A server bumped me, trotted back, and offered a mumbled half apology. She was one of several in fantastic shape, her body barely covered with a tight-fitting costume. Something leather and red and resembling the devil. Some kind of club thing maybe, costumed demons walking around tempting the patrons.

What I tried not to see were the tiny pairs of holes in the necks of the serving ladies, their wrists, and the low middle of their backs. Not-so-nice thoughts entered my mind as I watched the women walk with the sway that all seductresses master. Air circled over us, large scented waves washing around of lust and cherries, and I found myself bopping my head to the rhythmic pounding of the music.

It was sick, how this place seeped into you.

I walked around, catching glances here and there from vampires alone, vampires with people. Male and female alike, all of them drinking from tall glasses filled with a sluggish red liquid. Which I guessed was the Witch's Brew Johnny had told me about. All of the vampires looked drunk, or drugged, with hazy stares and lazy smiles. It was weird, seeing vampires like that. Normally I got a predator feel from them, a kill-or-be-killed instinct. Even from Gabrielle, though she clothed it better. Seeing these vampires drugged was just, odd.

And the Witch's Brew was everywhere in this club. It made me certain Jen had found something here. She had been looking into it and had found out something that had put her on Raphael's radar. Since the drug was here in this club, I was here, and I wanted to find something that linked her to it.

Something that might lead me to where she was. If I could find the link, I might be able to find her. Or find something that I could use to bargain with Raphael to give me Jen. I might not make it out of Grafton, but I could make sure she did.

Some people I recognized. Some vampires, mostly humans. All of them from school, back in the day. None of them seemed to remember me. Maybe it was the drinks and the drug, or maybe they just didn't care.

I worked my way to the back of the club, where a couple of figures stood behind the bar and funneled drinks to servers and patrons. A huge mirror rested behind them. In between the bartenders and the mirrors was a large black pot holding a pair of super-sized glass pillars. Each of the tall pillars had a picture of two large, sharp teeth etched on their fronts, and inside the glass a vermillion liquid shimmered. A light fog bubbled out of the cauldron's top. A witch's cauldron. I snorted. It was a corny piece of club art.

A person at the end of the bar recognized me. And smirked. Grant stood with Rand and a few other vampires. A few other humans. A couple of girls, half naked, kissing next to him. Grant pointed his finger at me and said something to Rand, who apparently was Big Papi. I would have figured Jake for that name.

I walked on, heading up the passageway that led to the theaters. As I walked past the theater doors, half-naked people entered and left them almost at random. I took a peek in the last theater and wished I hadn't. The room was dark, but lasers picked bare limbs out of a crowd of people writhing around each other. A movie was playing on the screen. A naked girl sat astride a man and leaned against his chest, her teeth bared and pointed.

A server bumped into me as I shut the door. A half-naked man wrapped in red leather holding a tray of Witch's Brew. He apologized, then looked down the hallway to see if anyone else was there before turning back. "Are you Fergus Grimm?"

I checked him out more closely. He was my age and in great shape, a well-defined chest tapering to a narrow waist. Tiny twin punctures marked the side of his neck, and a slight drizzle of blood leaked out of the holes. His nose had been broken, though, a long time ago, and that clued me in. Andrew Billings. "Andy?"

"So you remember." He circled around to put himself between me and anyone who might walk up the hallway. Andy had been someone we had hung with in middle school until he had moved to the next town over. If I remembered right, Jacob had broken his nose after bullying Andy, and Andy's mother had moved the family shortly afterward. "I thought it was you. Jen called you, didn't she?"

My heart rate sped up. "You know about Jen?"

"Of course," Andy said. "She's the reason I'm here. She found out that I was doing some male modeling."

All of a sudden I was jealous, and felt a slow heat rise over my skin.

"She called me and asked if I wanted to help her out," Andy said. "Said it was a chance to get back at Raphael and Jacob and the group. I jumped on it."

"So, where is she?" I asked. "Do you know?"

Andy shook his head. "No, she disappeared right after I told her what I heard."

"What did you hear?"

Andy looked around some more. The hand not holding the tray fidgeted in the air with nothing to hold. "Raphael and Cole were talking outside the club. I was walking out. Raphael was telling Cole they needed more women, and Cole was telling him they were hard to find. Raphael was complaining about the schedule."

"Just women?"

Andy shook his head. "No, they started out talking about women, but then Raphael told him he needed more witches, and Cole had better find them."

Witches. Jen. The pictures in her room came back to me, and her knowing where I was, everywhere I had been. I became really scared for her.

"Where are they taking them?"

"I don't know," Andy said. "I might have an idea. They bring in the drinks in these big plastic tubs. I found something on one."

Just then the door opened, and two naked guys came out. With their arms wrapped around each other, red liquid poured all over them. One of them grabbed two glasses from Andy's tray and dumped the contents over himself and his friend. The pair laughed and headed away from us, toward the main room.

I looked back at Andy. "Tell me."

Andy froze. At the top of the hallway, Grant had appeared. He smiled. Andy started fidgeting with the empty glasses on his tray. I stepped to the side and frowned at Grant.

"I'll come find you in a bit." Andy grabbed the empty glasses and put them on his tray.

I nodded and walked past him, headed to Grant. "You're pretty brave with Big Papi around."

"I was going to say the same for you, coming here." Grant smirked. "And you got no one else."

I walked on, letting my shoulder bump Grant. It was petty, but I was in the mode for petty things. I headed back down the hallway and into the crowd, around the bar. Everyone was drinking from the tall glasses, and in the short time I had been in the hallway, more people in the club had lost their clothes. Humans and vampires locked together all over the place, sometimes in larger groups, and I could see where the evening was going to go.

Walking, I could smell the cherry-cinnamon-whiskey scent like a thick perfume. It fogged up my lungs, and I took shallow breaths until I was past it. It amplified my anger. I could feel the scent *wanting* me to swing at someone, to maim, to kill. It drove a need for sex. I salivated at the women scantily clad in tight leather. The feelings were hard to control, as people bumped into me around the bar, and I fought them all the way back to the table.

Gabrielle was gone. Johnny leaned back in the couch by himself, arms to the sides. Hands tapping a little to the beat of the music. They had tall glasses of the Witch's Brew on their table, still full. Johnny had a beer in his hand.

"Gabrielle?" I asked.

"She's around," he said. She and Johnny had their own plan going on tonight, and I wasn't going to learn anything more about it, other than the drug in the drinks was at the heart of it. "Find anything?"

"Maybe." I told Johnny about Andy.

"I've seen Andy in here from time to time." Johnny squinted, as in memory. "Didn't know he was helping Jen."

"Why wouldn't she tell you about Andy?"

Johnny shrugged. "I don't know." We both looked at the empty glass next to his. Gabrielle was a vampire. And Jen's search was about the drug. If she knew about Gabrielle, maybe she felt like her connection to Johnny was a little too close to be giving Andy up.

"How many times have you been here?" I asked.

"Plenty." He grinned. I could see his eyes look around as if he was trying to figure out what he could say. Maybe what he wanted to say. He settled with repeating himself, waggling his eyebrows a bit. "Plenty."

I rolled my eyes. "Great." We didn't trust each other, but maybe we were feeling a little like old friends do after they get past how much they've changed.

We were silent for a few moments. The music was giving me a headache. It was an incessant pounding rhythm that rapped inside my skull. Somehow I could hear a looped track of a woman moaning under it, over and over. At least I hoped it was a looped track.

"What the hell happened, man?" Johnny asked.

"My face? I told you, Raphael welcomed me back home."

"Nah," Johnny said. "I'm talking about us now. There was a time I would've trusted you with anything. We were the Wolverines, remember? And now we're here, sitting at the same table, and I don't know what you're doing here and you don't know what I'm doing here and neither one of us trusts the other enough to say anything."

"Johnny," I said, "you know why I'm here."

"Maybe I thought I did," Johnny said, leaning forward. "But for a guy who's here to find Jen, why would you be spending all this time with Raphael?"

They had seen me at the highway with Raphael. Which explained why I was getting the protective feeling I had gotten from Gabrielle earlier.

"I don't have a lot of friends here, Johnny," I said slowly. Was Gabrielle watching me, or were they watching Raphael and had seen me with him? "I was hoping I could count on you as one of them. Jen would tell you the truth."

"I know," Johnny said. "But Jen's not around right now. And I'm thinking if Jen had meant to you what I thought she meant, you would have been back sooner. I would have thought we deserved that, right? But now, *right now*, you're here, Jen's gone, and Raphael has got you around the collar."

Johnny saw something in my face and took a step back. I loosened my jaw and took a deep breath. Fuck Johnny. Fuck all of them here except for Jen. None of them understood. No one realized I had cared enough about all of them that I had stayed away. I had run for *them*.

And I was angry at myself as well. That decision to run had been worthless. I had thrown away my life, and they, in turn, had thrown away theirs. And Johnny had no idea about any of that. Nor would he. I sat there and swallowed a couple of times, and Johnny finally looked past me.

"Look, Grimm." Johnny talked low. Like he had made a decision. "Things are happening here."

"I've noticed."

"No," he said. "Other things. Things you might complicate."

I looked at it from his side. Ten years ago I had left when Danny was killed. That's almost all Johnny knew of me until I arrived back in Grafton. A lot of time for change. A lot of time for mistrust to build.

"Things I might complicate?" I asked. "Or things Jen wouldn't trust you around?"

"Hey." Johnny sat, offended.

"Fair's fair," I said. "You say you can't trust me, and here you are, rolling around with a vampire as your girlfriend. And now I find out Jen had a plan she didn't tell you about. Instead, she called me."

Johnny took that in for a moment, looking at the crowd. I finally understood he was keeping an eye out for Gabrielle. And maybe thinking more about something. The music seemed to quiet down some like we were in some private bubble. It was just a dull roar.

"You can't help who you fall for, man," Johnny finally said. "But you can go along on their ride."

"So you're helping her against all this." I waved my hands over all the vampires and thralls around us. Johnny was a jokester, a kid I remembered as more round than tall. "You?"

"Don't sound so derisive." Johnny clasped his hands together in a tight ball. One of his thumbs rubbed the top of the other. He looked at me over his fists and frowned. "You haven't been here."

Right then there was a shift in the crowd, a change in tension like a rockfall had broken loose and tumbled down a mountain. A gathering emotional avalanche the drinks and the drugs and the sex had started but couldn't finish. Something animal and angry. A teetering of emotion that would not seesaw long before it collapsed.

"You can feel it, can't you?" Johnny said. "Every night, it always starts like this."

Gabrielle came out of the crowd at that moment, elegantly sliding into the alcove seat and situating herself—just so—around Johnny. In one hand, she held a couple more bottles. She opened them both and gave one to him.

Apparently I wasn't thirsty.

They talked together for a few moments. After a bit, Gabrielle leaned forward. "Johnny tells me that this Jen, she and you were like him and me."

I looked at Johnny, who grinned. "I guess."

"You guess." Gabrielle kept glancing at Johnny like they had some hidden wager, and her arm rested on his. The motion reminded me for some reason of Jen and me watching television together, answering the same question on a show, her arm nestled inside mine. "What would your future be, with her?"

I rubbed my arm where the memory of Jen's arm had rested on mine. Gabrielle and Johnny lay back, relaxed. It seemed unfair that the two of them could be here, enjoying the evening, while Jen was held hostage against my good behavior.

Life had been a succession of one-day runs for me. Each day a little ahead of a demon. Every day running from Azazel. Even now, knowing I was stuck in here, I wanted to go grab the Key out of the Vault and run. Being trapped by Raphael in this town, being the messenger between him and his father, my life span probably counted in days. I couldn't plan a future with someone when just making it through the next day was an accomplishment. "What makes you think we have a future?"

"Don't you think about it?" Gabrielle asked.

"Think about what?" I said. Jen for me was a moment in time: picking a flower because it was the color of her hair; a summer rain, honeysuckle on a breeze. It wasn't three kids and a mortgage. "It's not like I'm the house-with-a-picket-fence type of guy. I don't live in that kind of world."

"Which world is that?" Gabrielle's tone grew a little cool, and Johnny rubbed her arm a bit. "This world?"

"Sure," I said. "A world of vampires and drinks and demons and monsters. How can anyone have a future there?"

There was a long pause. Johnny reached his hand down Gabrielle's arms, and their fingers intertwined. I rubbed my arm again—the memory of Jen leaning against it had been strong—and took another drink of my beer.

"Humans." Gabrielle's voice cut through the music. Angry, for some reason. "Never thinking of what is to come. Always living in their moment."

"Why are you asking me about this?"

"I am curious about these things." Her face said she had another reason though. There was some pain there.

"I didn't know vampires got curious." I said.

"Hey, now." Johnny kicked my leg. "Play nice."

"Fine," I said. "My apologies."

Johnny slid a hand around her back, rubbing it. Gabrielle turned up to the ceiling, her eyes searching the fake frescos of ancient Greece. God, this place was gaudy. After a moment she took a deep breath, let it out, and then looked back at me. Her eyes glistened a little, and the look was oddly human.

"What do you know about the families?"

"You mean the vampire clans?"

"What you call the clans—yes."

"Clans exist all over." I replied. It's what everyone knew. "Some are small, some are large. The larger ones rule territories under a head vampire. I've never heard of them called families."

She frowned. "Choosing to live in ignorance doesn't excuse your lack of knowledge of us. What you call clans are actually families. What you here in America call thralls"—here her mouth twisted in distaste—"we call brothers and sisters, mothers and fathers. We complement each other. The Dumont family has existed for thousands of years, and we work together with our vampire brothers and sisters. Each generation, one or two of the family are selected to be born again as a vampire, to keep our line, our legacy intact. That is how we have children. How vampires should properly propagate their line. That is how my father had me."

My experience with vampires had started with Raphael and had migrated from there to the rogue undead I had found while on the run. I had never heard of vampire families like Gabrielle had described, entire clans working with the familial brothers and sisters, aunts and uncles, perhaps like a corporation. A company that could think and plan long term, and brought others into the fold as generations passed.

But the important thing might be how Gabrielle had been born. "So your father had you while he was human, then was selected to become a vampire?"

"Correct. And then I was selected many years later for my rebirth."

"It was kind of a special case," Johnny said. Gabrielle flashed him a frown though, and he stopped himself.

"Dominic, his family line had run out after generations of wars between the families. He was one of a few remaining from his family. They were Spanish. He fled here hoping to start a new family, and most of the larger families had brushed him away from their thoughts. You see, he had no complement. No legacy."

"Until Raphael." I got it. "He found some way to have a son, even though he was already undead."

Gabrielle nodded. "Yes. What Dominic has done has caused a panic amongst the families. If vampires break from tradition, if they forgo their human complement, if their complements are no longer needed, what next?"

"But there are vampires that don't have families, right?" I had run into them most of the time and had killed more than a few. I would assume those vampires would love to know the secret of having undead sons and daughters to follow them.

Gabrielle waved a hand. "Of course. Just like humans have muggers and thieves and murderers, those exist in the vampire world as well. But the best of us, we are complete only with our families."

"So, when I ask you about you and Jen," Gabrielle continued, "I ask because I was never afforded that chance. I grew up knowing I would be a vampire, and I would never have the kind of life humans would have. What you could enjoy every day with Jen, the future you pretend you don't have, those are brief moments for us. And those moments are treasured, when we find them." She placed a hand on top of Johnny's.

I looked away, over the crowd of vampires and thralls all leaning too close to one another, bodies moving to the music. I couldn't let myself think about a future with Jen. Life would always be better with her, but life was unfair. I had accepted that for a long time now, and that wasn't going to change while I looked at a bunch of drugged-up vampires and thralls dry-humping each other to pulsing music.

A server walked up with three new beers, set them down. Andy. He nodded for me to head back to the hallway and left. After a moment I got up. And bumped into Raphael. I stepped back. The corner of his lips twisted up. "Heard you were here, Grimm. Something you want?"

"I can't be here?" I said. "You want to order me back to Parker's? Give me a time-out, maybe?"

"Not at all," Raphael said. "Sit down, enjoy a few. Everyone deserves a night out on the town."

After a moment, when I didn't move, Raphael pulled a chair up from the table next to us and sat down. "Grimm, I asked you to sit. Should I ask it less politely?"

Andy disappeared up the hallway, torn. Raphael wanted a chance to order me to sit down. I couldn't give him the opportunity to hold me up. I sat back down. My foot tapped impatiently under the table. Andy would need to wait.

Raphael grinned. "There you go. And they said you can't teach an old dog new tricks."

"What do you want, Raph?"

Raphael ignored me and pulled up a chair from a nearby table. "You don't stop by enough, Gabs."

Gabrielle smiled in return. "The world is such a large place. But I try to stop by here when I'm around."

"No one formally told me the Dumonts would be back in town. Are we still negotiating?"

"Not this time," Gabrielle said coolly. "I'm here for something a little more personal."

Raphael glanced at Johnny. "I get it. New toys are tough to put down, aren't they?"

Johnny put a hand on Gabrielle's knee and kept it there. The female vampire's face struggled. Raphael leaned back casually and waited.

Johnny squeezed her leg once, then twice. Gabrielle swallowed once. Then again.

"Aren't you tired of being your family's flunky here, Gabs?" Raphael said. "I know what they want. I even know why you're here. I say let go of old traditions. Bring in the new."

"That's what your father never got either," Gabrielle said. "There are reasons traditions are in place."

Raphael just waved his hand over his shoulder.

"I laugh as I watch your story play out, though," Gabrielle said. "We all know. Son deposing father. Such a terrible trope."

He shrugged. "It's hardly a secret."

"You will be a victim of the same cycle," Gabrielle said. "It's what Dominic did, and it's what your son will do. It's what happens to those like you. Those of us with *traditions* know this."

"I doubt there's been anyone around like me."

"Such a large ego, for me to hear it over all this music."

Raphael's jaw locked. He leaned toward Gabrielle. She held her spot, but at that moment I could see how much larger Raphael was than the female vampire. Gabrielle projected an elegant confidence from her slick black dress. Raphael was raw force contained in a tailored suit and a loose tie.

None of this vampire ego contest was helping me right now. I looked back over the hallway. Andy had long disappeared. I moved to get up, and Raphael immediately held out his hand to me.

"I told you to just *sit*," he said. His voice intoned the same command he had used on the hill. My legs folded and I almost fell back into the seat. I could breathe, but my arms and legs were locked in place.

Gabrielle noticed the exchange. Her body went slack as if someone had surprised her with shocking news.

Raphael signaled the waitress over. "I see you guys are drinking beers. Another round?"

Johnny looked over at me. I couldn't move. I stared straight across at Gabrielle as the waitress brought a group of bottles over. Gabrielle watched me in return, her brows narrowed, as Raphael popped open the beers and place them in front of us.

Johnny took his. "Don't drink your own product, Raph?"

"It's not that." Raphael winked at Gabrielle. "I just require something a little more ... pure."

My mind flashed to Sarah in the back of his car, two tiny wounds placed precisely over her carotid artery. I took a deep breath and watched Raphael out the corner of my eye.

The vampire shook his head a bit at me and chuckled. "Apologies, Grimm. Feel free to move around. After you enjoy your beer."

I fought the command, even as my hand grabbed the beer and brought it to my mouth. Then I gave in and drank it, just to ease the compulsion.

Gabrielle still stared at me. I frowned back at her. "What?"

She shook her head and looked at Raphael. The commanding presence she had held earlier had disappeared. Her gaze now was speculative, perhaps the glance of a lawyer as new evidence was presented in the courtroom.

"You guys remember playing Hickam High School?" Raphael took a swig and drank.

"Sure, Raph," Johnny said.

"I miss those days, man," Raphael said. "Something easy about getting up and going to school and playing ball."

"Where the hell are you going with this, Raph?" I said.

"Just remembering, Grimm, just remembering." Raphael leaned back and let us all take him in. Nice jacket, shoulders relaxed, just drinking beer with his buddies. "We had a pretty good year that year, and Hickam came in. They were undefeated, talking a lot of shit. I remember Coach telling us they had us scouted. You remember what happened?"

"They lost."

"Who put them down?" He smiled.

I sighed. "You did."

"Damn right I did. Set them all up, put them all down. That's how pitchers work."

Johnny rolled his eyes at me.

Gabrielle gathered herself again. "What you are doing? It's not a game now."

"It's only not a game for losers, Gabs." Raphael smiled again. "Remember that."

With that, he set his empty beer bottle down, got up, and left. Gabrielle whispered something quickly to Johnny, and left herself. The club music seemed heavier, there was more of the subsonic pounding of bass notes underneath the moaning vocals.

"I'm out of here," I said.

"Yeah," Johnny said. "You can feel it, can't you?"

"You coming?"

"Nah." Johnny stayed lying back against the couch, tapping his hands to the beat. I could see part of him surveying the crowd, and part of him trying to not see what was actually happening there. Still watching for Gabrielle.

"Go on ahead," Johnny said. "This ain't my first rodeo."

I got up and pushed through the crowd. They didn't part as easily, this time. I shoved and swung an elbow here or there until I finally got to the hallway. There I hurried up and turned the corner. Andy was nowhere in sight.

I got a bad feeling and ran down to the last theater. I opened the door and walked in to an empty room. The orgy earlier had disappeared. Well, not everyone was gone. One person sat up on the front row, facing the screen. The snickering of an eight-millimeter film reel rolling ticked through the space and the screen flickered white and black in front of me.

My bad feeling grew worse as I walked down the aisle. I recognized Andy's hair. I called his name, but he didn't turn. As I circled in front I saw his eyes wide-open, blank, staring at the white screen in front of him. A lanyard was tucked tight under his chin, and a thick trail of blood snaked its way from two punctures on his neck.

He was dead. He had likely been dead when Grant saw me talking to him. I kicked the chair next to him, and a laminated piece of paper fluttered down behind the seat. I looked at the lanyard and saw it was one of those ribbons people wore identification badges on. The badge had been ripped off, and that was what I picked up from the floor. An old picture of someone I didn't recognize was on it, and on top of the badge were the letters GTF in bold black type.

Grafton Tire Factory. A place that had been closed for years. Likely something Grant had picked up when he and Rand came looking for Andy.

I had lost my chance at finding Jen. And someone had been killed because I was still looking for her. Johnny was still out there in the crowd. Nick drifted alone out in the town. Miss Tammie or Parker. Maybe even Sarah or even Jen. It was only a matter of time before someone else bought it if I kept looking for Jen. And yet it was the only thing I could do.

CHAPTER FOURTEEN

It had been a long day, and I decided to get some sleep back at Parker's. When I got there Parker was on the porch, not rocking, just sitting there with his head tilted back and his face looking up. Nick was sitting on the porch railing across from him, leaned up against the column. Neither of them moved as I pulled the Camaro up and shut it off. Listened to the car quietly chug its way to sleep. I patted the dash and got out. In the back of my skull, I could still feel the faint rhythm of the club music echoing over and over.

Nick watched me walk up, and as I neared the porch he got up off the rail and went inside. I stopped, looking at the front door swing back shut.

Parker didn't really move, and his voice was low and quiet. "That boy don't like you much."

I took Nick's place on the railing. "Isn't that the case for both of you?"

"Nah," Parker said. In the dark, his face was a mass of shadows and scars. "I've always liked you, Fergus. Just never liked the choices you made."

"That's what we are, right?" I couldn't keep my tone from being sarcastic. "The choices we make?"

"I guess people say that." Parker kept his head back, his whole body barely moving. Crickets chirped out from the woods, an echoing call of back and forth. We stayed there for a while, and the chirping song only got louder. Soon enough, the club music faded away.

"Thing is," Parker finally continued, "if you have to think about something to do the right thing, I'm not sure that's who you really are." He cocked his head slightly, and the rocking chair creaked a bit as his body leaned forward. He seemed to be thinking of something far, far away, and his voice grew distant. "If you are what you choose, then you can be any old thing you want, just by making the choice to be it. I don't know if I believe that. I won't not say a person is defined by the choices he makes, but I believe it depends on the *type* of choice. The kind of choice you have to make without thinking, *in the moment*, I think that's the person you're stuck being for the rest of your life." The old man leaned back a bit, and his eyes were far away. Thinking maybe about a young Parker, and a moment when he had made a decision that had led to this.

This was the most open Parker had ever been. I figured I knew how he felt about me, and I figured I deserved it. As a kid I had always been stubborn. I had been someone who made up their mind on their own and did things their own way, and Parker and I had butted heads many times. I had made bad choices, and he had too. I wished for a moment he knew the full story about me, and maybe what his thoughts would be after hearing it, about the type of person I was. I looked up at the dark night, the open sky, and thought about a young kid hitchhiking his way out of town.

"That's the moment," Parker said again, out of the blue. Still in his past. "The choice someone makes in the moment, that's what defines him. That's who you are."

We waited. The air was cool around us, but not cold. There was a bubble of pressure around us, one that muted the crickets and everything else around me and Parker. My thoughts turned to Danny and that day, as Raphael swung, and I had been frozen in place.

Inside I winced, over and over, thinking of my life since then. Was I punishing myself for Danny? Did I run to protect those I cared about, or was I selfish, too afraid to stand and face what chased me? Grafton was a mess, and my friends were in trouble, but what would have happened had I stayed? Had the person I was now been created in the swing of a bat and the death of a friend? Or had that moment simply revealed who I really was?

"Why are you telling me this?" I asked.

Parker snorted. "Grimm, I was charged with raising you. And I've done a pretty piss-poor job of it." He worked his jaw like he was swallowing down something. "And I'm not sure I like who you are, or what you've become, but I'll be damned if I let you run off again without telling you how to survive in this world."

We were quiet then for a bit. Parker leaned his head back against the house. The wind picked up, whistling a low moan and carrying hints of cool moisture. In the moments where it died off I could feel the air settle a little, heavy and just a touch wet. Then the breeze would blow again, a natural ebb and flow, nature's rhythm. We both were quiet for a long time.

"Nights like this," Parker said, his voice soft, almost a whisper, "feels better on my scars. Cools them a bit." There was a long pause and a sigh. "Or so I imagine."

I didn't know what to say to that. Those scars on his face were there because of choices I made. He had lived with pain for a decision I made, and I had never known. And here I was worrying about what had happened to me, what I had become, because of those same choices. "I'm sorry about those."

"They're not your fault, not really," Parker said. "My life led me up to this point, how I've lived it." He grinned, and the movement twisted his face up sickly. "You can't take other people's choices away from them, son. Bad as they are, we all make 'em."

"Even mine?"

"Especially yours," Parker said. "Son, you got plenty of time to right those wrongs. But you got to make a choice, and you got to stick by that choice. Life ain't fair, it ain't never fair to those of us like you and me, but you make your peace and you make your stand. You go down swinging, no matter what."

"Always?"

"Always," Parker said. "Because you got strength, boy. And fight that other people don't have. So you got to be strong so they have something to latch on to."

I held out my hands, palms up. "You weren't there that day, Park.

You're not there now. Being strong got Danny killed. Being strong got my ass kicked by Raphael the other day."

Parker waved that away. "There's strong and there's dumb, boy. I loved Danny just like the rest of you, but Raphael had it hard for that boy and you were just the match that lit that fuse, that day."

"Bullshit," I said. "You weren't there."

"You listening to me?" Parker spat. "I don't have to be there. You think you're the only person who's had a rough life? I been around people like Raphael before, and I'm telling you, they do what they want until someone stands up to them. You could've been that person, but you ran. And now look at you. Look at your friends. They're running around like a chicken with its head cut off, trying to stop Raphael. You think Sarah would be with that boy now? You think your Jen would've had to stay and pry her sister away? Or Nick? None of them ain't got no direction."

I shook my head. "And me being here would have fixed all that."

"That's what I'm saying. You just ain't listening." The rocking chair creaked as Parker leaned forward. He looked past me, out to where the swing hung from the tree. "You got to stand and fight for what's right. Otherwise, the other guy always wins. Show others the way, and they'll hold you up. They can be the foundation you need. But you got to make the stand first."

I followed his gaze to the branches of the oak tree, thick dark fingers clawing up into the night. The swing silently rocked left and right, left and right, in a breeze that always seemed to be blowing there. Whatever Parker hadn't faced, it ate at him. And maybe he thought if he had followed his own advice the swing wouldn't be empty now. But I wasn't sure Parker's advice helped me any. Staying in town would have gotten me killed sooner, and likely Nick and Johnny and Sarah and Jen. He hadn't been there that day, hadn't stared into the crazy eyes of a teenage vampire drunk on power, hadn't realized what someone could do if they just abandoned any sense of right and wrong.

So Parker could fight his own demons. I would keep running from mine.

CHAPTER FIFTEEN

I woke up late the next afternoon. Almost dusk. I had slept hard, a hibernation with no dreams, no restless sleep, no nightmares. For long moments I lay in my bed, not wanting to move and break the peace, not wanting to feel the first shot of pain from my sore body.

I would have to fix that today. It was time to heal up a bit, and there was one place I was sure I could do it. Every cemetery in the world had a ghost. I groaned, pushed myself up. A rib seemed to be poking somewhere it shouldn't be. My jaw was swollen enough the top teeth on the right side of my mouth wouldn't touch the bottom teeth. I took a deep breath, winced again, and let it all out.

There was no one in the house, no Nick, no Parker. I grabbed a quick shower, and an even quicker bite to eat. There were some apples on the table. My jaw winced just looking at them, so I broke a banana off of a bunch and got into my car. I would heal up, get a cup of coffee, and then pull on another string that could lead me to Jen.

The car rumbled along the road like a panther, pleased with the hunt. Andy had been a dead end. I grimaced at that particular thought. Thinking of the dead, though, Father Benjamin might be able to answer some questions. The wards in the diner, the conversation with Greg. There were plenty of strings to unravel there.

I took the long way around, avoiding Main Street. The church loomed up before me, perched on the side of the northwest hill. I came out of a side street and merged onto County Road 48, heading away from Main Street and out of town. Toward some other small town, hours away, whose name I had forgotten.

The road to the church came up on the right, quick. As I turned up the road it pointed me toward the water tower, a little farther west of the church and a little higher on the hill. I navigated a couple of turns and finally pulled into the little loop-around circling in front of the church. There was no road past here, just a dead end.

A short time later I was at the church. It was one of those days when there wasn't a cloud in the sky, just a haze of blue and gray, and a sun dimly hid behind the haze. A darkness gathered in the east. The colors of the trees had begun their change, and the yellows and browns rattled as a wind picked through the leaves. The water tower tilted like a drunken soldier behind the church, in the distance, poking out over the trees. I got out of the car, shut the door, and walked up to the church. The air felt moist and cool and smelled a little like the ocean.

The building was an old Catholic church, redbrick with stained glass windows circling the sides of the building. The tan sedan I had seen at the diner was parked behind the church. A steeple stood guard over the roof. Brown leaves scattered across the entry, twisting and twirling before me. The front doors of the church were thick oak things, with heavy brass knockers.

I tried to open one, then the other. Neither budged. It felt odd not being able to walk into a church. Normally I would stop by and enter a church to sneak a bit of holy water out to sprinkle over my ammo, and I hadn't yet found a church I couldn't enter in the middle of the day, though there was a wedding once I had slightly interrupted. So I knocked with no response. I tried one of the brass knockers. The thump echoed hollowly from inside the church.

No one answered. I walked around to check out the cemetery. It would be dark soon, and ghosts typically came out at night, after the last of the sun slipped over the horizon. The closer it got to what vampires called true night, or midnight, the most spirits seemed to appear. I put a hand over my jaw and felt the hard swelling there. For me, graveyards made the best hospitals.

The ground was a little moist, and I sloshed through dead and broken leaves as I headed around to the back of the church. Encircling the cemetery was a nice wrought-iron fence, the kind you see around a thousand small graveyards all around the world. There were a few statues, here and there, tall somber figures in granite robes. Tombstones dotted the lawn. Very few flowers filled any of the vases, though.

The graveyard here was fairly large. The town had been around a couple of hundred years, and everyone who had died here was buried here. Or, I thought as I stopped before the gate and looked out over the hill, everyone *had been* buried here.

Mounds of mud lay next to all the burial plots, some of them overgrown with weeds. The cemetery was more like a plowed garden, fresh dark earth turned up in long furrows, quite a few headstones cracked, some tipped over. From here it appeared as if every plot had been unearthed and robbed.

The breeze fluttered around me, picked up dead leaves, and flung them around the graves. I huddled in my jacket. Who would take these bodies? Why? The gate to the cemetery opened silently as I slipped in and walked around. Every row had been opened up, large trenches cut into the dark earth as if the whole graveyard was waiting for a mass burial. I peered into the first and saw weathered coffins tossed aside and broken up, rotten wood and cloth twisted together in bits and pieces. No bodies.

I searched the place. Every row, every plot was the same as the first. Every coffin broken into. Every casket picked clean. Everything in Grafton was tied around the drug Raphael was making. Could he be making it with corpses? That didn't go together with what Andy had told me, about Cole and Raphael talking about needing more women. Maybe additional women were only part of the rite, and corpses were needed as well? The whole thing seemed more demonic in nature, and less chemical.

A bench lay off to the side, and I found myself sitting there as night settled around me. The farther away I could sense a ghost, the stronger the spirit seemed to appear, and even though I hadn't sensed any in town, I hoped one or two weaker ones remained. It had been a long time since I was without a spirit around, and here in Grafton, right now, I felt a little like a tightrope walker without a safety net. Before me on the rope were Raphael, Rand, Jacob, and Dominic, and Jen lay on the other side, and I felt like a hint of a ghost would help me get to her.

In the beginning, when I had first accidently tapped a ghost and used it to heal myself, I had freaked out. Living their memories was never a positive experience, and I wondered why it happened, and what it did to me. Living someone else's life, even for a moment, I wondered if I walked away from that without keeping some of the evil the ghost had done in myself. I wondered if, by looking into the monster, I slowly became one.

Every ghost I had tapped had been evil, to a degree. I wondered what kept them from hell. I used to worry about using the energy that seemed to sustain them, and wondered what kind of parasite that made me, but over the years I had used them more and more.

Especially when I had found the Key, and Azazel had appeared. Each time I used a spirit up the memories made me hate myself a little more, but the next time I needed one, I always tapped another. When it came down to it, I always chose to live.

The moon appeared like it always did, fading out of the night as if it was always there. For a bit I stood as darkness overcame the skies, an inky blackness rising from the east and blotting out the blue of night sky. For those who can see true night appear, it grew as a dark blob from the horizon, from which it would swell out like a slow wave. I looked around, not seeing a single spirit. I checked my ethereal radar. I blinked and turned on my ethereal vision. I got up and walked around and checked in all the trenches.

Nothing.

No ghosts, no specters, no spirits. No footprints running around the empty graves, except for my own. There should be some ghosts here. Spirits were more likely to be tied to the place of their death than their burial, although there didn't seem to be a hard-and-fast rule covering that. There were always ghosts in a graveyard.

I looked back at the church. A golden shimmer blanketed the bricks under the black night, like the building slumbered. I blinked back to normal vision and took a breath. I wasn't going to heal here. And likely not in Grafton at all. The entire town had been purged of ghosts, and that concerned me. Did Raphael know how I got my powers? Could he have gotten rid of all the spirits here? I hadn't gotten that sense from him, and that spoke of another player in the game. Dominic? My mother? Could she do what I could?

I let out a deep breath, staring at the moon. It hung slightly behind the water tower and the hilltop, the tower a huge, shadowed metal shape sticking out of the backside of the hill. Long ago I would climb up there and look down on Grafton, watching the town lights wink out one by one in the coming night. Later on, I would take Jen there, and we had spent a couple of teenage evenings holding hands and talking, sitting side by side, legs dangling in the open air. It was chilly up there, and I could still remember her body nestled next to mind, with the whole world spread out below us.

I stood there looking at it, stuck in the memory so hard I could feel Jen's hand in mine.

Fuck it. I had nothing better to do.

I left the graveyard and headed back to the car. The breeze that had stirred up the leaves earlier was gone now, dead. No crickets chirped, no frogs croaked, no owls called out their questions to the air.

I slid back into the car and started it up. It answered with a low chugging, something it did sometimes on a quiet night, a sound that always made me think the car was trying to be stealthy. Quiet. As if an eight-cylinder engine from the sixties could ever sneak up on someone. "Still," I said, patting the dashboard, "points for trying."

I drove the Camaro a little past the church, turning off on a dirt road that led to the water tower. Two ruts in the ground where maintenance trucks had driven, once or twice a month, heading to the far side of the hills. I flicked on the headlights and followed the road carefully, lunging in my seat as I drove over a little washout in the road.

Soon the steel metal struts came into view, poking out of the hill. I pulled right up to the fence surrounding the tower and shut off the car. Patted the dash while she quieted down, and then got out.

The fence had been whole, a long time ago. It now sported several collapsed sections where it had toppled over. I walked through the gaps, feeling the brush of long, dry grass blades against my jeans, and stepped all the way to where the old water tower stood. Underneath the tower was a concrete pad, the pad surrounded by packed, hard dirt, and here and there, lines of weeds snaked through the dirt toward the concrete.

On one edge of the concrete was an old steel ladder. I grabbed hold of a rusted rung, feeling the slight rasp under my hand as it circled around the metal. The motion transported me back to when I was a kid, climbing it first by myself and later with Jen. The edges of flecked-off paint pressed into my palm, just like it had ten years ago.

I took a step up, then another. My ribs creaked, my side ached, but I kept pulling myself up. Slowly, but consistently. As I got higher I could feel the wind pick up, a chill breeze, and with it the lush scent of the forest. The concrete pad below got smaller and smaller, and soon I was up top.

There was a majestic sense up here, a feeling of being over the world, of looking down upon things small and insignificant. A ring of rusted iron grate surrounded the top of the tower, the walkway fenced by thin metal wiring, pulled tight at each post. A slight breeze pushed past me, past the tower. I felt like the wind was trying to pick me up and carry me out past the town, out of Grafton, away from this crazy place and somewhere safe. The scent of the forest grew stronger as the wind whispered through the trees.

I got to the top and walked the ring a few times, looking for a sign from Jen, and found nothing. There was a crumpled piece of paper, and when I first saw it I had hoped it was a note, but it was a missing kid poster. Someone I didn't recognize, a young girl, dark with dark hair. I wondered briefly if Jen had been trying to find them, but there was nothing telling me that. There was nothing, nothing painted onto the metal, no message from Jen hidden somewhere where only I could find it. Nothing.

Grafton lay before me, sprawling outward from the bottom of the hill the water tower perched on. To my left was the Antonados' manor, hundreds of acres on a hill west of town. Lights blazed around the compound, ringing a high concrete wall that encircled the house. As I stood there, the town came alive, lights flicking on in homes on each block, thralls stumbling out of doors and heading to where they might get a fix. A tan sedan left the diner and drove south on Main Street before heading out of town. I wondered if it was Greg and if Father Benjamin was with him. I followed the car until I lost it beneath the trees.

I felt lonely all of a sudden, which was odd. I had been alone a long time. But standing there, looking out over the town, an imaginary circle surrounding Grafton past, which I couldn't leave, I *was* alone. Somewhere, through the last ten years, I had felt I always could come back here, at least back to Jen. I felt like I could show up one day, one day after running from the demons and the vampires and the undead, and just say hi. And she would say hi back, and I would lean into her. Put my cheek on her shoulder and rest for a minute.

And she was gone. I was worried that she was gone for good, and if she wasn't I was hurting enough to worry I might not have enough in me to find her.

I was tired. It was late September and cool, but not cold enough that I would freeze. I had definitely slept in colder places, and with less, than on top of a water tower. Some places were strong with my memories of Jen, and this was a place we had sat together, looking over the town, watching people walk the world underneath us.

I sat down on the cold iron grates of the walkway and huddled in my jacket. The moon rose high over the small town of vampires and thralls and unknowns, and I thought about the ghosts I had left behind in this town. Spending the day at Partisan Rock with my friends, camping. Laughing around a campfire. The arguments with Parker. The fights with Raphael. All things I thought I had left for good.

All those thoughts tangled together until there was a huge ball of string surrounding me, and I was looking for the one piece that would unravel everything if I just tugged it. But I couldn't find the one piece, just memories that wound around me and around me and around me, tighter and tighter and tighter. I looked deep into the night sky, staring at the stars, wondering if Jen was somewhere else and looking at them with me.

I took a deep breath and let it out, slowly, into the night air. It was cool enough for slight wisps of breath to lift silently in the purpling sky. In my mind, I had known the water tower was the place, the place I would find something, even might find Jen here waiting for me. But she wasn't here, and I tried not to get used to disappointment. I didn't have long before Dominic arrived, and I didn't know what would happen then. I needed to rescue Jen before I became so tightly wrapped in Raphael's machinations that I couldn't save her.

True night arrived. I leaned back against the tower and watched it. The inky blackness born of midnight absorbed everything it touched, like a giant slow-motion wave building from the east. It rolled over mountains and trees and enveloped them whole. It even swallowed up a brightly lit area around where the old Grafton tire factory used to be.

I cocked my head and peered closer at the fields where the tire factory had been. A tiny glow rose over a hill, like the lights of a stadium or parking lot. It was odd that the lights of the factory would still be on if the plant was shut down.

Andy had had a lanyard tied around his neck. And the identification badge in the chair next to him. With three bold-type words at the badge's top.

Grafton Tire Plant.

A place Raphael controlled, a place he could manufacture his drug, a place he could control access to. A place he could hide someone if he wanted to.

I pounded the railing. The metal of the catwalk vibrated in response. I had found where Jen was hidden. I leaned out over the rail and tried to see more from the east, but all I could see was the glow. A van headed down the road from the factory, toward me. Now that I knew where I was looking, I picked up details like a police car idling at the old gas station, at the corner of where the factory road met the state road. Maybe waiting on the van.

All I had to do was sneak through the fields and into the factory. I was sure I would find Jen there. I would time it for early in this morning, just a few hours from now when vampires and thralls were getting ready for day sleep and most people would be less than aware. It would work. I could save her and still get out of town alive, with the Key.

And then a deep, rich voice echoed through my mind.

Come.

A commanding voice that resonated through my bones.

Come-come.

The words pulsed like a heartbeat, from the center of my chest.

Come-come. Come-come.

I had a moment of wonder. That wonder quickly turned to fear as I lost control of my legs. My feet took a couple of steps on their own. I moved like a broken marionette. I headed toward the railing, as if the command just wanted me to come, and didn't care about how I arrived.

This was like when Raphael had commanded me, but much, much more powerful. When Raphael used his voice I could sense what the command was moving in my body, but here I couldn't feel my legs at all, or the will controlling them. They were separate from my body.

I grabbed the railing with both hands. Looked to the east. I grabbed onto the railing even as my legs slid themselves underneath it. Each leg moved like I was pedaling a bike, trying to pull me off of the walkway, dragging me little by little over the edge. Pulling me toward town. Toward Parker's. Where I was sure Dominic waited for me.

I looked east, toward the tire plant, and screamed aloud. I was *this close*. I had found where they were hiding Jen. I knew it. Just too late to do anything about it.

Come-come. A rhythmic heartbeat. *Come-come*.

The harder I fought, the more my body shook. One leg off the side. Then the other. My stomach slid underneath the rail and I hugged the railing for dear life. My legs hung in midair but still tried to walk toward the voice. My elbows ached from the metal railing that dug into them. The ground waited for me to drop like a rock and spatter over the hard-packed earth.

Come-come.

I didn't want to give up Jen. Not now. But one arm slipped off the rail, and I could feel the rail slide out from the crook of the other. That elbow was all I had left. Every other part of my body was trying to fling itself toward the ground below in an effort to head toward town.

Toward the bearer of the command.

Come-come.

My elbow slowly began to unhinge, my body fighting against me until I was seconds away from tumbling to the earth. From there, I imagined, whatever was left of my body would probably still try to wriggle its way toward the speaker of the command. Though I would be long dead before that, and the voice might get tired of waiting for me. I pressed my eyes tight and gripped my slipping arm with everything I had.

Come-come. The pulse of the heartbeat continued, the rhythm working faster and faster. *Come-come. Come-come-Come-come-Come-come*.

"All right!" I screamed. And immediately the force stopped. I could still feel the command pulsing in my veins, in my chest, but it was more subtle. Waiting, like a snake, to take over and strike only when it felt I wasn't doing what the geas wanted me to do. I was allowed leeway, but there would be limits.

I had seen a lot of scary things, and I had walked away from them all with nightmares. But at least I had been able to walk away under my free will. What I felt now was a greater fear of anything I had ever felt. I had just been shown that my body was not mine to control. And never would be. Someone could control my every action, and I feared who that person might be.

Slowly, painfully, I pulled myself back onto the catwalk. I stood like my legs were perched on stilts, and managed my way to the ladder. I carefully crept down the rungs and made sure to have a solid grip and footing before moving to the next step. The command lurked in my mind, waiting for me to slow down so that it could force me to move faster. My hands shook as I waited for the command to strike and force me off the ladder because falling to the ground was much faster than climbing. On and on the command pulled, toward Grafton, toward the bad side of town. Parker's.

Finally I got to the ground. The command allowed me a breath before pushing me toward town. I stilt-walked my way to the car, fired it up. I drove like I had had a few, weaving all over the road. I managed my way down the back roads to the south side of town, going around Main Street and heading toward Parker's. The command stayed inside me like a backseat driver, looking for every chance to correct me.

The commanding voice quieted as I neared Parker's. The closer I came to obeying, the more *normal* I could move my body. Only if I fought the voice would the command force my body to move. I was still shaky, and my driving was still a little wobbly, but finally I got to where the voice was bringing me. I drove up the gravel driveway of Parker's, seeing the house far down at the end of the headlights. The house was dark, and no one was on the porch.

A black limo parked before the house, lights off. The car was the standard limo black, the wheels and accessories nicely chromed out, and the windows well tinted, to the point where they reflected my headlights. If I had to guess I would say the windows would be tinted enough to keep all forms of ultraviolet light outside the car. I had a bad feeling about who would be behind those windows.

I stopped my car a little down from the limo, more scared than I had ever been. I fought the desire to run. Part of me, a part I was ashamed of, thought I could always came back later. More prepared. But I knew I couldn't. I knew the voice would stop me if I did. Still, I wanted badly to put the Camaro in reverse and streak out of here, out of Grafton, never looking back.

Come-come, the voice begged quietly from inside my chest. *Come-come.*

I wondered what Jen would think of me now, fighting my hand on the shifter. *We both know what you can do.* I snorted and threw the car into park. It shut down with a shudder. I opened the door and got out.

A slight wind picked up and blew across the porch, rustled the leaves of the tree in the front yard. It brought a chill, one affecting the body and the soul. The moon had pulled itself halfway up into the night, a three-quarter moon bright in cloudless skies. I wondered if Parker was home, if he was inside, watching. Or if he had left to be somewhere safer tonight. The wind blew harder, a slight moan through the night, and I shivered.

The door behind the driver opened first, and a woman got out. She shut the door and walked around the limo to me. The moonlight fell brightly around her, and everything else seemed dim in comparison. She was tall, with long blond hair tied back in some kind of warrior's braid. Each of her steps was firmly placed in front of the other in an elegant, timeless motion. She didn't walk the earth; the earth revolved underneath her step.

She was dressed in a mix of black leather and blue-black steel; her whole outfit brought up an image of a Valkyrie. The handle of a blade tilted out over her shoulder. Her face was beautiful, but stern, with arching eyebrows and piercing blue eyes. High cheekbones framed an angular face. Her lips were pressed firmly together, and she did not smile. She appeared to be maybe thirty years old. Just a little older than me.

She stopped in front of me. Each of her steps had been light, crisp, almost soundless in their perfection. She nodded and stared at me for a long, long moment.

"Son." Her voice was musical, but not light. More like the mournful melody of a dirge, the soprano tones of regret.

I looked at her, took a deep, shaky breath, and let it all out. I didn't know what to say. Couldn't know what to say. I had never felt the need to have a mother and didn't know what to do with one now. I could not sense the bond that all kids had with their mothers. Whatever tether mother had to son had been cut for me long ago.

Her eyes seemed to search me out, seemed to understand what I was thinking, what I was going through. Maybe she had gone through the same. The wind died down around us. Of its own accord her hand reached out, and a finger trembled slightly as it pushed aside a lock of my hair.

I leaned back, just a bit.

Her hand retreated. Her eyes moved everywhere except to me. I pulled at my ghostly sixth sense, and ethereal energy steamed off her in tiny wisps. So she was like me. I was no longer unique.

"Know," she said simply, sadly, softly, her eyes still looking past me, "that I will be sorry."

The other car door opened. The driver, a man of normal build and perfect carriage. He walked around and opened the other passenger door, stepping aside to let a figure step out. My mother sighed and stepped back. Whatever time she had wanted with me, it was over.

Dominic Antonado strode down the gravel driveway toward us. The crunch of his steps on the stone was like the cracking of bones. He was tall, shoulders somewhat hunched with age. There was a resemblance to Raphael in his face, classically Roman, small rounded chin, a protruding nose. But where Raphael was young and full of energy, this man was thin and hard. He radiated an unyielding will, a cloud of power that pulled those around him to him.

I have faced evil beings before. Other creatures of the night. Half vampires, demons. Azazel. I do not know if any of them held the pure malignant force Dominic Antonado radiated. He was ancient, far older than any vampire or undead I had seen before. Something darker than night swelled around him, forcibly pushed me back a step or two. Stars winked out behind him. Hate shed off him and slapped against my chest like a large ocean wave hits the shore. I knew, deep inside, this man lived off pure hate, pure evil. A malignance. And I stood frozen before him.

He stopped beside my mother. She had taken a step or two back, like a guard, and continued to look out at the surrounding area. Perpetually watching. In my ghostly sense, I could see a dark cloud mask the center of Dominic's body, a pulsing of something purple and thick from his chest. I had seen it before, in other vampires, but Dominic's held a thick blackness deep inside the purple I had never seen before, a dark inkiness of old, ancient evil.

"Fergus Grimm," Dominic said. His voice was surprisingly deep, even pleasant, resonating like a chord from a harp. It was the voice of command, of expectation to be obeyed. "You are home again."

He stated it as a fact. There was no emotion saying it, no satisfaction. It was like someone was commenting the night was dark, or the grass was green.

I was quiet as my mother's eyes flicked over to me. Her ghostly white essence encircled her in a way that kept itself from the dark cloud around Dominic. It shrank in on itself, a tight white globe in the pit of her chest next to the huge purplish-black bruise of the vampire's cloud. Looking closer, I could see my mother's cloud streaked in lines of black, little twirls of dark energy that were compressed tightly in her aura, like a ball of marble.

And, oddly enough, there was a dark tendril connecting my mother to Dominic. Something large and thick that pulsed in rhythm with the geas. The leash of the curse? I looked up and down myself, and saw nothing, though I still felt the pulse of the command.

I wondered if she saw all these things, like I did.

"I am," I finally answered.

Dominic nodded, once. The purple miasma bobbed up and down beside his head like thick smoke. The motion made me nauseated, and I flicked my ethereal sight back off. The vampire waited a long moment, the twin black orbs of his eyes shining with some inner thought. "I wonder," the pleasant voice rumbled, "why you've decided to come home now."

"I didn't decide," I said. "I came because I was asked."

"By my son?"

"No," I said, and the word sounded braver than I felt. "But that doesn't matter now. Your son asked me to stay, *wanted* me to stay until you got here. So here I am."

The old vampire cocked his head. Like he was listening to an inner voice. The seconds grew long, felt like minutes, began to feel like hours. I looked over at my mother and thought about the people I had talked with in the past few days. Especially Johnny. I wanted to find Jen more than anything, yet I had left her in order to protect her.

I wondered about how I had seen the essence that had surrounded the pair before me. The pure white tucked around my mother, the evil black-ness emanating from Dominic. The tiny cracks of black splintered across the white marble of her aura. I wonder if she had been around as long as he, how she had kept herself from that taint, or even if she ever could.

"My son," Dominic said, "*asked* you to stay?"

"Yes," I said. Feeling the tiny *come-come* beat of command deep within my chest, faint.

"Do you understand who you are?" Dominic asked. The power and the hate thickened his voice, but it still resonated, made me want to like him. "What it is you are on this earth for?"

I waited a moment, shook my head.

"Thousands of years ago, your forefathers were hunted down and bound in an ancient ritual," he said. I felt the words in my bones. "This ritual binds your kind to us, to each of the vampire clans. Your mother is completely, utterly my servant. She is my protector at all times, she kills who I want to kill, she breathes only when I want her to breathe."

I looked over at my mom, who stared straight ahead while Dominic was speaking.

"And when you grew of age, you were intended to be the same servant for my son." He paused a moment. *"Kneel."*

In the blink of an eye, I had dropped to my knees. I had had no choice in the matter. My nerves had fired on their own, disconnected from my brain, controlling my legs like a puppet on a string. I could feel sharp points of gravel cut into my knees, but could not move my legs.

"I have had ten years to think of something that might convince you to do this," he said. He picked his words carefully, and as he went along, each word gathered a deeper and darker hate. "To convince you of your duty to my son. And I have had ten years in order to convince my son of his duty to his people. To me. But it has been a wasted ten years, in many ways."

"Dominic," my mother said. One word.

He looked over at her, then shook his head. I waited, unable to move.

"I cannot see a way to reconcile either my son or you to your duties." There was a slight pause, in which the corner of Dominic's mouth lifted in a tiny smile. "And I never reward those who fail to perform their roles, as I have set them."

The vampire focused on my eyes, and I imagined his dark oily cloud enveloping me, running over my skin. Dominic's smile grew wider, sinister as he glanced at my mother. "Kill him."

I heard the vampire speak the words, yet I still couldn't move. My heart beat faster with fear as I watched my mother draw her sword in a fluid motion, a single-edged samurai blade, and then take two quick steps toward me. Light steps, like raindrops pattering across water.

Her eyes blazed fiercely. I couldn't even raise my hands, or turn away. Her hands moved in a blur of motion. A slight tickling sensation pinched the skin over my heart, followed by a hot, growing burn in my chest.

A second later my body rocked back as the sword shot through me and the hilt thudded against my chest. Almost as an afterthought, seconds after it had happened, I raised my hands in defense and turned half away. Far, far too late to have avoided the blade that knifed through my heart.

Cold pulsed through my veins, accompanied by the numb tingling of dying nerves and failing muscles. I gasped once, twice, and stared at the sword hilt punched in my chest, hard and pointing straight out from my heart. Something beat irregularly there, a staggered loping of a muscle torn in two. I looked up at my mother, and her eyes stared carefully, coldly past me.

The only thing holding me up now was the blade on which I hung, her hands carefully placed over each other in a swordmaster's grip. One of my hands pawed weakly at hers, trying to grasp her hands, pry her fingers from the handle of the blade. My vision dimmed, and I was swallowed by a numbing weakness.

"Release the sword," Dominic said simply.

Her hands let go, and I tipped to the side, face slapping the ground. Gravel dug into my cheek, but I felt the tiny pebbles more as an abstract thought than true feeling.

"I do not think you are worth the effort, Fergus Grimm," Dominic said. He looked over at my mother. His mouth frowned. "There are always more of you that can be made. I had thought, raising you here with my son, that the two of you might form a stronger bond. Perhaps that was my mistake. Perhaps servants do not *require* bonds."

I coughed, and something thick and red burbled from my throat, warm and salty on the back of my tongue. I had failed Jen. I had been so close, and now I had failed everyone. Anger cut through the pain, and I felt my leg kick a little. I coughed some more, blood bubbling out of my mouth to the ground, and used my anger, one last time. I focused on my hand, placed my palm on the ground, and pushed as hard as I could until I was kneeling again.

From there a felt my heart lope one hard time, then stop. Pain shot through my chest. I gritted my teeth and screamed inside at my heart to beat again. I poured more and more anger into my arms, forcing my hands to grab the sword hilt and try to pull the blade out.

"Ah, spirit," Dominic said. Glee edged around his voice like he was watching an entertaining show. "I can always admire spirit."

Spirit, hell. All I wanted to do was pull out the sword and take a wild swing at the vampire. Go down in a blaze of glory. *It's the way I'm made.* I grinned, feeling my lips slide over my teeth, hot with blood and saliva.

Dominic's eyes widened, ever so slightly. His lips curled, in a minute motion, into a tiny smile. A genuine smile. My mother's eyes blazed beside the vampire. Inside my chest, my heart beat once more, then again.

I no longer felt the giant hand press over me. The closer I got to death, the further the vampire's spell seemed to affect me. I forced one leg up, caught myself with one arm on the ground, and then stood. Both of my legs trembled, barely holding me up.

I grabbed the sword hilt with both hands, hard.

"Your son …" My voice came out thick from my throat. "… right now plans to take your life."

I pulled the sword hilt, and the blade slid free. Blood spurted from the wound. A thundering crack of pain shot through my body. My heart sputtered. I staggered a step, swinging hard and fast at Dominic's head. Who never once moved.

There was a metallic clang. I blinked. My mother's arm was raised against the sword, catching the blade on her armored forearm. I coughed another bubble of saliva and blood, let it drop out of my mouth to plop to the ground. Her eyes looked past me, out into the night sky. My arm wavered, and in a quick motion, she disarmed me of her blade.

I dropped to my knees and swayed before tipping forward onto my hands. My arms shook from trying to hold me up. Dark liquid leaked from my mouth and pooled on the ground beneath me. The agony in my chest was so great I couldn't comprehend it, the pain something I was aware of but lacked the capabilities to feel.

My mother's feet stepped back again. Into her guard position. My heart moved in my chest like it was trying to find a way to turn itself over, but lacked the spark. I fell to my side. Rolled over to my back. Stared out into the inky blackness of true night.

Dominic's face appeared over me as leaned forward and held out a finger. A hard, curved fingernail rested at its tip. He smiled. "Now," he said, "you will see the full power of what controls you. Of what controls your mother."

Blood soaked my shirt. I lay in a red puddle that grew ever larger around me. My inside was empty and grew cold.

"I command your body to live," Dominic whispered, staring into my eyes.

The power of those words shot through me. The pain was incredible, indescribable. It overwhelmed everything I had felt just moments ago. Pulses of lightning traced through me, as nerves fired and commanded organs to work, commanded muscles to pump, commanded skin to close. Commanded more blood to be made, to replace what was pouring out of me. My heart was a drunken drummer pounding wildly out of beat. I screamed a voiceless scream. The pain was incredible, but deep inside I prayed this was a chance for me to live.

But the damage was too much. Far, far too much.

"I always wondered what would happen, if I said those words in a moment such as this. What the geas that controls your family would do. I was always tempted to try this on your mother, but she is ... valuable." Dominic placed his mouth against my ear, in a motion faintly resembling Raphael just a few short days ago in the jail cell. I could barely hear him past the thundering in my head. His breath, oddly enough, was minty. "I know about my son. Every vampire lord's son tries to kill his father. It is our nature, once we come into our power, to own. To overthrow. To dominate."

I smiled and lifted my head one last time. I no longer could make out Dominic or my mother. "That might be true," I said, not really sure if I was saying it or thinking it, "but your son is going to win."

CHAPTER SIXTEEN

Death is a lot like a dream, I thought. It is also a lot of blackness. I lay under an inky blanket of darkness. I felt more than saw other shapes moving around in the darkness with me. All of us under the same burden. All of us meandering in the same direction. Somewhere, the rushing of water echoed upon itself in the dark.

Only the darkness kept me safe. I knew if the other creatures could see me, if they touched me I would know exactly how they had lived, how they had died, and how they wanted to regain their life by taking whatever I had left of mine.

I drifted, and it felt a lot like swimming in a thick black soup. After a while, tiny globes of light glimmered at the edges of my vision. Tiny pulses on the horizon of my little death-world. Swimming brought me no closer to them, but after a time one or two lights got larger, faster, like they were coming at me. Like an oncoming car in the night. Then they were screaming past me. And as they passed, I recognized them.

Danny, mouth cracked open in a scream. Bone jutting from his head. Joe from the army, bottom jaw gone, tongue flopping from the back of his throat. Suzy-Q floated by, another Ranger, scrunching up the side of her face like she was eyeing down a scope. Her chest cavity blown wide open. One by one all these faces passed me. I swam and ducked and dodged them all. Mrs. Cooper, the back of her head missing.

My stomach heaved. I was watching the final faces of those who had died, because of me. Because I had been near them. Because someone had wanted something from me.

A last light headed towards me. It grew stronger as it approached, like a locomotive in a tunnel. As it approached I could see blond hair, blond hair that I remembered very well. And maybe there was a scent of honey-suckle in the darkness. The inky black soup had hardened around me. My limbs were stuck with this last face fast approaching.

The light grew larger and larger. I tried to kick, to turn my head away, but the black soup imprisoned me. A voice whispered that I was too late, too late. The light now loomed over me and illuminated the blackness of my prison. I screamed, and the inky blackness fled the night, found its way into my mouth, clogged my throat, held my last breath inside me.

I could not breathe, I could not turn away, and I did not want to look at the light in front of me … did not want to see this face. I did not want to see this face …

The smile of a middle school student.

The scent of honeysuckle.

The feel of her lying back against me on a couch. Memories, fleeting, flying by.

I screamed and kicked hard against the blackness.

I jerked out of the dream so hard I almost fell out of bed. Daylight glowed through the curtains. I was in my room at Parker's. A hand reached out to grab me. To steady me on the bed. I could feel the hand, hard against my chest, a chest covered in sweat. Night sweats. Nightmare sweats. The sweats of the living.

I was alive.

I took a breath and another. Tried to settle my wildly thumping heart. I had really died last night, and in death I had drifted among the other dead in an inky limbo, all of us crowded together into a funereal world and waiting for the boatman to take us across the river, to whatever lay on the other side. I had felt the dead around me in the beginning, and I had seen those who had died around me, and in that dreamworld, I had maybe seen something I didn't believe.

My mother sat like a statue next to me.

I jerked again and slid a little to the other side of the bed.

"Son," she said. Simply. Her voice a whisper of softness carrying a sharp edge of death. She perched on a folding chair but looked tired. She still wore what she had worn last night, and in the bright light of morning, it looked more evil, less hidden by the dark. An assassin's garb.

I twisted and ran my hands all over me. *Looked all over me.* My chest, my jaw, my ribs, my heart. All healed. A tiny white line rested on my chest. I felt incredible. I wondered if my mother had been the one to heal me. She simply nodded.

"That one was troublesome." She looked at the twisted line over my heart.

"Why?" I asked. I had thrown a last roll of the dice at the end and had hinted that Raphael was going to beat his father. But I hadn't honestly believed that would work. Dominic had to know he was playing into Raphael's plan by keeping me alive. "Why?"

She took a moment and gazed out the window. Her profile was all edges. I could see her jaw move a little, like she was about to say something, and then changed her mind. After a bit, she said, "You have become useful to Dominic, briefly."

So once that usefulness ended, so would I. Again. My mother turned back to me. "There is something he wants you to do."

"Let me guess," I said. "You helped convince him of that."

"It did not take much," she said. "His son worries him greatly."

I remembered Raphael in the cell, wildly out of control. And I remembered Raphael calm and collected, outside the town. "He would worry me too."

There was a long moment. "I do not like the feel of this town," she said.

I understood what she meant.In the bright sunlight of day, in my room at Parker's, freshly healed, it was hard to feel the evil in the town. But later, as dusk fell, warring evils waited in the shadows of Grafton for their moment to strike.

"I asked Dominic," she said, "if his father was as confident in his powers, when Dominic killed him. If the possibility existed, where Raphael might kill Dominic. And then I asked, why waste a commodity?"

As we talked her body revealed, in certain motions, how uncomfortable my mother was around me. That she didn't know what to *do*. Her hand would pick up, move over to me, then quickly return to its place in her lap. She would take a quick breath, like she wanted to say something, then let it all out in a silent exhale. Her eyes never remained on me for long. I recognized many of those things in me, the inability to be close, the unknowing of *how*.

And I was just as uncomfortable. She was my mother, but I didn't know her. Was she a good person? Could she be? I had run from a lot of things in life, and a lot of it shamed me. Once I may have been a fighter, but I had never been a killer. How did I feel about myself, if I was born from someone whose existence was protecting something that evil? Who killed everyone on the word of that evil?

Raindrops pattering across water, and a large, gleaming blade ...

"So he's not worried about me?" I asked. "About Raphael?"

My mother shook her head. "Not with me there. And Dominic is still in his full power. A Vampire Lord. It will be centuries before Raphael can equal him."

I remembered Raphael in the cell, how powerful he had felt to me, and thought centuries might be an overestimate. But all that mattered was that I was alive, and given another day. And I knew where Jen was. Today I would find her, free her, and leave this town with moments to spare. But I wasn't surprised. In my last few years running with the Key, I had lived on last-second escapes and miracle vanishings, and Grafton would be the same.

"What kind of creatures are we?" I asked her. "How can we do what we can do? There are no stories of us in books, there are no fables. I don't understand."

She looked at me, really looked at me. Her eyes were a piercing blue. Like Jen's. She gathered herself and opened mouth. But no words came out.

Her jaw clenched. Her hand reached out and grabbed the bedsheet, twisting it in a tight grip. She opened and closed her mouth like a fish, trying to force a word out. A vein surfaced on her temple, and beat in time with her heart. But I could hear nothing.

The geas could do more than just command movement, then. Where Raphael used it as brute force, in the hands of a master like Dominic, it could control thoughts, possible actions, things you may or may not say.

That scared me. If someone could program a person in such a manner ... I wondered what my mother could have left in her, what was actually her.

"Try writing it down," I said. There had to be some way around the curse. I sat up and reached over to the nightstand. Pulled out an old pad of paper and a pencil.

My mother grabbed the pad and pencil, set the pad on her knee, and put the pencil to paper.

And stopped.

Then wrote out *The quick brown fox jumped over—*

Then stopped again, on the next word, in midstroke. As if she had tried to trick the geas and had tried to change the words in midsentence. The pencil dug into the paper until the lead broke. With a scream, my mother got up and threw the pad of paper. It fluttered through the air and landed softly against the door. She took a deep breath, looked at the pad, and then grabbed the chair she was sitting on.

And threw it through a wall.

There was a loud crunching sound. The chair hung there, vibrating slightly, the legs having punched through the drywall. My mother stood there for a long time, chest heaving, fists clenched. Then she took a long breath, let it out with a whisper. "This is too hard."

I didn't know if I was supposed to hear that. She turned back to me, looked around, and finally sat at the edge of my bed. One hand resting across my legs.

Her eyes sought mine. "There is a book that tells about us. What you'll learn about us is there."

So there was a book. My gaze drifted to her hand. It was covered in tiny scissor-like scars. A crooked white line curved around her neck. In all my time, the white scar across my heart was the only thing that hadn't healed fully. Anything I had broken, or cut, had healed without a scratch once I had access to ethereal energy. I wondered how many times she had been cut up, how many times she had had to heal herself, how *old* my mother had to be to have all those healed wounds.

Only fighters had scars like those.

"How do you survive?" I asked. "How do you not become them?"

"You find a little part of yourself," she said. "You tuck it away, where nothing can get to it. You hope the smaller part is greater than the evil."

There was a little silence then. I looked back at the poster. Luke, a small part of good, under an empire of evil. My mother reached out and straightened a little of my hair. I could feel her fingers shake, just a little, and knew that my hair was no straighter than before.

"So what am I part of now?" I asked. "What does Dominic want me to do?"

"Dominic wants you to get his son, tonight," my mother said. "Bring him to the schoolyard. At the baseball field. Alone. Tell Raphael whatever you want, as long as he comes there. Dominic and I will take care of him then."

"Why not go to their house?" I asked. "Their mansion?"

"It's Raphael's center of power now," she said. "Dominic will not risk himself where he shouldn't."

"If I get Raphael there, what will happen to me then?" I said. "Will Dominic let me live?"

My mother remained silent a long time. Her lips pressed tightly together. By her omission, she was telling me something she had been told not to tell me.

"I see," I said.

She nodded, and I could see her jaw muscles relax. Like she had been fighting them. Here was someone who could be my ally. Here was someone who might help me.

"Mother," I said, "I'm here to find someone, someone that called for me. Someone I—"

"Don't." She held out her hand, palm first. The irises in her eyes shimmered as they looked everywhere but at me. "Anything you tell me …"

Dominic would force her to tell him anything we talked about. If I had people here I wanted to protect, the worst thing I could do was reveal that to her. Whatever I was doing here, she would want to protect me. If she could. "I understand."

She nodded. "Be at the field tonight, at midnight. With Raphael. We will be waiting." She stood quickly, an elegant, precise motion. The blue-black of her armor glistened in the sunlight, and I wondered how I could have thought it evil.

"Remember," she said. "If you try anything, it will be me that kills you."

"I remember," I said.

She leaned forward, and one of her hands reached up to the side of my head, cradling it. Her lips pressed softly against my ear as she whispered, *"Be prepared."*

Her steps were light as they carried her to the door. Quiet and precise, she reached out, grabbed the doorknob, and swung it open.

Parker stood there, to the side, ugly face twisted up and pressed up against the door. He straightened as the door opened, looked to the side. One hand trembled, reached up, and held his face as if protecting it. Or hiding.

My mother walked past him. As if he didn't exist for her. I sensed then more than at any time before the capability of great violence she had, and the utter lack of remorse for her actions. I wondered if she could have healed him as she had me. Or if she even thought to.

I got up and got dressed. It was not yet noon, and I had a lot of work to do. Dominic would kill me tonight, for real, after I brought him his son. I had twelve hours to do either one of two things, find Jen and get out of town, or find Raphael, bring him to the football field, and survive the night. I didn't care to guess the odds on either of them.

Someone had brought some of my clothes from my car. Maybe my mother. I found a new T-shirt and pants and tugged them on. Then I went downstairs. Parker was sitting at the kitchen table, a cup of coffee held loosely in one hand. There was a smell of dark Colombian grounds in the air, and a bottle of whiskey was on the table beside the cup, less full than it had been. His dark skin was pale, and he stared at the wall beside me and shook some. His free hand kept touching his face.

He looked up after a moment. "I didn't want to spy on you. I didn't."

I nodded.

"It's just that, I did them all good. All good." Parker pointed to his face and stuttered a little, and tears ran out of his eyes. "I just wanted to understand *why*."

I could understand. Parker's face was a mass of twisted scar tissue. One side of his mouth had trouble closing on its own. He had to press it down to force it shut. I imagined he would always have to work to keep from drooling. And I wondered about the first ghost I had ever seen, the kid swinging out on the front tree, Parker's son.

"I did good for her." Parker began to cry, and he buried his face in his arms. "I did good for her. It was you that left. It was you." He said that over and over and over.

I didn't know what to do, watching Parker cry into his hands. His shoulders shuddered, and the sobs were loud. I didn't know what I could say; I didn't know why she did what she did to Parker. I didn't know anything about his past or his son or why he got those scars.

They were just another consequence of me leaving, another effect I had caused without knowing, a branching list of effects from a singled cause. Maybe once I had thought that I wasn't responsible for things I didn't know about, but I was starting to think that wasn't the case. I mean, the people in Grafton weren't aware of what I had been doing. They didn't know I had been protecting the entire world, keeping a stone prison from a demon.

Could I hold what they didn't know against them, and in the same breath wonder why Parker blamed me for his life? Why Nick hated me? Why Johnny didn't trust me? When I was running, I was protecting the world. But while I was running, people I cared about had been hurt. Could I say Parker's pain wasn't my fault? That I had nothing to do with it?

I didn't think so.

Parker's crying bothered me. Not just the scars, but because of his son. In some way I was responsible, maybe just because I had been born. Part of me wanted to reach over and hold him, but that kind of thing was something I had never learned, and in the end, there's something about watching a grown man sob like a child that will make almost anyone uncomfortable. So I left.

I made it to my car before the nerves hit me. Maybe watching Parker break down had started it. Maybe it was just time for it to happen. At the door, my hand slipped on the handle a couple of times. Then the keys trembled in my hand with a tinkling sound that crackled up and down my spine. It took a couple of times to fit the key to the ignition. The engine coughed a couple of times before turning over. I sat there looking at both hands on the wheel, shaking violently.

I had really died last night.

I knew I had, knew that I had taken damage far beyond what a normal person could take and live, knew it beyond a doubt. Just a few days ago I was some guy on the run, a guy who could tap the energy of ghosts to maybe heal a broken bone or two, but now I was someone who could die and then be brought back from the dead.

What was I?

I sat in the car and forced myself to take deep, even breaths. Every exhale shuddered on the way out. I had been in a number of scary situations, times when normal people might run, might scream, might beg for mercy, and each time I had come out alive. But what had happened last night, what I could be made to do, what Dominic had done to me, what Dominic had done with my mother …

I swallowed, hard.

It was more than I wanted to know. And I didn't know how to unknow it. I had one more day of full sunlight before I met with Dominic again, and my chances of surviving that meeting were low. Especially with no ghosts around.

Then I looked at my chest, imagining the white scar lying behind the Iron Maiden T-shirt. If my mother was like me—then *how* did she heal me? Did she need ghosts? Did I? Was there some way to store my power?

I knew too little. What drove me now was I believed I had found where Jen was being kept, and that daylight was burning. The fact that I had died, or that I was starving, and that I lacked knowledge I needed, all that could wait.

The Camaro spun out as I backed out of the driveway. I drove quickly through Grafton, seeing little to no movement from anyone. Then south out of Grafton. Then east on the side road to the factory. The sky was blue and the trees rushed by in flashes of green and gold. Up and down a few hills until I got close.

There I stopped, letting the car idle. A guard shack sat with a crossbar across the road, manned by a couple of guys sitting in a booth. The two had stopped talking and were looking at me with some interest. Behind the booth the plant rose in the distance, maybe a half mile, beige square blocks protruding from the ground with little figures across the lawn, some of them moving.

A lot of activity for a closed plant.

I waved a salute to the guards and threw the car back into reverse.

Headed back down the road to the gas station at the corner. It was closed and boarded up, so I pulled into the back lot and drove the car a little into the woods.

There I got out and popped the trunk. Grabbed my shotgun and some extra shells. And on second thought grabbed a few more. I figured this to be a quick in and out, and if it got messy it would get messy quick.

I ran through the woods, keeping just enough brush between me and the open field to stay concealed. One long step in front of the other, one after the next in a quick patter, I felt like I was flying.

I slowed down when the beige blocks of the factory showed through the trees. Snuck up the last couple of hundred feet, breathing a little heavy. I crept up to the edge of the woods and hid behind a large oak tree, peeking out when I got my breath.

And stared.

Surrounding the factory was an old chain-link fence, flopping over in places. Between the fence and the factory, scarecrow-like forms stood on the ground. Hundreds of dead bodies, standing and staked with a chain to posts driven in the ground. They were spaced apart in a weird fashion so that someone would have to zigzag through them to get to the doors.

Wights. Hundreds of them. Some of them even on the factory roof. I realized now why the graveyard had been dug up, but the sheer number of dead bodies needed to do this added up to more than what was in the local cemetery.

Wights would be good protection against vampires. Undead human bodies bonded to animal spirits. They were slow but strong. They had no blood for a vampire to drink, and an undead wight would fight until it was torn into little pieces. A part of a wight's hand had kept crawling after me once until I kicked it into the barrel where I had burned the rest of the body.

They had no human thoughts to speak of, just animal instincts. They would guard, protect, and hunt. Eat. Not a bad safety net, if you were worried about vampires coming and stealing something.

Or a lone human wanting to rescue an old girlfriend.

I looked down at my shotgun, then back at the field of undead. Who knows how many guards were inside the factory, once I got past those? My jacket pockets were full of shells; they still felt too light. Even if I could get past the wights, I'd never be able to get back out with Jen. Not through those fields. And the front gate was guarded.

I would need help to get in there.

But the wights weren't there to keep me out. They were there to keep vampires out. So the drugs were being made in the factory. Greg wanted to destroy those drugs. And he had asked for my help.

And time was running out.

I ran back to the Camaro and sped to the church.

CHAPTER SEVENTEEN

The tan sedan wasn't parked at the church, but I tried the church door anyway. It was locked shut, which was a surprise, since it was daylight, but I knocked anyway. To my surprise, Father Benjamin opened it.

"Fergus Grimm." Up close the priest appeared harried, worn. Lines that may have once been made with laughter now drew dark furrows in his cheeks. His voice was soft but carried well in the small church, perfectly heard above the silence in the room. "What brings you here this day?"

"I'm looking for Greg," I said. "Is he here?"

Father Benjamin shook his head. "He's not here. He probably won't be here for a bit. Is there anything I can help you with?"

I thought about the wards in the diner, the golden glow the priest's handprint had left on my shoulder. "I need a little help."

"Well, this is the place," Father Benjamin said.

I looked past him, at the church. It was empty behind him. "May I?"

The priest raised one eyebrow. "No need to ask, Fergus. Either you can, or you can't."

Ah, *the test*. Demons, vampires, and the like can't cross the doors of the church. Not willingly, and definitely not without an invitation. But why would he have to lock the door? I looked at him and took one step into the church.

Father Benjamin placed two fingers in the holy font, and I waited as he crossed me, murmuring something under his breath. I couldn't make out what. At the end, he pressed two fingers into the middle of my forehead. His fingers were surprisingly hard, like oak. The water droplets were cool, wet, and felt normal to me. But I had seen what the stuff could do to vampires, to demons, and to others of the underworld. I wondered if this was another part of the test, and if so I wondered more about the kind of creature who could actually invite itself into a church that holy water would affect.

Benjamin nodded. "Coffee?"

I was running on fumes, and still starving. But coffee would tide me over until I could get to the diner. Which would be one of the last places I could check for someone who might help me. "I'm in a hurry."

"It's already made," the priest said. He led me deeper inside the church. It was nice but sparse. Old oak pews lined their way toward the front of the church where an altar sat, covered with a white cloth. A figure of Christ resting on the cross above it. Two tiny alcoves sat to the sides of the altar, and the alcove on the right held the statue of the Virgin Mary. Confessionals sat in the back; to the right side of the pews, old wooden boxes. Stained glass windows ran down the walls, colored with biblical portraits.

The wooden benches were old, dark, a little scratched but still polished with a gleam. Bibles stuck out of the backs of the benches, sprinkled with a few songbooks here and there. A silence muted the church, a silence of emptiness, of a place that had not been used in a while but never abandoned. A few doors sat in the walls, two in the back of the room, two in the front.

I followed Father Benjamin through one of the doors in the front and entered a kitchen with a square table and a couple of chairs, a white fridge, and a stove. An old white Mr. Coffee sat on the counter, the carafe stained a dark brown. It was half-full, and Father Benjamin poured a couple of cups. "Black?" he asked.

"It's easier," I said, accepting the cup. It was thin and hot with the coffee, warming my hand.

Father Benjamin opened up a cabinet, pulled out a box of pastries. I arched a brow at the priest.

"We all have weaknesses," he explained, and offered me the box.

I pulled out a pastry. My coffee was strong and bitter and maybe a little burnt. My stomach rumbled. I sipped the coffee again, hoping it was better the second time around. "The pastry certainly can't hurt the coffee."

"It's why I started eating them." The priest laid his back against the counter. "What can Greg help you with?"

I ate the pastry. This was all new to me. Asking for help. The Templars. All of it. I spoke the priest about what Greg had mentioned to me, and about his offer. And that I could help the soldier, if he was willing to help me in return.

"He would be excited to have a hand," Father Benjamin said. "I'll let him know when he gets back."

"Do you know when he'll be here?" I said. "I'm kind of running on a tight schedule."

He shook his head.

"I thought you guys worked together," I said, remembering the wards. "Aren't you a Templar too?"

The priest snorted. "Not at all, Fergus. I'm just a lookout."

"What's that mean?"

Father Benjamin waved toward Grafton. "The Catholic Church has been around a long time, has seen a lot of things. When a town like Grafton pops up, someone with some knowledge of the supernatural gets sent. We like to keep an eye on things."

"But you've been here—"

The priest nodded. "Since you were born. Dominic has been on our radar a long time. Grafton was of particular interest to us."

"So why not send more Templars?"

"Fergus." Father Benjamin leaned forward. He was weary, but his eyes were laser-sharp. "Who says we haven't?"

I had seen the town. I had seen the wights. Were some of those the dead bodies of Templars out there, standing guard over the drug they wanted to destroy?

"The fact is, we just don't have enough soldiers anymore," the priest said. "We can watch, and warn, but fighting these battles, the Templars just don't have enough left."

"Can't you hire people?" I said. "Won't mercenaries help?"

"We could. And have," Father Benjamin said. "But the best work we do is done by people who believe. Something in short supply, in today's world."

I could understand that. I was never a believer—even though I had faced demons, I had never seen their counterparts. Hard to believe in someone who never shows.

It was easy in today's world to believe in it a little less, with stories in the media about pastors sleeping with children, nativity scenes being taken down, and prayer taken out of school. All little things, like the spores of a black mold. It was nothing when there was a spot, here or there, but over the years, as the fungus grew, it would infect everyone who breathed it in.

What could drive recruitment back up? Extra Sunday School? Someone leaping a tall building in a single bound?

I didn't know. I was just a guy on the run from a demon. In a town full of vampires. Trying to rescue a girl.

"Father Benjamin," I said, "I could really use a hand. I need to get into that factory before nightfall tonight. And I saw the wards you drew in the diner. Could you put something like that on me? My car? Something to keep the wights away?"

"Those wards don't do quite what you think." Father Benjamin stopped, then peered at me from lowered eyebrows. "You saw those?"

"Yeah." I flipped to my ethereal vision, looked at the kitchen window. A symbol just like one of the many at the diner sat there. I walked over and traced it out with my finger. "Just like this one here."

"Huh," the priest said. "Something like that, only Templars can see. Our wards are powered through belief, taught through long sessions where what we believe has power and can be used for good of all."

"Huh." It was my turn to be stumped. None of that sounded like what I could do. "Are people born Templars?"

The priest smiled, and I could see where his frown lines once had been lines of laughter. "No, son, it doesn't work quite that way."

I looked at the clear windowpane again, a thin layer of glass against whatever was outside that wanted in. "I don't see how belief could be much protection against vampires. Or demons."

"You might be surprised," he said. "Belief can do powerful things. You know once Einstein believed in dark matter, long before people could even possibly develop anything that could possibly measure it."

"Odd you pick Einstein as your argument."

"Think belief only belongs in religion?" he asked. "The American hockey team, back in the eighties Olympics, believed they could defeat an overpowering Russian team. They called it The Miracle on Ice. Belief can inspire, can empower, through a group of people, or just one."

"What's that mean with your wards?"

"I believe they keep evil out," Father Benjamin said.

"That's it?"

"We all have different ways to go about it," he said. "But basically, for me, that's it."

"So you've got nothing to fight wights."

"If I had something, Fergus, I would be happy to provide it. But Greg is likely to provide better assistance than I."

I took the last bite of the pastry and a last swig of coffee. I was still hungry. "If he gets back, I'll be at the diner."

CHAPTER EIGHTEEN

M iss Tammie had a small crowd that afternoon. I remembered a time when the diner would be full from opening until close. The place still looked clean this morning. If the floors didn't shine, they were at least swept and mopped, and all the tabletops had been wiped down. As soon as I came in Miss Tammie did a quick double take, I guessed at my newly healed appearance, and then went to fixing some casserole on a plate.

I looked over the crowd. I didn't see Johnny. Nick, however, was in a booth by himself. He was busy eating and drinking coffee, doing his best to look out the window and not at me. I thanked Miss Tammie as she reached a plate of food to me, grabbed a cup of coffee, and walked over to sit in front of Nick.

"Nick," I said.

He didn't want to for a minute but finally set his jaw and turned to lock eyes with me. His blue irises were so dark they were almost black. We both waited long moments. He broke first. "What?"

I came out and said it. "I need help."

Nick snorted. Munched on a roll. "You've been in town a day or two and you come begging for a hand. What makes you think you got that right?"

"I know you're mad at me," I said. "But I didn't come here on my own. Jen called me. And she's missing. And I think I know where."

"And you need help getting her," Nick said. "That's rich."

"I'm pretty desperate," I said. "I'm on a time limit here."

"What, until you have to leave again?" Nick kept eating. "Tell me something. We get Jen, wherever she is, you just leaving town right then?"

I looked at him. We stayed like that for a long moment.

"Thought so," Nick said. "You can go fuck yourself."

"Nick, she's one of us," I said, and Nick rolled his eyes. "At least she's one of you. She needs a hand, even if you don't want to help me. I mean, she called *me*, Nick."

"And now her mother's dead," Nick said.

"Yeah. Her mother's dead." Twice over, becoming a leech, and then getting her head blown off by Cole. I gritted my jaw.

"And Sarah's stuck with Raphael," he pointed out.

"Jen called me to come help with Sarah," I protested.

Nick shook his head before shoveling more casserole into his mouth. He chewed wildly. "Well, you're doing a bang-up job so far."

"Yeah," I said. "Yeah." Nick had always liked Sarah. Maybe like I had always felt about Jen. But Sarah had never thought of him the same. And then I had left.

"Nick, dammit," I said. "I know where Jen is. We used to be friends. Are you really not going to help me?"

He swallowed, then sipped at his coffee. He was always wiry, thin, rangy, but he had grown up hard. It was a hardness that was close to being brittle.

"I'll help you." Nick pushed his breakfast plate away, wiped his mouth with a napkin, and tossed the napkin on the tray. "If you just tell me what happened to Danny."

I pleaded with him. "Nick."

He raised his eyebrows.

I bit my lip and looked up at the ceiling. Took a deep breath and let it out. I had just lived that memory. I felt like if I admitted it to anyone, I would live it over and over. Over the past few years the nightmares still remained. I still would dream that Danny was alive, until that last swing.

A coldness broke inside me, rushed over my skin, little bumps popping up all over my arms. I swallowed.

"Nick ..." If it would save Jen, I'd tell him. "That day was bad. And I loved Danny. You know Raphael had it out for him, because of how he was. And that day, they had him in the alley."

I took a deep breath. Seeing Raphael hauling away with that bat. Danny's wide-open eyes.

Miss Tammie slapped something on the grill then, and I jumped.

"I can't, Nick." I would never not hate myself for what happened to Danny, and I didn't know how to tell Nick that in a way he would listen. "I'm sorry."

"Well," he said, "the great Fergus Grimm, not able to do something. Hard to imagine, that."

"Come on, Nick, help me out," I said. I took a moment, then looked up at him. His eyes were a mixed intensity of anger and wetness, maybe tears. "We used to be friends."

"Sure, we used to," Nick said. "Wolverines, right? All for one, one for all. Then Danny's dead, you're gone, Sarah's gone, Jen's gone, and then there's just me and Johnny. Wonder which one of us is next?"

"Nick, that's not fair."

"Life isn't fair, Grimm." His eyes had darkened. "But at least some of us stayed around and tried to make it even."

He got up so fast he was almost out of control, coffee swishing over the lip of his cup and splashing over the table. He rushed over and gave Miss Tammie her something from his pocket, then fled out the door. Miss Tammie looked after him and shook her head softly.

Strike two for people who might be able to help me rescue Jen. I wasn't doing a great job with people in this town. But what did I expect? Nick to fall over himself wanting to help an old friend who had abandoned him, had abandoned everyone?

I turned around and finished my breakfast quietly. Every now and then I would take the fork and stir the potatoes and the sausage and the cheese together before taking a bite. The food here was heartwarming. A deep, content feeling spreading throughout my body, uplifting me.

I got up and talked to Miss Tammie, asked her to tell Greg if he came in where I was going. I had to describe him to her. After breakfast, I ran down the street, to the bar where I had first met Johnnie. He wasn't downstairs, and I asked the bartender where he stayed. He gave me the number of a room upstairs and I ran up and knocked, but no one answered. After a few moments I tried the door, but it was locked.

I pounded the door a few more times until the bartender called up the stairs for me to cut it out. I kicked the doorjamb once, and then gave up. I didn't know where Johnny and a vampire would be staying in the middle of the day, but daylight was wasting, and once night fell I would be on Dominic's schedule. I ran back out to my car and drove it back out to the factory, to see what I could do on my own.

Up close in daylight the wights were uglier. They moved the same. Daylight didn't affect wights any more than nighttime. They stood. Walked one way until their chain tightened. Stood some more. Walked the other way until their chain tightened. Every now and then the breeze changed and I caught a whiff of rotting flesh and had to keep from gagging.

I was in the same spot as before. I had done a circle around the perimeter. It all looked the same. There was a maintenance door on this side, if I could get past a dozen or so wights. And that was the problem. I couldn't drive straight in, and I couldn't get past all the undead guards. Even if I shot the lot of them, I was sure someone would stumble out of the factory and see me.

A number of cop cars drove up and down the factory road at random times. They drove up to the factory, circled the lot, and then headed back down the road. A circuit of sorts.

So I sat there and waited. Tried to talk myself into just doing it. But I knew it for a fool's errand. I would get caught at best, and dead at worst. I tried a couple more laps to see if I had missed an opening, and after each lap, the chances of me getting through lessened. There were just too many wights. As the sun fell I began to feel like Dominic's deal had the better chance of me surviving.

I kicked the tree. One of the wights closest swiveled its gaze up. Shambled over. Sniffed the air a couple of times.

I was going to have to face the truth. I wasn't getting into that factory. I wasn't rescuing Jen from there. If she was there, which I believed wholeheartedly. I sat there and stewed and talked myself into running for it and then immediately talked myself out of it and the whole time the sun sank toward the horizon behind me.

Dusk was coming on, and somehow I would have to survive the night to get to Jen. I got back in the Camaro and drove toward town, listening to the rumble of the engine, comforted by the sound. We had been together awhile, and the car had never failed me. With the windows down, breathing in the cool fall air, I could almost pretend I was going over to see Jen on a cool fall day. Maybe watch some football and eat some cinnamon toast.

Her house seemed empty now. Habit had me knocking on the door before I opened it. There was a chalk outline of Jen's mother by the couch. I wondered who would care enough to follow through on police procedures here in Grafton. Maybe Frank.

I stepped through to the stairs, trying to avoid the sickly sweet smell of blood mixed with the alcoholic smell of disinfectant. The light over the stairs remained lit, and I walked up to Jen's room slowly, each foot sinking a bit into the thick carpet over each step. The house still felt cold. The air conditioner was still set low, and I wondered if the bill would get paid. And who would pay it.

At the top of the stairs, I could smell the honeysuckle scent that always made me think of Jen. I opened her door, hoping to see her sleeping in bed, one arm tucked over her face, hair spread over her pillow. But the room was empty. I could still see the depression where I had sat in her bed, and I found myself sitting there again for a while.

This room was a portal to ten years ago, to a time when things were simpler, when there was just me and Jen and the rest of the group, and all we had to worry about was homework and what we were going to do that Saturday. I sat in the same spot on her bed and thought about the many times we had sat together here, her arm pressed against mine, talking about teenage stuff and laughing at stupid things. Each of us feeling something exciting and raw and scary inside is, both of us too young to understand how to commit to those feelings fully, maybe worried they were so strong they would consume us both and everything around us.

I blinked on my ethereal sight, maybe hoping to see some evidence of Jen. A reminder she was here, and alive, and real. But the only echoes here were my fading footsteps from before, entering from the window and walking out the door. Anything Jen had left had faded long past where I could see it. I peered closer at her dresser. Some smudges of fingerprints lay around the middle drawer. A lot of smudges, as if someone had opened and closed the drawer so many times it had left a long-lasting ethereal echo.

I opened the middle drawer and reach my hand deep inside the bureau. A manila envelope had been taped to the underside of the top drawer. It was thick and it crackled as I pulled the tape away and emptied the contents on the bed.

A few newspaper clippings slid out, some magazine articles, old photos. The first clipping caught my eye when it slid out. It was a news piece of the Ranger battalion I had been a part of in Iraq. A list of those attached was at the bottom of the piece. Gus McNulty was circled as if Jen could be closer just by tying a knot of ink around my name. I wonder how she had known that particular name was mine.

The next thing I found was an article describing a robbery at a donut shop. I recognized the shop because I had been there that day. The robber hadn't been a robber, but a certain demon showing up when I was getting a cup of coffee. There was a bad description of me in the paper as a drifter in an army jacket, and a little joke about the robber taking Halloween costumes to a serious level. Again, the picture was circled and a little smiley face put next to it. I smiled. Jen's handwriting had all the flour-ishes of a teenage girl writing a Valentine's Day card.

Somehow she had been tracking me, had known where I had been and where I was going. Did Jen have some kind of power that I hadn't known about? She had always represented a life I dreamed about when I was sleeping in the car off some back road somewhere. A normal life of green lawns, white picket fences, and an apple pie in the kitchen window.

I grabbed all the pictures and jammed them back into the envelope. When I did, a wallet-sized picture slipped to the floor. A rounded heart traced the backside of the picture in thick pink ink, the initials J and G nestled next to each other inside. Underneath, the heart-curved line snaked back, smaller and smaller until the line was just a whisper of ink.

I flipped the picture over. It was a photo of just Jen and me. There were hints in her girlish figure of the woman she would become. She leaned into me on the picture and smiled an impish smile, a smile that said something wicked this way comes. She had braided her hair back then, but that day part of the braid had come loose in the wind and had landed smack across my cheek—right when the shutters of the camera had snapped. I had been caught trying to blow her hair off, my eyes kind of crossed in the picture and my lips pursed to the side, and the resulting picture looked ridiculous.

Danny had taken that picture. Jen had loved it. I had hated it then; I would do anything to go back to that moment in time now. The two of them had laughed when they got the pictures back. I remember Danny's big smile and Jen leaning against my arm, still chuckling hours and hours later. I held the picture, and a deep breath escaped me and I wiped the corners of my eyes with the palm of my hand.

I wondered how I could have given that up. I knew the answer, but my mind still reflected on how I had felt with Jen. Could a feeling like that between two people continue even while they were apart, or would it disappear? Would it be more like a tool, which once set aside, would dull and rust with age?

All I had to do, I promised myself, was stay alive tonight. Just until the sun rises. If I made it to the morning, I'd go into that factory with or without help. Guns blazing.

Dusk turned to night outside. A tendril of consciousness uncurled itself, made me aware I had a job to do. To bring Raphael to Dominic. The longer I ignored it, the longer the request would become an unbreakable command.

I forced myself to get up. I walked down the hallway and opened the door to Sarah's room. There was no answer there either. I opened that door and entered a different portal, to a different place, to a different girl.

Sarah's room was cluttered, the bed unmade, clothes strewn over the place. It looked like someone had started to tidy it, putting piles of clothes in one corner of the room, though that was as far as they had gotten. Pictures and posters splayed over the walls, of boy bands and pop stars. A guitar sat in one corner, an older thing of faded wood. The closet door hung half-open, revealing more clothes stuffed into a space too small to hold them all.

More pictures sat over her dresser. There was one of our group, and one of her and Nick. That picture was older and must have been taken long after I had left. Nick's smile was worse than mine. His lips were thin and pressed tight together, his face sharp, edged. His eyes burned with an intensity I had not known in him before. In the picture, the two were close, but not touching, a best-friends kind of pose.

There were other pictures in frames around, Sarah with other men, older boys. A couple I remembered from school. Some were obviously later, maybe taken inside the past year, as Sarah posed in front of the movie theater with a young gentleman, pale, a dark jacket.

Next to the pictures was a stereo, and I reached out to push Play. Guitar chords echoed out of the speakers, a strumming soft rhythm of loneliness and the need to feel, a raspy voice that ached for someone, or anyone. I listened to the sadness and looked over the pictures, ending up on the one with Sarah and Nick.

Nick, I thought, *I might understand you, now*. It must have eaten him alive, seeing Sarah like this. Ten years ago he might have had a chance, but seeing Sarah in these pictures, I could imagine her checking the club out. Getting sucked into that life.

If I had had to watch Jen do the same the past ten years, I might feel much like Nick myself.

The geas grew and became slightly uncomfortable in my chest. I left the house. There was nothing there that led me to believe Jen had returned there, and little else left to learn. The sun had sunk below the horizon, and I could feel the air shift with the chill of the night.

There was a car parked behind mine, something dark and sleek with tinted windows so dark that I had begun to associate them with vampires. The car was off, and Johnny was leaning back against the hood of my Camaro, waiting. Arms crossed.

"Didn't want to disturb you," he said when I got near.

"How'd you find me?" I asked.

"Not hard in this town," he said. "Diner, Parker's, here. Where else are you going to go?"

"You got me." I grinned a bit, but it was a grin without any humor in it. "Look, I need some help."

Johnny held up a hand and shook his head. "I heard it from Nick. I can't, not tonight."

"Johnny," I argued. "This is Jen. It's one of us."

"Some things are bigger than us," Johnny said. His expression turned grave. "I think you probably understand that."

"Johnny—"

"Look," Johnny said, "I'm just here to warn you. Things are happening soon."

"What the fuck do I care about things?" I said.

"Look, Grimm, we were always friends," Johnny said. "I'm not Nick, but you don't have the right to come at me on a high horse here. You've been gone too long."

"Johnny." I let out a breath. "It's Jen. It's one of us."

"I know, man," Johnny said. "I know. And I wish I could help tonight. But I can't. I got something else to do. Something you need to stay away from."

"Whatever," I said.

"I'm serious." Johnny was a long way from the funny kid I had known, the kid with a joke, the kid who never took anything seriously. He was calm, quiet inside. Centered. "Tonight, stay away from the club. Stay away from Raphael."

"You're kidding," I said. I had to get through tonight alive, and there would be no way I could do that if I didn't obey Dominic. "Johnny, I can't do that. Not tonight."

Johnny frowned. "Grimm, whatever you've got going on, let it wait one night. I'm trying to help you out here."

"Johnny, I can't." I wondered what he and Gabrielle had going on. *Personal business,* she had told Raphael. "It's just not possible. Maybe it's something where I can help you, and you can help me."

Johnny looked back at the car, making a decision. Eventually he shook his head. "You got to know too much is riding on this, Grimm. I can't. Things are in motion that can't be stopped. And I promised I wouldn't tell you what."

"That's a shame, Johnny," I said. Did Gabrielle know about the geas? Was that why she left the table after Raphael had used it on me? That I could be forced to tell Raphael what I knew?

But if she knew about me, or my mother, she might know more. But I couldn't find that out right now. I looked right at Johnny. "I've got to be wherever Raphael is. It's life or death for me tonight, brother, or I'd listen to you."

His eyebrows dipped. "I hear you."

A moment passed between us. Johnny looked away for a bit. I looked toward Main Street, where everything would be begin tonight, for me.

Johnny rubbed his forehead with the palm of his hand, then looked back at me. "Remember when Gabrielle was asking you about you and Jen?"

"Yeah."

"I wanted you to know she didn't mean to make you feel bad."

"I get it," I said. Even if I didn't.

Johnny laughed. "Man, you don't get it. I know you were angry. You get this ruffled-feather look when you hear something you don't like. Like you want to punch something."

"I don't do that."

"You're doing it right now."

I looked at myself. Maybe my chest had swollen a bit. Maybe my jaw was a little tight. But I wouldn't say I was angry. At least, not really angry.

"I wanted to tell you," Johnny said. "Something happened to her, when she was young. She wasn't always Victor Dumont's heir. What happened to her, man, it was tragic."

His voice died off, and Johnny looked over my shoulder for a moment. Then he gathered himself, and shook whatever it was off. "And man, don't tell her I said this, but she really loves kids."

My look must have looked really disbelieving.

"I mean it," Johnny said. "She would love to have a family, man. It's something we talk about."

"You and Gabrielle?" It hit me. If Dominic could have a real son, and Gabrielle could figure that out, then she could as well. But then, all that talk about the family. "What about the clans? Her speech on the families?"

"She believes that wholeheartedly," Johnny said. "She believes in duty. But she also believes in family. She hates what the drug does to her kind … but there's a part of her that wants to be a mother. Raphael has her contradicting what she believes. It eats at her."

"Huh," I said. A vampire who was disgusted with what the drug did to her kind. A vampire who loved kids enough to think about having them with Johnny. And living proof in front of her in Raphael, born human and vampire. And he was the same person creating the drug she hated.

Johnny sighed a bit and lifted himself off the front of my car. He reached out, and we clasped hands as we had back in the day, each grabbing the other's forearm. His dark skin seemed too muted in the afternoon light, and his smile was a sad, quick flash of white. "Anyway, if you see us later tonight, I wanted you to understand that."

The chances were I was going to see them. "Let's get out of it in once piece, then."

Johnny crossed his fingers and rolled his eyes

CHAPTER NINETEEN

I dreaded the nights here, but they came on fast in Grafton. Gray clouds of dusk had rolled in quickly, heralding the darkening of the horizon and then what would be true night. I started to feel like the sun was only around for an hour or so out of the day, and the rest of the time it was either dusk or dark.

Johnny started up the car and drove away. I took a deep breath. The geas was stronger in me now, a choking knot at the bottom of my throat, and when my lungs expanded it felt like they pushed against that knot. There was one goal tonight, to get through it and watch the sun rise, and then back to the factory. I had no plan. No imaginative way out of what was going to happen tonight. No last-second miracle. I was going to do what I was asked to do and then react as fast as I could. The one thing I had going for me was, after the past few years, reacting to things was a well-honed skill.

The geas tapped again. It was time.

I headed over to the trunk of my car and pulled out my shotgun. There was no being too careful tonight. Raphael, Dominic, my mother, Johnny, Gabrielle, there was a lot going on from a lot of different angles. I loaded the gun with my silver buckshot, each cartridge having drops of holy water dribbled onto it. I then made sure my .38 Special was loaded too, spinning the cylinder and snapping the pistol shut. At the last second I put a grenade in the inside of my jacket pocket. Careful was now my new middle name.

I shut the trunk of my car and climbed into the driver's seat. Right between the seat and the door was a little place that I could lay the Benelli down and grab it if I needed it. An option that maybe was standard back in 1968.

I fired the car up. I felt a nice energy from the Camaro. My knee was bouncing up and down, and I worked the pedal a bit. Even small decisions, once made, empowered a person. Tonight something was going to happen. I would either live, and move on to finding Jen, or die for good. At least if I did I could let go of everything, of the Key, of running, of having abandoned my friends. And then I shook my head. I might run, but giving up was something else. That wasn't something I could do.

I felt the rumble in the engine reverberating inside me, tapping into a primal power deep inside my chest. Things were happening now. I would find something out tonight. I backed the car around, pointed the Camaro down the street and spun forward with a roar. In moments like this, I was free.

I swung into town, passing a few outlying houses. Lights were on in some windows. I could see a television here and there. Figures kind of stood outside, on porches and driveways, staring at me as I passed, thralls and vampires alike. Scarecrows in the night, lit by the moon where they were poking out of the shadows.

I parked the car in an alley across from the club, got out, and kept my pistol in my jacket. I probably wouldn't get in with the shotgun. I walked across the street, noticing the long line of thralls and vampires outside, and headed up to the bouncer at the front of the line.

The rhythmic bass was again pumping from inside the club. A powerful wave sifted off the people waiting in line, a mingling of lust and desire, of drugs and alcohol, of sex and sweat, cinnamon and cherry. I was ready for it this time and braced myself. It was a heady mix, and I breathed as little as I could of it. What I didn't breathe felt slick and heavy against my skin.

The bouncer studied me, a different one than the other night. Little crosses were tattooed down from the corner of one eye, which was odd for a thrall. Maybe it was a road-to-hell-paved-with-good-intentions kind of tattoo.

"Fergus Grimm," I explained. "Raphael needs to see me."

He raised his eyebrows farther, then turned around, jerking his thumb at me. "Hey, Jacob. This guy says Raph needs to see him." He mixed the tone so that it sounded like a statement and a question.

I sighed. Nothing came easy. Jacob glowered down from the top step, next to where the booth used to be in the movie theater. He had been talking to someone inside it. When he saw me he rolled his eyes and turned back to the booth.

I strode up the stairs, heading toward the door to the club. I made it up to the booth before the vampire stopped me.

"I see Miss High and Mighty ain't around tonight," Jacob said. He was grinning, like a cat, and started in motion with slow grace. A careful planting of each foot, a springiness to his step. "You sure you're safe to go in there without her?"

"I'm going in to see Raphael," I said.

"That's kind of up to me." Jacob stopped inches away. There was tension inside him, something my body responded to. My heart beat faster, and the edges of my nerves tingled. Like a fight was coming.

"Jacob," I said. I made eye contact with him and held it. My hands were in my jacket pockets, my left hand on the gun. "Do you really think you're going to stop me?"

Jacob broke our gaze and then noticed that I wasn't beat up anymore. Which introduced some doubt into the equation, and bullies never operat well off doubt. He had to wonder about me, and then he had to wonder if he could take me, and that was far too much thought for a guy like him.

"We can have it out now," I told him, my tone perfectly neutral. "But I'm going to give you one warning. I'm going to be the guy that walks away from this fight."

Whether it was how I looked, my tone, or something else, Jacob backed down first. "If you're coming in, you'll follow me."

He reached down and swung the door open, cinnamon and cherry blowing out over the pavement, punctuated by the pounding bass. It was heady, and as prepared for it as I was, I still paused as Jacob went in. The vampire looked back, rolling his eyes. "You coming?"

I pulled back, making a face and mimicking the words "You coming" a couple of times with my mouth quietly when Jacob turned away. Childish? Could be. Did it make me feel better? It sure as hell did.

Jacob drifted through the crowd, some vamps taking notice of him, other vamps too far gone to notice. I looked around to see if Johnny was here, or Gabrielle, and I didn't see either. I wondered what they were setting up, and if it was something that would help or hurt my chances of making it to sunrise.

Jacob led me down the other hallway, up to the other side of the theater from where I had found Andy. In front of the double doors to the movie screen stood a large, thick man. Well, vampire. He was blocky with muscle, a tight T-shirt on and half a foot taller than me. Darian. The last of the stooges. He had the same slight sneer as his friend and opened the door so I could follow Jacob into the theater.

This one had most of the chairs removed at the bottom of the theater, close to the screen. The screen had some black-and-white movie playing, but no sound. A large card table sat on the flat area under the screen, with twelve or so vampires ringing the table, playing cards. The rest of the chairs formed a balcony of sorts over the game, though most of those chairs were empty.

The table was a large red velvet thing, surrounded by nice leather chairs. A few thralls, lightly dressed, stood behind the players. A busty woman in a tight leather bodice leaned precariously over the table, gathering the chips from the last hand, and a thrall outfitted in a black-and-white suit was shuffling a deck.

"Hey." Jacob stopped me and jerked a thumb. "Up there."

I looked up into the chairs, saw Raphael sitting in one, half watching the game, half watching the screen. Sarah sat in a row behind him, quiet, and her gaze darted away when she saw me. He held one of his drinks in his hand.

I walked up. "Thought you didn't drink that stuff."

Raphael snorted. "Tonight's going to be a little different, Grimm." His voice was slow, murky. The voice of a man who had drunk too much while contemplating dark things. "Have a seat."

The geas twitched. "I'm here to take you to your father," I said, and at Raphael's look: "Like you *asked*."

"Have a seat, Grimm," Raphael said again. "Don't make me order it."

Stay alive, I thought. And sat. Raphael took a sip of his glass, and a couple of deeper drinks, until it was empty. And when it was empty, a waitress brought up another, and he started on that.

I flipped on my ethereal sight and got a surprise. Where Dominic had a tightly growing purple miasma as the core of his essence, Raphael's essence was more a deep red, tinged with violet, but it was occluded, like a blood moon during a lunar eclipse. It looked like a black disc, blacker than night, had slid across Raphael and blotted out anything that was him. His entire body was black in my vision, black but swimming with tiny bursts of white, which looked like it came from his drink. And tendrils reached out from Raphael to all the vampires below him, dark tendrils invisible to all but me. I had never seen that before. I didn't know what that meant, and all of a sudden I became terrified of tonight.

Whatever Dominic was planning for his son, it wasn't what was going to happen.

Behind Raphael I could see a tiny glow, a whitish spark burning his dark silhouette. Sarah. She was still human, then, or as human as she could be.

I blinked back to my regular sight. Raphael looked at me strangely. He appeared so normal now, but beneath the skin, something supernatural and deadly lurked. A power fed by whatever he was drinking. He should be glowing, there was so much power concentrated inside him.

Raphael turned to the game below. Piles of chips moved in and out of the center. Players were knocked out, bought back in, and threw larger piles in the next time around. A vampire had just thrown his cards down after a seven of clubs was flipped up on the river.

"Chance is a funny thing, isn't it?" Raphael said, after a bit.

"What do you mean?"

"All that money," he said. "Lost on the flip of a card. You'll never see me gamble like that. On some flip of a card, or a coin. On a chance."

"What was all that bullshit the last time I was here?" I asked. "About baseball, and setting them up and knocking them down? Any game is a gamble."

"Nah." Raphael took another drink. "You play a sport, you know something about yourself. About your opponent. You work on things. And in the end, you know what your chances are when you come into the batter's box against me."

"No batter bats a thousand," I said. "And no pitchers strikes everyone out."

"It's still not a gamble," Raphael argued. His eyes had taken on a faraway look. "Because you can do something to affect it. A card is just a card, and when you flip it up it is what it is. The game is over, and you've won or lost."

Another drink. "You think I have a soul?"

That was a large tangent. "What?"

"I know what they say about me," Raphael said. "I'm part human and part vampire. Humans have souls, don't they? Shouldn't I have one?"

I didn't know if they had souls, but some of them definitely had spirits. "I don't know."

"I wonder sometimes," Raphael said. He tossed back his drink. Once more it was filled in front of me. I imagined the demon inside him swelling with power.

"Can we go now?" The conversation was going to an uncomfortable place. I didn't know how to be with Raphael like this.

Even though Raphael was quiet and introspective, he was holding a whole lot of crazy behind his gaze. Maybe not holding so much as constraining. He was going to face his father tonight, along with my mother, and he knew what the chances of walking away from that alive were going to be.

Unless he had stacked something against it. Unless it wasn't a flip of a card for him, but a game. One where he knew his opponent and knew his strengths and weaknesses, and even though the opponent was on a long hitting streak, Raphael could take the mound with some confidence.

"Why are you so eager to get there?" Raphael asked me. "You know my father will kill you."

"I like to rip the Band-Aid off," I said.

He finished his drink, and sat there for a few moments, over which his face got more focused, his eyes narrowed, his jaw flexed.

"Well, then, let's rip it." Raphael stood up, and motioned for me to go. Sarah wobbled as she got up. She was extremely pale, and I looked down at Raphael's hand.

His glass was empty, but his smile was not. "As I've mentioned, I like my drink to be pure."

Sarah. She had been his drink for tonight. I clenched my jaw hard enough that my teeth hurt. *Stay alive.* I caught her eye and did not like myself when she turned away. *Stay alive.*

Darian followed us out of the theater and into the central part of the club. Raphael's bodyguard, apparently. He hadn't said much when we were kids, and steroids hadn't gotten his jaw muscles working any more now. The music pumped out a rhythm, but it seemed as if the club lacked energy now. Vampires lay back, lax. Vapid. Thralls did most of the work on the dance floor or hunched over a vampire. Tall glasses, some still full of the dark red liquid, scattered across the tables. Most were tipped over, the liquid pooling over bare stomachs, smeared and dripping across all bare skin, flailing arms, grasping hands. There was a different feel to the room.

I blinked on my sight and shaded my eyes from Raphael. My eyes followed the tethers, from him to all the vampires. Each strand pumped to an invisible heartbeat as if they were long arteries running from each vampire to Raphael, and I felt more than heard a sucking sound on reach rhythmic pump. I shook my head. I didn't think my mother or Dominic was really ready for Raphael. I didn't know what the odds were on a son taking on his father in vampire terms, but Raphael had definitely stacked the deck.

Raphael looked back at me as we reached the doors, one corner of his mouth turned up, and winked.

Outside, there was still a small line to get in, mostly thralls and half vampires. They looked used, old, wasted. Thin. They would not get into the club, and still, they waited. Darian ran around the side of the club with car keys in his hand. I took a deep breath. It was nice to get some fresh air, away from the choking cherry cinnamon of the club.

We waited at the sidewalk, and I could feel the damp morning chill surround me. The night was old, maybe somewhere midnight and two in the morning. Closer to sunrise than sunset. I wondered again where Gabrielle and Johnny were and wished I knew what they were up to. Hell —I looked over at Raphael—it would be nice to know what *anyone* was up to.

"Where does my father want you to bring me?" Raphael asked.

"High school ballpark," I said.

"The old stomping grounds." Raphael smiled, perhaps in memory. He stood there, maybe in his own world, weaving just a little bit to and fro. I wanted to look at him again with my ethereal sight but was afraid of what I might see.

"You know what happens between father and son, Grimm," Raphael asked, "if you're a vampire?"

"Whatever it is," I said, "remember our deal."

"Sure, Grimm." Raphael smiled, a little lift of his lips. "You held up your part. You and I are good." He definitely seemed somewhere else. Playing something out inside his head, like he was thinking and moving a little faster than everyone else and had to slow down to answer me.

"Just so we're clear, what do you mean, good?"

"I mean after you deliver me, you can go," Raphael said. His eyebrows rose. "Provided you survive, that is."

"When are you giving me Jen?"

Raphael's eyes opened wide, a surprised smile on his face. "I'm not giving you anything. Except your life."

I stepped up right in front of him. "You said Jen would go free."

"I said I'd kill her if you ran." He shook his head. "I told you that you could be free."

"That's bullshit," I said.

"That's the deal." Raphael seemed bigger now, standing beside me. We normally stood the same height, but I felt as if I had to look up at him now. "If you think differently, then we're going to have issues."

Just then there was a thumping of a tire running over a curb, and a few shouts of the thralls as they jumped away from the Cadillac, taking the corner sharply. Darian stopped the car suddenly by slamming the brakes, and the car rocked a bit. He got out quickly for a man of his size and opened the back door for Raphael. I started to walk over to my car in the alley, feeling a tingle in my spine like someone was watching me.

One of the back windows of the Cadillac rolled down.

"Where you going?" Raphael asked.

"I was going to follow," I said. "In my car."

"Nah." Raphael grinned again. "You'll be with us."

I looked at him, watching him stare at me with a blank face. Like we were all acting a play, and Raphael was the directory. Nothing left to chance. He wasn't going to let me out of his sight. I looked wistfully at my Camaro and thought of the shotgun nestled inside it. The armory in the trunk. *Damn.* I hadn't been careful enough, it seemed. I looked back at Raphael. He had slid back against the far door and motioned to the seat next to him with an exaggerated gesture.

I took a deep breath, walked back over to the car, opened the door, and got in. Darian got back behind the wheel, and Jacob slid into the front passenger seat

"Buckling up?" Raphael asked, still with the far-out gaze and the grin.

I wasn't sure if he was drunk with power, drunk with Sarah's blood, or just drunk. I looked straight ahead. I was sitting next to the man who had killed Danny, and I hated myself for it. I was doing this instead of searching for Jen, and I hated myself for that. And I was sitting in the backseat of a Cadillac while Sarah had been drained of her blood for some drink for Raphael, and I hated myself more and more. I closed my eyes at the memory of Sarah's final stare, her eyes shimmering and sad.

The Cadillac was plush, all tight black leather and gold fixtures. The backseat was more comfortable than most beds I'd slept in. Raphael sprawled on his side, leaning against his door a bit, relaxed. He looked almost asleep.

Some classical music was playing in the car, faint strings of notes threading through the low hum of the Cadillac. It was hard to hear after the pounding music of the club. Violins sang softly together, their slow bows sliding back and forth through a long measure, a dying, mournful wail. Raphael's hand drifted in the air to the sound.

Main Street grew worse as we rode by, the closed sports store, the bar where I had met Johnny. The car windows were mirrored one-way, so I could see out, even at night, at the cold sleep of a dead town.

"You ever wonder, Grimm, how this all could have turned out?" Raphael asked. I turned to look at him, and I could see him staring at me with the earnestness of a drunk who had rethought his life. I wondered if it was the drink, or what he was holding back inside himself.

"What's that mean?" I said.

"You and me," he said. His words came out slow. "I have no illusions about myself. I am who my father *made*." Raphael spat out the last word. "Sometimes I wonder what would've happened if I had been a bit more like you. Someone who people like."

"Me? You think people like me? You see anyone here helping me out?"

"Maybe." Raphael was serious. "Maybe not. You had friends, Grimm." He waved his hand up to the front seat. "I have cronies. People who will do what I tell them, whatever I tell them. It's *boring*."

"Must suck to be you," I said.

"It does." Raphael sighed. He hadn't caught the sarcasm. "It's why I wonder if I could have changed things if I had just tried to be different; if I had not tried to please my father. If I had been just a kid, and not what my father created. I wonder if I'm tired of my world now, what I'll feel like in a few hundred years."

"Maybe you'll get lucky," I said, looking at him with more bravado than I felt, "and it won't be that long."

"Heh." Raphael slapped his leg, barking out a short laugh. "There's always that, Grimm, there's always that." He turned his face to me, and even though my ethereal sight was off I could feel the pressure inside the car swell, and all of a sudden the backseat wasn't large enough to be sitting next to that man. "You going to be that guy, Grimm?"

"I'd like to be," I said. Trying to keep my voice even, to let my hate overcome my fear.

"Ha." Raphael laughed, pumped his fist a couple of times, then punched the roof of the Cadillac. Didn't notice the huge dent he put in it. "*This* is what I miss, Grimm. You and me. That never got old."

Our high school passed behind Raphael's head. The yard was trashed, and most of the windows were empty and gaping. Darian turned left after the school, headed into the parking lot. I could see the stadium over his head, a small group of stands around a baseball diamond. The lights over the field were on, illuminating Dominic's limo, in the outfield behind first base. I could see the slim shape of my mother, leaning against its hood.

"Man, this is going to be fun," Raphael said to himself, smiling.

The Cadillac bumped up and down as Darian drove us over the curb and onto the grass, the car curving a trail around the limo, between second base and the stands. As we neared the dugout the Cadillac slowed down a bit, right over third base.

My mother kept resting against the limo's hood. She was outfitted in her black armor, the sword that had killed me angling out from over one shoulder. She had been looking into the night, past the bright lights of the stands, and turned our way just as Darian switched off the car.

"It's game time," Raphael said, his words pronounced with the focus of someone who had drunk heavily. His eyes were glossy and a little unfocused. Everything he had drunk seemed to catch up to him in one moment.

Jacob turned in front of me, jerking his thumb to the door. "Out."

"Great." I rolled my eyes and got out. My mother looked me over carefully. I didn't know what anyone wanted me to do here, so I raised both my hands and walked to the front of the Cadillac, right over home plate. My mother stood almost a hundred and thirty feet away. The engine of the car ticked and pinged against the backdrop of the night.

"Son," she said. Even that far apart, I could see her focus on everything and nothing. Alert.

"Mother."

"You're late." She glanced back at the limo, back to me.

"Wasn't much I could do about it," I said. "Takes a while to pull a drunken vampire out of his own poker club."

"*He* will not like it," my mother said.

I didn't know what else to tell her. Tonight had all the feeling of walking into the O.K. Corral, without the backup.

Darian got out behind me and opened the back door for Raphael, who pulled himself out by the top of the door. Jacob got out as well, and we all watched Darian have a hard time keeping Raphael standing without falling down.

The back door of the limo opened and Dominic got out. His door shut hard enough the limo rocked. The old vampire was dressed the same as the night before, and his face was twisted with disgust.

"Father," Raphael cried out. He threw open his arms and stumbled a couple of steps. Darian reached out and steadied him. "Welcome to my humble abode."

"You're late," Dominic said, stalking forward. He turned his gaze to me.

"I said this already," I explained. "I can't control your son any better than you can."

The jaw of the vampire flexed, briefly. *"Down."*

I fell to the ground without a second thought. Or even a first. My body immediately relaxed, like I was a puppet and someone had cut my strings. I tumbled to the ground, and my cheek pressed against the cold, packed dirt.

Dominic stared at me a moment. Then looked back to my mother. Then back to his son. I wasn't sure anyone was meant to hear what he said, but I did.

"Acorns." Dominic headed toward his son. "Sometimes fall far from their trees."

Jacob stepped to intervene. Dominic lashed out, and Jacob quickly stumbled back, holding a hand to the side of his face. Darian then stepped forward, all three hundred pounds of bench-pressed muscle. Dominic reached out and threw Darian thirty or so feet into the bleachers, the aluminum seats buckling with a gong-like sound.

Jacob came forward again and threw a punch that was more likely to connect with a cloud than Dominic. The Vampire Lord blurred, and Jacob was flying through the air and somewhere over the batter's cage.

"Ten years." Dominic stopped in front of Raphael. "Ten years, and this is all you do. All you learn."

It was quiet then. A heavy silence, the kind of silence that hid an evil, the kind of silence swollen with the birth of a monster. Raphael looked at his father and grinned.

My mother pulled herself off the limo and headed toward Raphael. A few steps at first, then faster. Her steps the quick pitter-patter drops of rain before the storm. As fast as she was, I could see she wasn't going to be fast enough.

Raphael winked at his father.

Dominic swung.

His fist hit Raphael's chest.

Raphael's grin spread out larger.

My mother was almost there.

Raphael grabbed his father with one fist. Dominic placed both hands on his son's arm and tried unsuccessfully to yank himself free. Raphael pulled a syringe out of his suit with his free hand and stabbed it into his father's chest.

Immediately feeling restored itself through my body and I could move. Dominic fell to the ground, convulsing around his chest. My mother reached Raphael, her sword arcing through the air, impossibly fast.

Raphael swatted the blade with the flat of his hand, then punched my mother in the face. She rolled backward with the punch and immediately launched back up at him, ducking a couple more of his swings before one Raphael's fists found her again. Her blade fell out of her hand and went flashing across the infield. As fast as she was, he was impossibly faster. And much, much stronger.

I blinked on my ethereal sight and saw Raphael standing there, the blackness inside him swirling like mad with the white sparks I associated with the drug. He held so much of the drug inside him, all I could see was something that looked like the Milky Way, spinning way too fast to track. What was more, the tethers still reached out from Raphael, hundreds if not thousands of them, all leading back toward the club.

Each of the tendrils seemed to undulate or pull back toward Raphael. I went back to normal vision and worked my way backward toward Raphael's Cadillac. At the same moment, my mother shrugged back up and launched herself at Raphael. Each of her hands held a long, slim dagger. She dodged a couple of his swings and got in close to Raphael so that as he swung she could twist around and score a couple of long, deep cuts. For a few moments, my mother and Raphael danced that dance together.

Until my mother missed a beat.

She overextended with a thrust and Raphael caught her with a knee. Again she went spinning, this time toward the outfield. Dominic crawled back to the limo, half curled up and shaking from whatever Raphael had injected into him. The drug, I guessed. Raphael laughed and squared his shoulders and headed that way.

"You feel it now, don't you?" Raphael asked. "Feel it coursing through your veins, feel the *need*?" He smiled, leaning over his father's bent form. "Have I learned enough for you now? Am I what you envisioned when you created me, Father?"

Dominic flipped over on his back. The syringe still stuck in his chest. His eyes wide-open in fear. One of his hands twitched constantly, like a bird flapping uncontrollably.

"You wanted the perfect son," Raphael said. "I hope you're satisfied with the result."

He dragged Dominic over to the front of the limo, leaned him up against the bumper. Went and did the same with my mother, who was out cold. Squatted down in front of them.

"I'm a bit torn," Raphael said. "There's something about keeping you around that's tempting me. Part of me knows that once I kill you, I can't go back and do it again. And I'm afraid that killing you once won't be enough for me."

There was movement in the stands by first base. Right across from me, over the top of Raphael. Forms like purplish blobs in my ethereal sight leaped across the seats. I blinked back to normal vision. The figures were clad in black and snuck through the bleachers. Someone stood tall on the top-most bench, holding a long, cylindrical tube over a shoulder.

Raphael didn't notice any of it, though. He squatted in front of his father, their gazes locked. Dominic opened and closed his mouth like a guppy, as if he was trying to make a sound and couldn't, the same hand flapping at the syringe.

And then Raphael smiled, reached out to grab one of my mother's daggers that was lying nearby. "And I just told some friends I'm not really one for traditions. But vampire sons killing their fathers—that's one I'm going to follow."

Raphael plunged the dagger down. At the same time a flash of light flared from the stands, leaving behind a plume of dark smoke against the stadium lights, a rocket tracking toward us too fast to see. And then Dominic's limo burst into flames.

I covered my face with my arms just as the limo exploded. The blast picked me up and threw me backward over Raphael's Cadillac. I slid up the windshield and tumbled across the roof before hitting the ground back by the trunk. The car rocked back and forth.

I shook my head to clear out the ringing. All I could hear besides the ringing was a slight roar. I leaned over and looked down the side of the Cadillac, seeing Dominic ten yards away, on his knees, one hand on the ground, another finally pulling the syringe from his chest. I didn't see my mother. Raphael had ended up on the pitcher's mound. All around him flames licked the ground and sputtered out on the dirt. The young vampire straightened out his coat and looked out over the bleachers.

"Gabrielle!" Raphael called out. "I didn't know we scheduled a doubleheader tonight!"

The single figure at the top was reloading the tube. Dozens of black figures leaped the fence and raced toward Raphael. All of them had pulled out blades that flashed under the lights, like out of some ninja-samurai movie.

Raphael faced the oncoming tide, jogging his shoulders up and down like a boxer before a fight. He seemed to swell in front of me, and as the tide arrived he screamed out a challenge.

Blades flashed—some hit Raphael, most missed him. In turn, Raphael tore through the figures attacking him, literally. The vampire waded through the wave of attackers and seemed to instantly kill anyone within reach. Swords missed him, bullets missed him; he was too fast for all of them and too strong for any of them.

His scream echoed in the distance, but it wasn't a real echo, but an imitated roar pronounced by hundreds of other voices. We were about to get company. Raphael stood surrounded and yet still grinning. The rest of the vampires had pulled back a minute when they realized someone else was headed this way. One of the vampires surrounding Raphael had long black hair.

Raphael grinned at the vampire. "Gabs, you thought this was only personal *for you*?"

Hundreds of shapes flew over the dugout then. Vampires, in various states of undress. I paused. I had seen these vamps back at the club, and I could see the ethereal outlines of tendrils reaching from Raphael to each of them. He was controlling all of them. A side effect of the drug. Or maybe the real effect. An image of Sarah, holding her neck and looking at me. *Something purer,* Raphael had said.

I could feel something similar in the tethers that I felt when I was being controlled. I blinked and saw the tethers, all stretched razor-thin reaching from Raphael to the crowd. The strings pulled tightly. They radiated a leashlike control, almost like the same kind of control he had over me, but not as elegant. Something brute force required. He pulled all the vampires to him, and they came. Willingly, unwillingly, it didn't matter. The vampires came, and they killed.

The vampires flowed over everything like locusts. There was a metallic bouncing sound from the bleachers as the creatures pounded down the stands. Screams and cries called out as Gabrielle's group was overwhelmed. Here and there knots of people dressed in black banded together against the horde, and Raphael waded through all of them.

Bullets popped and pinged into the side of the Cadillac. I lay down, hoping people would think I was dead and not worth an extra bullet. My mother staggered back onto the field from where the blast had thrown her. With each step, she moved a little better, and when she got to Dominic she was able to throw him over her shoulder. The elder vampire's mouth was moving, but no sounds came out, and his eyes were blank.

My mother looked at me for a brief moment, set her jaw, and took off, blurring as she ran. It only took a moment, but they were gone.

More vampires fluttered from the stands, and I could see Raphael dance in the middle of the fight like a warlord. Like death itself. The drug gave him not only power but the ability to command others, much like he could command me. I wondered at his power, and what he had become.

But I could find all that out later. First things first, staying alive. That thought occurred just as a pair of feet slammed down in front of me. I looked up into the face of a grinning vampire, incisors bright white in the lights over the field.

I rolled over onto my back, stuck my hand into my jacket pocket. The vampire reached down just as I squeezed my hand around the grip of the .38. I pulled the trigger twice.

The silver bullets blew through the vamp, two blazing trails of fire punctured out from his back. The vampire spun and fell to the ground.

Stay alive. I got up and ran. I had no specific direction in mind, just anywhere but inside the lights of the park. As I ran into the shadows past the outfield, I looked back. The bleachers were full of vampires from the club, running down Gabrielle's team, and the field was littered with the dying and the dead and the dying flames of the limo. The stadium seemed too small to hold all the bodies. In the middle of everything, Raphael stood on the pitcher's mound, facing the stands, holding both hands above him like he was conducting an orchestra.

CHAPTER TWENTY

I ran a bunch of blocks before the screams died into the distance. No one chased me. I kept seeing Dominic's face back at the field. Pale, scared, mouth moving soundlessly, eyes recognizing something his mind failed to grasp. Fear. Defeat. Dominic had lost before he had known losing was possible.

Raphael had used me as bait. And as a distraction. He had put together a masterful performance and drawn his father to Grafton, alone, and suborned him. Had used me to distract my mother. Had acted like a spoiled brat for years, building and building his performance, until his father had to come discipline him.

Raphael had taken the ten years I was away and had set a trap for his father, with a vision I didn't believe Raphael had. A type of complexity I wouldn't have believed he could have had, in the past. Either he had good help, or he had changed.

And he had set us all up. Me, his father, my mother, Gabrielle. He had pulled us all together for one night, a night that Raphael meant to rid himself of all his enemies in one go. Raphael had kidnapped Jen just to get me into town for this night. When he knew his trap was ready, foolproof.

Which meant Jen hadn't found anything that could have stopped him. I had been wrong there. He had hunted her down because he needed me in town, and he had likely applied all the pressure he could until she had called me. Which made me question if I really knew where she was at all.

I had stayed alive, on the one night I would have bet against it. And it was temporary at best. Daylight would come soon, and if I stayed in town much longer than tonight I was sure Raphael would come after me, promise or no promise. I had today, and today only, to get to Jen and get her out of town.

The edge of the eastern sky was colored in red when I finally got back to my car. I was surprised to see Johnny there, leaned up against the Camaro much as he had been earlier. He looked worn-down, tired, much like me. His jacket had a couple of tears down it and was covered in smoke and familiar dark red blotches. He was dark-skinned but looked pale in the predawn light.

"Hey," I said.

"Hey," he said.

"So that's what you were warning me about," I said.

He nodded. "Didn't go the way we expected, did it?"

"I wouldn't think so," I said. "At least you can't blame me, right?"

"Not the way it went down, I couldn't," Johnny said. "Not seeing Raphael like that. I'm not sure we could have taken him with twice what we had."

In my memory Raphael grew in size, swelling as his fists splintered bone and tore flesh. He had been a monster unlike any I had ever seen. "I can believe that." I looked past Johnny, looking for Gabrielle. "Gabrielle okay?"

He acted surprised, maybe that I had asked about her. "She made it out."

A little trail of blood leaked down his neck. I realized Johnny didn't just look paler than normal, he was actually paler. "Are you all right?"

He saw where I was looking and wiped his neck. "Close to sunrise."

My eyes followed his. Far in the distance, a little slip of a yellow orb peeked over the horizon, surrounded by clouds of crimson and ochre.

"So," I asked, "a rocket launcher, huh?"

"Yeah." Johnny chuckled, a harsh coughing sound. Like he had swallowed some smoke somewhere. "Can't believe I missed."

I wasn't sure a direct hit would have done anything. Raphael had torn through meat and bone and metal like all of it was just thin papier-mâché.

He had thickened, grown faster, stronger, taller. And all those invisible tendrils had encircled him and reached out to control a mass of vampires. They had been almost zombielike in his command and wolflike in their intensity.

I had to get Jen and get out of this town, soon.

"Johnny," I said, "I need your help."

"Man, you know it's not the best time to ask," Johnny said. "I'm not sure I could walk ten feet. Was thinking about some breakfast."

"It's Jen," I said. "She's at the factory. I've got to get her free, today."

Johnny took a deep breath. "I get it, man."

"If we hurry we can get there before daybreak," I said. "There won't even be any vampires there, after tonight."

"Vampires are the least of your worries there."

"I know about the wights."

Johnny shook his head. "Man, you know Gabrielle was sent here to get the formula for that drug. She's been trying to get into that factory for weeks. Nighttime it's guarded by the wights. Daytime it's guarded by the wights and dozens of cops."

"Why that many?"

"Something that big cop set up," Johnny said. "The cops protect it during the day when the vamps are sleeping. You're better hitting it right at nightfall after the cops head out to patrol the town."

"If I do it then, I've got to do it quick," I said. "And then I've got to go. If I stay around, Raphael or Dominic … one of them is going to get me."

Johnny rubbed his stomach. "Let's talk about it over some breakfast. I got to get some food in me, and then go check on Gabrielle."

"If you're sure that we shouldn't go now."

"Man, I couldn't go now if I wanted to. And I'm telling you, it's a bad time. Trust me," Johnny said. "Diner?"

I did trust Johnny. Though my body was screaming for me to get over there now, I would do this right. I had one chance to rescue Jen, and I would not mess that chance up. "Sure."

Johnny picked himself off the hood of my car and walked around to the passenger side, peering into the backseat. Then he looked over with an eyebrow arched.

"Yeah, I know," I said. "It's a mess."

"When you find Jen," he said, "you're going to need to clean this up."

It was my turn to look back at him.

"Women like a clean car, man." He smiled a little. "Wouldn't hurt if you cleaned yourself up some too."

We got to the diner and took a booth. It was pretty empty, which maybe wasn't a surprise this early in the morning. Too early for the elder folks, and too daylight for the other crowd. Miss Tammie looked excited to see both of us and brought over a pot of coffee and two cups.

"Now, Johnny," she said. "You don't come by enough."

Johnny waggled his eyebrows at me. "More than him."

"He's got his reasons." Miss Tammie raised her eyebrows and shifted her bulk. Waiting on Johnny.

I grinned at him. "Yeah. I've got my reasons."

"You want to tell me you got reasons too?" Miss Tammie said. "Or you just want to come back a little more often?"

Johnny grinned back at her, and that easily the two of us felt young again. Like before. "You got me," he said. "I'll come back a little more."

"Good," Miss Tammie said. "I'll go get you boys some plates."

We poured ourselves some coffee. Both of us still had little boy grins on.

"Some things never change." Johnny's eyes were a mixture of memory and loss.

"Yeah," I said. "You ever wonder what might have happened to us if Grafton was a normal town?"

"I stopped wondering that years ago," Johnny said. He looked out the window. Dawn had finally arrived, the bright yellow rays of the sun burning away the last tinge of red from the sunrise. I looked out the window too, and both of us for a minute just sat and drank our coffee. I could feel a warmth from it that maybe was more than just the temperature. A comfort.

I thought about what the infield might look like in the sunlight, layered with dead vampires and a burning limousine. Wondered if anyone would go out there and look at it closely, or clean up the black stains in the grass where dead vampires had burned away to ash under the dawn.

Scores of vampires that Raphael had slaughtered, by himself. Dominic, under his son's drug. And my mother, who had killed me only the night before.

I shivered. Johnny's eyes had a faraway look as well. Behind our booth, Nick open the door to the diner. The little tinkle of the bell cut short as Nick held the door out a moment, looking at us and frowning. Or scowling. Then he let go of the door and walked over to the counter, ignoring the two of us.

Johnny turned around to see what I was looking at, then turned back, shaking his head. "Nick," he said. "Another one of us this town has fucked up royally."

Nick and Miss Tammie talked a bit. Their conversation was just low enough that I couldn't make out the words, but I could guess the topic. As she talked Nick kept shaking his head. He looked at us once and his brows lowered.

Miss Tammie sighed, a huge shifting of her chest. One hand reached out to tousle Nick's hair, and he jerked back a little at the touch. She withdrew her hand, smiling a sad smile, and filled up a foam container with some casserole. When she was done packing food in it, she folded the top over, tucked in the tab, and handed the food to Nick.

He said something, ducked his head, and turned to leave.

"Nick." I waved him over to the booth.

Nick paused a second and looked at me. Looked at Johnny sitting with me. For an instant something warred within him. Something marred his scowl and I couldn't read what it was. Then he turned back to the door.

"Nicholas Franklin, you go sit with your friends." Miss Tammie's voice was loud, insistent, and firm.

"They're not friends," Nick mumbled, sullen. Miss Tammie stared at him, with her arms crossed over her large bosom, one eyebrow arched.

Nick looked down at the container in his hand, then back at Miss Tammie. Finally back to us. "Fine." He shook his head and headed over and took a seat next to Johnny in the booth.

"Hey, Nick," I said.

"Fuck you." Nick grabbed a fork, opened up the foam container, and started shoveling in casserole. Johnny smiled a little smile.

Miss Tammie came over and slid a plate in front of me and Johnny.

Both of us dug in. I surveyed outside as we ate, seeing a dead town stay dead. The sun was up but spread no warmth. Everything was gray or brown, the sky a chilly blue, the three fall colors of Grafton.

Nick ate with a vengeance, barely stopping to chew. Johnny glanced over at him once or twice.

"Nick, man," I said, "we're trying to be nice here."

"Maybe you missed what I said a minute ago," Nick said, food almost falling out of his mouth. "Fuck you and your vampire-loving friend."

"Hey," Johnny said, looking a little miffed. "You casting the first stone, Nick?"

Nick looked at Johnny for a bit. He stopped eating and sighed. "No, man ... No."

Sarah came to my mind, standing pale in the club, surrounded by vampires, her neck beckoning to them. Nick had always liked Sarah ten years ago, a teenage crush, and all of a sudden I could understand Nick a bit better. What Nick was looking for in Sarah was different from what Sarah was looking for in Nick. But he had stayed around to change her mind, and had watched her become the plaything of a vampire he hated.

Suddenly I feared finding Jen. That maybe she had changed and what we'd had once no longer existed. Maybe she had moved on and become more like her sister. I admired Nick a little more. He stayed in this town and tried to protect Sarah even when Sarah wanted something that wasn't Nick.

I leaned forward. "Hey, man, whatever it is, whatever it was, I'm sorry."

"Yeah," Nick said. He sneered slightly, or maybe the look was just permanent on him. "I'm sure you are. It's easy to be sorry after the fact, right? Maybe ten years from now you come back and apologize again."

"Look, man." I took a deep breath in anger, and I tried to clamp down on the feeling. "I'm only here—"

"Because Jen called," Nick finished. "Yeah, I know. Guess the rest of us are just lucky you're back, right? All your old *friends*?"

Johnny saw it. "Come on, Nick, why's it got to be like that? Grimm being here or not wouldn't have changed you and Sarah."

Nick turned to him, red-faced. "You don't *know* that."

"Of course I do," Johnny said. "You do too if you think about it. For whatever reason, Sarah wanted the life."

Nick pushed at his food, threw it all over the bench, and stood. Some of it landed on me. "Shut the fuck up."

"Fine," Johnny said. "Keep throwing those stones, man. You're good at that, right? Everyone's fault but yours."

I made myself unclench my hand and take a deep breath. I had clamped down on my jaw, and I worked to loosen it and say something.

Nick turned to me, though, and bent over the table. "You want to be friends again, Grimm? You want me to forget it all, Johnny? Fine. Tell me about Danny."

"You know what, Nick? Fuck you." I pounded the table one time with both my fists. The diner went quiet. Johnny and Miss Tammie and Nick all looked at me. "You weren't fucking there. You weren't the guy who they beat with a bat before they killed him. You weren't the guy they left with Danny's body bleeding out all over the place, and him just looking at me …"

I put my face in my hands, felt my fingers tearing into my hair. I tried to take a deep breath, but it felt like I couldn't get any air, so I just kept trying. My chest kept swelling, but nothing filled my lungs. Fuck Nick. Fuck them all.

It was several long moments before I looked up from my hands. Nick still stood there but looked out the window, away from me. Johnny's eyes held concern. He started to reach out and then pulled his hand back. I finally got a good breath in, and Johnny nodded at me before I put my face back in my hands. After a while, the clatter of forks hitting plates resumed.

I felt more than saw Nick push back from the table and leave the diner. Even the bell rang harshly when the door shut after him.

Miss Tammie came over to grab Nick's dishes. She patted me on the shoulder, and I wiped my face with the back of my arm, still not looking at anyone.

"That boy," she said. "Something done twisted in him, and I hope he can twist it back."

"I understand," I said automatically. Thinking of just a short few days ago, when all I had to worry about was staying ahead of Azazel. Before I had gotten trapped in this town.

"Of course you do." Miss Tammie patted me again, her hand big and warm on my shoulder. "You know the secret there?"

"The secret?" I snorted. All I could see was Danny lying in a pool of blood in front of me, eyes open and not seeing anything.

"If you know what makes people wrong," Miss Tammie said, "then you also know how to make them right."

A moment later she had picked up our plates and walked back to the kitchen.

Johnny sat before me, pale from his relationship with Gabrielle, and her need for blood. Sarah, with the same needle points on her neck. Nick, angry at the world.

And what happened in this small town held reverberations beyond my close friends. My mother, jaw clenched against what she wanted to say. Parker, sobbing at his table. Miss Tammie, holding on for her kids.

Danny, killed right in front of me. And then there was Jen, who needed me while I sat and ate food in a diner.

Johnny leaned forward. "We'll get her, man."

"Will we?" I sighed, utterly exhausted. The kind of exhausted that happens after emotions run wild and then disappear, leaving just an empty shell.

"Hell yeah." Johnny grinned. "You know why, man?"

I looked at him, shook my head.

Johnny waved out the window. "Look out there at Grafton, man. You see what it's like. A bunch of bad guys out there, a bunch of bad things happening. But then there's us here too. Me, Nick, Sara, and Jen."

"Yeah?"

"You know what we all have in common?" Johnny pressed on. "You, man. You brought us all together. And here we are, ten years later."

"I couldn't help Danny," I said.

"Wolverines die, man." Johnny's face was open and earnest, his eyes locked on mine. He really believed what he was saying. "You're not seeing it. There's a group of us still left, still fighting the fight. And you started it. You started *us*. You're the reason we're here. You'll be the reason we win it."

"This isn't a movie, Johnny," I said. "Life doesn't work that way."

"Maybe, maybe not." Johnny grinned a shit-eating grin. Something from back in the day, when he was cracking some joke. "But it'd be great if it did, right?"

We were both silent. He believed in good over evil. I had lived too much to believe the same. Peace was a concept I was unfamiliar with. All I had were tiny moments of survival threaded between fights with monsters and flights from demons and whatever else got tossed in along the way. If good existed, it avoided me.

Johnny was tired and was hanging in, though, for me. And that was enough for now, for me. "You need some sleep," I told him.

"That's both of us."

"I'll get some at Parker's," I said. I wondered if we would talk some more. What did he know about my mother, about my geas? "You probably need to check on Gabrielle. We can meet up later."

Johnny nodded. "How about the gas station outside the factory?"

"Not here?" I asked.

"Nah." He got serious. "I'm hoping Raphael needs to rest too, after last night. But he'll be looking for us later. For Gabrielle. It'll be safer to stay out of town come sundown."

Shit. I hadn't thought about that. After last night, Raphael would likely want to find anyone left from the massacre. Unless he was too tired, too excited, or worried about his father still being out there. And here I was asking Johnny to come with me to the factory when Raphael might be hunting him and Gabrielle down.

"You sure you want to go?"

"Definitely, man." Johnny stood and gave me a little wave. "We got to take care of each other. It'll all work out."

I finished my cup of coffee while Johnny left. He turned down Main Street. He put his hands in his jacket, huddled into himself, and disappeared down the street. I wondered briefly how bad Gabrielle was hurt, and if anyone else had survived the massacre at the baseball field. Wondered where my mother and Dominic were, and if they were far enough away that I wouldn't have to worry about them, for at least the day.

While I was watching Johnny, the tan sedan pulled up next to my Camaro, Greg in the driver's seat. Things were looking up. I had survived the night, and I might have more help to get into the factory. I got up and stopped at the door, turning back to the counter and the lady working the grill behind it.

"Thanks again, Miss Tammie," I said, smiling. "It feels good, being here again."

"You're welcome, Fergus." She smiled back and looked years younger. "You bring the whole gang and eat when you can. Then take them as far from this town as possible."

"If I can, Miss Tammie, I will." I walked out the door, heading toward the sedan. Tony was driving this time, and both of them had cups of coffee in their hands. I wondered where they got it from in this town.

I came up on Greg's side. He watched me in the side-view mirror. I got the same feeling as when I first met him, that he was a hard and capable man. The car was still running, and some news channel was in the background.

Greg nodded. "I heard you were looking for me."

"You back in town?"

"Recruitment is low," he said. "Been busy."

"I'll get to it, then," I said. "I'm breaking into the factory tonight."

His heavy-lidded eyes opened with interest.

"I could use some help," I said. "It's where they make the drug, so you help me, and I'll help you make sure they can't keep making it."

"There is something really wrong in this town," Greg said, looking at me. "More than just a drug. Something evil."

"Then help me take a part of it out."

Greg took a moment and sipped from a foam coffee cup.

"You won't get a better chance," I said. "I even have another hand to help us."

"I know this factory," Greg said. "But destroying the drug, it will not be enough."

I clenched my jaw. "Not enough? What more do you want?"

"You misunderstand. There is too much to fight in this world to try to defeat all of it. Part of what we do ..." Greg's eyes flicked to the empty passenger seat. "Part of what *I* do is find the place where I can tip things back to the good. I'm a fulcrum. I find the tipping point, and I apply pressure."

"You're a fulcrum." I put my hand on the roof of his car and leaned in. "Have you seen what this drug can do? I have. And I haven't seen anything near as dangerous."

Greg snorted. "Just because you have not seen it does not mean more dangerous does not exist."

"And recruitment is low," I added for him.

Greg bowed his head as if to say, *You understand.* "The drug is the symptom here, not the cause. Taking it out will not give these people back their town."

"Look, I don't care if we destroy the drug or not," I said. "I'm here to rescue a girl that's there. I wanted to help you destroy the drug if you'll help me rescue her."

Greg took a long sip and looked back at me. He nodded a moment. "I can help you rescue the girl."

"And destroy the drug?"

He shrugged. "Destroy the drug, do not, it may not matter here. But I can help you with the girl."

Inside I wanted to shout for joy. This had a real chance of working, with Johnny and with Greg. Even if I had to wait until this afternoon.

"There's a convenience store out on the road by the factory," I said. "We're going to make it right around five tonight."

Greg sighed and smiled. "It is better," he said, "than drinking this piss-poor coffee another day."

"Great." I slapped the top of his car with my hand. Things were looking up. "See you tonight, then."

"Tonight," Greg echoed.

I tapped the car hood a final time and headed around his car to mine. While doing so I glanced over at the side of the diner, where the pay phone stood, metallic cord swaying back and forth in a slight, unfelt breeze. To where it all began.

I stopped, and remembered the call again, Jen's voice, the crackling and sizzling, and the abrupt end of the call. After a moment I walked toward the phone. As I neared I could see nothing had changed: the tiny black marks tracing up and down on the wall beside the phone, the metallic end of the phone cord, sharply severed, the smell of brimstone, a choking charcoal burning the hair in my nostrils.

The sedan pulled out of the lot behind me, Greg heading into town and likely back to the church. I turned back to the metal cord to the phone, a black scorch marking the severed end. I held it up; if I looped the cord right, the phone line ended right in the middle of a black mark on the wall. As if someone had been standing there, holding the phone and talking to someone, when they had been attacked.

I stood there, wondering if this was where Jen finally stood, here on

earth. If my search was a foolish one. I believed, like all those foolish
enough, that somehow I would know if she was dead. But maybe, like the
millions of fools in the world, it was just a dream. The reality of the situation was Jen had found out something someone else didn't want her to,
she had called me for help, and she had disappeared. After a few days, I
still didn't know any more than that.

I thought of being with Jen in her house, sitting on her bed, the feel of
her all around me. Memories swarmed me of her and me sitting together,
her bare arm touching mine, the warm smoothness of her skin. The scent
of honeysuckle and cool rain. I remembered just a few nights ago when I
had blinked on my ghost vision and seen the traces of evil in Jen's house.

I almost slapped my head and blinked on my vision now.

I was surprised by what my sight revealed. The entire side of the
building was painted in brilliant blue jagged lines, overlying the scorch
marks. It was bright enough I had to squint and raise my hand to shade
my eyes. The scorch marks had an ethereal blackness to them, like huge
blobs of dark clouds. But blue streaks of lightning traced along the bellies
of the dark clouds, up and down the wall. I looked at my feet and saw
clumps of blue in a path along the gravel of the lot, and about five feet
from the phone a dark shadow lay on the stones. Like a black chalk
outline.

I squinted some more in order to mask the bright blue light reflecting
off the gravel. There were prints from a woman's shoe, outlined in bluish
white, standing before the phone. As if someone had been standing there,
making the call.

I backtracked those prints. They had come from in front of the diner
and headed back north on Main Street. They faded as they led out of town
and toward the closed motel I had passed when I first drove into Grafton.
The King's Lodge. It looked like Jen had left the motel and headed down
here, running immediately to the phone on the side of the diner, just a few
nights past.

I did slap my head this time.

I looked around. No one seemed to be interested in me. At least, there
was no one else in the streets, and nothing else but flaps of cardboard and
foam cups on the sidewalk. The morning was still gray and cool, even
with the sun out.

I headed back to my car and fired it up, backing out of the parking lot and onto Main Street. The front end of the car pointed to King's Lodge, and when I used my ethereal vision I could see a dim outline of blue-white steps tracing their way up there. I pushed the gas and drove on up the hill.

As I drove up I saw a police car heading back down, and I instinctively slowed the Camaro. Cole sat in the other car, the huge cop driving around with the window down, arm over the door. He looked over and grinned nonchalantly at me as we passed, like we were old buddies, and cruised on by.

Closer up the motel looked just the same as it had when I drove in a few days before. Plywood covered the windows on the motel office, and most of the doors were chained tight. A few room windows poked out from behind broken slats of wood, and those windows had been broken, long ago. The walls of the motel were grimy and in places sprayed with graffiti: exaggerated pictures and words that didn't make a lot of sense to me.

As I pulled through the lot, I followed the prints around the back, and I parked the Camaro near the back stairs. The prints led up them, and I walked up the concrete blocks, past old cigarette butts and wads of gum. A weird déjà vu slipped over me from a few nights ago. I was losing count at all the times things felt familiar to me. I went up the stairs and down the backside walk of the second floor of the motel. All the doors were locked as I tried them, and my palms came away covered in dust.

The footsteps led to a door in the middle of the walkway, number 218. The doorknob was clean, as if had seen recent use. A weird tingling crawled over my skin and I had trouble breathing. Jen could be in there; she could be dead. My heartbeat sped up all on its own.

Some of the window showed behind the plywood cover, and I could see the curtain closed behind it. The room was dark inside. Jen had to be at the factory, but still, I knocked and called out her name.

No answer. I knocked louder. I glanced quickly around the back parking lot. There was no one in sight. I pounded the door. "Jen. Jen. *Jen*."

Maybe she really was in that room. Hurt, unable to answer. She might even be dead. All kinds of things entered my mind, and I cursed myself for not thinking of the motel when I first came to town. I could have found her then. None of the rest of this had to have happened: the geas, the town, Raphael.

I kicked in the door. I followed it as it swung inward. The room was dark, and I paused after hearing a large zapping sound. Then a bright blue lightning bolt sizzled out of the corner of the dark room and struck me in the chest. The bolt threw me against the frame of the door, and I fell to the floor.

My chest felt funny. Light electric traces of blue ran over it and down to the floor beside me. A blue afterglow seemed to light up the room. I moved my head a little and saw the bed was stripped. The room was empty. No sign of anyone having been here at all. I looked at my chest and saw blue lines tracing themselves over my chest before flaring out.

I tried to move my feet. I felt more than saw them flop around. A strange numbing sensation spread out from my chest, quieting the trembling in my feet. Was this a trap for Jen? Or something she had left for someone else? I tried to fight it, breathing hard and fast, trying to force oxygen in my slowly receding consciousness. My eyes flicked left, then right, and then they closed.

CHAPTER TWENTY-ONE

I woke with a start like someone had hit me with the electric paddles they use to jump-start a heart. It was dark out. I was still sprawled across the hotel room floor, my arm numb where I had lain across it, and my feet still part of the way across the motel door's threshold.

I had a headache. A large thumping headache that echoed and rolled around in my skull, like crashes of thunder, or a heavily beating heart. I groaned, rolled over, and sat up, looking at my chest. My shirt was all burned up where the bolt had struck it, like a Taser gone wild. I smelled burned chest hair and saw little traces of burns sparking out from the center of my chest. I groaned and pulled myself up. Past the door I could see it was full dark out, the sky over the back parking lot a deep, dark purple. None of the lights were on in or out of the motel.

I shook my head, trying to clear it. I was supposed to meet Johnny and Greg and now I was late. It had to be much closer to eight or nine at night. I pulled myself up, shaking my arm out to get feeling back in it. As I moved, my jacket rubbed up against the raw skin on my chest. I looked down and saw a good blistering there where my shirt used to be.

There was enough light in the night to slightly illuminate the room, and I took a look around. Some clothes folded on the dresser, smelling like honeysuckle. A backpack near the bed that smelled the same. Other items, like a finger-thin iron rod that twinkled with dark blue electric lights as I twisted it around. A torn piece of paper with a phone number scribbled on it.

Jen had hidden here for a bit, then, before they got her at the diner.

I grabbed everything and put it in the car. I shouldn't have let Johnny convince me to wait today. I should have headed to the factory as soon as I realized Jen was there, when I was up on that water tower. Never mind Dominic controlling me, or Raphael. I should have found a way and rescued her. Now it might be too late.

A minute later my car was fired up and I was rolling down the street. I made a quick pit stop at the diner. Miss Tammie hadn't seen Johnny, but Greg had stopped by for a minute before leaving. She wanted me to eat, but I wanted to be on my way, so I smiled and waved at her and told her not to worry.

I was worried, though. Johnny hadn't shown. What would have kept him? Had Gabrielle not made it? Had Raphael somehow found him during the day, or had Johnny had to leave quickly?

The Camaro hummed, as it always seemed to do when I had a purpose. The steady thrumming of the engine soothed me a little. The cool air of dusk flowed through the broken window. To the east the moon rose, bright white and almost full, and as I took a series of turns the light threw the shadow of my car wildly across the road like I was out of control.

The trees and brush grew closer to the road as I headed south out of town, the forest reclaiming its territory. Another couple of miles to the turnoff for the factory, with the closed service station sitting right at the corner. What used to be a twenty-four-hour Stop and Shop. On the way to the plant, you could stop and get coffee and a donut, a couple of sodas, that type of thing. On the way home get an energy drink to stay up long enough to get home.

The little shop was as I remembered it, sitting in a big lot to the left of the cross-section of the main street and the factory road. It sat silent, quiet, all lights off in the lot that was empty except for a tan sedan almost hidden to the side of the building. The little car was hard to see but looked empty, sleepy, the sedan nestled right against the station. Greg was here. If I was lucky Johnny would be inside too. Though I didn't see another car.

I turned in slowly, letting the Camaro idle as it pulled through to the corner of the lot. I was thirty feet or so from the sedan, the shadows of the car from my headlights thrown up against the side of the station. The car itself was empty, and I wondered if Greg for some reason had decided to press on.

The night felt odd, tense, like something was out there, like I could feel someone looking through a scope at the back of my head, a finger light on the trigger. My spine tingled, and my hand reached down to where I hid the Benelli and picked it up, almost on its own.

Long minutes passed. No light showed from the shop, no one came out to say hello, the imaginary guy with the scope on my neck didn't pull the trigger, no one was doing anything anywhere. The door to the shop was half-open, though the rest of it was boarded up. I was pretty sure if Greg was in the shop he would have heard me drive up and come out. Unless he couldn't. Or it was a trap.

The gas station door swung shut. Maybe it had been the wind. My chest still burned with whatever bolt had hit me earlier, my spine tingled with the sense of being watched, and my gut was telling me in no uncertain terms to throw the car into drive and move on. But something was wrong.

I sighed and got out of the car, leaving it running and the driver's door open, the lights falling just short of the station door. I'd rather have my car ready to go than a quarter more gas in the tank. I'd seen too many movies where the victims dropped their keys at the last second. The warm *chug-chug* of the engine helped to ease my nerves in the quiet night, it was nice to know I could jump into the car and roll at a moment's notice.

My feet crunched gravel over the parking lot as I walked to the front door, my shadow long and lean in front of me. It was cold out, and something smelled foul in the air. Like a busted sewer line. I pumped the Benelli as I neared the station door, passing an old cigar store Indian who had stood watch over the station for as long as I could remember.

I couldn't see through any of the windows that weren't boarded up. The glass was dark with years of grime. No light was on inside. Carefully I placed my ear against the pane on the door.

I had to take a minute to relax and to tune out the Camaro, chugging quietly away back in the lot. I took long, shallow breaths, felt the cold of the glass against the lobes of my ear, and then I heard a noise from inside.

A slapping, sickly sound, like a wet mouth crunching down on dry twigs. Almost like snacking.

I gripped my shotgun handle harder and left my ear pressed tight against the glass.

My heart *tha-thumped* in my ear and the sound was followed by the moist, wet crackling sound, and maybe the sound of something heavy being dragged over a wooden floor. I didn't want to go in there. I tried again to look through the window. The Camaro's headlights threw my shadow against the dirty glass. I kept listening, hearing more wet crackling. Maybe multiple things eating multiple things. A single heavy footstep on a hollow piece of floor, an echoing reverberation of a heavy weight. I pressed my ear even tighter—

A hand crashed through the window, grabbing the back of my jacket and hauling me through the top part of the door, raking my side over broken glass and old metal. I grabbed the arm as it pulled me through. The flesh felt squishy, but the grip was as hard as an oak. As soon as I was through the broken door, whatever had me took a giant swing and threw me into the depths of the store.

It was dark back there. I bounced off a wall, tumbled down a shelf, got the wind knocked out of me, and then fell on something soft, like warm clay. The clayish something was covered in a warm wetness. I did not like where that thought took me and tried to spring up. My legs slipped on the same wetness, my feet stumbling over what felt like a body, my free hand slipping over a blood-soaked chest. The other hand, luckily, still held the shotgun. The whole time I was trying to stand, my lungs were trying to dig deep and pull a large breath out of the air.

The hollow floor pounded behind me, echoes reverberating as whatever had pulled me through the window came after me. Little sparkly spots swam in my darkened vision in the lightless store. As the pounding got louder my only thought was wherever I was standing, I couldn't stay there.

I raised the Benelli and pulled the trigger and jacked the next round in for all I was worth. The gun bucked hard in my hand. In the flash of the fire, I finally saw what I faced.

It was human-shaped, had been human once, but the resemblance ended there. It had huge gaps in its flesh, with white pieces of bone jutting out of paper-thin skin. Pieces hung out of it in places. Clogs of dirt clumped over wispy gray hair and dirty white orbs of eyes. Uneven, jagged teeth, dark and pitted and stained in a crimson red. Something tiny, like the tip of a finger, hung on the bottom of one pale lip like someone might mouth a cigarette. The flash of gunfire had caught it facing me.

The wight screamed.

Quickly I scrambled back from where I lay, skidding back on elbows and pushing with my feet. I didn't know if I had hit it. Then its hand grasped my leg, the fingers curled around my ankle, and I felt myself getting pulled back toward it.

The hand grasped my ankle tighter, and I cried out in pain before firing again. I pumped frantically. The shotgun was all I had. The silver buckshot didn't seem to affect the creature, nor the holy water, but the tremendous force of the buckshot blew chunks of it away. I kept firing over and over, even after the Benelli had emptied and the only sound was the snapping of the trigger.

The creature had let go. It no longer moved.

I took another second to pause, another to take a deep breath. I pulled some shells out of my pocket and thumbed them into the tube. My breathing slowed and I stood up again, slowly. And then the hair on the back of my neck rose.

There was more wet munching somewhere in the dark of the store.

It was a munching and a crunching, a tearing, and a gnawing. A messy feast. A loud boom broke the room, the breaking of a large bone in something's jaws. A slurping of what I imagined was marrow. I swallowed slowly and backed down the aisle, trying to make it closer to the door. My ankle protested a bit, swollen already from the wight's grip. Around step four or five, something else grabbed my leg.

I tried not to scream, just barely. Whatever held my leg wasn't the hard claws of the undead, but fingers barely able to ring the cuff of my pants. There was a weak groan. I bent down to one knee.

"Shhhhhhh," I whispered. The weak hand patted me for a minute, then pulled softly at my jacket. He wanted me to move closer.

"Grimm." I recognized Greg's voice, weak and gurgly. He held back a cough. "Should have waited for you. Thought you were in here."

"Nah." I was softly patting around him, feeling huge bloody puddles on his stomach and chest. My hands came away warm and sticky. I would need some light to be able to bandage him. "Just late."

"You're the lucky one, then." Greg coughed and couldn't control it. It was a large racking cough, and a warm wet spray hit my face in the middle. "I wonder what I heard."

Johnny. I had to check. Somewhere in the back of the store came a soft crunching and slurping.

"Fucking *wights*," Greg said.

"What happened?"

He arched, and his whole body tightened under my hand. His jaw shut tight as if he could keep back the pain by the force of his will. A low moan leaked from the back of his throat. I held him down until his body slackened and he let out a deep sigh. "Just heard a scream."

The munching had stopped. I listened harder, turned to the door, flicked on my ghost sense, but couldn't see anything except maybe large rows of shelves. Wights had no ghosts for me to see. Could Johnny still be alive back there? Was that why I couldn't see a ghost?

From far away, my headlights broke through the shattered glass of the door and illuminated a short area into the store, but the light didn't fall far enough to help us back where Greg lay. All I saw was dark shapes on darker shapes.

Whatever had stopped eating would be coming this way. "Can you stand?"

"Fuck no." Greg snorted, then coughed. The sound was raw and loud enough to echo through the station. "You need to get out of here, Grimm."

"We'll both be out of here in a second." I needed to check if the other body was Johnny. I had to know. Even with the slow, settling creaks of wooden boards around us, the subtle tell of an animal stalking its prey.

"Hold on." I took a deep breath and stood. "I'll be right back."

I held the Benelli in both hands out in front of me and walked toward where I had last heard the eating. I moved light on my feet, seeing darker shapes against the blackness that surrounded me. Did wights breathe? Could I hear them? I strained with my senses, but all I could hear was Greg letting go an occasional moan over the rumble of my car outside.

I found a set of shelves and kept one hand on them, walking back down the aisle. Down from me, a piece of flooring creaked. I pulled back the shotgun and kept it tucked inside my arm. The last thing I wanted to do was walk into a wight and have my gun ripped from my hands. Another step. Then another. And finally my foot hit something soft.

I squatted. I didn't know how I would identify who this was, but I reached down and started patting my hand around. I first grabbed a shoe and found the part of the leg the foot was attached to was no longer attached to the body it belonged to. Acid rose in my throat and I swallowed it down, reaching farther up the body.

My hand found another shoe. And then another. There seemed to be an excess of legs, but no body. I found something I thought was a hand, and then a boot. The boot was part of a leg that was cold and thick, flabby. A person who never exercised.

It was one of the more disgusting things I've done, but I forced my hand to go through the entire pile. All the skin was cold but soft, like the gelid fat on the back of a rump roast. Blood had congealed here and there. Limbs were glued together and came apart only with a wet smacking sound. I held my breath, but every now and then I had to breathe in and when I did I gagged on the smell of rotted meat. And after all the searching, I didn't find a head or a body in there, just a pile of limbs. Like someone would put in place to feed an animal. Or animals.

It was a trap. Johnny had never shown. Which worried me more. But first things first. Back to Greg. Quietly. And then get Greg out.

An arm brushed against mine. The wight, coming back for something to eat. I stood up too quickly and bumped into the creature. It screamed, and I fired point-blank into it with the shotgun. For a second I saw a superimposed flash of the creature's face in the darkness, mouth covered in gore.

I fired twice more, scrambling back down the aisle. My hand shook as I pulled a couple of shells out of my jacket pocket and thumbed them into the tube. The wight crashed through the shelves down from me. And then a second crash came from behind me.

Another wight. How many of them could possibly be in this fucking store?

I spun and my foot kicked Greg. He bit back a scream. I reached down, and both of his hands gripped mine.

"We're about to run for it," I whispered.

"I can't move," Greg said. "Just go."

"I can't do that," I said. Heavy footsteps pounded toward us from the second wight. I pulled my hand away from Greg and pointed my shotgun that way and waited, crouching. The floor shook under me. This wight was a big one.

"Grimm," Greg said, "I can't feel my legs. I'm not making it out of here."

"We'll talk about it outside," I told him. I felt in my jacket pocket, but I had used all my shells. I had what was left in the tube.

The first wight had stopped crashing. Instead, it screamed and started running my way. I couldn't point the Benelli both ways. I would have to hope to get the big one and worry about the first one later.

I fired at the big wight and just kept ratcheting the pump and firing. The large booms echoed in the station. I felt the steps stagger, but the big wight kept coming. I kept firing, knowing that in a moment the first wight would be on me.

Two hands pushed me. Greg screamed with the effort. I toppled to the side just as the big wight fell onto the floor where I had been. I felt more than saw the first wight fall over the big one. I ratcheted the shotgun and heard it answer *shik-shik*. Empty.

"Greg!" I scrambled to my feet.

"Grimm." Greg's voice was thick, wet. There was an unmistakable tinking sound of grenades bouncing against each other from his hands. "Just run."

"Greg." I couldn't see him, just shadows fumbling over each other. Which was wight and which was human, I couldn't tell.

"Run!" Greg screamed.

I stood, frozen. Until I saw the dark blur of Greg's arm as he jerked out a couple of grenade pins, followed by the heavy thumps of metal bouncing off the floor.

I took off for the door. Behind me, the wights screamed, Greg screamed, and even I screamed before a heavy hand picked me up and threw me through the station door, followed by a fiery blast of heat that tumbled me through the air.

I landed and rolled in the parking lot. Down was up, up was down, until I came to rest on my back. The detonation still rang in my ears. Bits of wood sprinkled the ground around me with the little tapping ticks wood makes on rock.

I groaned and leaned up. The top of the store had exploded outwards and the sides had all been blown out, like something from a cartoon.

Flames licked the edges of the store's frame, at the top of the walls and windows. The sedan to the left of the store was now buried under its wall. The cigar store Indian, having stood guard at the store for decades, landed in one piece to my right with a loud thump.

A shadow fell across me. Someone stood between my car and me. I hurried to get on my knee but had a little trouble finding my balance. It couldn't be Raphael. Maybe it was the cops.

"What the fuck did you do, Grimm?" Nick asked, looking at me and the burning building behind me.

"Good to see you too, Nick." I pushed myself up to one knee. Something between a grumble and a groan leaked out of my throat. "What are you doing out here?"

His eyes flicked to me, to my car, back to me. He finally answered. "Johnny talked to me."

The look on my face must have said what I was thinking. Nick rolled his eyes.

"Just because I don't like who Johnny sleeps with," he said, "doesn't mean he isn't my friend."

He reached down and pulled me to my feet. My ankle flared in pain when I put weight on it. The wight had done some damage there. I dusted myself off, looked back at the store. A lot of the flames had died out quickly, but inside there was still a good bit on fire.

Greg. I took a step toward the station, and Nick held me back.

"Whoever is in there isn't coming out," he said.

I looked at the flames inside the station. They whipped back and forth with no rhyme or reason. Greg was dead and had died saving me. He had come out here to help me, after not wanting to. And now he wouldn't get his chance to move any fulcrums. It seemed pointless.

His death brought Johnny back to mind, though.

"Johnny okay?"

"He is," Nick said. "His girlfriend isn't. Raphael is hunting them. Johnny called and asked me to come help you."

I snorted. "You're going to help me?"

"Don't act so surprised." Nick's lips were thinly pressed together. "My friends are my friends."

We both heard a siren in the distance. Blue and red lights flashed from behind the store, down the road heading to the factory. I looked and found my Benelli, collected it, and limped to the Camaro.

"Come on." I waved Nick to follow. If this was a trap, someone was coming to see who it caught.

I got in quickly. My hands shook trying to buckle my seat belt. Nick hopped into the passenger seat and watched me with funny eyes. I didn't know what I was doing. I usually didn't bother with seat belts and now I just kept trying to get this one to work and my damn hands couldn't click the buckle in straight.

Finally I let the belt go. I was glad I had left the car running, but I flicked the headlights off. A second later we spun out of the lot and headed back down the road toward town. I went fast enough to handle the road but slow enough not to hit the brakes. Maybe a mile later I slowed down enough to bump the car off the shoulder and into the tall grassy area by the woods, driving it as deep onto the grass as I could before parking the car and turning it off. The Camaro went silent. It was as hidden as it was going to be.

"What are you doing?" Nick asked.

"Someone set a trap," I said. I gripped the steering wheel tight in both hands. "I'm going to find out who, and why."

"You think it was for you?" Nick snorted. "Don't kid yourself."

"Me or not," I said, "I'm looking."

I got out and popped the trunk, got some more ammo for the shotgun. As much as my pockets could carry. I grabbed a nine-millimeter from a bag and a bunch of magazines as well. The .357 was nice, but I left it. Tonight was a night for volume over damage. Without waiting for Nick I shut the trunk as quietly as I could, and then hurried back on foot to the store, hoping to catch those who were hoping to catch me. I worked out my ankle as I walked, limping a little.

A minute later Nick was following me. It was still dark out, but the moon lit everything with a silvery luminescence that outlined every blade of grass and every leaf in a ghostly shadow. The light was enough that it was easy to walk inside the tree line without being seen from the road. Soon we arrived at the edge of the woods beside the parking lot of the store.

The wisp of smoke and explosive was strong, as well as the stench of burnt flesh. A few cop cars were scattered across the lot. I looked at Nick, motioned him to be quiet, and watched him roll his eyes. Carefully we moved around the trees and the brush, staying a good distance from the edge of the forest and the cops.

One cop car sat in the lot almost where I had parked, lights off, with someone on the walkie-talkie. Another cop car sat on the other side of the lot, parked at the corner next to where the factory road crossed the main road. A couple of others were talking next to that car. It struck me that neither of these cars had come from the road out of town. They all had to have been at the factory.

Another guy was looking into the crushed sedan, moving bits of blown wood and burnt roofing to perhaps see if anyone was inside. Maybe doing a body count.

Flashlights flickered all over and I hunkered down, my ankle twinging at the shift in weight. A big shape walked around from the other side of the building, neck craned as if he was looking at things inside the fire. As if he could peer through the flames. At one point he pulled himself up to the front door and pointed a flashlight deep into the burning building. The heat didn't seem to affect him. He shook his big, thick head. Cole.

"Tell the fire department not to make the damn effort," Cole shouted. The cop in the car nodded. "It'll burn itself out. A couple of you need to hang around and keep an eye on it."

"What was it, Chief?" This from the cop by the sedan.

Cole looked over at the cop. "Grenade. Maybe a couple of them." He must have caught the other cops in his peripheral vision because he then turned to the men standing around the car. "Hey, you fucks! You all walk the perimeter yet? See if any of the wights are out here? Or are you okay with standing the fuck there and getting eaten?"

The men at the car grumbled and dispersed. They apparently had thought the show was over. Cole watched them until he was happy, then wandered over to the cigar store Indian. After a moment the cop pulled a cigar out and lit it. He toed the Indian a couple of times with a boot. And smiled after a particularly deep drag.

"When did Cole get here?" I asked.

"A few years ago," Nick said. "Raphael brought him in, right around the time the drug started showing up."

"He doesn't seem to fit."

"He's a cocky bastard," Nick said. "Screams Raphael's type to me."

I ducked down lower into the woods. We were behind thick brush and a couple of trees, but it wouldn't take much for someone to see us. My hand knuckled over the guard of the Benelli. If someone saw me, we'd have a little shoot-out, and we would be a lot outnumbered. It was time to go. And with everyone here at the station, maybe it was a good time to visit the factory.

I backed away, and Nick followed. Both of us kept low and made little noise. Nick was thinking the same thing as I, and when we got far enough away he whispered, "If you want to get to the factory, now's the time."

"You helping me?"

"Let's say we're helping each other," Nick said. "Sarah might be here."

"Why do you say that?"

He just shrugged. "They bring her here a lot. She won't tell me why. But she disappeared from the club last night. And she usually will text me." He laughed, something bitter and choking. "I think I'm her lifeline, should something happen."

"So we're helping each other, then."

"Sure," Nick said. "First time for everything."

If those cops were going to look for possible free-roaming wights and wait for the fire to burn out, then we had some time. It would be a while before the fire burned down enough for them to get in there and see who was dead. If I was lucky, I'd have the rest of the night. Even without luck, I should have a couple of hours.

I took a last look to make sure. A few of the cops had begun walking to the trees. Slowly, in small concentric circles, like they were afraid scores of wights hid in the woods. Cole had turned back to the shop, one hand tapping the ash from his cigar, seemingly intent on watching it burn. Maybe waiting for me to crawl out. Maybe waiting to report to Raphael I was dead.

CHAPTER TWENTY-TWO

Rescuing Jen was going to happen now, or never.

In a little under twenty minutes, we topped a rise and the lights of the factory glowed over the edge of the field surrounding it. It looked like something was going on at the factory tonight. The parking lot held a few parked cars, and lights were on in the front, where most of the offices would be. A van pulled out of the docking area, drove through the parking lot, and headed out toward the main road. The van had been parked next to many other trucks just like it, small vans and larger moving trucks.

Wights populated the fields around the factory. There seemed to be more than before. Hundreds of them circling the plant, staked on the roof, out to the woods in places. It was like an undead minefield that Nick and I had to try to cross.

I hadn't realized how bright the lights were that surrounded the factory. Large lights shone outward over the outside of the plant and reached out to barely touch the first row of wight guards. No place to hide, even if we made it past the undead guards. And the wights worked pretty well against what I could do. They lacked the ghosts I could pull energy from, and they combined unremitting hunger with formidable strength. The wights were all chained and moved just occasionally, but there was no way to travel through them without getting in reach of one or two.

"Fucking wights," I said.

"So how do we get in?" Nick asked.

I just stared over the rows and rows of wights and closed my eyes. I didn't have a plan.

"Fuck, Grimm," Nick swore. "Really?"

I had come this close before. I wasn't leaving this time. "I'm going to run for it."

"Come on," Nick said. "You're not running past any of those things, not with that ankle."

"Those things are slow to react," I said. "I'd bet they're mostly a deterrent for vampires."

"You won't make it." Nick let out a loud sigh. "Dammit."

"What?"

"Do you know why I'm here, Grimm?" Nick finally said. "Why Jen's here? Why even Johnny is here?"

I took a second and then shook my head.

"We're here because of Raphael," Nick said. "We stayed to face him. Even after Danny. Even when you left. We saw what was going on and *we stayed*."

I didn't say anything. Johnny's words came back to me from that morning. *You put us together.* And I had left them to face this. It didn't matter that I hadn't known at the time. It only mattered that I had abandoned my friends to this. I could use any excuse I wanted, but a person is what he does.

They all were much better people than I could have been. Than I *should* have been. I could make amends, though. Maybe.

"One of us can make it in," I said. "Give me a head start. I'll distract them. When I do, just run past me."

Nick shook his head. "I'll distract them."

"I'll do it," I said. "If one of us makes it in there, it should be you."

"I'm not asking your permission." Nick glared at me. I avoided his eyes. He was a different person now, than he had been as a kid. He and I were more alike now, than in the past. We both shouldered different burdens, but for maybe the same reasons.

"You can't run from them, Grimm," Nick said. "I can."

Nick loved Sarah, much like I loved Jen. Part of me wanted him to be the distraction, and the other part of me was ashamed of myself for wanting to let Nick do it. I sighed. "Nick, let me do this."

"You always got to be the sacrifice, right?" Nick's eyes burned with an intensity that made it hard for me to look. "We all *stayed*, Grimm. And we're all still alive. You remember that. We did all this *without* you."

He took the Benelli from me, holding my gaze until I finally looked away. I handed Nick the extra shells, and he put them in his pockets like he had done all this before.

A few seconds later we slid through a gap in the fence, quietly slipping around to the side of the factory where it seemed like the wight herd was thinner. If that was an actual thing that could be measured. We both stopped twenty or thirty feet from the first line of wights. There was a row staggered enough that, if one or two of the wights were distracted enough, someone might make it through.

"You better have a better plan once you get in there." Nick didn't try to hide his sarcasm.

"I'll figure something out," I said. It was what worked for me.

"Are you taking Jen out of Grafton?"

"I'm going to try."

"I thought so," Nick said. "You should think about staying."

I looked at him, but he had looked away. He might be thinking about all of us back in the day. How we had all been together. Maybe some small part of him wanted us all back together too, wanted to know that someone cared about him in this dead town, that he was worth the effort too.

I had blown that ten years ago, and I wasn't making it easier for him now.I wanted to give him what he wanted. That he was my friend. That he was worth it. And yet a part of me resisted. A man is what he's done. I had run once. I was planning on doing it again. I didn't want to lie to Nick.

My jaw clenched, and I looked back at the factory. Away from Nick. *Jen.* "I probably always should have."

There was a moment of silence. I turned back to the wights, flicked on my ghost vision. Normally I couldn't see the ghosts of animals. Whether or not they had spirits after they died was something I had no idea of. But I had never really had the opportunity to see a wight up close, and have the time to study it. The ones back at the store hadn't really volunteered themselves for it.

The wights. There was a slight shimmer to their frame, maybe something like a ghostly dew that covered their undead bodies. A glistening. I focused, but that was all I could get. A faint echo of what had been, maybe.

I pulled back, blinked, saw the night regular again. "You sure you want to do this?"

"Yeah," Nick said. "I'll handle it. Just look out for Sarah for me, okay?"

The feel of needing to find Jen washed over me like a large ocean wave. It was almost all I could think of. But I would help Sarah, if I could. I nodded, which was enough for Nick.

"You ready?" he asked.

I nodded again.

"Then it's showtime." Nick took off, loping through the shadows. I followed as quickly as I could, but Nick moved faster in the dark than I thought possible. And he just got faster, seeming to move within the shadows, almost becoming one with them.

My eyes had trouble tracking him as he wove through the field. It was like trying to pick one shadow from a hundred. Nick was one with the darkness. He was fast. Supernaturally so. He flickered in and out of my vision. Before I could blink he was at the first wight. The creature didn't have time to respond as Nick fired the Benelli point-blank at the chain holding it.

The wight was free. For good measure, Nick popped the wight on the side of its head with the short stock of the shotgun.

My, my. I smiled. *Nick has balls.*

The wight roared and took off after Nick. He led it deeper into the wight field, to the next wight in the way. I ran as fast as I could after him. Nick blurred in my vision, and then there was a second boom of the shotgun, and another wight freed. And then a third.

At some point, we ran right past each other. Nick leading the wights into each other and away across the field. Freeing a wight here and there as he ran with a blast of the shotgun. The wights tumbled into each other, wrestled with each other, and the whole side field of them started baying into the night like a dead pack of wolves.

I ran as hard as I could. The wights I ran past sniffed and stretched toward me until their chains strung out in the air, taut. I ran past them all in a limping, lurching jog, with my ankle protesting each pounding step. As fast as I could I reached the wall. Right by where I stopped there was a small, thick emergency exit door. A sliver of a window sat right above the door handle, light shining behind the glass.

I jiggled the handle and found the door locked. A shadow blocked the glass right then, someone coming toward the door. I stood on the hinge side and waited, listening to the wights scream and yowl behind me. If a few broke free and came at me, I'd be trapped between the field of wights and this locked door.

There was a snap of a thick lock turning. I stood ready. The door opened and a man's head popped out, a ball cap pulled down tight around his forehead. He obviously didn't want to step out to see what the disturbance was, and I couldn't blame him, but in my case, a head was all I needed. I brought the butt of the nine-millimeter around to the side of his head, there was a solid thump, and the man collapsed. His head was nice enough to keep the door open for me.

I moved quickly inside, stepping over the man. No one else was in the room. The guard was dressed in some old coveralls, like old factory clothes, and a jacket. A funky smell wafted from him. I dithered about it a minute, then decided to go all in. I took his jacket and his ball cap, wincing at the smell of both, and picked a second nine-millimeter out of the back of his pants.

After that I rolled the man out the door, leaving him outside and making sure the door was locked. With any luck the wights would smell him and keep up their cries, maybe pulling more people from inside the factory to the outside. At best it would distract the wights and anyone interested in what was getting them rowdy, and worst it would keep this guy sitting quietly. Either way, it bought me time.

I shut the door to the outside and found myself in a large, dark room. A couple of boilers stood off to one side, as well as a number of old condensers. A smaller room with glass windows square on my right, with its lights on and some car magazines on the table. It looked like the power house to a factory, where things like steam, vacuum, and air-conditioning were produced. It was empty now, dark, the factory not having a need for those things for a long while.

A huge roll-up door lay in a huge wall between the power house and the rest of the factory, for larger carts and cranes, and another smaller door stood right next to it for people. I headed that way. The wights still howled outside, but the sound was faint through the thick walls of the factory. I looked back at the outside door and set my jaw. Nick would be fine. He had told me he would be fine, and I had to trust that.

We stayed. And we're all still alive. He would make it. I needed to not let him down.

I got to the door and opened it a little to take a peek. The factory had been constructed like four big boxes in a row, each box the size of a football field and having roll-up doors at both ends so you could travel from one area to the next. I found out I was right by the third area, with the last area—that being the inspection area—last. The roll-up door was down, but there were lights showing beside the people door.

I walked into the area, shutting the door quietly, and got a good whiff of dust and old rubber. Faded lightbulbs hung from the ceiling, swaying slightly in an unseen current of air. A good many of the bulbs were out, but a couple threw a weak yellow light as they drifted back and forth on invisible currents.

A concrete floor rolled away from me and across the area, plotted like farmland with rows and rows of machines, each the size of a small house. I walked quietly among the inanimate panels and sleeping motors, catching glimpses of rust on metal arms that hung in the empty air, abandoned.

A good many of the machines looked like they were still ready to make tires. Rubber lay in flaps across drums, and round rubbery shapes hung on mechanical limbs above me. It looked like someone had just turned a switch and shut the plant off.

Light kept flickering beyond the roll-up door to the last area in the plant. I heard voices from the next area. Something was going on there. I made my way through the machines and snuck closer, recognizing I was headed to the warehouse. Tires would get inspected there and then packed into eighteen-wheelers to be shipped across the nation.

It was likely people were close to the door, and I wondered how I could sneak into the inspection area without getting noticed. Or shot. As I walked closer I looked across the area I was in, and noticed a large trench running like a river straight through the wall into the inspection area. My ankle throbbed on the concrete, and I limped along machines that looked like they had stopped in midmotion, dropping finished tires onto a conveyor belt in the trench. That trench looked like it would carry tires through the wall and into the inspection area. Or even a person sneaking in.

It took me a few minutes to drop safely into a trench, protecting my bad ankle as much as I could, and it was much colder down there than I had expected. Chill, cool, and moist, like the feel of cold earth under a heavy dew. I snuck through the corpses of dead curing machines, smelling more melted rubber, and a thick scent of decay. Like something had died nearby.

It was quiet enough for me to hear the sound of a door unlatching, not far away. Pairs of boots echoed through the area. Two pairs, by the back-and-forth of the voices. Every now and then a flashlight beam waved over the top of the trench.

The presses were huge machines with round molds at the top and bottom. Walking through the trench, they loomed over me like metal scarecrows, warding me away with angled arms and clublike molds of hands.

As I walked down the center of the trench, the decaying scent grew stronger. Just as a flashlight beam waved overhead, I looked up and stopped, seeing bodies hanging from the arms of the presses. I looked down the row and saw more bodies, each hanging from the arms of a press, each chained with what looked like silver links to the bodies of the metal scarecrows.

Vampires. Likely ones who had come to the factory and tried to steal some of the drugged blood drink. Addicts who couldn't control themselves any longer.

The wight guards made much more sense now.

I had never seen so many dead and dying vampires in one place. It was early because no flies buzzed around the undead. As I moved forward an eye would roll, or a hand would flutter. I tried to walk on the farthest side of the belt from those. All the vampires still leaned in the direction I was walking, as if the drug still called to them.

I felt my back crawl, a shiver build, and I forced myself closer to one of the vampires. The one I looked at was aged, old, even for a vampire. Or maybe he just appeared that way. They looked similar to how a meth junkie looked on the street. Face pitted, hair stringy, teeth pitted and dirty in a gaping mouth.

And then the mouth moaned.

The flashlights stopped their dance and focused on some of the presses above me. I quickly and quietly ducked under the side of the trench, listening. The voices got louder. I could hear the tapping of boots on concrete, and above all, I could feel the chained vampires hanging in the cool, dead air above me.

I looked up at the vampire who had moaned. He had forced his head down against the silver cord on his neck so he could see me, and his mouth made dry, clicking noises. His eyes where almost a full white, with veins of black, and the intensity of his gaze forced me to duck lower.

The guards were coming closer. I could feel the hunger of the vampire above me, heard the snap of his jaw. The back of my neck tightened. All I could do was duck down and lie in the dark shadows of the concrete trench. Nothing would hide me here. I pulled out the nine-millimeter and gripped it tightly.

The vampire moaned again, a long, low trawling sound that broke a few times as it sank into a whisper. I looked up and saw hands appearing over the lip of the trench, holding flashlights. Both beams focused on the vampire. I could see how desperate the vamp was through the flickering shadows. It screamed and forced its face toward the guards, snapping at the air between them.

"It's this one, for sure," one of the guards said.

"It ain't going anywhere," the second guy said.

"We should report it, though, right?"

"I'm not reporting it," the other guy said. "They'll probably tell us to go check him out. And I didn't sign up to be some chained vampire's lunch."

"Me neither," the first guy said.

"So you heard nothing too?"

"Exactly."

"Works for me," the second guy said, and both flashlights turned off at the same time. After a long moment or two, footsteps started fading with distance.

As soon as I felt safe I slid out from under the press, avoiding the moaning vampire, and crept along the trench until I reached the part where it bored through the large wall into the inspection area. I snuck quickly along the length of the belt, staying in the middle where the belt was loose and softening my steps. A few seconds later I ducked through a hole in the wall between the two areas, and I was in the warehouse.

The warehouse, like the tire building area before it, was as big as a football field. There were square racks of tires all over the place. Some of the racks reached as high as the ceiling. More lights hung here than in the previous part of the plant, and the area was better lit. But the brightest lights came from somewhere in the middle of the room, beyond a bunch of tire tracks. Some sounds as well.

The boxes of tires formed nice, tight alleys, and I navigated through them to the center of the warehouse. The area was warm, and the air was thick with the smell of rubber and grease. As I got closer to the center, the sounds became voices, and then the voices became words.

"Raphael's not bringing the girl over." I recognized the speaker. It was Cole. *That guy is everywhere.* "He's busy tonight."

He was busy chasing Johnny and Gabrielle. I hoped they were okay. Part of me wondered if Johnny knew that keeping Raphael busy was helping me rescue Jen. He was a good man, and a friend I still had. Johnny knew what he was doing for me, for Jen. My right hand opened and closed a couple of times, knuckles tight. He was a good friend. Unlike me.

The other voice sounded frustrated. It was an older, weasel-like voice. "He knows he has to bring her, right? He knows she's got a schedule."

"He does." Cole's answer was short.

"Fuck," the other voice said. "Just fuck. He's probably chasing his vampire bitch and her toy. Dammit!"

"What's it matter to you?"

"It matters because she's got to get her treatment." The voice got angry. "He knows that, dammit."

"Does she need it, though?" Cole asked. "Or do you just need yours?"

There was a pause.

"I could use a treatment."

"Thought so," Cole said.

"We can't all be in perfect health," the older voice said. "I deserve what I've worked for."

I peered around the corner. A large area opened up in front of me, full of hospital beds and medical apparatuses. Here and there a woman was tucked into one of the beds and tied to the rails with Velcro straps. Cole was standing next to a much older guy in a white lab coat. I recognized him as the guy with Sarah in the car earlier. Both of them were maybe twenty feet away and facing away from me, in front of one of the beds. An arm hung off to the side, dark-skinned, lifeless, with a red tube leading away from it.

"This one's dead," the doctor said. He reached out and flicked a few switches on a machine next to the bed.

"You're working real wonders here, Doc," Cole said.

"Raphael keeps demanding more. We can't keep up." The doctor waited a moment. "He really needs to bring her."

"Call him up and tell him that, then."

"She's going to end up turning, and then he's going to come after me." The doctor's voice became really nasally. "You know he will."

They had to be talking about Sarah. I wondered what he meant about turning, and whether he meant into a vampire. She still had looked human in my ethereal site. And what had he meant about her needing to be on a schedule? What had they done to her?

I had left Sarah twice, once in the car at the hill, once in the movie theater with Raphael. She had told me to go, and she looked away at the theater like she wasn't worth saving. I bit my lip until my eyes moistened. She was a friend. She was Jen's sister. I was so tired of running. I was so tired of letting down my friends. They all deserved better than who I had become.

"If you're going to get blamed, you might as well do something to get blamed for, right?" Cole asked.

A long pause. "Fuck this," the doctor said. "We're going to do the other girl."

Cole laughed. "Look who actually has a ball or two. I'll be interested to see if they're still around when Raphael shows up."

"Fuck him. He should know better. He's going to need one of the sisters with Dominic still out there," the doctor complained. There was some kind of machine standing between him and a cot, with a rack and plastic tubes hanging from it, and he had started fiddling with it. "He fucked that up too."

A couple of guards came in then, from the direction of the roll-up doors in the area I had just been in. I couldn't tell if they were the guys holding the flashlights earlier or not. They both wore security ball caps and dark gray overalls. One of the guys filled out his uniform a little too much. The back of his shirt flapped behind him. The other guy was thinner and had his uniform tucked in.

"The wights are still screaming," the heavyset one said, breathing a little hard, like walking fast had been more than he could handle. "Something's got to be out there."

"Did you all send Mark?" Cole asked.

"He's not back," they both said.

The cop shook his head. "So you ran all this way to tell me nothing?"

"We thought you'd want to know."

"What, are you Sherlock Holmes now? Deducing shit from thin air?" Cole said. "If you didn't see it, I don't know it. So go out there and find Mark and get me something to go on."

"What if those things ate him?" the thinner guy asked.

"Then you better hope you can outrun your friend," Cole said. "Either way you guys go check it out. Or we'll have two more wights posted out there tomorrow night."

The fat guard looked at his friend, who half shrugged. They left much slower than they had come in.

"Something is happening out there," Cole told the doctor. "I'm going to walk around."

The doctor nodded, not really paying attention. He still was fiddling with the machine next to the dead girl and complaining to himself. "This thing isn't set up right at all. Would it hurt Raphael to get me some real nurses? Where the hell is Drew?"

Cole followed them out. The doctor swore and headed off in the other direction. When they both had left and I could no longer hear Cole's boots thudding on the concrete, I moved closer, as quietly as I could.

Women lay in the cots. There were at least ten of them, all set up next to machines with IVs hooked into their arms. Low plastic bags filled with an amber liquid hung from the racks next to each, with multiple tubes going in and out of each person. Most of the women were pale, almost white, and even though they were asleep their faces were scrunched up in pain. One of the women couldn't have been more than thirteen or fourteen.

I checked the woman the doctor had been standing next to. She was definitely dead. Her body was so thin and wasted her veins showed through her skin. Her hair was stringy and looked like it had come out in clumps on her pillow. My jaw flexed and I covered her face with the thin sheet.

Quickly I searched around. Arcane symbols had been traced all around the beds and the concrete underneath each cot, all done in thick blackish-red ink. Like a child had finger-painted them all with blood. Dark magic whirled through the air. I swallowed a few times to keep what was in my stomach in my stomach.

It was hard to figure out if the women were filling the bags or if the bags were filling them. Both of the bags hooked up to each woman were dark red in color. Possibly it was a little of both. I looked ethereally. The red bags pulsed with a rich red glow.

A variety of footprints circled the beds. The doctor's recent prints led away from me and across the floor. The same with Cole, although I smiled at Cole's footprints. They seemed much too small to carry a guy that big.

I ignored those trails and followed a channel of older footprints. They led me from this area and down a row of tire racks, and the number of steps was such that there must have been a lot of traffic over the years this way. This row of tall tire-rack sentries went on, and I walked down it, following the herd of prints. Finally I reached an area where the racks had been removed, forming a larger square theater-like room.

This room felt like an operating area. In the center was a large sigil, with dark red edges traced across the floor, all the way out to the very edges of the space. The center of the symbol looked like a bloody sunburst and glared an angry crimson. The lines of the symbol were thicker than my fist and glowed blackly.

The pattern seemed to pull at me. I tried taking a step backward out of the room and felt resistance like I walked through a deep pool of water, or blood. Sharp corners of the symbol cut everywhere, radiating a jagged menace in the ethereal plane.

In the middle of the symbol was another hospital bed. The tiny magics inscribed on the bed seemed outweighed by the dark symbol on the floor. In the bed, a body glowed a subdued blue, the sapphire blue of Caribbean waters, or maybe a cool summer day.

The scent of honeysuckle washed over me. I blinked back to normal vision and realized Jen lay in the cot, asleep. An IV with a clear liquid ran from a bag into the back of one hand. Equipment and trays lay around the bed, the same as you would find in the operating room of a hospital. Her arms and legs were strapped to the bars of the hospital bed with Velcro. Everything had little arcane symbols across them.

I forgot to breathe, I think. A large gasp came from my lungs, waking me. I took a step forward. Jen slept, pale in the yellow light, her bed angled up a little bit. A thin white cotton blanket covered her body. Her hair drifted around the pillow and surrounded her. I was struck by how much she reminded me of the young girl I used to sit by, and at the same time, I was highly aware of the beautiful woman she had become.

I clasped her hand like we were back in school. Her fingers slipped naturally through mine. Her hand was warm and soft to the touch. Her eyes opened, sleepily at first, as both of us fastened our hands to each other.

"Hey." Her lips curved in a little smile. Her voice was soft, quiet, and yet it still vibrated through my body.

"Hey," I said back.

For us, that had always been enough.

Jen tried to look around, to move, but whatever they had pumped her full of kept her down. Or maybe it was the magic around her. She still struggled a bit against the straps. For those moments I held her hand and kept telling her everything was going to be okay. Her movements slowed. Her hand gripped mine hard, and then finally relaxed.

I smiled to myself. It was time to get her out. I had had plenty of experience in sick bays and medical wards overseas. I turned off the IV before carefully removing the cannula from the back of her wrist. A tiny spot of blood welled up and I quickly bandaged it. I looked down. The cot was in the middle of the dark symbol, so I pushed it toward the edge a bit. Away from the IV bag, the machines, the center red sun, and the concentrated magics I felt there.

As I parked the cot, a motion caught the corner of my eye, and I looked across the room to the opposite corner. A large cage perched there, holding a group of both young and old women. Maybe ten or so. They were thin and huddled and collapsed. Most were sleeping.

An older lady stood against the bars and waved at me to come over.

She had dark gray hair tied up in a bun. I didn't know what they were here for, but from the look of them and the cots next door it was part of the process of making the drug, and that process was going to end tonight. I would have to figure out a way to get them out too. I put my index finger to my lips. She nodded, but waved once more, urgently. I nodded in return.

Jen would come first. And she was strapped to the hospital bed. I winced each time I peeled a Velcro strap off. No matter how careful I was, each one made a loud, long scratching sound as it came apart. First her legs, and then her arms. And then I smiled and let out a deep breath. Jen was free.

Then the old lady called out a warning. I looked over at her, angry, before seeing that the doctor and another man were headed this way. The second guy wore a security guard outfit with his ball cap on backward. They passed the cage with the women and stopped as soon as they saw me.

There was a moment of recognition by the doctor. The security guard started talking into his walkie-talkie. I pulled out both nine-millimeters and stepped toward them, keeping myself between the two of them and Jen. Backward Ball Cap chewed gum with a smacking sound, like the ticking of an extra-large clock.

Ball Cap kept talking into his microphone. Unless I was ready to shoot him he didn't look like he was going to stop. And not much I could do about it now. I had lost the element of surprise.

So I walked toward the center of the room in measured steps. I moved so that Jen continued to be behind me. The old lady gripped the bars in both hands. She looked frustrated. I got within a few steps of the doctor and the guard before stopping, holding a gun on each.

"You ain't got much time." Ball Cap let go of the walkie-talkie and grinned at me. The ticking sound I had heard was actually him chewing gum with his mouth open. The sound instantly put me in the *I don't like this guy* camp.

"That all depends on what I need the time for," I told him.

"Fergus Grimm." One side of the doctor's mouth didn't move as well as the other. That side of his face seemed stiff, and the eyelid drooped a little. His coat had a name tag that read Browner, M.D. "Raphael's not going to be happy you're still around."

"I'm sure Raphael knows I haven't left," I said. "But I hear he's busy with other things."

"You shouldn't move her." The doctor looked over my shoulder at Jen and stepped toward her. Closer to me. "She's not ready."

"Hey." I wiggled a gun at Browner, M.D. "Guy with a gun here."

"Raphael's not going to like it," the doctor repeated. His voice came out extra-nasally. His eyes had winces at the corners, and it looked like the wince was permanent.

"If you keep walking that way, you won't have to worry about being the one that tells him," I said. I pushed him in the chest with a muzzle of the gun, and he finally seemed to realize I actually had a gun. He stepped back.

I looked over at one of the empty medical cots, Velcro straps hanging to the side. I looked at Ball Cap. "I'm going to need you to get on that cot."

Ball Cap shook his head, chomping gum like a cow chewing cud. I had no idea a person could make the sounds coming out of one side of his mouth while grinning with the other side. "You're going to have to shoot me, Chief."

"Nah, I don't have to shoot you." I swung my pistol. The butt of the gun connected with Ball Cap's temple. His eyes rolled up in his head and he tipped over on the concrete. "I just have to do that."

The doctor was looking down at the guard. "You've knocked out the only help I had."

"You don't get it," I told him. "You're not going to need any help tonight. Unless it's the kind that comes back and unties you."

"Just shoot him!" the old lady yelled from the cage.

I rolled my eyes. There was always a backseat driver. The old lady had pressed herself even tighter to the bars, both hands white-knuckled. Like she was trying to pull herself through to get to the doctor. I waved downward at her, the gun hanging in my hand, in a settle-down type of motion.

I looked back at the doctor. He peered at Jen over my shoulder. I wondered what Cole meant when he had asked the doctor if he needed his treatment.

I asked him, "What are you doing with these women?"

"Them?" The doctor sneered. Or maybe that was just how he looked, with part of his face frozen. "You look like you can breathe on your own. I'm sure you can guess."

"Here's what I think," I said. "You use these women here to make the drug you feed to all the vampires. Something in that drug allows them to be controlled. And whatever you did to Sarah, her blood allows Raphael to control those vampires."

The doctor shrugged.

"So why is Sarah on a schedule?" I asked. "Is it something in the drug? Do the other women have one too?"

"Them?" The doctor shook his head. "No, no. Only the controller. And only because Raphael is using her too much. She just needs a little maintenance."

He talked like Sarah was a car, getting an oil change. I squared my jaw. "So she's okay as long as she checks herself into the demon Betty Ford Clinic every once in a while?"

This factory was a one-stop demonic shop. And this doctor was at the head of it. This place was littered with demonic symbols and bathed in dark magic, some weird blend of modern science and the supernatural. They had used medicine and magic to twist Sarah into a human IV bag, one that gave power to the person who drank her blood.

And Jen was about to be next. I nodded back to her. "What about her? Have you done anything to her?"

The doctor swallowed. "Not yet."

I put the barrel of my gun square on the doctor's forehead. "I don't really like you, Doc. How can I make sure you're not lying?"

"For heaven's sake, just shoot him!" the lady called out.

The doctor's closed his eyes briefly under the barrel. "Would you shut that witch up?"

I waved the lady down with one hand. If all those women were witches, and the drink was made from them, then that was one piece of the puzzle. Live supernatural creatures from which a drug was made that helped control vampires. But also—in the process—allowed the doctor to reverse his symptoms a bit. Maybe something he learned during the creation of the drug. Or had he learned it performing another ritual?

What else was common to the drug, to Sarah, to these witches, in this town? What common thread tied everything together? Gabrielle had told me Raphael was unique to the vampire world. A real human baby born to a vampire.

It clicked. "You were the doctor that created Raphael."

"I was at the very beginning of my understanding." The doctor smiled. Proud. "I have learned so much since then." He lightly touched the stiff side of his face.

The witch in the cage wanted me to kill the doctor. And now I wanted to. Here was the guy who had started everything that had happened in this town. The man who had created the monster that was Raphael. Who had threatened Jen to get me here, and ultimately kidnapped her. Who had kidnapped Sarah and made her into some drug-blooded junkie. Who had killed Danny.

The doctor leaned back from me.

"So, why Sarah? Why Jen?" I asked, my voice cold. "What's special about them?"

He waited a long moment. "What's different about all of us? Why do you have black hair and not red? Genetic code."

I kept the barrel against his forehead. My finger stayed tight on the trigger. This man had done so much to destroy Grafton and the lives of my friends and family. He had done it maybe unknowingly, but I wasn't concerned about how he paved his own road to hell. I just wondered if I could be the one to send him there.

The doctor swallowed then. His tongue licked the side of his lips.

"Well, well, well." A deep voice resonated through the factory. Cole. "Seems like I keep running into you, Grimm."

I looked over to where the doctor and Ball Cap had first come in. Cole stood there, smiling an easy smile. Like he was coming in to settle some friendly neighborhood dispute. Behind him came the guards from earlier, who had reported the guard missing.

I looked at Cole but kept a gun on the doctor. "Probably my dumb luck, I guess."

"Probably is," Cole agreed. "You think you'd learn one of these days."

The two guards behind Cole walked tight like their knees were locked. Both of them had their pistols out and held in both hands, their arms too straight.

"Why don't you tell your friends to lower their guns before someone accidentally gets shot?" I said.

"Let me tell you how this usually works," Cole said. His hands were on his belt, one hand next to his holster. "The guys with more guns get to tell the guy with a couple of guns what to do."

"I'm not a fan of that." I moved one of my guns to cover the group of them. "Got another idea?"

Cole lifted one shoulder and let it down. His whole uniform moved with the motion. "We could always start shooting."

I frowned. It didn't look like this was a situation where they cared who I had hostage. I kept the gun on the doctor anyway and looked at him. "Hard to believe you don't have more friends."

"Be interesting to see where this comes down," Cole said. "Seems to me like you're not the shoot-it-out type. I got you pegged as more of a cut-and-run."

The big cop looked relaxed, though one hand rested close to a big .357 strapped to his hip. More boots slapped concrete, coming from the entrance of the other area. Then some behind me. All of a sudden, the echoes were everywhere. Police started to appear, some from the gas station, others in body armor and carrying assault rifles.

"The longer this goes, the more people you're going to have to shoot," Cole told me.

My eyes flicked around. The old lady was frozen to the bars. I pointed for her to get down. She did, pulling the other women in the cage with her to the floor.

"You enjoying this?" I asked Cole.

The cop grinned. "I won't lie, you've been a lot of fun for me."

Cole raised a hand and waved a finger in a circle. The three policemen in black flak jackets split up, two to one side, one to the other. They began to circle me, ducking behind machines, flanking me. A few moments from now I'd be surrounded.

I looked back at Jen's cot. Right now I was still between everyone and her. But in a few seconds, she would be in the line of fire. And I was outnumbered and outgunned and had no ghosts nearby.

It seemed such a waste to get this far, to get right here, and have it all be taken away now. I could lie to myself and say that I had been running from a demon to protect the world from the Key, but I had really been running from the world and using the Key as an excuse. I saw that now. People I loved and cared about had been hurt because I hadn't been brave enough to stand up for them. Because I had seen what had happened when I failed.

A man is what he does. Parker's words.

I had a chance to become something else now.

And I took it.

I glanced at the doctor. The guy who had set all this in motion.

So there weren't any ghosts around. I could always make a few.

The doctor's eyes opened wide just as I pulled the trigger.

His head ricocheted back at the loud crack of the pistol, a pattern of blood instantly painting the floor behind him. The faded outline of the doctor knelt before me for a brief moment, his eyes wide-open, his mouth about to say something.

I tapped into the doctor's ghost even as it slipped its human shell. Wisps and motes of glowing ethereal light around his spirit became a stream; the stream became a torrent. With it I hardened my muscles, my skin. I had always been able to make myself stronger, faster, tougher. I didn't know if it was possible, but this time I wanted skin hard enough to stop bullets.

Only a brief moment had passed, but in my slowed-down senses, the shooting had already begun.I pulled as hard as I could at the ethereal energy that rested behind the ghost of Browner, M.D. Power began to run through my muscles, my skin, but I needed more.

Slowly, the bullets spun their way through the air toward me.

Slowly my skin hardened around me.

The doctor's ghostly face looked much the same before his death. Eyes slightly open in realization. A recognition of what had happened to him. And then something changed.

His eyes focused and his face twisted in rage. Like a child throwing a tantrum, his arms snatched at me, but passed harmlessly through my body. At that same moment, I pulled enough to consume him.

I, or Browner as me or me as Browner, whoever and whatever I was in his life's memory, we looked down at a young girl on a cot, red hair tumbled across the hospital pillow, and the doctor's crotch swelled up with anticipation.

Tiny red tubes ran into her wrist, and her eyes opened back at me, at

Browner, and they were drugged and hazy and yet a fury and hate still shone behind the clouds. She worked her mouth in disgust as the doctor leaned over and traced his thumb around her lips, grinning and imagining the things he would do as he drank on her blood and lay with her on the cot ...

A fleeting memory of a younger Browner, looking at himself in the mirror, feeling a side of his face with his hand, poking and prodding, and watching the face not respond at each touch ...

Memory after memory of Browner in a medical cot here in the factory, with a different girl. One of the girls who flickered by was Sarah.

A vision of Dominic, shaking his head no at the doctor, with Browner holding the frozen side of his face and demanding to be made a vampire and the Vampire Lord laughing and laughing back at him ...

A last vision of Browner injecting himself with some of the red stuff. Only it looked a little different in the vision. A body behind him on the cot, covered in blood, the cot itself lit up by the arcane symbols underneath it. The doctor pushed the needle into his skin and smiled. In the vision, his face was unfrozen ...

And then his ghost was gone. Popped like a soap bubble.

It was just in time. Dozens of bullets tattooed me. And then ricocheted off my body as flat little coins, tinkling around me on the floor.

There was a pause as everyone who had shot at me waited for me to fall to the floor. And a longer pause when they realized I was still standing. The *tinking* of the last few bullets bouncing around me filled the empty air.

I looked at Cole and grinned. Cole looked back in fascination. Everyone else started to reload their guns.

I began shooting. Ghosts popped up around me, and I pulled at each one. The fire alarm sounded and the sprinkler went off.

I pulled and pulled at every spirit that showed. Time slowed again. The air around me was still. The dead guards stood like ghostly statues of their human counterparts. Drops of water hung in the air around everyone.

The live guards began firing again. Bullets arced their way toward me. I could see them submarine through each drop of water that hung in the air.

Each ghost I pulled fought me much as Browner's had. But I kept pulling. All that mattered was I had another ethereal source to power me. I would use them all up until I could get Jen safe and out of here. I shot and pulled and danced through bullets and shot and pulled until the air was full of rounds and casings and fine mists of blood hung in the air around each corpse.

I stood over someone on the sidewalk, kicking someone's side over and over. The man curled into a ball, and something red and bubbly slipped out of his mouth as he tried to gasp another breath into him.

I twisted and shot again and pulled, using the nine-millimeter to bat aside a bullet and emptying the magazine into the cops behind me. As each cop died, I pulled and pulled and was taken from memory to memory:

I forced the kid's head down, making him take my belt with his teeth and pull open my pants ...

I was loading women into the back of a large moving truck, women with silver circlets on their wrists and their heads down, and I grinned at the ass of one ...

I was in a dank kitchen, punching some woman over and over in the mouth, teeth scattering on the floor below us ...

I couldn't help it, somewhere I stopped what I was doing and dry-heaved, all in slow motion, all with bullets nosing their way through the air above me. Something stung me along my ribs, and then my thigh, and then something slowing dug into the meat of my arm.

I screamed at the pain. And at the memories. I pulled more and more and felt like I needed to get faster, stronger. I needed my skin to be harder than steel.

Armor grew out of my skin. Black and blue plates, like the sleeve of a gauntlet, slid over my arms, my chest. Bullets hit the armor and dropped to the ground. I didn't know what it was, and I couldn't stop to look at myself, I just kept tapping ghosts and pulling the trigger.

These memories would haunt me. Whoever those people had been, they weren't cops. They were evil in intent and deeds, and I felt their lusts and passions and joy as they beat and killed and did unspeakable things to others. I got angry and pulled at each of them until their ghost popped and they longer could be seen in the ethereal world.

Good riddance to all of them.

The entire time I stayed in front of Jen, making sure no bullets passed me. The guards watched a man blur before them, a man too fast to see clearly, gone before they could aim and pull the trigger. Bullets started going everywhere.

Cole popped up from behind a rack of tires. I paused for a moment as we faced off. The water from the sprinklers ran down Cole's face and seemed to reveal another face deep inside him, like his bones underneath the skin were structured wrong. We both shot at the same time. Bullets thunked into me and fell off as little discs. I pulled the trigger again and again until Cole ducked behind the tires and I lost track of him. I tapped another ghost.

This entire time I felt alive in a way I had never felt alive before. Supernatural. Unstoppable. Bullets bounced off me and I was something otherworldly.

Then after a last pull an electric pain shot through my entire body. Blue-white light arced across my skin. I felt a tug on my back and the entire plant dimmed as something flapped over my head like a hood or a back of a cape.

Moments later a wave of energy burst out from me in a ripple of blue-white force, rushing outward like an explosion. The concrete floor below me shattered into a thousand circular cracks. The force blew back bullets hanging in the air, tossed bodies into crates and machines, broke machines apart, and slung parts of metal frames to dance across the concrete floor. The cage of women crashed against a machine and slid away from me a bit, only stopping when they hit a rack of tires.

Then it was over. I stood there, leaning over one leg, breathing deeply and barely hearing anything through the echoing roars of dying gunfire. My clothes lay ragged on me, torn to shreds by bullets. The sprinklers sputtered above me and finally died out.

I looked at my arms. The blue-black armor still hung around my forearms. I knocked on one, and it was dense, almost like bone, but there was a tiny metallic ping, like a soft bell. It seemed to ring forever. A quick second later, the plates disappeared back under my skin. It happened so fast I didn't believe what I was seeing.

Between them and the explosion, I had no idea what I had done. I didn't understand what had happened. Nothing like that had ever happened to me before.

And I had no idea who I was. I had seen things in sketches here and there like the armor that had appeared on my forearm, on demons with evil-looking twisted armor, curved and spiked and black as night. And fucking armor had just grown out of my arms, blue and black and hard as steel.

It took a long moment for me to move after that. Not one of the guards or the cops who had stayed were alive. I couldn't see Cole anywhere in the wreckage around me. Smoldering flames threw shifty shadows across the far wall.

I looked back at Jen, still lying on the bed, asleep. The water ran down her like a liquid sheen, pasting her clothes to her skin. Her hair lay around her head as if she had just risen from a pool. I could see every outline of her, the curve of her hip to her stomach, the swell of her breasts pushing against the thin cotton of her shirt. Something in me stirred, hard, and I swallowed it back down.

Whatever had happened to me, whatever I had become, I wasn't sure I could do it again. Wasn't even sure what it was. Or if I wanted it back. I could worry about later. For now, I had to get Jen out of here.

I turned back to Jen's bed, trying to get her to wake. Her eyes opened, unfocused. As I leaned over her bed, she reached out and brushed against my arm, her fingers trailing down without direction. The touch was electric.

"Hey," she whispered.

"We already did that," I told her, and picked her off the bed with both arms. She snuggled against me, and the warmth of her body pressed against my chest.

I turned around and saw the cage of women. The older woman with the dark hair stood at the side of the cage closest to me. I hurried over. The fight was over, for now, but Raphael was still out there. I wouldn't be surprised to see him pop in at any moment.

The older woman stayed at the bars. Arcane symbols were intricately carved over the bars and lock. Water glistened over everything in the pale light. The lock on the door was thick and black and had four dials for numbers as well as a hole for a key. Tiny etchings were cut over the metal, symbols that looked hieroglyphic. I jiggled the lock. As thick as it was, the explosion looked to have broken something in the mechanism itself and the tongue of the cage flapped loosely.

"The big guy has the key," she said. *Cole.* The way she talked, her air of certainty, reminded me in some way of a stern librarian.

"We'll figure something else out," I said. I laid Jen down against a sideways-flipped cot. Then I found a thick metal bar and set it between the bars of the cage and the lock of the door. After a few jerks, and one final pry, the lock snapped and the cage door popped open.

"Thank heaven," the woman said. I helped her get the rest of the women up, and the older lady led out a younger woman, with red hair. They had similar features and I recognized the younger girl from Browner's memories.

I was glad I shot him.

The older lady held her daughter for a moment, then walked off. She held up a finger when I asked her what she was doing. After a moment, she found the doctor's corpse and spat on it, cursing.

"Though maybe it's a blessing, of sorts," she said. Her voice was like steel. Hard, without a trace of an accent or flexibility. "If he hadn't been so interested in my daughter, he might have bled her to death. At least she's alive."

"For now," I said. I picked up Jen, who stirred a little in my arms and murmured something in my ear. "We've got to get moving."

"After we free the others," the lady said.

I looked back at where I had come in. Some of the tire racks had flipped over after the explosion, but the path was manageable. "Let's hurry, then."

We got to the first area and the older woman organized everything. Had each person who could walk unhook the women who could walk. There were a few that couldn't, and they had a couple of women push each of those cots. We headed toward the roll-up doors.

I pulled Jen up slightly on my shoulder, resetting her weight, and heard her moan, low, like a whimper in the middle of a bad dream. I turned around, saw the rest of the women behind me, waiting. Those on the cots were being carried by a group of women. The older lady stood right behind me.

"We go out the front," I said. "Stay close."

The older lady nodded. "Just keep us with you."

We took off.

We rushed through the plant, moving as fast as I dared. I wondered if

Raphael knew what was happening right now. If he was headed this way. I wondered if Cole had survived and if, even now, he was waiting outside the factory to start a fight that I wouldn't be able to finish.

The entrance to the plant still was another area away. My feet started feeling like concrete blocks, harder to move with each stop. Jen lay across my chest, the featherlight touches of her hair brushing my cheek. Her skin was warm to the touch, and there was a rightness to how her arm hung around the back of my neck.

The area with the large tire-building machines was the size of a couple of football fields and took forever to run through. The emergency lighting was far weaker here, the pale yellow globes of light barely reaching the huge, dark shadows of the machines. Here and there small red strobes turned, spinning and throwing out flashes of alarm. A cop could hide anywhere in that.

We finally reached the end of that area and ran through the double doors leading to the front offices of the plant. The women followed me as fast as they could. All of our shoes made the little squishing sounds shoes make when they are wet, a spitter-spatter kind of sound.

I carried Jen toward the front entrance. A short hallway held a pair of time clocks, and past those were the doors to the outside. And then we were in the parking lot.

A quick fear ran through me as I walked out to a couple of police cars parked in the front of the lot. The entire group of us stopped as one as soon as we saw them. All the cars were empty, and I let out a big breath. They likely wouldn't need drivers for a while.

I didn't think I could drive cop cars unnoticed around Grafton for too long, but it turned out that I had something even better. The familiar rumble of my Camaro fired up from the back of the parking lot. The car pulled out from between a couple of the factory vans, and the hideaway headlights flipped up and over, flashing their brights twice.

I turned back to the women. The older woman had stayed in the front, her black-and-gray hair beginning to curl as it dried. She, with the help of her daughter, was holding a third witch up between them.

"Stay here a moment," I said. She nodded.

I ran over, and even as fast as I was moving I kept expecting to hear the crack of a gunshot, to feel the tearing of flesh as the bullet ran through me. But the lot was empty of everyone but us. I got to my car. Nick sat behind the wheel. I was impressed that he had made it. Maybe I shouldn't be. What did I know about him, really?

Carefully I laid Jen into the backseat, placing her against the side panel of the car, snugging the seat belt around her to help hold her in. For a moment her eyes opened, little slivers of blue, catching mine. Her eyes were clearer than back in the factory, and I wondered how much of her slumber was drug-related, and how much was the dark magic inscribed there. Nick tapped impatiently at the wheel. The wights howled in the fields around us.

"A couple of cops ran out a few minutes ago," he said. "Jumped in cars and took off. That Cole too."

"Damn," I said. I had hoped he had been caught in the explosion. "Hold here a minute, would you?"

"Might want to hurry," Nick said.

"I know."

I shut the door and ran back to the women. The older lady who had talked to me from the cage was going through the group. Maybe taking stock. She turned when I got back.

"There's a few of the factory vans there." I pointed. "I was thinking we could use those to transport everyone."

"We know them," the lady said, shortly. "It'll be better to be taken out of here in one than taken in, I guess."

The memory of one of the guards leading women into one of the vans came to mind. I moved in to help carry one of the women who was drifting in and out of consciousness. She was much lighter than Jen, bony, her hip digging into my side as we hurried to the vans.

I opened the back doors of the cargo vans and found them empty. There was a faint earthy smell from them, like freshly turned earth. I laid the bony girl inside one, ran around to the front, and opened the door. Found a key tucked into the sun visor and gave it to the older woman. The rest of the women all got in the back, smell of graves or not.

The older lady turned and held out her hand.

"Tabitha," she said.

I arched an eyebrow.

"Tabitha." She nodded to the back of the van and held out her hand. "Thank you. My daughter will live. Two hours ago, I didn't believe that would be the case."

"Grimm." I shook her hand. The rest of the women piled up in the van, and the woman with the key got in and fired it up. "Best of luck to you all."

"Where are you going?" she asked.

"Find a place to hole up," I said.

"Are you going to go after *them*?" She left no doubt who she was talking about. The creator of the drugs.

Killing the doctor had been the first step to cleansing Grafton. Getting rid of the vampire plague would be next. Ultimately this fight would end up between Raphael and me. And maybe it was fitting, coming back to where all this was started.

So somewhere along the way, I had decided to take this all the way. Strangely I felt a certain peace. "I am."

"Then I wish you luck," Tabitha said. "If you find yourself in Lewiston, look us up. If we can help you, we will."

I had no idea where Lewiston was. But I nodded my thanks and headed back to the car. The van's engine started behind me.

I got to the Camaro. Jen was huddled against the inside of the car. Her eyes opened as I got in. The car rocked underneath me for a moment. She was coming out of it.

"We need to hurry." Nick still tapped the steering wheel.

I buckled up. Nick pushed down on the gas and the Camaro spun down the road, heading past the security shack at the front entrance to the plant. In the night the shadowed trees passed like quiet sentries.

In the distance, the taillights of the van flashed and then they disappeared as the van rounded a corner. It was silent, and I looked back, seeing the factory dwindle in the distance, imagining tiny figures chained around it. Crazy.

Soon we passed the burning building of the service station. I had stopped the drug from being made, and by killing the doctor I hoped I would keep it from ever being made again. Did it tip the scales back onto the side of good? Maybe a little. And Jen was safe now. Would Greg think all of that a poor trade for his life? I didn't know.

I reached down, felt around both my arms. My fingers touched warm skin and solid muscle. I felt nothing abnormal like the armor that had somehow come out of me. My body felt, well, real. Like itself. Had I imagined what had happened?

It wasn't like armor grew out of people every day. My jacket and shirt were shredded with bullet holes and where the armor plates had slid out. I wiggled my finger through one of the holes in my shirt. The edge of the hole felt a little charred. I couldn't have imagined the plate, I didn't think.

"Did you see Sarah?" Nick asked.

"What?" I was still wondering what it was that I had become. A few days ago I had been someone who could see ghosts and could use them to tap into some kind of ethereal power. That was all I had been and known. Now I wondered if I was even human.

"Sarah," Nick repeated. His hands grasped the steering wheel tightly. His voice was strained.

A flush of heat washed over my face. Sarah wasn't there, but I had killed the doctor without finding out how to help her. And Sarah needed him to be healed of whatever had been done to her. She needed some kind of reset. I just hadn't had the time to find out what, or how.

It was too late now. The place was destroyed. An explosive force had burst out from me, something I couldn't have controlled and had no idea how it had occurred. It had left behind cracked and lifeless demonic symbols and broken machines.

The guy who had created it all was dead now. I had killed him to save Jen. I had destroyed the drug and what they were doing at the factory. I had saved the other witches there. But had I doomed Sarah at the same time?

"You fuck," Nick said.

"Nick." I didn't know how to begin telling him what I had overheard. Or how it all had gone down. The vision of Browner having sex with Sarah ran through my mind. How could I explain any of that to Nick?

Nick shook his head. "Fuck you, Grimm, I should have gone in myself."

"She wasn't there, Nick," I said. I still struggled with how to tell Nick what I had seen, when I didn't know enough about it myself. What had the doctor meant, turn? Turn into what?

Nick's knuckled tightened on the grip of the wheel.

"I know you feel bad, Nick," I said. "You'd have never made it."

He turned to look at me. "What makes you so sure?"

The trees raced by the window behind his head. His stare was angry, intense, the stare of someone who had looked into the abyss and liked it. *Nick is a dark fucker,* I remembered Johnny telling me.

Nick stared at me long enough that I began to worry about the car drifting off the road. I remember Nick running through the wights, almost too fast to see. I wondered what Nick was now, and who he might have been had I stayed. Did I rescue Jen and leave her sister? Did I forget all about Sarah? These thoughts all jumbled together into one, and through all of it, I felt ashamed that I had let him down.

"Look, Nick," I said. He wasn't wrong. I had rescued Jen, and everything else had come second. I had a chance to find out more about what had happened to Sarah, and I had killed the man responsible with no thought to the consequences. I had done that even after Nick distracted the wights for me, knowing Nick had asked me to help him, and knowing what he felt for Sarah. "She's alive, right? We'll find her, and then we'll figure out what they did to her."

"What's that mean?" he asked.

"I don't know, man," I said. "I didn't get a chance to find out. I'm sorry."

"Fuck you and your sorry." Nick took a curve too tight. We all slid to one side. I checked on Jen, saw her place a hand out on the seat to keep herself steady. "You are sorry, a sorry piece of shit. You always just did what you wanted anyway. Just like Raphael."

I opened my mouth and he cut me off.

"I figured it out, over the years. You always talked a big game, and yeah, you looked out for us, but it really was all about *her*." He nodded to the backseat. "You could have cared shit about the rest of us."

"That's bullshit, Nick," I said. Wondering inside how much of what he said might be true. I had been in my share of childhood fights, and a lot of them had seemed to be protecting our gang, but maybe I was lying to myself about why I had done so.

In the end, memory smears a lot of things in a way that makes it hard to remember exactly what happened, and I couldn't say how much of what I really did was to impress Jen and how much was really to protect people I loved.

Nick was driving faster and faster, and I could hear his breathing, raging swallows of air in and out.

"Nick, we'll find her." Jen's voice, shallow from the back. I looked back and her eyes were open. Less drugged.

"Are you sure?" Nick's eyes flicked to the rearview.

"She's my sister," Jen said. Simply. Her voice was weak, though it still resonated in my chest. "She'll be up the Hill."

The Hill. A nickname from the Grafton folk, naming the place up on the hill where Raphael's family mansion stood. A gated place, a guarded place. And now, I knew, a place full of vampires.

Nick knew it too. He hit the brakes, hard, and the car slid down the road, nose down. We all leaned forward, put our hands out, and rocked back as the car stopped.

The Camaro sat in the road and rumbled.

"Fuck," he shouted, then punched the steering wheel a couple of times. *"Fuuucckkk!"*

Jen leaned up. "Nick, we'll get her back."

"We can't go to the Hill, right?" I said. That was where they would all be. I had made the decision to stay for my friends, but running up into where Raphael could summon all those vampires. And he had bested my mother, easily. What hope would I have?

Nick looked ready to swing at me and somehow looked darker, dangerous.

"We just have to be smart," Jen said.

"Smart," I said. I had no excuse, and Nick yelling at me that he couldn't trust me had struck close to home. Part of me was ashamed at having chosen Jen over helping Sarah, but I would do it again. I looked out the passenger window. "Was smart what got you trapped in that factory?"

Even as I said the words, I instantly regretted them. I had a habit of saying things before thinking, but I had never done it to Jen before. The corner of Nick's lips turned up a little.

"Gus," she said softly, surprised.

"Yeah." I caught her eyes in the rearview mirror; they had widened slightly. I looked down at the floorboards. "I'm sorry, Jen."

"We don't need him, Jen," Nick said. "Can't trust him."

I looked away and tried to make an excuse. "Been a rough night."

There was a long moment when I could feel her staring at me, even as

I ducked my head. Her voice was soft as she near whispered, "Gus, I've never known you to be afraid."

She got to the core of it, that fast. I shook my head and closed my eyes, tight. I had lived a life where I couldn't afford to be brave, where my only option had been running, and running, and running. Being brave meant dying, and dying meant giving a demon a parting gift, the Key. Being brave meant getting held down while your friend gets beat to death with a rock. Being brave meant losing friends, and I couldn't lose them. I couldn't lose Jen.

No matter how that shaped me. And I was too far down that road to be able to turn back. Who I had become was the person I had to live with.

"You don't know," I answered her.

"I don't know what, Gus?" she said. Her eyes were soft, but her voice held a needy edge.

"You don't know what I've done," I said. My voice took on a hoarse growl. "What I've done, what I've had to go through. What I *am* going through. What I've sacrificed. *You don't know*."

"Maybe I don't know," she countered, "but you don't know what we've been through either. But we all can. Friends share it all, Gus."

"I don't trust him anyway, Jen," Nick said. "We'd be better off without him."

"Be quiet for a moment, Nick," Jen told him. "You once told me you couldn't run, Gus. That you weren't made that way."

I shook my head. Thought about night after night of being alone, of living in cheap motel after cheap motel, of what had happened in my service overseas. Thought about back in the factory, of the slicing, thrilling pain of something sliding out from under my skin. Of feeling the amount of force that had burst out from me in one, frozen instant, when bullets had been flicked away from me, guards and policemen whirled through the air, machines had cracked apart ...

I was scared, I was alone, I was afraid, and I didn't know if I was human.

"Gus," she said, "you've got to share it."

I shook my head, felt my eyes water. Swung my door open and got out of the car. The night air was cold and wet, and I could feel the weight of the dark skies press down on me. I took a big breath of the scent of the fresh green of the forest and a little of the exhaust of the Camaro. I took a couple of steps away from the car.

"Jen," Nick said, the Camaro chugging, "we can't wait here long."

There was the pop of a seat leaning forward. Cloth slid against leather. In a moment Jen was beside me, her hand on my arm. I didn't look at her.

"Gus," she said, "you don't have to tell me if you don't want to."

I shook my head, kept looking up. Hoping that by doing so the water in my eyes would stay there and not spill down my cheeks. If I looked at her right now I would lose control and cry, and at that moment it felt important to have control over something.

She had known where I was all these years. I wondered if she knew about that day with Danny. How could I tell her I was there and couldn't stop it? I had told her I couldn't run, but that had been pure ego. There was no way I could tell her I had watched Danny get his head beaten in with a bat.

If we headed up the Hill, Raphael could stop me with just a word, turn me against my friends with *just a thought*. He could derail whatever plan we came up with, just by talking to me. I would be leading my friends up to their certain massacre. And Raphael would make me watch, again.

Here was Grafton, dead and dying. My friends, the last good people left here in town. And me, a person who once told a girl he couldn't run, he wasn't made that way. Maybe a man is what he's done, and can never be who he wants to be.

Jen slid her arm around my back, leaned into my shoulder. Her other arm wrapped around my chest, and she hugged me tightly. She was warm against the night, and her arms encircled me as though inside her grasp was another world where none of what was happening mattered and all that existed was she and I.

"It's okay," Jen whispered. "Hold it in, if you have to."

I held it in. I was afraid of letting it all out. I was afraid if I did I would become something less and fail them all, that they would all die, that they all would be killed in front of me, despite anything I wanted.

Then the demons and vampires would win, and I would be the only person left standing, and standing at the right hand of Raphael. It was a horrifying vision, and one I couldn't share because I was too scared of it. I had been alone for so long, and I was afraid if I let them in, it would only lead to their deaths.

Maybe we stood there a minute. Maybe it was hours. It was quiet in her arms, and warm, and the faint scent of honeysuckle swirled around me. Finally I took a deep, shuddering breath in, then let it all out in one big exhale.

"Better now?" Jen asked.

I wasn't sure, but I nodded, once.

"Then let's go." Her arms opened and let the night back in. Her hand dragged across my lower back, then patted my arm.

"Anytime, princess." Nick rolled his eyes and pointed to his wrist. I think he had forgotten he was the reason we were stopped on the road to begin with.

Was I imagining this too? Was any of this real? Could any of this actually have happened to one person in just a couple of days? Numbly I slid back into the passenger seat and shut the door with a solid clunk.

Jen looked at Nick. "Take us to the church. Father Benjamin will put us up for the night."

"Why not Parker's?" Nick asked.

"I don't care if you don't like the church, Nick." Jen's voice strengthened. "Just take us there."

Nick turned forward with a sigh and pushed the gas. The car jerked, slid a second on some loose rocks, the front swiveling left and right for a second, pointing one way, then the other. I felt the shift of the machine around me, the weight of the car as the tires took hold and shot us down the road, the press of force as I was pushed gently back into my seat, and the Camaro took as all up the hill and into the night.

CHAPTER TWENTY-THREE

Father Benjamin opened the door on the first knock, took one look, and let us in. He was dressed much the same as I had seen in the diner, dark slacks and a priest's frock. For a moment he looked past us as if searching for someone. I caught his eyes and shook my head.

While we stood at the doorway the priest blessed himself at the holy font and made sure to press wet fingers on each of our foreheads. I tensed up as his fingers neared. All of a sudden I feared I wouldn't pass this test, after what had happened at the factory.

A moment later, though, his fingers left a cool droplet to run down the side of my nose. I let out a sigh of relief. Jen took her test with a smile. Nick seemed ill at ease during the process but didn't burst into flames either.

The old priest forced a laugh. "Well, none of you seem to be demons. Or vampires."

Nick wiped a drop of water off his face, snorted, and walked past us all.

"Thanks for having us, Father," Jen said.

"Always a pleasure, Miss Cooper," Father Benjamin said, and shut the doors to the church and then slid a thick wooden bar behind them. "Glad to see you well."

"I'm sorry about Greg," I said, and told him about what had happened at the store. Jen held my arm as we spoke.

The priest nodded near the end. "It was a good death.""You say that," I said. Greg had gone into the store likely looking for me, but it seemed such a large mistake by a guy like him. A veteran killer of the supernatural. "But it seemed pointless, to me."

"His partner's death really caught him." The priest said. "He may have just wanted to make a difference, somewhere."

"But he didn't."

"I would argue he thought he had," the priest said. "He would be happy, I think. To be a part in the rescue, the destruction of the drug, all that."

"Sarah didn't tell me," Jen told Father Benjamin. "I'm not sure she knew."

"Knows what?" I said. "About what her blood does to vampires?"

Jen looked at me funny. "You've seen it?"

"Up close and personal," I said.

"We just thought, for the longest time, that all Raphael was doing was getting vampires hooked on something like meth to humans," Jen said. "None of us had any idea, even when they kidnapped Sarah, what that could do."

"Until right before you called me," I said.

Jen nodded. Father Benjamin asked her something, and the two of them began talking. I walked around the church, wondering if it would be enough to keep us safe tonight. The thin stained glass windows held the dark night at bay, a narrow line dividing life and death. I had straddled that line, and the thin, fragile glass seemed about right.

A set of stairs led upstairs to an alcove. There was another set of stairs there, which took me up to the little bell tower of the church. A trapdoor rested between the tower and the inside of the church, with a sturdy lock on this side. The door felt stout, snug to the ceiling above me, and definitely locked.

I headed back. The priest and Jen were wrapping up their pleasantries. The church echoed with my steps. Nick was nowhere to be seen.

"I'm sure you all are tired," the priest said. "There's some old cots and blankets in the schoolroom off to the side. It's not much, but it has a flat surface to sleep on."

"Thank you, Father," Jen said.

"More people used to come here," he said. "They just kind of dwindled away. There's not many of us left in Grafton now."

It wasn't a great stretch of the imagination to know the priest meant humans.

Jen grabbed my arm and led me down the main part of the church, to a door off to the side. That door opened into a small room with an outdated green chalkboard. Faded chalk outlines of erased words ran from left to right, ghosts remaining of a past lesson.

Real windows lined the outer wall, with no curtains, just flat black panels of glass reflecting the night. A sturdy oak desk, tabletop scarred by years of use, sat by the chalkboard. A few little plastic tables, like a child would use, were stacked to the side of it.

A number of cots lay here, at least a dozen. Old thin things with blankets of gray wool. Each one was carefully made as if Father Benjamin had been expecting people to come back and fill them.

Jen and I grabbed a couple and slid them together, in the corner of the room. She turned off the light, and after a moment we both were standing there with the cots beside us. Moonbeams lay slanted across the room, revealing and hiding everything.

"What?" She smiled.

I took a breath and let it out. The moment felt surreal. Here was Jen, a girl I had always loved. Someone I had never thought to see again when I fled Grafton. But somehow I had been lucky enough that she had called me back.

I couldn't talk, and she realized it. She reached out and grabbed my hand, tugging me down to the cots.

"Hey," she said.

I swallowed once. Twice. "Hey."

Her hand slid up and down my arm. Her fingers caught in the holes in the jacket, and she helped me shrug it off. There were holes in my shirt too, and where her fingers touched, my skin tingled.

"Gus." Her fingers poked and prodded the shirt, which was more a rag than anything else. Torn in the sleeves, torn clean in half through the back, holes all over the place from who knows how many bullets. "What happened in there?"

It was then that I realized I had almost died. Again. I lived again not knowing how, or why. Which had me wondering what I was. Azazel flashed in my mind. I had shot him many times in the past few years, and he kept coming back to haunt me.

Jen saw the exact moment I began to panic. I tried to hold it in, but I know my skin turned pale, and a cold fear burrowed deep into my chest. I wrapped my arms around myself and tried to hold it all in. When it seemed to be too much I just gripped myself harder and rocked back and forth a little.

"Hey," she said softly, "hey."

My jaw was so tight my teeth began to ache. I breathed in and out so fast I wondered how my lungs got any air. My eyes watered no matter how hard I tried to blink it away. It was everything I could do to not moan aloud.

Jen leaned forward. Grabbed me. Held me close. Her heart beat softly through my skin, and her warm breath nuzzled my neck. In and out, in and out.

After what felt like a long time I relaxed my grip, relaxed my legs, and leaned back into her. We moved a little until we both had our backs against the wall, wrapping our arms around each other, loose, but also tight.

Her arms formed a barrier where the rest of the world couldn't get in. I was warm and safe. At peace. I took a deep breath and let it out slowly. I nestled my head above Jen's chest and felt the warmth of her body against the side of my face. I listened to the deep beat of her heart, a slow, rhythmic pulse; the pounding of my heart slowed and slowed until it matched hers.

Jen's hand moved up, started smoothing down my hair from front to back. Front to back. Her fingers slid through my hair, and it just felt good to have that, someone holding you, taking care of you. I had almost died, but I was alive, and here now. With the woman I always had loved.

Jen held me. What had happened in the factory seemed like a lifetime ago. She murmured soothing sounds into my ear, just told me it would all be okay over and over and over. I relaxed, my ear against her chest, and felt her chest rise and fall with deep, slow breaths.

I counted each swell. One, two ...

Three.

CHAPTER TWENTY-FOUR

I woke slowly. A warm body nestled next to me. A beam of sunlight crossed my face. I had an arm around Jen, and I left it there, just breathing in the scent of her. Always honeysuckles, always spring and the rain, and the feeling of renewal.

After a few minutes, my other arm stirred, and I realized it had been doing so the entire time I was lying there. Likely even as I slept. The arm stretched out from my side like an arrow, and the fingers walked like they were trying to drag my body along. Deep in my chest, beating to the slow pulsing of my heart, I could feel Raphael's demand for me to come to him.

I frowned, wondering how I could resist him so easily now, even when I wasn't aware of his call, when it had taken everything I had in me before. My mother looked to be completely under the geas, and I was born of her. Was it just because the geas hadn't reached its full power in me yet? Was it because I was in a church, with all the protective symbols?

"What're you doing?" Jen asked, her voice sleepy. She had been watching me watch my arm.

I didn't say anything for a long moment. She moved to say something, then looked at me, waiting.

"Raphael and his father, they have some kind of hold over me," I finally said.

"You mean like blackmail?"

I shook my head. "No. Something darker." I told her everything in reverse. Raphael commanding me at the club. Dominic, commanding me to live. My mother, and the geas power over her.

It all led back to the day with Danny. I got to that part and swallowed. Jen stayed quiet, eyes locked on to mine. Her hand moved across the blanket and squeezed mine.

And I told her about that day. Why I had run. What I had thought I was doing then. Why I thought I was protecting them all by running away. And my biggest fear, what would happen now if I stayed, if we went up to the Hill to battle this out, if Raphael or his father could command me to stop. Or even worse, kill.

"Gus." Jen leaned across and placed a kiss on the corner of my mouth, her breath hot against my cheek. Her voice was a whisper. "You fear so much making a mistake."

"It always costs so much."

"You have to live your life, Gus," Jen murmured. "Be brave."

I was not sure I deserved that kind of love. I wasn't ever giving it up again.

She patted my chest then, smoothed out my shirt. She pulled back from me, her nose furrowed with disgust. "You need a shower."

"Yeah, I do." I laughed a little "Not all of us can smell like honeysuckle all the time."

Her hand kept rubbing my chest, in small smoothing motions, her head nestled next to mine, and her breath hot in my ear. It was disconcertingly erotic, and a spike of desire shot through me. Her eyes recognized it, and Jen gave me a knowing smile, placed another kiss on my forehead, and then tucked her head into the nape of my neck.

Her voice was somewhat softer than usual, slower. "Hey."

"Hey," I said back, my voice low. For a long moment, we sat like that, her breath hot against my skin. My heart thudding loud in my chest. I reached up and ran my fingers into her hair, cupped the back of her head. Jen let out a shuddering sigh across my neck.

I swallowed hard.

"You okay?" Jen asked.

I kissed her. Her lips pressed back against mine. We both laid back against the cot. She lay across me, and I rolled a bit to be on top. Somewhere in that roll, I hit my head on the desk.

A loud crack echoed through the classroom.

Jen looked up at me, her face startled. I fingered my scalp and winced. The desk was solid oak and had a sharp corner.

She tried to hold it back, but finally started laughing. "The one thing in this room harder than your head."

I had to laugh too, and pretended to be more injured than I was. "That hurt, you know."

"Come on, now." Her smile had a delicious, devilish quality to it. "I didn't think you'd grow into a big drama queen while you were away."

"I didn't." I waggled my eyebrows at her and grinned. "I was always a closet drama queen."

She laughed some more, and I laughed with her. It wasn't the best joke, but she laughed some more, and I laughed with her, and at some point, the two of us were laughing so hard Father Benjamin peeked in on us.

"Brought some breakfast," the priest said. He had a couple of mugs of coffee and a pack of toaster pastries.

I rolled my eyes. "You've got to try this coffee, Jen. Especially if you want food to never taste right again."

That set off another bit of laughing. The priest handed us the coffee and we tore into the toaster pastries and used them to muffle the bitterness of the brew. We were high school sweethearts again, sitting next to each other and just enjoying the moment. I had been alone too long, and being this close to her was both incredible and also frightening. At some point, we started talking about little things, which led up to the bigger things.

Jen began talking about the last year of high school when Sarah had started seeing Raphael. It had destroyed Nick, who had withdrawn more than normal after Danny was killed and I disappeared. He waited for Sarah to choose him over Raphael. Sarah partied and did drugs and hung around Raphael and his crowd, almost to keep away from Nick.

For his part, Raphael ignored the group who had been my friends back then, and after a while, the group all had drifted apart. Nick had become obsessed with rescuing Sarah. Johnny had lost his job at the factory and pretty much spent his days at the local bar. Jen and her mother were trying to identify a new drug going around Grafton when they realized it was targeting vampires specifically.

Then girls started disappearing. Then young women. Then older ladies. Jen's mother taught her how to take precautions and to stay in all night, how to set wards and protections. I understood without Jen telling me that she was a witch. Jen for her part tried to contact other witches outside town, trying to learn how to fight what was going on, and then those witches started to disappear.

Witches and priests weren't usually allies, but Jen had still become friends with Father Benjamin. By then the drug had taken off and Grafton was swelling with vampires. Neither of them linked the missing girls as witches, nor witches with the drug. Only right before she had been captured had Jen made the connection.

So it started out little, and then as little things do, they somehow became huge overnight. Things changed, drastically. Sarah started coming home with bite marks. Jen and Sarah fought, more than once. Mrs. Cooper started warding the house against vampires, and Sarah moved out.

Raphael had bought most of Main Street and turned it into a strip of sorts, with little bars all leading to the main club, where he held court every night. Time seemed to fly by. Sarah disappeared for a few days, and Jen went to Raphael asking about her sister. Raphael had brushed her off, which had led Jen to dig deeper.

Jen sighed, from something deep inside her that had been around for a bunch of years. "Sarah just got hooked on Raphael. I can't even tell you when it happened, but all of a sudden they were together and she shut me out."

I opened my arms and she leaned into me, waiting a long time before talking into my chest. Little words at first, then low mumbling sentences, and finally something sharp and angry. Angry words at her sister, at herself, at Raphael. Sobbing at finding her mother, not dead in the kitchen, but a leech. I just held her and let her finish.

"You called me right after finding her," I said.

She nodded into my chest.

"Crazy, how that timing worked out." I told her a little about what had happened to me. My time in the service. Finding the Key. Being chased by Azazel. I told her about the last fight I had had with the demon, right before she called.

"So this Key is on you now?"

"No," I said. "I buried it in the Vault."

"What happens when this is all done?" she said.

"You mean if we all live?"

Jen punched my arm. "Of course I mean if we all live."

"I got to go back and get it," I said.

"And keep running."

"Who's to say?" I said. I hadn't figured that part out yet. I was here for my friends now. For as long as they needed me. But the Key would never be safe buried under a rock.

Jen's eyes focused behind me. I turned to see Nick standing there, for who knows how long, and a dark cloud seemed to have followed him into the room.

"Where've you been, Nick?" Jen asked, smiling at him.

"Walking around," he said, his fist absently opening and closing on something. A key—the key to the door in the belfry.

"You were up in the belfry?" I asked.

"Yeah." Nick looked like he wanted to say something, or maybe start something, and then he just shrugged. "Couldn't sleep."

He was looking at me oddly. And his accusation last night still bothered me. I had looked for Sarah. Even if I had shot the doctor and maybe cost Sarah her life when I had. My voice was curt enough Jen pinched me. "So you spent the night there?"

"What of it?" he answered.. "Besides, if I hadn't been up there, I wouldn't have seen them."

"Them?" Jen asked. We looked at each other. It was impossible for Raphael to bring his vampires here in daylight, wasn't it?

"The cops," Nick said. "They're headed this way."

CHAPTER TWENTY-FIVE

Jen and I followed Nick up to the Belfry. The police cars had been heading down Main Street, and as they got closer the trees obscured them, so we could barely see the vehicles begin their winding up the old road to the church. There were two police cars, both moving at the same slow rate of speed, with their lights flashing and sirens off like they weren't in a hurry to get to the inevitable. The church was safe enough against vampires, but Cole and the other cops could easily solve that problem for Raphael

"Looks like they stopped at the diner first," Nick said.

The whole setup spoke of someone about to deliver a message. I swore and headed back down, taking the stairs a couple at a time. Nick followed close on my heels.

Father Benjamin waited by the thick oak doors. He stopped me. "The glyphs don't keep out bullets, Fergus."

"Relax, Father. I'm just talking," I said.

The priest raised an eyebrow. He was looking at my jacket and all the holes in it.

I took a step out of the door. Nick followed me. I stopped and looked back at Jen. She was right behind Nick. We had been together less than half a day. She and I locked eyes, and I could see she knew what I was thinking. I looked at Father Benjamin.

"You're not getting rid of me that easy," Jen said.

The high-pitched whine of an automatic transmission downshifting echoed up from the cars at the bottom of the hill. We didn't have a lot of time.

"Fine." I led them all to my car and popped the trunk. I grabbed my .38 and handed Nick the Benelli. He checked it over and pumped a round into it while I loaded up the .38 and put it in my jacket pocket. The pocket without a bullet hole in it. I put the nine-millimeter in the back of my pants. I dug around in my army surplus bag and pulled out another shotgun, one with a long stock and regular slugs, and handed it to Jen with my eyebrows raised. She nodded and took it.

"What are you going to do?" Nick asked.

"I don't know yet."

"Let me cross the road," Nick said. "We can pin them down, shoot them all."

"Jesus, Nick," I said, "this isn't some movie."

"We can't trust them," Nick said. "Not any of them."

"I know, man," I said. "But we can't get into shoot-outs either."

Nick looked unconvinced. "Why not?"

He was looking at my jacket, and my shirt as well. Maybe he thought I could deflect bullets all the time. The truth was, I didn't think I could pull the same trick in the daylight. It wasn't impossible, but it was harder to find ghosts during the day. They came out at night, true night more often than not. Maybe there was something in the dark they could relate to. Or maybe it was just the rule.

Whatever, I didn't want to have to find that out the hard way.

"Nick, just no shooting, okay?" I looked at him. "Trust me, man, I'm here."

Jen put her hand on Nick's arm. "We're going to get her tonight. But we got to get there first."

Nick looked back and forth and finally nodded.

I shut my trunk with a thunk. The police cars showed up down at the turn to the church and the motorcade headed in.

"We'll figure it out after, man," I told him. "Do me a favor ,Nick. Hang out here, behind the car. And don't get her shot all up."

I looked at Jen. "I need you at the church door. Keep it open, stay behind it, and get ready to cover us if things get messy."

She cocked her head for a moment. Then she smiled and turned back to stand with Father Benjamin inside the door.

Nick knelt by the trunk of the car. "It's all right if I still *want* to shoot them, though, right?"

I grinned at him as the police cars rounded the last curve and pulled up in front of us. "If it wasn't, both of us have some confessions in our future."

Both black-and-whites rolled to a stop maybe twenty feet away and turned off the lights at the same time. Cole was in the first car with Marks driving. A couple of other cops sat in the second. As soon as the motorcade stopped, Cole got out of the passenger side with a squeal of the suspension springs, waving a white handkerchief in the air.

"Can't trust him," Nick said. I wondered what the parley was for. Some of the cops had to have been in the factory last night. They all had seen what I could do. Could it be a surrender?

Marks got out too, red-faced but grinning. "You done fucked it up now."

I walked around to the front of the car. Marks grinning worried me, made me feel like there was an ace in the hole I was missing. I was sure Marks had either heard what happened last night or was there, and either way, he shouldn't be wanting to provoke me. "I didn't see you last night. Were you at the plant? Or can you just run really fast?"

Marks lost his grin.

"Let's cool everything down," Cole said. "We're just here to talk."

"Peacefully?"

"Scout's honor," Cole said. He held up two fingers. "Just delivering a message from the boss."

"Then let's hear it," I said. "We're burning daylight."

Cole continued. "Raphael wants the women back."

"That's all?" I said. "No *or else*?"

"It is what it is," Cole said. "Unless you want me to get creative."

"Well, if that's all you got to say, you might as well head back and tell Raphael those women are long gone."

"Look, Grimm," Cole said, "we figure the women to be in the church. You bring them back tonight, and maybe Raphael doesn't blow his stack and come after everybody."

"You were there last night," I said. "You saw what I could do. You should go back and tell Raphael he better hope I don't blow my stack and come after him."

Cole laughed, but it was an odd laugh. He stayed on his side of the car and was big enough to lean his arms on the top. His eyes bored into mine. The irises seemed black, and his laugh never reached them. "I never figured you as a guy with balls, Grimm. And I told Raphael you'd need some convincing. Lucky us, we have something handy."

My stomach sank. As soon as he spoke the words I remembered where the cops had come from. I took a step forward.

Marks spoke into the walkie-talkie on his shoulder. Immediately we heard a gunshot crack across the valley. Then a second one. They were tiny sounds from so far away. A few more pops after that.

Marks grinned again. "I told you, you done fucked up."

A large boom blasted the air, and the small cop's head disappeared. A splash of blood and splintered bone painted the door behind him. His body bounced back against the car and fell to the ground.

An immediate smell of sulfur flooded the air. I dove behind the Camaro just as the other cops started shooting. There was a ringing in the air, but I still heard a shout from inside the church and turned to see Jen sidled up behind the door, shotgun pointed down toward us.

I turned back to the police car, grabbing the nine-millimeter from the back of my jeans. The first thing I did was look for Marks's ghost, but no spirits appeared. Rule or preference, no ghost was going to help me now.

Nick fired again, blowing the lights off the police car, where Cole had just been standing.

Nick ratcheted the Benelli. A couple of bullets hit the other side of the Camaro.

"You done over there, Grimm?" Cole shouted out from the other side of his car.

I peeked over the hood of the Camaro and felt a bullet whine past my face. I ducked back down. When I did the bullets tracked up the grass and cracked off the bricks of the church. Jen and Father Benjamin were tucked behind the door.

"Cole!" Nick screamed.

The big man laughed. Nick fired again. I lay back against the car, staring at Jen and Father Benjamin in the church. The water tower loomed in the distance. And all of a sudden a plan hit me. I waved Nick down.

"You go back and you tell Raphael I'll be there tonight," I said. "With the witches."

Nick stopped to look at me. "What?"

"You going to shoot the messenger?" Cole asked.

"I'll settle with you tonight," I said.

"All righty, then," Cole said. He shouted something, and the other cops stopped shooting.

Nick fired again, and the cops fired back, half-heartedly.

"Put it down, Nick." I said.

"What?" he said again.

"Put the gun the fuck down." I looked over at Nick. His hands were tight around the stock of the shotgun.

"You guys know Raphael still has that girl," Cole shouted out. "It'd be best for her if I made it back and gave him your answer."

"All this guy does is kill and lie," Nick said.

"I liked her too, Nick," I said. Miss Tammie had always been a friend. And just because she knew me, she had been killed.

"Fuck you, Grimm," Nick said. "What the fuck you know? She's been here the past ten years." He swallowed, hard. "The past ten years she's taken care of us ..."

"Nick, let that go. Just for now," I begged him. "Let's get to tonight, and we'll get our revenge then. I promise."

Nick looked me in the eye. His jaw was shut so tight his cheekbones stood out. Tears ran from his eyes. He snorted and looked away. "What do you think a promise from you is worth to me?"

"We just came to give you the message, Grimm," Cole called out. "Remember it was you that made the decision to say no. And it was you that pressed it further."

I looked over at Nick, who was barely holding himself back. His hands were trembling on the gun, and white knuckles poked out from the fingers on the trigger guard. I stepped over and pushed the barrel of the gun down. It resisted the movement haltingly.

"You know they're aren't going to let Sarah go," he said softly.

"I don't care what they want," I said softly in return. "What we are going to do about it is another thing."

"We can't even get in there," Nick said. "Even if we could, how are we going to get out?"

"I've thought of something," I told him. And my idea was like a boulder, gathering other boulders with it, becoming a landslide. For the first time, I felt real hope we would all make it out, alive. "It's good. But we got to get through this right now first."

"So, are we good here?" Cole asked.

"You tell Raphael we'll be there at his place at midnight," I called out, flashing a look at Nick. Keeping a hand on the top of the Benelli.

"He said sundown," Cole said.

"And I'm telling you midnight," I said. "It's going to take a while for me to get all the women together. And I'm sure they won't be easy to convince, you know?"

"Raphael isn't going to like it," Cole said.

"He doesn't have to like it," I said. "You just tell him we're bringing them at midnight. He needs to have Sarah out front. I'll drive them all to his front door myself."

"Grimm," Jen said from behind. She pointed north, where a tendril of black smoke twisted its way into the sky. There was no doubt now, if there had been, that the gunshots had come from the diner.

"Cole!" I shouted out.

"Yep?" The cop's voice was rumbly and calm.

"Make sure you're there tonight," I called out. "I don't want to miss you again."

"Don't you worry, Grimm," Cole answered. "This time no one is overlooking anything."

Nick pulled the shotgun out of my hands. I looked at him, concerned he was going to start shooting again, but he just lay back against the car and watched the tendril of smoke climb higher and higher into the sky. Jen looked that way as well, tucked beside the doorjamb of the church.

"Then take your men and go," I told the big cop. "The dead one too."

I stayed behind the Camaro, keeping an eye on the cops. Cole told the pair to grab Marks and put him in the trunk of their car. They did it with little mumbling and a few glances at us. Cole walked over to the driver's side, ratcheted the seat back all the way, and got in with a creak of the suspension and a slight rocking of the car.

Cole looked at me through the window. I stared back at him over the hood of the Camaro. He put two fingers to his temple and saluted me with a sideways grin. A moment later both cars were pulling back onto the road and heading down to Grafton.

He would get his tonight. He and Raphael and the rest of them. I took a deep breath and got up, feeling the slight shake that happens after adrenaline spikes through you. Jen and Nick and I all wandered to the side of the church, staring at the black smoke curling over Grafton. For long moments the three of us stood there together, nothing moving in the town below, and the hillside quiet except for the fading rumble of the police cars

CHAPTER TWENTY-SIX

W e headed down to the diner. We all were in the car, Jen in the passenger seat, with Nick and Father Benjamin in the back. Jen's hand covered mine on the console. There was a slight off-kilter thrum to the Camaro, even though I had checked to make sure no bullets had gotten into the engine.

No one spoke during the ride, which gave me a little time to flesh out the plan that had popped into my head. Daylight was wasting. I had seen what Raphael could do with vampires, and I was sure that he would have his vampire army ready come nightfall. I was sure he thought that if any of us managed to live through this, he would come in and finish the job, so we would have to take care of the army first. Tall order.

Jen squeezed my hand a little. The air whipped in through the broken window of the car and ruffled her hair. Nick sat behind me and said nothing, just stared out the side of the window, eyes narrowed against the wind. The priest himself sat behind Jen. He didn't say much, but at some point he had become part of the group.

We had too many things to accomplish, and too few people to do it. A newspaper blew across the street in front of us, and I wondered when that paper had actually been printed. The town felt emptier than ever, as if nothing human lived here anymore, just sleeping vampires waiting for nightfall.

Jen's hand squeezed harder.

"Hey," she said, "we're here."

"I know," I said. "I was thinking about tonight."

She gave me a sad smile.

In the rearview mirror, Nick gave a half shrug. I turned onto Main Street, looking at the trail of black smoke on the far end the street from where we were. A slight ash smell winnowed its way into the car, beginning as a faint charred scent and getting thicker in the throat as we drove up to the diner.

No one was standing around watching the diner burn. I pulled into the parking lot and put the car in park. The diner was a busted ruin. Flames licked the edges of broken windows, and black soot had sprayed down the outside of the walls. There was a déjà vu feeling between the diner and the gas station from last night.

We all got out of the car. The fire in the diner was dying out, but a wave of heat still washed off the restaurant, only getting stronger as we neared. I got as close as I could stand the heat. A gust of wind blew a puff of smoke directly into my face, and a hot ashen taste flooded the back of my throat. I coughed, inhaling more smoke, and coughed some more.

I put my shirt over my mouth and nose. The wind shifted and the smoke flickered in another direction, lifting away from Miss Tammie.

She was sitting on the floor, in the middle of the diner, leaning back against her counter. At least what was left of her was. I don't know where she had been shot, but someone had poured grease over her, and even now she was a combination of a charry, fatty soup and blackened, flaky skin.

I had nothing in my stomach, but it tried to empty itself anyway. I swallowed hard once, then twice, and it was all I could do not to throw up. I leaned over and tried to take deep breaths through my shirt. Jen came up to me, shirt over her nose, and patted me on the back.

"Grimm," Nick said, nodding to the side of the diner. A darker man sat in the booth there, skin blackened and burned, hands in front of his face, trying to stop the bullets from crashing through his scarred face and into his skull.

I imagined Parker sitting there, eating his breakfast when the cops came in. Not knowing what I had done the night before. Not knowing there would be a reprisal for something he had no part in.

There was the man who had raised me, as much as anyone had. The two of us hadn't gotten along a lot of the time. He was gruff, single-minded, and strict. There had been very little give-and-take. I wondered back when Raphael and I were just kids fighting it out at school and Parker had realized the impossible task he had been given.

My last vision of the man who had raised me was him crying into his hands at his breakfast table. We both had made decisions that had come back to haunt us. Yet even at the last, he had tried to teach me something.

I did throw up this time. When I was done Jen was still patting my back, still holding on to me. Letting me know she was there.

"Dammit, Jen," I said. "Just … dammit."

"I know," she said, softly patting my back.

"Was this always going to happen?" I asked. "Or was it because I showed up?"

Jen stopped patting. I wiped a thick string of bile from my mouth with the back of my arm. My mouth tasted ashy and charred and bitter with vomit.

"It's just evil," Jen said. "It doesn't have to have a purpose. It's like a tornado. It comes into being. It destroys. There's doesn't have to be a rhyme or reason to its path."

Father Benjamin began the Lord's Prayer, standing as close to the heat from the diner as he could. Nick was far to the side, in the middle of the smoke. He stood straight like the smoke was emanating from him and swirling around his body. He stared, unblinking, at what was left of Miss Tammie.

As soon as I noticed him, Nick looked directly over at me. His eyes were a mix of sadness, crazy, and hate, and envy. It was strong enough I looked away.

While the prayer was going on I took a final look at Miss Tammie, and at Parker. Made sure to keep those images in my mind, to make me as hard and as angry as I could be. Just a few days ago she was tousling my hair.

"Gus," Jen said, taking her hand off my back. I looked up, saw a figure standing off to the side of the diner. The wind gusted, and the smoke cleared to reveal Johnny, looking a little forlorn, sad, lost. His arm had a big Ace bandage over it, which he hadn't had the day before.

I nodded, and he came close enough that Jen reached out and gave him a hug. We all stood there, silently, listening to the prayers of Father Benjamin over the dead. And like that, we all were back together again, or as close as we would get after all this. We just had one more member to get.

"Wolverines, right?" Johnny said. Echoing my thoughts.

"I never liked that movie," I said. Looking up at the ridgeline where our hideout had been.

"Me neither," Johnny said. "Everybody dies."

I laughed, he laughed, and even Jen snorted a bit. Nick shook his head.

"You here to help?" I asked Johnny.

"Yep," he said. "Gabrielle too, as much as she dares."

"Thanks for last night," I said. "It gave us time."

"Wish I could have been with you." Johnny's lips curved in a very sad, very small smile. "But at least one of us is back."

I looked back over at Main Street. Saw the road as it left the far end of town and began to climb out of the valley, up past the large water tower and toward the church. Heard Father Benjamin praying over and over again, a murmur over the crackling of the dying flames in the diner.

The water tower perched over the church, almost a part of the skyline, swollen and portentous. Standing so long it had been forgotten. I could feel the hunger of hundreds of vampires in the dead houses around us, too many to try to kill before nightfall. The chill autumn wind swirled around me with the fiery heat of the diner. Things were coming to a head. And then it hit me.

I could avenge Miss Tammie. For the first time since coming to Grafton, I had a plan. A real plan. Something that would surprise Raphael and would give us a real edge. It was risky, but maybe less risky than normal, for me. Something that could actually come together, with a little luck. A corner of my lip turned up.

"I know that look." Johnny's sad smile strengthened into a strong, purposeful grin. His eyes lit up.

"Tonight," I said, "everyone's going to know it."

CHAPTER TWENTY-SEVEN

I t was a few minutes to dusk. The vampires would be stirring before long; after they felt the first shadow of nightfall upon them. We were all on Main Street, in front of the movie theater, watching and waiting. The entire town rested silent around us, maybe with anticipation.

I sat on the hood of my Camaro, looking down the street toward the diner, watching a few puffs of gray smoke twist up into the twilight. They tell you when you see the gray smoke, the fire's dead. Part of me knew something still smoldered there, though.

No one else had come to see the diner today. I wasn't sure anyone human even remained in the town other than our small group and what was left of the police. And I wasn't sure I was even human.

I bounced up and down a bit on the hood of the Camaro, testing it out. The springs squealed a little on each bounce, but they seemed to squeal less than they used to. I wasn't sure. Nick had used to work in the garage in town, earlier this afternoon he had given my car a once-over. Even with bullet holes down one side, he proclaimed it was good to go.

I had stolen a lot of cars, and this one was my favorite.

Nick sat in a car next to mine, an older Mustang, maybe from the nineties. He had the car running and the windows up and was listening to some music, though he wasn't bobbing his head to it, which looked strange to me. He just internalized it. He looked through the passenger window at me. There was a coiled tightness to him, action waiting to spring beneath his surface. He had been through as much as any of us today.

Johnny leaned against the hood of the Mustang, twisting a bottle in his hands, a rag lilting from the top of the bottle. He looked at Nick too. "He just keeps things bottled up, doesn't he?"

"I can't blame him," I said. Nick had done some of the hard parts today. He had been fearless that night with the wights, and he had been fearless today as well. Although maybe hate and anger had hidden some of the fear.

Johnny shook his head. "This is one crazy plan."

I grinned. "You had most of the day to come up with a better one."

"Yeah." Johnny sighed. "That's one of the things that bothers me the most about this."

After I had broken out the plan, we got ready, as much as we could. Toward midafternoon we were on the water tower, watching over the town and waiting. Finally a few cop cars headed from the factory up to the Hill. To wait with Raphael.

Johnny had let us know that was all of them. Jen and I had run down then and taken as much of the drug as we could, piled it into one of the vans. Johnny and Nick had run down to the club and broken in, doing the same.

We spent the next few hours putting bottles of it in both cars. Johnny had found water balloons, and we spent some time filling those up and stacking them in each car. Each of us had fifty or so of them.

"Should be soon, right?" Johnny said.

"Just waiting on the signal from your girl," I said. Johnny's relationship was his, whatever I thought of thralls. He had gone through a lot in this town, and Gabrielle had been there for him. I couldn't be high-and-mighty on someone for making the choice he thought best, thrall or not. "She going to be okay?"

"She's in a shitload of trouble with her family," Johnny said. "But they aren't here. She is. And she wants to make sure Raphael gets taken down."

He raised his eyebrows at me. "It helps that someone else destroyed the drug and the factory for us."

"Well, maybe she'll be lucky and I'll take care of Raphael for her too."

Johnny laughed. "There's always hope."

We waited a little longer. The air darkened around us. I could almost feel the time coming, the moment when all the vampires would rise and Raphael would command them to hunt us down. Like when an autumn breeze gets a winter's bite to it. "It's getting close."

Johnny looked at Nick, then bent toward me. He told me quietly, "You know, Nick left me for a bit today."

I threw a questioning look at him, and Johnny explained. "While we were at the club, before you guys got there. He went out to get the car, he said. But it took a while. Just kind of wanted to give you a heads-up."

"What's he going to do?" I said, watching the last of the sun fade to the west. "Let's go ahead and light this thing up."

We both grabbed our bottles and walked to the front doors of the old theater, Johnny taking out a lighter and lighting the rags on them. I opened one of the doors, and Johnny grabbed another.

"Just felt like it took longer than it should," Johnny said. "You know, that Wolverines movie, someone turned."

"Maybe he went to look at the mansion," I said. I looked back to the Camaro, where Jen sat in the passenger seat. "I would understand it if he did."

Johnny shook his head a little. Both of us were letting the rags get a good flame going. The inside of the club smelled like gasoline, which made sense, seeing as we poured a lot over the floors in there. "Maybe it's nothing, but I didn't like the feel of it. And I've learned to listen to my gut. Not sure he's all together."

"Just keep an eye on him in the car," I said. "You guys know where you got to go. The timing is the most critical thing."

"I know," he said. He raised his eyebrows. "I'm just letting you know, in case something happens."

"Ah." He meant, in case something happened to him while he was with Nick.

I tossed my bottle to the left in the huge center room. It flipped end over end, the flame swirling in the air, before the bottle crashed against the far wall. Which immediately lit up in a sheet of fire.

Johnny repeated the process to the right. For a moment we watched the flames spread across the floor, like a fiery wave. Then we both headed back.

"Don't worry, man," I said. "This is an all-or-nothing kind of plan. We'll all get out or we all won't."

"That's got to be good enough," Johnny said.

Johnny and I got into the cars, he into the Mustang with Nick, and I into the Camaro with Jen. I fired it up and felt the happy chugging of a car knowing it was about to do what it had been created for. Jen was sitting in the passenger seat, strapped in, and waiting with one hand on the windowsill and a bucket of balloons between her feet.

She gave a quick smile. It wasn't a nervous smile, it was more like she was happy to have me there. A Sunday drive kind of smile. I half grinned, a twisting of the lips that I always used to call my smile, and she caught the gesture, punching me lightly on my arm.

Our eyes locked, and my breath got shorter like there wasn't enough air. I could see her taking shallow breaths too, her shirt swelling and falling quickly over her breasts. For that long minute, something primal came over both of us. Her mouth parted slightly, her tongue rested just behind her lower lip, and I had a growing urge to lean over into her seat. Jen's warm hand fell onto my arm, and her fingers tightened around me.

"You guys going to make out?" Johnny shouted from the Mustang. "Maybe wait until after the big battle?"

Nick chuckled beside Johnny. I took a deep, ragged breath. Looked back out the front window and let all the air back out. Hearing Jen do the same. Waiting for the sign. It was inching ever closer to evening. Dusk was slowly dropping its curtain over the sun, and the moment was going to get dark soon.

"I can't believe we're going to fight vampires with water balloons," Jen said.

"Don't forget beer bottles," I said. "It's a shame we couldn't find any of those paintball guns around."

"Yeah." Jen smiled again, the glad-to-have you smile. "That would have made this whole thing feel much less half-baked."

I grinned. "Hell, Jen, half-baked's kind of been my life for a while now. This feels almost normal."

"Do you like the plan because you came up with it," she asked, "or because it's harebrained and crazy?"

"A little of both."

"That's the Gus I remember." Jen smiled and placed her hand on my arm again. Just resting it against me, a friendly gesture carrying a hidden electrical current, a small resonance from our moment earlier.

"Yeah," I said. "I needed to remember him too."

Her hand moved down my arm and lay on my hand. She gripped my fingers, hard, her thumb on top of mine. At that moment the last of the sun slipped over into its nightly abyss. And fires began to blaze out around town.

"Is that Gabrielle?" Jen asked.

"That's the sign." I looked over at Johnny. He and Nick were ready. He had rolled the window down and was wincing at the music Nick had on.

Behind the Mustang the flames licked the inner panes of glass of the blackened movie theater windows. Anticipation stirred in my chest, something cold and hard and sharp. I called out, "It's time, guys."

"You mean it's about time," Johnny said, giving me a thumbs-up.

"Remember," I yelled over the noise of the cars, "stay on schedule."

Nick flipped me off, shifted into gear, and sped down the street, burning rubber and having the back end of the Mustang get a little squirrely on him on the blacktop.

I looked over at Jen. "This is about to get dangerous."

Jen gave me her serious look. The one that told me she could take care of herself.

"Jen." I wanted to say something about how I felt, how I missed her, how I wish I had never left. Tonight she could die. I could die. But both of us could live. I just wasn't sure how to start it.

Her hand gripped mine, then relaxed. "We going to do this?" Jen asked.

I looked at her, really looked at her, and saw what I had seen when we first met. A heart-stopping smile and a serious, studious face. A mind that knew what it wanted, and had found him. Had never given up on him. Faults and all.

I squeezed her hand in return, then nodded. "Wolverines."

Jen grinned. "Together again."

I turned back to the burning edge of the town. The smoke trails swelled and swayed like large ribbons. The first part of our plan was easy.

Gabrielle knew where most of the vampire lairs were, and she and the group she was with were going to smoke them all out. I wanted all the vampires up and awake as soon as they could be. The more we could get now, the less Raphael would have at the mansion.

I put the gear into drive and gassed it toward the diner. The car took off with a squeal as rubber grabbed the road, and we were racing to the north side of town. Where I had first come into Grafton days before. The beginning.

Nick had already peeled off, heading into the northwest part of town. Jen and I turned northeast. Both sides of the town had suburban neighborhoods. The side I chose just had shabbier ones. Gabrielle and her vampires would light the outside of the town on fire, all the houses on the outside of the neighborhoods, a big noose of fire surrounding Grafton with the knot of the noose at the church. It was our job, the four of us in the two cars, to give the vampires stumbling out of the houses somewhere to go.

Smoke gusted around the streets like a gray fog. I could smell the ashy, acrid flavor of it in the air. We drove along older suburban homes, and I slowed down as we entered the outermost cul-de-sac of the outermost neighborhood, stopping the Camaro before a circle of houses on fire.

Forms raced from the farthest house, six of them. They had the fluid, loping motion of vampires that was hard for me to track, as they moved faster than your eyes could follow. I had learned it was easier to follow your intuition tracking them, more of a *feeling* where they would be instead of *knowing*. Like my eyes had taken all the information they could and given me a best guess of where the vampire might be next.

"We're on," I said to Jen. "Go for it."

She grabbed a water balloon, which held maybe twelve ounces of the drug made from the blood of witches. She leaned out a bit and threw it toward the vampires. It arced into the air and then splattered maybe a couple of dozen feet from the car, about a couple of hundred feet from the vampires.

I looked over and raised an eyebrow. "It's a bad time to throw like a girl."

"Shut up." Jen smiled, and threw another. Farther this time, though.

As far as it was, the vampires still sensed the drug when the balloon broke. Every form instantly paused, then moved like a junkie fighting a need. The vampires would jerk back and forth and then stumble toward the splatter of blood on the street. It wasn't long before the stumble became a run.

"They got the scent," she said.

I nodded, looking in the rearview. Most of the vampires had stopped where the balloons had splattered against the pavement. One kept on coming, though, racing after our car, sensing the mother lode of the drug we had in the backseat.

"I might have underestimated their need for this drug," I said. I pulled out the Benelli, switching the selector to semi-auto.

I leaned out as the vampire leaped, pulling my foot off the gas to let the vampire's leap carry it farther toward us, and then pulled the trigger. There was a large blast, and the silver buckshot tore through the side of the vampire, spinning it and throwing it to the side. I leaned back into the car, hit the gas to spin the Camaro around, and took back off.

I lay the hot barrel of the shotgun across my lap. Jen threw another balloon, letting it plop and burst behind us. She kept up a nice trail of spatters as I navigated the neighborhoods.

I checked the rearview mirror. More forms ran from houses, some breaking off to where the balloons splattered on the street, others sprinting after the car. A crowd had gathered behind us. I tried to keep a slow enough pace to lead them on, and a fast enough speed to keep them from swallowing the car. When one got close enough, the shotgun made up the difference.

Then the game changed. We were still driving through the neighborhood, throwing fewer balloons now, watching more and more vampires follow us by the dozens, then hundreds. There were so many I had to keep a careful eye to stay ahead of them.

It was during one of those moments, while I was glancing up to the rearview to see how close they were, when all the vampires paused. Like they had all just been tuned to the same station. I could even almost *feel* the message, sense some hidden transmission over a wavelength that I could barely fathom.

"Uh-oh," I said.

"What?" Jen asked, looking back.

"Raphael's taken over the vampires," I said. "All of them, I think."

"Is that even possible?"

I nodded back at the crowd of vampires. As one, they erupted in a shrill scream, the same scream out of the same mouth. They began flowing toward us like locusts, running in the same steps, overtaking anything in front of them in synchronized leaps and bounds.

I floored the gas, felt the tires grab the road and shoot the car down the street ahead of the vampires. In the mirror, the vampires sped up to keep pace with us. I was so focused on them I didn't see the vampire in front of us until the front bumper hit it and I ran it over. A second later I swore and swerved the Camaro onto a sidewalk, and then back onto the street.

Jen shook her head at me, one hand braced against the dashboard in front of her.

I pointed out the vampires ahead of us. "They're coming straight at us now."

They launched themselves from windows of homes, rushing through the yards to try to stop us in the street. Each time one of those groups ran at us, I would jam the pedal down and swing the car away. Jen tried a few more balloons and bottles. They all landed and broke and the vampires ran right over the drug, ignoring it. Raphael was definitely in full control of all of them.

Jen looked back, reached over, and grabbed my arm. Held it tightly. Instead of taking a corner at the end of the street, I cut through another yard, trying not to lose the time I might spend cornering. We both jostled up and down and pressed against our seat belts as the car bumped up the sidewalk, over the yard, and down the other sidewalk.

I grinned. "Well, the plan's working."

"So far." Jen still looked back. The horde was fascinating in its movements. Every vampire moved exactly like the one next to him. "It's the staying alive part that I'm worried about now."

"That is my favorite part." We took a last turn and swung onto Main Street, pointing toward the church. It was now completely night. Yellow and orange flames dances across the roof of the theater, down the street.

I looked to the side. Black forms flickered through the yellow shadows cast by the streetlights. At times I would let them get within inches of the Camaro before I pressed the gas and took off. Screams echoed behind us, down the street.

Just then, way ahead of us, the Mustang spun onto Main Street, bumping over the corner of the sidewalk and knocking over a parking meter. A bottle flew out of the window and broke into the street. The car accelerated smoothly past the club and headed out of town. Nick and Johnny were headed toward the church.

The flames from the club spotlighted the Mustang. Dozens of vampires were following Nick and stumbled into the street, some of them stopping at the broken bottle. In the same second, though, they all paused, then turned as one to face us.

"Hold on." I hit the gas. The Camaro leaped forward. "It's about to get bumpy."

Jen put one hand on the dash, grabbed my shoulder with the other. The Camaro shot through the street with a rumble of three hundred and fifty cubic inches of power, its headlights picking up a few of the vampires standing there. They all opened their mouths in the same scream.

We barreled through them, knocking some down, running over some more. Jen and I bounced against our seat belts, and my head hit the steering wheel at least once. The Camaro squirreled around a bit on the street. One of the vampires spun off the hood and bounced off the windshield, spiderwebbing it.

Then we were in the clear, and we were catching up to the Mustang. Both of our cars started pulling away from the horde. As fast as the vampires were, they couldn't run at seventy miles per hour. Or eighty. If we were fast enough, we could get a minute or two of time. And that would have to be enough.

There was a shrill, raspy roar behind us, like the sound of a million locusts. I looked in the rearview at the swarm of vampires flying after us. Each vampire ran in the same exact loping motion, taking the same number of steps on the same foot. Almost military in their precision.

"That's definitely weird," I said. And powerful. Raphael was far more powerful than I had guessed, even after watching him on the football field the other night. He had shown the ability to call on vampires taking his drug, and even to command them to some degree, but watching then lope behind us like a synchronized battalion was far beyond what I had thought could be done with the drug.

"Is weird going to get us killed?" Jen asked.

"It's likely." I took the turn onto the road to the church hard enough the rear wheels skidded across the road. The car downshifted and picked up some acceleration, but we weren't going to win this race by that much, if at all. Not when the vampires could cut across a field I had to drive around.

I looked downhill. They were gaining fast. "We're going to have to go off-script."

"Off-script?"

"Yeah." We were pulling up to the church. The Mustang sat out front, taillights on. Nick leaned out of the church door. I beeped the horn a couple of times, hoping Nick would understand I had to change the plan. I hoped he got it enough to shut the door and keep everyone else safe inside.

I swung the Camaro off the blacktop. The car rocked as it bounced over the edge of the road and onto the grass. The feel of the car switched. The usual hard resonating grasp of rubber on road I could usually feel through the steering wheel was replaced by a soft, earthy sensation. Like the tires were swimming through turf.

"Oh," Jen said. "You mean *off*-script." She hurried and rolled up her window. My window was permanently down.

I wrestled the wheel a little and pointed the car to the old dirt road that led to the water tower. The headlights spotlighted weeds and tall grass as the Camaro ran them over, a fast black boat splitting a sea of green.

Earlier today we had laid a lot of open bottles of the drug on this trail, as well as poured some of the drug liberally into the dirt, thinking it would help lead all the vampires this way. Since the vampires weren't paying attention to the drug anymore, I'd have to replace it with better bait. Namely Jen and me.

The car's suspension jostled, rocking both Jen and me, and a strong scent of oak and wet leaves came into the broken window from the night. In the mirrors, there was nothing but shadows, but I could feel figures leaping through the grass, flickering through the woods behind and around us. The vampires ignored every morsel of drug lying in the road, following Raphael's will. We had just seconds before they sprang onto the car.

The car rumbled, then gave out a high whine and broke out onto an open piece of flatland. The water tower loomed ahead of us. A sign flashed by, warning us we were on city property. And then the Camaro busted through the chain-link fence surrounding the tower and onto the concrete.

The chattering clink of the fence bounced behind us, and I spun the steering wheel and pumped the brakes so the Camaro did a one-eighty, sliding backward under the water tower. We were still moving fast, and I felt the back of the car collide solidly with the mound of plastic tubs of the drug we had taken from the warehouse earlier. One of the tubs burst, spitting a curve of red onto the gray concrete.

I flicked a quick grin at Jen as we both looked out the windshield at the oncoming vampire horde, the Camaro idling directly under the center of the tower. Now that we had stopped, the vampires slowed a bit and circled us. They all were in various states of undress, and in the headlights their chests heaved, and blood and mud ran down their bodies, but all of their eyes burned with hate.

I kept my shotgun in my lap, pointed toward my window. The horde piled around us, thin and pasty in the light, surrounding the car and standing almost rank and file around it. Circling and circling, tens, twenties, hundreds. Until they were all there. Lit up by one headlight and red taillights.

Up close the vampires had a sickly look to them. Not the normal pastiness of a creature that rarely, if ever, saw the sun. A hollow look. Like something was eating them from the inside. They were thin, wan, their skin stretched tight over sharply protruding bones.

One began to lick his lips. A few others on the backside began to do the same, looking at the drug spattered over the concrete pad. Shuffling a little toward it. So Raphael didn't have complete control. But he had a good amount.

I shut off the car. Jen muttered something under her breath, and something like the scent of rain washed over me.

Then all the vampires smiled, precisely at the same moment. The same smile. A smile I had seen before and knew to whom it belonged. The smug smile of someone who had everything going according to plan. And then all the vampires opened their mouths to speak.

"Grimm," Raphael said from the vampire by my window, the voice echoed by hundreds of vocal cords. The sound resonated through the car like a bass guitar. "Now you see what you're truly up against."

"Come on, Raph," I said. "Having me here to lure your father so you could kill him? Isn't that a little too much Greek tragedy for you?"

Behind us and all around us I could see the vampires loosen up, just a little, from under Raphael's control. They slunk closer to the puddles of the drugs on the concrete. And then, in the next instant, they all went back to standing ramrod straight, fangs out.

"Good-bye, Grimm." Raphael's words echoed through all the vampires as they all moved toward the car.

"Hey, wait a minute," I said. "I wanted to give you a chance at another deal. One you might abide by, given proper incentive."

The vampire by my door held up his hand, and all the vampires froze.

"The way I'm figuring it, you probably need the drug to keep recruiting and maintaining your vampire army," I explained. "And I'm thinking it's going to take a while to find someone who can do what your buddy Browner was doing."

"So far, there's still no reason to keep you alive," the vampires answered. "Unless you're volunteering."

I grinned. "Nope. Let me finish. So you need someone to make the drug, and you need a place to make the drug."

"A place?" Though it was Raphael's voice, the nearest vampire looked past my car, toward where the factory would be. "Why would I need a place, when I have the perfect spot in my own town?"

I looked at Jen, and she pressed a button on a radio receiver. Something small and very military in appearance. A second later, a thunder of an explosion rolled over us, and a jet of fire appeared over the hill.

Raphael realized what happened, and the vampire by my door reached in to grab me. Before he could, I had the Benelli pressed tightly against the vampire's chest, and the vampire stopped. Each of us straining against the other.

"Grimm," Raphael said, out of just that one vampire's mouth, every other vampire standing like mannequins, looking at the explosion over the hill, "you've only given me more reason to kill you."

"Not true." I kept my finger tight on the trigger. "You see, you'll need the witches you held captive in the factory a lot more now. In fact, they'll be the sole source of your drug, from now on, right? That and the fact that I'm holding some tubs still, to get you by."

"And that's your deal?" the vampire said.

"That's it," I said. "I'm coming up to your mansion. I'm bringing the truck of witches, and the rest of the drug that I have. I'm telling you now to have Sarah there. We meet, and we all go our separate ways."

"That's it." The closest vampire looked behind the car at the huge barrels of the drug, not worried at all about the barrel of the shotgun balanced against his chest. But Raphael wouldn't be worried, it would be this vampire that took the buckshot of silver. "What's to keep me from just killing you and taking everything, right here, right now?"

"Oh," I said, smiling, "this other thing."

At that moment Jen pushed the other button.

"See you in a few," I told Raphael. "Make sure Sarah's out front."

Then the bottom of the water tower exploded.

Waterfalls spurted down around us, spraying over the crowd. Vampires screamed as maybe a million gallons of water, recently blessed by the kind Father Benjamin, began to rain down on us all. Holy water in the form of Niagara Falls. Raphael stared at me through the nearest vampire's eyes, the flick of a smile, and then he was gone. Leaving all the vampires here to their fate.

Something metal gave with a torturous screech and the bottom of the tower opened up. A deluge of water plunged down and picked up the Camaro, pushing it down the hill. Jen grabbed me, or I grabbed her, as the headlights bobbed up and down in a dark night sea, tubs of the drug bobbing around us. The car only went a few dozen feet before the water began to subside and the tires ground again, but the car twisted and spun in the current and it felt like forever. Even after we stopped, it still took a while for the large river of water to bleed out from the tower and run past us.

It was over. The car was pointed back toward the tower, and nothing moved in the headlights. Even in the night, we could see a huge sheet of metal hanging down from the bottom of the tank, and not much left underneath the tower itself. No vampires, at least.

"It's hard for me to believe I'm riding in a car with a guy who drives around with an arsenal in his trunk," Jen said. "Including military-grade transmitters."

"Not much to it," I said. "I live a life where it pays to be prepared."

"What kind of life do you have," Jen asked, "where this is what you stay prepared for?"

"You know what?" I said, turning the key to the car. Miraculously it fired right up. "I've asked myself that same question a lot lately."

Jen raised her eyebrows at me, and I grinned.

We found out a '68 Camaro didn't handle all that well driving through soupy vampires and wet grass. But it managed well enough.

We idled the Camaro up to the church and parked next to the Mustang. Its door was still open. Nick stood in the doorway of the church, the light from inside lighting up around him, then walked down to where we had stopped. I turned the car off and let it chug its way off. I smiled and slid my hand around the wheel a second. Every time I parked the car, it loped for a second or two more. Like it always wanted to run.

Nick appeared at the window of my car. He put his hands on the inside of my doorframe, then pulled them up, dripping wet. "Is this actually a vampire?"

"I don't know," I said. "Probably some of it."

His mouth twisted in disgust. "Ugh. So it's done?"

I nodded.

"We went off-script." Jen grinned. She patted my hand and got out, heading up to the church. I hoped she was looking to head Tabitha off before the earth witch saw how messed-up the Camaro had gotten.

"So we're on to phase two," Nick said.

"We are as soon as Gabrielle gets here," I said. As dangerous as what we had done, it wouldn't compare to what we had to do next. Gabrielle and her friends had stayed far away, not wanting to risk the temptation of the drug.

Nick squatted down next to me. His face was for once open, without its usual set jaw and scowl. "Look," he said, "I know that you don't have to do this. And that you're doing it mostly for Jen. But I know some of it is for Sarah, and that means some of it is for me too. So I wanted to let you know I appreciate it."

"Nick—" I started to say.

He stopped me with a shake of his head. "No. No, man, I know. Look, I know you came here for Jen. But you staying and doing this, that's for us. And you and I know, we all are given choices in life. Sometimes we don't make the right ones." He looked back at me. "This one you're doing right."

And he was right. This *felt* right. All those years on the run I had been dwindling away. Becoming less and less. Until a good burger had seemed too good to be true. I shook my head.

My friends and I might die tonight, but I wasn't worried about it. Because I was doing the right thing. And maybe I had felt like I was doing it before, running with the Key, but doing it alone wasn't right. If a person could do the right thing, he should do it. And by doing the right thing with others, it became more than right. It became a force.

I looked up at the church, lit up against the night. Something that would make a difference. Shift the fulcrum. Give others a chance. Make the world a better place.

"I got you," I told Nick.

His and my eyes met, Nick's eyes a little moist in the moonlight. He patted my shoulder, once, twice, like a lost brother might after finding his sibling after decades apart. Then he headed back up to the church, leaving me to think.

A long time ago, I had liked the fact that my friends looked to me for help, and that I could protect my friends from Raphael and his bullies. I had liked the fact that they looked to me as their protector, and that I was strong enough to do it. That I had made decisions that had kept them safe. When Raphael killed Danny, he had shattered any illusion I had about my ability to protect my friends.

I had been on the run from that ever since.

I had done the wrong thing then. I liked being responsible for my friends. I also liked them being responsible for me. Now I just had to keep them alive a little longer. And rescue one more.

I got out of the car, shutting the door. Wet bits of what I hoped was mostly water splattered the ground around me.

The group headed down from the church. We met somewhere in the middle. Jen, Nick, Father Benjamin. Johnny, grinning at everything and nothing. A slight form materialized next to Johnny. Gabrielle. Her straight black hair was tied back in a knot and she was covered in tight black leather.

"Thanks for the help, Gabrielle," I said.

She nodded, one of her hands holding Johnny's arm. Maybe the drug was still on me, or the car.

"You guys ready for the next part?" I asked.

Gabrielle nodded again. "We are ready."

"I don't like it," Jen said.

"I know you don't like it," I said. "But you understand it, right?"

"We should go in with you."

I shook my head. "We've been over this. Raphael can control me. I'm not going to let him make me stand there while he tries to kill any of you, or worse."

"You're going to be all alone, in front of Raphael and everything he can bring."

"I won't be alone. We got a good plan. Gabrielle and her team will be shooting from the fences."

"I was able to reach out," Gabrielle said. "But I don't know if my message was received."

I nodded. The way I thought about this, Raphael's father would still be around. He might want to know what was going on, and Gabrielle could connect to his house from channels within hers. He would need to feed himself with the drug, but stay far enough away to be outside his son's control. He and my mother would be hovering somewhere, waiting to take their chance.

I was going to provide them the chance, tonight. I was going to go in and be a big distraction. In a way only I possibly could. I had told Raphael enough times to have Sarah out front that I knew he wouldn't have her there, just to do the opposite of what I suggested. But he would have her close by, and if I could distract him long enough, Nick, Johnny, and Jen could all get in and find her and get her away.

Jen's hand found mine. I squeezed it. "That'll have to be enough."

Jen and I had argued about this earlier. I wanted her nowhere near Raphael's. She wanted to be with me when I faced him.

I reminded her she had called me here for my help. She appreciated the reminder but wondered if I could possibly have a larger ego. I was also told she could handle herself. I pointed at all the bullet holes in my shirt. So somewhere during the argument, we compromised. I would go in alone with the distraction. She would go in with Nick and Johnny.

"When the balloon goes up, it's going to get hectic," I said. "I have no idea how long you'll have, so you've got to get in the mansion and burn through it until you find Sarah. After that, we all meet up here and get ready to drive out of here as fast as possible."

"I'll be coming with you guys," Johnny said.

"Really?" I looked at Gabrielle. She looked like she had had the same argument as I had had with Jen, and lost.

"Yeah." Johnny grinned. "Wolverines, right?"

"Some people," Gabrielle said, staring at me, "when they ask, you do it."

I felt the force of the stare. Remembered me saying those same words when I had met Gabrielle in front of the movie theater. Johnny meant more to her than someone who was just a thrall.

"No matter what." I nodded back to the vampire.

"No matter what," she echoed.

"Okay, then," I said. It was an hour before midnight, but we might as well start moving now. I didn't care about arriving at midnight so much as wanting to have the time to pull off the first part of the plan. And Raphael might be ready now. He might not. They might even have their own surprise. So now was as good a time as any. "Take a minute, get ready, and then let's roll."

Father Benjamin went back inside the church. Nick wandered down to the Mustang. Johnny and Gabrielle broke off. Jen stayed where she was. I looked over at her.

"Twelve hours, huh?" I said, and smiled.

"What?"

"I was just thinking. We've been apart for ten years, and now we've spent twelve hours together. A crazy twelve hours. It'll be nice to wake up in a room with you and maybe go get a coffee."

She reached out, and I reached around her, and in the next moment, we were holding tight around each other. "Are you sure you'll be safe?" I whispered into her hair.

"You'd be surprised." I could feel her lips next to my ear, and her warm breath against my skin. And a tiny electric pulse between her and me that promised something amazing. "Are you?"

"I can handle myself," I said.

"Me too." Jen stared me in the eye. "Promise."

"I promise." I held her some more, and she tucked her head under my chin. After another moment she spoke low, into my chest. "I'm a little scared."

I rubbed my hand up and down her back. "I think we're all a little scared."

"They killed my mother," she said.

I kept quiet.

"I don't even know where her body is now," Jen said. "And they've got Sarah, and we've got no idea whether she's alive or dead or a vampire or not."

Her voice got a little louder, and a little out of control. "And we're going in there, and I might lose you too."

"Hey," I said. "I know." For a moment I just ran my hand through her hair, feeling the strands slide through my fingers. Looked down at her for a minute, just as she was looking up at me.

And we kissed. Not a burning kiss of passion, well, not only a burning kiss of passion but something else as well. Her lips were warm, soft, and wet. I ran my hand down to the small of her back and pulled her tightly to me. She gasped, I whispered her name, and for a moment no one else and nothing else existed but us.

We broke off at the same time, breathing heavily, and she tucked her cheek aside my chest again. Her hand rubbed small circles into my skin. Her palm was soft and warm. I grinned a big lopsided grin.

"A small room, soon. And some coffee the next morning." Jen's eyes shone with a bit of mischief, and the corner of her lips turned up in a wicked grin. I saw nothing else.

"Promise." I crossed my heart and winked at her.

She nodded, and her grin disappeared. Her eyes opened a little and she took a deep breath.

I leaned a little closer to her and whispered into her ear, "We're both scared. We are about to do some crazy shit. In a crazy town. But I'll let you in on a little secret."

"What?" Her voice was muffled against my neck.

"You're holding on to someone who's got a lot of experience with crazy." I squeezed her with one last hug. "You're not going to lose me tonight."

She laughed once, loud, then chuckled against my neck. She couldn't stop laughing. She started giggling trying to hold back the laughs, and Jen hated giggling. And I knew she hated giggling, and she knew I knew that, so of course she giggled more. A tiny puddle of hot wetness spread over my chest, from where her cheek pressed hard against it. Jen was both laughing and crying and I felt much the same way inside.

"Let's go get the troops," I said after the giggling and the laughter and the crying had all been worked out. "The sooner we do this, the sooner it's done."

She waited as if she didn't want to let me go. "Okay," she said.

CHAPTER TWENTY-EIGHT

Not a half hour later, I sat in the driver's seat of the factory truck, parked off the street a few blocks from the bottom of the driveway to Raphael's house. I wanted to give the others enough time to get into place. While I waited I stared up the long incline. Lots of trees bordered the road and surrounded the property, dark shadows under the moonlit night. The road wove up the hill like an old piece of ribbon candy, and behind the trees, a tiny crescent of yellow light revealed where the mansion lay.

I missed my Benelli. It had always ridden in the saddle with me. I had given it to Nick. There was a chance I would be relieved of it in the near future, and it would protect him and Jen and Johnny far better than it would me. Instead, I had my .38 Special in its regular spot in my army jacket, which I still wore, holes and all, and the nine-millimeter.

I patted myself down and made sure I was ready. Checked the guns again. Checked to make sure I had extra magazines. Finally I took a deep breath. I had to trust that Gabrielle's team would take out any surprises outside Raphael's walls and that my friends would be able to sneak in safely. At some point, it was time to go. Now.

I fired up the truck. It was something like a person would use to move homes with. The engine coughed a bit and then started a rumble, a light churning with a tick-tick-ticking sound like a loose valve cover. A faint scent of ash and heat came through the vents.

I flicked on the headlights. They were a soft yellow and barely lit ten feet in front of the truck. A couple of thumps pounded from the back of the truck. I grinned a little grin at the rearview mirror, then pulled out of the spot and heading west. The hill was steep, and the truck turned much like an old whale, slow and sluggish.

The driveway to Raphael's was new. Paved well and smooth. A contrast to the rest of the town with its pitted roads and potholes. The side-view mirrors reflected parts of the town on fire. Likely it would stay that way for some time, though. Main Street was clear of any fires.

I pushed down on the gas. As the incline increased, the truck whined further and downshifted itself with a jerk. A thump or two came again from the back. Our captives were not liking what they found.

I made a last turn. In front of me lay the brick walls of the Hill. Two sides of brick joined by a beautiful wrought-iron gate across the driveway. Floodlights lit up the entrance, intricate loops and whirls spun around each other, linked up, and ended in short tiny spikes at the top. Very sharp spikes.

They would easily see me coming. I was counting on that. A good distraction wasn't a good distraction unless it was loud and obvious and over-the-top. I felt those were three things I could do, very well.

I hit the gas. The truck lurched forward like a drunken sailor. A couple of guards stood in front of the gate. The gate itself looked like it might be slightly open. Which wouldn't matter much in a minute.

I beeped the truck horn. For the fun of it I beeped out the rhythm of some random tune, maybe from a song I had last heard on the radio. The truck picked up speed slowly as it climbed the hill. I pushed the gas pedal all the way down and listened to the engine whine.

The guards jumped out of the way. Then the truck rammed the gates, at a top speed of fifty miles per hour. There was a huge grating sound, the squeal of rubber on the road, the cry of metal unhinged. The truck shuddered its way through the gate.

I was thrown forward, the seat belt tight against my chest. The tip of one of the gates swung around and crashed through the windshield, blowing little bits of crystals into the cab.

I closed my eyes and felt the truck swivel a little on the road, and tried to steer it in the direction of the slide. There was a huge grinding wheel sound, like a knife pressed hard against a sharpening stone. I overcorrected on the first slide and the back of the truck swung farther out the other way, and then I tried to turn the front wheels into the direction of that slide.

I kept my foot on the gas, and one slight oversteer led into the next as I tried to keep us from flipping over. The back of the truck rocked as the weight inside it shifted. For a second the truck righted itself and I thought I'd had it, but then it overcorrected and I swung the wheel back the other way for everything I was worth.

It wasn't enough.

All the weight in the back of the truck tipped it over onto its side. We slid up the driveway until the front of the truck clipped the wall of a large marble water fountain in front of the house. There was an immediate jerk and my head bounced as the truck tipped up a little in the air, swung around, and landed on its side.

I let out a deep breath. Thumping came from behind me. The engine flooded in a high whine and cut off.

There was an odd moment of silence.

From where I hung on my seat belt, I watched guards running down from the house. Almost in view to the right, the large fountain poured into the air like a fire hydrant had been opened.

Questioning pounding continued from the back of the truck, and the metal sides reverberated in hollow sounds of thunder. The driver's side-view mirror had made it intact, and I watched all the guards run up from the gate.

Distraction achieved.

I carefully wiped my face and hair as free of glass as I could. There was a wet stickiness on the side of my head, accompanied by a sharp, tender pain. I probed the area, wincing a bit, but finding no deep gash and no huge sliver of glass jutting out of my skull. I took a deep breath.

Hard boots clicked on pavement. The bite of burned rubber pushed in from the broken windshield. Vampires surrounded the truck. I unclicked my seat belt and fell to the passenger side. While I was figuring out where to go from there, someone decided to help me, and a hand reached in through the windshield and pulled me out.

The rest of the glass broke as I came through it, large webbed chunks of it falling to the ground. A couple more hands grabbed me and stood me up and a pair of them loosely patted me down. Jacob took my nine-millimeter but missed the .38. He stood there and smirked at me.

Raphael stood a little behind Jacob, smiling. Jacob was big, but Raphael seemed bigger. The mansion lights threw his shadow over all of us. Cole stood a little behind both vampires, with some of his policemen spread out around all of us. The big cop tipped his hat to me.

Sarah was nowhere to be seen. Which meant, in my mind, everything was going according to plan. I would stall as long as possible, at least until the thumps from the back of the truck became too loud to ignore.

"What is that?" Jacob asked, looking at the wreck.

"It's your delivery," I told him.

Raphael looked at the truck. Tiny strips of water spurted from cracks in the fountain wall and snaked down the driveway. The vampire nodded to himself. "You can't ever do things the easy way, can you?"

"That makes two of us," I said. "I don't see Sarah out here."

"Turns out, she had another engagement."

"There was a deal, Raph," I said. "A way we could all walk away from this."

"You call this walking away?" Raphael kicked the front of the truck, after which another round of thumping came from the back.

"You've had your fun with me. I figured I was due."

"I get it," Raph said. "You knew you wouldn't get what you wanted. So you drove the truck in through the gates. Did some damage. Wrecked some things. Threw a tantrum."

He should be angry, but he seemed excited. Eager. "You've had your fun too, you know. I have to go find another geneticist. They're going to have to reverse-engineer the drug. Then I have to build *that* supply up again and start this all over. Hell, Grimm, you've even wiped out the army I had here."

He seemed awfully happy for someone who had had all that done to him.

"But I'm not angry, not really. Know why?"

"I know you're going to tell me.""Because all the damage you've caused can be fixed. Because all it needs is time and resources. And I have that in plenty now. Because you did the one thing I needed you to do. You brought my father to me."

I glanced to the side. The vampires surrounding us had started moving toward the back of the truck. They moved like they were going to check it out. The thumping inside the truck grew louder and more insistent. Like people needed to get out.

"So," Raphael continued, it doesn't matter that you've killed Browner. Or that you destroyed the factory. And my army. I don't even care if you've brought the witches or not. I've got time on my side now. An empire to manage. And a lifetime to manage it. The whole point of getting you here was that. And it's done."

The vampire took a deep breath and let it out, slow and relaxed. "I didn't realize how I would feel right now. Always before, it was about getting to this moment. About getting my father here. Now ... now the whole world is open."

"What about me?" I wanted to distract Raphael from the crowd gathering around the truck.

Raphael grinned. "That part goes on like before, You had a chance to leave, and you didn't take it."

"You knew I wasn't going to leave without Jen," I said.

"So you made your choice," Raphael said. "She was my ace in the hole. I knew if you came back, you would never leave her again. It's all coming out just like I wanted it to."

He paused. "Just like I command."

And just like that, I became a statue, unable to move. Like in the back in the club, or back in the parking lot with Danny. I had resisted Raphael in the church, and I had hoped I could do it tonight. But while Raphael didn't have the reach or the finesse his father had in controlling me, he did have brute force when I was close enough. And I didn't have Father Benjamin's wards helping me.

A corner of Raphael's lip curled up. His eyes twinkled. "Anything else happens tonight, whatever surprise you think you've got cooked up, that'll just be the icing on the cake."

Jacob grinned at me. Cole winked.

Goose bumps tickled the back of my neck as a thrill of fear ran through me. I hadn't expected Raphael to have Sarah, but I hadn't known what he would be prepared for. He could guess, from my friends and Gabrielle, what resources I might have. So it was a good thing I had come up with something out of the ordinary. Way out of the ordinary.

"Any last words before the party starts?" Raphael asked.

He allowed me to move a little. I still took a long moment to answer. "We both knew neither of us was walking away from the other, not this time."

At that moment all the guards had piled around the back of the truck. Where I had smeared the drug liberally, had poured gallons of the drug all over the walls inside. The smell of cinnamon and cherry grabbed the guards one by one and drew them light moths to a flame.

"Something's happening." Jacob took a step toward the back of the truck. Raphael looked at Jacob, then back at me. A vampire by the rear of the truck instantly got tight, like he was on alert. Next to him, a female vampire sniffed, loudly, like she had caught a scent.

I curled up a corner of my mouth at Raphael. Earlier I had opened a plastic tub of the drug inside the truck, had punctured a bunch of five-gallon buckets of it, and the crash had tipped them all over. The pounding continued inside the truck. One of the police wandered that way. And vampires paused, strung on the same taut string like a drug was calling for them and it took everything the vampires had to hold back.

Raphael took a step forward, his chest out, biceps flexing. He cocked his head at the back of the truck. Then all hell broke loose.

The vampires at the back of the truck gave in to their urge and yanked the roll-up door sideways, sliding it along its track and opening the truck. The drug poured out the opening. All the vampires at the back of the truck got on their knees to start lapping it up, fighting over each other to get closer.

Dozens of wights exploded out of the back of the truck. The drug dripped off all of them; they were coated in it. We had used Nick as bait to get as many as possible into the back of the truck before shutting the door on all of them. Which was enough to get them here.

While trapped in the dark, and with their sense of smell muted by the drug, the creatures had been relatively docile. Now, though, they were wide-awake and angry, and hungry. They burst from the truck like a heard of buffalo, tramping and tearing everything in their path.

None of the vampires even tried to flee. The drug on the wights hypnotized them. They were reaching out to lick the drug off the wights even as the wights ripped their limbs off. The cop got a few shots off before stumbling and getting torn apart as well. The vampires with wills strong enough to flee found themselves tripping over each other as they fled.

I grabbed the cop's ghost as soon as he fell, quashing the memories. Next to me Jacob opened his mouth in rage and launched himself at me. He landed on me and took me to the ground, and we wrestled around until I got my hand into my jacket and fired the .38 several times.

Blessed silver bullets make short work of vampires. Jacob exploded into a cloud of fiery mist and ash and disappeared on the whirl of a breeze. Good riddance. I took the opportunity to get as far away from the truck as possible, scrambling to the front lawn of the house.

Furious combat surrounded me. Wights tore through the vampires around the truck and ripped into everything else in sight. Dozens more vampires rushed into the scene, firing into the wights, but regular bullets just thudded into the walking corpses. It actually seemed to make the wights angrier, getting hit by something they couldn't see. The creatures would reach out and flail around them. Any vampire caught too close to a wight fell prey to the scent of the drug, stopping just briefly enough to be quickly dismembered.

Some of the vampires got smart. They pulled back far outside the battle and aimed their rifles at the wights. Where the bullets hit, bits of dead tissue blew outward from the creatures.

But I had a plan for that. As a vampire lined up a shot a hole burst through his forehead. A tiny sonic boom echoed through the air. Then another vampire, farther out, toppled over, followed by a second boom. Gabrielle's people, sniping from outside the wall, safe from both the drug and the wights.

Raphael waded into the fray, impervious to the drug. Like in the baseball diamond, he was a one-man wrecking crew, tossing wights aside and tearing them apart. But even he seemed to be slowed somewhat by their raw undead strength and their numbers. We had packed that truck full. Raphael slowed more and more as the bodies around him pressed on him. As soon as he stopped I pointed my .38 at him and lined up the shot.

A blackjack knocked the gun out of my hand.

Cole stood a few feet away. His feet planted solidly, uniform pressed. His deep voice rumbled through the fight. "Can't have you ruining something that easy."

This was the man who had ordered Miss Tammie shot. Parker killed.

Burned. I blinked back an image of Miss Tammie tousling my hair and ran at the big cop, screaming.

Cole was faster than he looked and bigger than me, but in close and with ghost, I was a match. He tried to pull his gun. I slapped his hand away and pounded his ribs with my fists. He blocked some and then tried a punch. I ducked and swung and felt bones break in the cop's jaw.

He staggered back and fingered his jaw. I dove right back in. He swung again and I bobbed up and down before driving my fist deep into his stomach. Air whooshed out of the cop and he bent over to spit out a bunch of bile.

I took that moment to kick his kneecap sideways. He screamed and wobbled a few steps before falling to the good knee. Cole tried to pull his leg back up under him, but the bottom of the leg lay at a sharp angle to the top of his leg.

He didn't seem dazed. Just curious. I stepped closer to him. "You didn't have to kill Miss Tammie. Or Parker. They had no part in this."

Cole blinked. "I never have to kill anyone. That's just one of the perks."

I pulled as much ghost as I could and picked the cop up. I slammed him one time on the pavement and felt his body give at the impact, and a puddle of blood spurted across the blacktop. I screamed and threw him. Cole spun through the air and bounced off the top of the fountain and disappeared under the water. I stood there, chest heaving, waiting for him to rise again.

"You keep killing my help, Grimm."

Raphael. I turned to face him, taking deep breaths. Wights ran rampant around all of us. More vampires had come down out of the mansion and were laying fire into the undead. The driveway was a mess of dead bodies and twitching limbs. Vampire fought vampire and wights fought everything, and all of this just gave Nick and Johnny and Jen more time in the mansion to find Sarah.

Right now it was just Raphael and me in the middle of all the chaos. I looked around and found ghosts of a few policemen standing over their bodies in around the truck. All I had to do was stay alive and keep the distraction going. And hell, I was even winning some fights here. Pressing my luck just seemed like the thing to do.

I grinned at Raph. "Just working my way to the top."

298 CHRIS J. CRANFORD

Raphael's eyes had swollen into a solid black, the lenses mirroring the lights of the mansion. "You think so?"

"I do." He could always control me if he wanted to, but I felt like Raph and I both wanted this to come to this. "You can always use your safe word if you need to."

The vampire nodded to me. "Go ahead and give it your best shot."

I grabbed as many ghosts as I could.

An older man at a schoolyard, leaning against a tree, waiting for a bell to ring ...

A needle, freshly wiped, sliding into a vein in an arm bearing many such marks ...

A man waiting for someone in a cheap room ...

And the two of us fought.

I had watched Raphael fight my mother, and I wasn't as elegant or as fast as she was. No matter how much ghost I could pull. But I was tenacious. And I could take a beating. Those qualities would have to be enough.

When I pulled enough ghost, I knew other people saw me as a blur of motion, but I hadn't realized how that actually looked until now. As fast as I moved, Raphael was faster. I was a breeze; he was a tempest. I would move, and he would be gone. I swung and missed, and what felt like a dozen fists hit me at the same time.

I staggered and reset and tried again. We stood toe-to-toe. Again a miss and a hundred fists. I spat out blood and tried again. Swing, miss, a dozen fists. Swing, miss, a dozen fists. Rinse and repeat. I kept pulling ghost to repair the beating I was taking, and still I was coughing up blood. I couldn't take much more. Though there was a rhythm to this dance.

And any rhythm could be broken.

I ducked and led back with an uppercut. Raphael's head flew back with a large snap, and the vampire stumbled a bit. His eyes lost their black luminosity.

I grinned and wiped blood from the side of my face. "Round two?"

Raphael fingered his jaw. He looked a little surprised. But also focused. And focused Raphael worried me just as much as crazy Raphael did. "You ever miss this, Grimm? Just the fight? Us?"

I did. Maybe not fighting Raphael, but the fight. Here I stood facing a demon from my past, and maybe insurmountable odds, but I was helping my friends. I was right where I was supposed to be, and I wouldn't have wanted to be anywhere else.

Raphael nodded. "I thought so. Where it started is where it should end."

And we fought again. He was smarter this time, though. I never got a chance to stand in front of him and take a beating. First Raphael was here, then there, always where I wasn't swinging. And I was pulling ghost as fast as I could, just to keep taking the beating.

There was no rhythm to it this time.

But there was some luck. I got thrown onto his lawn. I rolled a bit and turned to see some of the wights jump Raphael. He had been so focused on me that the wights took him to the ground easily, and I lost him for a moment as the herd pulled him down the driveway.

Then scores of vampires dropped down from out of the night air, wearing similar colors as my mother had worn with Dominic. Black and blue leather. As they dropped they fired assault rifles, and bullets tore into the blacktop. Others held a variety of martial weapons, swords and axes, and all shapes of blades, all gleaming in the moonlight.

I had won my second gamble.

For the few moments I had met Dominic, I knew he would not run from his son. He would fight the drug and his son and find the right moment to strike back.

I had provided that moment for Raphael, earlier at the baseball diamond. It was only fair to offer Dominic the same opportunity. And it looked like Gabrielle had been able to send the Vampire Lord the message.

Then the gamble took a bad twist.

A cold, weightless hand was placed on my shoulder. Undead lips pressed next to my ear.

"Kill my son," Dominic whispered, his voice unyielding. And the geas took over.

I swore. The command swept through me, with all the strength and control Dominic had.

I watched myself get up and kick up a shotgun on the ground nearby. I ratcheted a round in the chamber and headed down to where Raphael fought the group of wights. One of the creatures dove at me. I burned some ghost and sidestepped it. The wight bounced off the fender with a roar. I put my foot on its shoulder and broke it off in a crunch of dead bone and leatherlike ligaments.

I kicked the creature aside. I wasn't sure if the wight was out of commission, but the command wouldn't let me turn back to it. Even though I wanted to kill Raphael, I wanted to do it in a way that kept me alive. The geas wasn't concerned about that triviality.

Raphael's back was to me. I pulled the trigger and pumped the shotgun over and over, the twelve-gauge bucking at each shot. Each shell tore through Raphael's back. Dominic's words had burned into me and I waded the twitching limbs and blood-soaked bodies, pumping the shotgun and burning ghost like I was a forest fire and the spirits were saplings. The vampire's command ran through my body and forced me to his will.

I didn't know how many times I hit Raphael. It seemed like he staggered once or twice, turned, and then was right next to me. My arm cracked and the shotgun flew out of my hand. I didn't see the fist that dug into my stomach and caused me to throw up. Than Raphael's elbow connected with my temple and I spun through the air.

I rolled to a stop in the driveway. I tried to get up, but one of my arms wouldn't respond. I looked at it and it was bent all funny. I reached for more ghost and found, unfortunately, there were none left.

"Father!" Raphael's voice echoed in the chill night. "Kill your troops, if you please."

The whole battlefield fell silent, except for pieces of wights wrestling each other on the ground, pulling themselves closer to anything they could kill or eat. Every vampire had stopped fighting, some of them looking back at Raphael and Dominic with tilted heads.

And then the former Vampire Lord started killing. A puppet, now. Some of his soldiers ran. Some fought. All died. Raphael laughed and watched it all.

I turned my head and saw Nick, standing in the front door of the mansion, looking out at everything with lost eyes. When he saw me he shook his head slightly. Next to Nick, Johnny lay against the doorjamb, pressing a towel against his side. It was wet and dark. Jen should have been with them, and a dark fear ran through me, even with the geas.

Dominic's curse still bound me. Johnny and Nick would have to keep looking until they found Sarah. I had to find a way to give them more time. I had to hope Jen was okay. I gasped at the pain in my arm and tried to get up, almost passing out with the effort.

Vampires screamed and ran and fought in the front yard. Raphael's troops went around finishing off what was left of the wights. Dominic was a blur, running from blue-black-leather soldier to blue-black-leather soldier. If Gabrielle and her friends were still here, they wouldn't be much longer.

Raphael looked over at me and grinned. Like he had planned all this all along. Like I had helped him execute it, to the letter. My good arm reached out to a gun lying on the pavement. Raphael shook his head and came over, kicking it away. Then he held me down with one foot, surveying the battlefield that was his front lawn. "Come to me, Father."

There was a rustling, of thick leather armor scraping against the driveway. Out of the darkness, and into the yellow lights of the mansion, Dominic came to his son. Crawling. Fighting it every moment.

Raphael smiled, once Dominic was fully in the light. "Father. You can stop now."

Dominic stopped. His face was seething in anger and hate. A cool breeze picked up and blew across the yard, rattling leaves and carrying a mist that promised rain.

"Don't be angry," Raphael said. "Be proud of your son. Stronger than you have ever been, or ever will be. What every father should want, right?"

All Dominic did was grit his teeth.

"Now be a good dad and tell Fergus here he can quit trying to kill me," Raphael said.

Dominic frowned before he told me to stop. As soon as he spoke the words, I felt my body release a deep breath and I lay flat on the road. Exhausted.

I had put everything I had out there. And it hadn't been enough.

Nick and Johnny hadn't found Sarah. So the plan, as well as it had worked, hadn't been good enough.

Raphael stood on me and laughed. He had beaten me, even with the geas driving me like a berserker. He had beaten us all.

I wanted to scream. To cry. And when a few drops hit my cheeks, I felt like they were tears. But a long, low rumble of thunder echoed along the hills and valleys around Grafton as it began to rain.

The skies opened up and let out an ocean of water. Thick fat drops hit the pavement like a thousand hands clapping together. Raphael laughed, and held out his hands, and stood there in the middle of the downpour, getting drenched. The whole world stopped and watched the man who was going to rule the world.

And then a lightning bolt struck him. Not just any lightning bolt but a cascade of forked blue streaks, thundering up the pavement and thrusting through Raphael. He screamed as the explosion hurled him somewhere over the mansion.

Dominic struggled against his son's command. I flipped over, wanting to get to the father before the older vampire could command me to do anything. Blue streaks arced everywhere and illuminated everyone in a raving blue flash.

Jen appeared, both feet planted at the bottom of the driveway. Her body was covered in tiny arcs of blue lightning, a neon blueness that raced around her and dripped from her fingers. She started walking up the driveway, jaw set. Lightning struck around her, exploding wights and throwing vampires aside.

I stumbled toward Dominic. Nearby, Jen stalked up the driveway. Each arm moved in a concerted motion, calling sheaths of lighting to pound over the grounds, tearing vampires apart.

An ax lay on the ground near me. I gritted my jaw against my broken arm. I leaned over, picked up the ax, and staggered toward Dominic.

Dominic was still bound by Raphael's command and struggled to move. I grinned and raised the ax over my shoulder with one hand. I looked at Jen and smiled. She threw some lightning and winked.

Then the lightning went out.

One last sheet of lightning died across the night sky.

Jen tumbled to the ground.

My mother stood behind Jen, sword angled to the side. Her wrist quickly flipped the blade in a blood-cleansing motion. A tiny trace of lightning flickered down the blade and disappeared.

I forgot about Dominic. I screamed and charged my mother. She strode toward me, every step for her a precise beat, every step for me a maddening stagger. I ran like an elephant; she ran like a panther. Raw anger and force coming against precise and controlled energy.

We collided. I twisted around her blade and beat on her with my good arm. In close, the blade would be worthless. She hit back, but in controlled motions, focused. It was a few moments before I realized she was allowing me to work out my anger while getting me to use up all the energy I had left. Like a parent might do to an angry child.

I didn't care, though. I swung and swung. She took each hit carefully, on her shoulders, in her lats, on the sides of her arm. Her fists drove precisely into me, into my stomach, into my kidneys, and into my solar plexus. Not hard enough to kill, but hard enough to sap whatever I had.

I ran out of screaming, and my lungs sucked in air. My mother clipped me on the side of the head with the butt of her sword. I stood there, letting her go, not realizing what was going on anymore, and not knowing where I was. A swaying sensation came over my body like I was on a ship as it rolled upward into a huge wave. Then I tipped over and crashed into the ground.

My face bounced off the concrete. All I could see were tiny pinpricks of light at the end of a large, dark tunnel. I fought to stay conscious and my limbs moved like a baby learning how to crawl.

My mother flipped me over and grabbed me by the collar of my jacket. I briefly saw Jen lying on the concrete, soaked in the rain, face hidden by a thick swath of hair. My mother swung me around and dragged me back up the driveway, to where Dominic waited, still not able to leave his spot. Something burst inside me and I threw up blood.

My mother kept pulling me up toward the front of the house. I hung from my mother's grip and watched her face as she dragged me. Her face had purpose. Every feature, from the corners of her cheekbones to the line of her eyebrow, to the slight crow's-feet, was firm. Resolute.

Dominic looked at my mother. He still couldn't move, still stuck under Raphael's last command to stop. They stared at each other. Her jaw clenched, and her blade twitched, once. It was quiet around the mansion as if we were the only people left.

Like turning a faucet, the rain slowed down from a downpour to a shimmering haze. And out of that haze walked Raphael. His clothes were black and torn and shredded. His arms had swollen out of his shirt. His dark eyes shimmered with madness.

My mother paused.

A splashing sound came from the fountain. Cole pulled himself out of the pool. His face looked broken, and he spat out some teeth. So I hadn't even taken care of him.

Other figures came forward. A smaller number. Just who was left. The evening air was filled with the expectation of a prizefighter getting up from the mat after being knocked down for the second time.

There was a gunshot and another. Raphael staggered back once or twice, then screamed in rage. Either Gabrielle was still around, or Dominic still had a few people left. Whichever, it was going to be them versus Raphael.

My mother released her grip on me and grabbed her sword with both hands. I fell to the ground and stared up into the black empty night. I was so exhausted the driveway felt like a bed from a nice hotel.

My mother disappeared from view. I heard the slip of her sword through the air and Raphael's maniacal grunts. Other screams surrounded me. Gunfire. Shouts. Somewhere people still carried on the fight.

I was empty. I had given this fight everything I had, I had even gambled on a few things that had come through, and all of it hadn't been enough to beat Raphael. The sounds of fighting went on around me, but they dwindled fast. The fight inside me had died out faster. I looked over to Jen's inert form on the concrete and struggled to pull myself over to her, but nothing in me responded. Empty.

Raphael swore in pain. My mother's sword no longer cut the air. He screamed again, this time in anger, and there was a pitter-patter of her steps heading off into the night.

A long moment later Raphael appeared above me, an arm held tight to his chest. His skin looked burned in places, but his eyes looked as sane as I had ever seen them.

His lip curled up, and he shook his head. "Grimm, you're no use to me like that."

I looked away. "Just get it over with."

"Oh, I'm going to keep you around a bit." Raphael looked to where my mother had disappeared with Dominic. "At least until I get your mother under wraps."

A busted face appeared next to Raphael's. It looked demonic. Parts of Cole's cheekbone had been crushed, and blood dripped from the socket, and the face was bruised enough that it appeared as if Cole had put on another face over his. I thought I had killed him, but it seemed as if Cole was unkillable.

"I'm going to go after them," Raphael told the cop. "Put Grimm somewhere safe."

"You got it." The big man grinned at me through his broken jaw, and his teeth were oddly perfectly even and white. "You just can't get rid of me, can you, Grimm?"

I let out a big breath and turned away.

The cop leaned closer. Blood crawled down from the side of his eye, but he smiled and grabbed my broken arm, yanking me off the pavement. Cole threw me over the shoulder and walked us over to the side of the mansion. A few cop cars sat there. He opened one and tossed me into the backseat. I almost blacked out when I landed on my arm.

The cop got in and fired up the car. "I told you, Grimm. I haven't missed a thing."

I dragged myself up and put my face against the window of the car. The air was muggy after the rain, and my breath fogged the glass. I couldn't see much, but the car bounced as Cole drove us past the factory fan and down onto the main driveway.

It was a short trip from there to the jail cell. I spent the entire time half in and half out of the waking world. The exhaustion and the pain were too much, but I couldn't just let go either. I spent the trip in a gray-limbo world, all the way until Cole tossed me into the cell and clanked the bars shut.

CHAPTER TWENTY-NINE

For a while, I thought I had become a ghost.

I rose high into the dark night through the cell, shivering as misty masses of blackened clouds passed through me on the wind. I rose higher and higher. The how and why and where were all nebulous questions. I had no idea where I had started or where I was going, but as I rose the haze around me cleared, revealing an atlaslike image of Grafton lying flat on the earth below me.

Shimmering blue lines outlined the town, each block, and every street, lines that I normally would associate with ethereal vision but that now traced the city like a glow-in-the-dark map. The night was black, but I could see the shape of each building, each corner, each street clearly in blue-white dotted lines. Like everything was connected in some way. Red and orange flickers muddied the lines here and there like a child had taken crayons and colored over the lines, and purple and black blots dotted the map below, most of them congregating around Raphael's home.

The fires around the town had died down a good bit, as if the storm had put everything out in its thundering downpour, short as it had been. Little red and orange blotches were all that remained below me, and around the mansion the red and orange mixed with thick masses of purple and black blotches, with little fingerprint smudges of fading purple dying into darkness.

The thickest smudge lay directly underneath the water tower, the water droplets around the tower itself shimmering slightly as they fell to the ground. Lines of glowing light curved and split where tiny streams of blessed water slipped and flowed to the bottom of the hill, fading into the earth there.

I felt timeless, but time passed around me. Crayonlike colors of red, orange, and yellow swirled around the church. Figures moved there, bluish sprites racing away from a burning building in a familiar roar. Like I was watching some stop-motion film. The Camaro itself was outlined with ethereal lightninglike edges and raced down a black road.

Purple and black blotches stumbled after them, and an inky black shadow blossomed behind the vampires, and all of them stopped moving. The shadow would fade and blossom again, fade and blossom again, and everywhere it appeared the purple smudges would cease to exist. I focused and the shadow became a young man with wire-rim glasses and a shotgun spitting balls of silvery fire.

Nick in the shadows was a deadly thing to watch. A dark fucker indeed.

The outline of the Camaro raced to the north side of town, alone. One after another, the purple miasmas fell and soaked into the black earth behind the vehicle. I found myself rising in the air again, against my will, until I could see over the hills that encircled Grafton.

I thought I was dead, and I was unsure of what direction I was headed.

I was dragged through the air, over Raphael's mansion. I looked hard for Jen's body, but try as I might I couldn't see her. Things were happening there, large things, impactful things. Purple blotches surrounded a swallowing darkness, a large sparkling white and purple and red shadow that overtook everything around it. Raphael, full of the drug and Sarah's blood, commanding the stage.

The stop-motion movie continued, and the sky brightened as I flew. The Camaro pulled around to the backside of the King's Lodge. Three blue-and-white figures got out, one slowly, stumbling, arm around an inky shadow. I had no idea who they were, other than Nick, but I hoped they all made it. That the sacrifices the rest of us made, Jen and Tammie and Parker and even Danny, had given them a shot.

A purple miasma swiftly appeared by the car, followed everyone into *the motel rooms. Gabrielle? After a little time, one of the blotches walked out of the hotel room and stared alone at the Hill. It seemed for a long moment the blotch could see me, high above the mansion.*

The sky brightened around me until it was a concentrated white glow, enveloping me and hiding everything else from my vision. Like a spotlight. Everything was blank and white and I wondered where I was. Long moments passed, and I could still see the edge of twilight around the white glow, and feel the peeking eyes of the warm sun as it woke from its nightly slumber.

I woke to the orange-yellow rays of the sun trickling through the bars of the cell to fall flat across the gray concrete floor. It was the same cell Cole had thrown me in on my first night of Grafton. The one Raphael had beaten me half to death in.

I laughed, but it was a dark chuckle, a laugh without humor. I was empty. I had never been empty like this. It was the cold emptiness of a dead star hovering by itself, surrounded by cold, dead space. Different memories warred within me.

The flick of a smile under a bright blue summer sky …

The flick of a blade and sun-yellow hair awash on the ground …

I slumped on the bench in the corner of my cell. My forearm swelled on my lap like a misshapen balloon way too full of air. The rest of my body hurt, but it could move, though I lacked the effort to try.

There was movement in the front of the station. The outside doors slammed shut. Hard rapping of a big cop's shoes across a tile floor. An office door opening and closing.

I shivered. The cold concrete and lifeless metal bench leached away any heat my body could generate. The predawn light barely illuminated my cell. The window bars cast black and yellow shadows against the floor. There was very little light and no warmth.

Inside, if I hadn't given up, it was close enough to not make a difference.

Jen winking at me, a fistful of lightning in her hand …

My mother taking every hit I could land on her until I collapsed …

I had been alone for a long time. That was how my life was supposed to be. Who else could have done what I was doing? Who else could have run for as long as I had from Azazel, and kept the Key safe, all on their own?

Other people always got hurt around me. Even killed. So I had protected everyone by staying on my own. It was what I could do, and I thought it had been noble. That sacrificing what my life could have been was worth it, if it kept the world safe.

But what had it been really? A selfish punishment. I had been running, but not from Azazel. I had been running from the truth. From responsibility. I had failed Danny. And I had justified my cowardice by telling myself running kept my friends safe, and wasn't protecting the whole world worth that?

But my friends had needed me this whole time. When I had run from Danny, I had run from them. I had abandoned them to whatever fate was going to deal them. And I had realized that too late to help them.

If I was honest with myself, I could have come back to Grafton at any point in the past ten years. I might have been able to stop this long before it happened. I could have kept the world safe from Azazel and the Key and also helped my friends. I could have come to Grafton at any time. I had been scared to. I had been selfish not to. I had lacked the fortitude to face myself, and that had cost my friends dearly.

Life wasn't about who won or lost. It wasn't even about who I could or could not protect. I thought I had been saving the world by running with the Key. I thought I had been protecting my friends by running. Hell, I had even tried to protect them all last night by demanding to be the distraction.

Sacrifice was noble, to some. But I wasn't doing it right. I was sacrificing myself for a selfish reason. And life wouldn't reward that kind of selfishness. My life proved it. No matter how much I tried to take onto myself, the people I cared about could always be hurt. There was always danger.

True sacrifice was love without reservation. Making the most of my time with friends and family. Living in a way that they would be proud of. Giving everything I could without fear.

I finally understood that. Just too late to help my friends. To help Miss Tammie, Parker, Sarah. Too late to help Jen.

Oh, Jen …

I wiped my eyes with my finger and thumb. I held my hand against my temple for a long moment. Jen had called me just a few days ago. I had come to town and found a vampire launching a plot to take over the world. I had found my friends and had brought them together. I had found a connection with each of them that still existed, after all these years. Had in some cases even become stronger.

I wasn't sure I could have done anything different in the past few days. It was all slated to happen the way it happened. I could relive it a hundred times and at the end, each time, I would be here in this cell, with Raphael the victor.

Every strand connected another person to me. Tied another event to me. Raphael kidnapped Jen to get me here. I connected Raphael, Dominic, and my mother. Parker and Miss Tammie. Nick and Johnny. Even Greg had died trying to help me free Jen. I had been a piece of each of their lives. Johnny had told me I had brought us all together, and look at the result. A tangled cat's cradle of loss.

I sat in the cell and felt all the strands connecting each of them to me, the threads that bound me tighter and tighter in this cell, thick strands that wove around me and fastened me in the center of the web that was Grafton.

And a web was always, first and foremost, a trap.

A slight chill rippled over me. My breath caught. I had missed something vital. There was a piece of the puzzle missing this entire time that, once placed, would terrify me in its reveal. If Grafton was a web, there had to be a spider to spin it. I had thought, several times, that Raphael wasn't someone who could plan something intricate, or bide his time.

Down the hall, the door to the cells opened with a slight metal squeal. Uniformed dress shoes clicked confidently across the concrete floor. The assured step of a big man who had it all under control, and had from the very beginning. Who could wait thousands of years, if necessary, and plan that far ahead. Who had told me, before taking me down to the cell, he had not missed anything, *this time*.

I had missed it entirely. Cole's face appeared between the bars.

I let out a breath. "Why are you still here?"

The cop's lips smiled, but it was a smile without smugness. One of satisfaction. "Sometimes it's about the appreciation of a thing."

I nodded. He had set this up from the very first. Had timed Jen's kidnapping so I would get the phone call at the exact moment I had finished the fight at the motel. Had pulled me back to this town and ensnared me in its web of lies. All for one reason.

I closed my eyes. It had never been about Raphael, or the drug, or Dominic. It had nothing to do with anything or anyone in Grafton. "It was never about Raphael."

"No," Azazel answered, "it was not."

I took a deep breath and let it out. Forced my eyes open. Cole was gone. In his place was the demon, wearing the same outfit he had worn back at the motel. The same white suit with black pinstripes I had seen him in at the hotel, the same black shirt underneath. His favorite ensemble. Short, dark hair, a little product making spike, the well-manicured Vandyke. Not a hair out of place. Dressed for success.

"You don't have it." I reached out and felt for the Key. I always could sense it, in a general direction. I still felt it north of me. The Vault.

"In just a bit, Grimm, in just a bit." Azazel looked at his watch. "Your friend Nick seems to think he can find it. And Raphael still has his girl, you know."

Nick was gone for a bit, Johnny had told me.

You can't trust him, Grimm, Nick had told me. *He lies …*

That was why we couldn't find Sarah last night. Azazel had made sure to have that part covered. Nick would have known about the Vault. I was sure he was the person who had scratched out Danny's and my names. If Azazel had been working Nick, it would have been a matter of time before Nick found where I had hidden the Key. And it would be easy enough for Azazel to talk Nick into trading Sarah for the Key.

"So you just here to gloat?" I asked.

His head tilted a little to one side like I was an object of study. The demon didn't look disappointed or surprised. I got the feeling Azazel might be a little sad either because I was figuring this out too slowly, or just because his game was finally over.

"Oddly enough, no." Azazel seemed to be in one of his more honest moments. "I've chased this thing so long, it's become part of who I am. Now that it's this close …"

He seemed sad. Or maybe he just didn't know what he would do, after he brought his fellow demons back into the world. Maybe ruling the world didn't have the appeal he thought it would have. I flashed something between a smirk and a glare at the demon. "Underworld problems, right?"

Azazel didn't get the joke. He was in his own thoughts. "This has been the most fun I've had in a few thousand years. You've been different, you know, than any of the other Keepers. Maybe that was part of the thrill, for me." His eyebrows relaxed, and his eyes had a faraway look. "I think I came here because I wanted you to know that."

"Fuck that," I told the demon. "I'll be happy to see you gone."

I was lying, though. A flame had kindled, a flame of hate and anger, where I had just felt empty. I latched on to that flame and stoked it. If Azazel was the reason this all went down, he would also be the reason I would go on. Jen was dead. Azazel was the reason.

"It's rare to find someone I can really relate to," Azazel said to me. Like we had been buddies this whole time. He seemed to miss the change in my mood. "Someone who can appreciate the lengths I go to in order to achieve what I want. The scope of the thing."

"I figured a whole crowd would be cheering you on."

"In hell?" The demon looked down, then shrugged. "There are fans, I guess. But very few artists, and those are too self-absorbed to note what I accomplish."

I cocked an eyebrow at Azazel. "Self-absorbed, huh?"

It took the demon a moment, but when he got it he laughed and laughed. "Hell, Grimm, I'm going to miss you."

"There's no need to miss me." I pointed at my arm. "Just heal me up. Let me go. We can keep the game going."

"All games come to an end, Grimm," Azazel said. His words were quiet and hinted at a deadly purpose. "No matter how long you play them, they all end."

This had been nothing but a game to him. Grafton. My friends. Miss Tammie. The flame in my gut burned hotter. Who knew how long he had been scheming something here? Before me? Before Raphael? "Vampires could never have real kids, could they?"

"They certainly cannot." Azazel chuckled.

So Azazel had been here long before I had been. He had been a part of Dominic's plan to create an heir, a true son.

"I always have something going on, Grimm. So many hundreds of thousands of schemes. It amuses me." Azazel frowned. "These vampire families, they all feel so *noble* in their traditions, when they are nothing more than undead carnivores. I felt like bringing them down to earth. Imagine my surprise when I found out you had been born here."

I hadn't been born here, but I guess a demon couldn't know everything. "I'm sure it didn't take much to figure out how to get me back here."

The demon looked over at me. "Even better when I found out Raphael hated you. The tough part was keeping him from killing you. Everything fell into place, though, almost like it was meant to."

Azazel was taking credit for setting this up, but my past was *my* past. I had lived day by day, going from one place to the next, not knowing or caring what I had left behind. My past had dug itself. It stretched deep below me like an abyss, packed with everything I had said or not said, everything I had done and not done.

I had filled my past with hate and anger and fear until it overflowed with all of it. I had avoided it until now. But I was face-to-face with it now, and I was ready for what stared back at me. It was hard to accept unless I was ready to make it right. Looking at Azazel, the reason I was here, the reason my friends here had suffered and died, I was ready.

Azazel hadn't looked at his past yet. He was a planner, a schemer; he looked ahead. He only appreciated the results of his plans. When he did look back, I wanted to be the man staring back at him. "Upset that your game is over?"

"All games end," Azazel repeated. Then he paused for a long moment and looked at me with that cocked-head stare again. "But a new game, maybe? That would be interesting."

I controlled my breathing. Hate and hope together burned in me. "I'm listening."

"I can feel your hate, you know." Azazel laughed. "Always easy to hate, you humans. What if your brothers and sisters were held hostage in the Key? What would you do differently than I?"

"I wouldn't go birthing baby monster vampires and destroying towns."

The demon shrugged. "I've been around since the beginning of time, Grimm. Grafton is small-time compared to what I've done for *my* family." He paused with a thought. "I wonder what you would do if I had something you desperately wanted back. What would you do? How far would you take it?"

I felt it then, what had occurred to the demon. His game, his trap, his chase. On his terms.

"There would have to be something balanced against the Key, though." Azazel reached up and held his chin in his hand, forefinger over his lips, deep in thought. "Some motivator, some reason for you to not want to chase me ... someone you love ..."

I froze then. It was clear that Azazel was talking about Jen. But I had seen her die. I had seen her fall from my mother's sword.

But I had not seen her body when we left. I had not seen it when I was floating above the town in a corporeal dream. *Could it be I hadn't seen her,* my mind whispered, *because Azazel already had her? Or did she get free? Is she even now at King's Lodge with those who made it?*

I shook my head once. Twice. It wouldn't clear. Rage and hate ignited a furnace inside me. I clenched my good hand. I wanted to be there when Azazel's past caught up with him. I wanted to be the last twist of that knife.

It was hard to remember this was all just a game to Azazel. He claimed his brothers and sisters were in the Key, but if that was true he would stop all these schemes and plans and just free them.

For me, I always understood the Key was what kept the world safe. Kept the worst of the demons locked up. And if that door was opened, I would be responsible for everything that happened in the world afterward.

Could I give the Key to Azazel, if it meant Jen's life? If Azazel had the Key, could I chase the demon, knowing he would try to take her from me?

"Ha!" Azazel slapped his hands together. "You see it, don't you?"

"I see it," I growled. "But it's all worthless talk if I'm stuck in here."

"I like this game," Azazel said. "The whisper of hope in your bones, your blood burns for it. *Sings* for it. The world's safety ... or Jen's?"

"Let me out and we'll find out," I told him.

"Part of me wants to, Grimm," Azazel said. He rubbed his chin, as if in thought. "I think in some ways you scare me, and I think that's a dangerous thing for me. To want to fear."

I waited, knowing that my fate was tied to the demon's decision and that nothing I could say or do would tip the scales in my favor. One moment led to another until finally Azazel's eyes zeroed in on me.

"I think I'll pass."

"Chickenshit," I said.

Azazel smiled. "Don't be a sore loser. I've gotten what I came for. *My* realization. *My* appreciation of a thing."

The demon smiled fondly, and my vision blurred, and then I was looking at Cole again. Back in his pristine uniform, creased to perfection. Azazel winked at me from Cole's dead eyes and disappeared down the hallway.

I lay there for a long moment, watching the soft morning light waft through the smoky gray air in the cell. And thought about what he had said.

Your friend Nick seems to think he knows where it is.

There wasn't a lot of time. But it wouldn't matter if there was. There was no one guarding my cell, but there didn't need to be, because there was no way out of it either.

CHAPTER THIRTY

Azazel was gone. Left in his place was the knowledge he would have the Key. And that I was stuck in this cell until sundown when Raphael would come to claim me. Rage burned inside me and withered into ash. There was nothing to fuel it. I was alone and empty and tired, and the night would likely bring my death.

The morning sun continued to rise through the bars of my cell window. The black and yellow shadow patterns on the floor faded into an indistinct gray. I sat and wondered whether Jen was alive. When Nick would trade the Key for Sarah. If my friends would make it out of this town alive. I slumped and breathed and watched the shadows on the wall.

Something slivered through the concrete wall underneath the window. The tip of a katana. It poked in and out in a little sawing motion and moved down through the thick concrete wall. Then it was pulled out and reinserted to cut across. Rinse and repeat, until an entire square around the window had been cut.

I watched all this with interest until the blade slid back a last time. The square of concrete worked its way inward with a rumbling, grating sound. The sides of the block were perfectly cut, the stone polished.

The cut block moved inward slowly, then gathered momentum, and in an instant a sliver of light shot through from behind the block. I stepped back. A moment later the stone toppled into the cell and fell over with a large, echoing boom.

My mother stepped precisely through the hole into the cell. Tiny beams of sunlight washed over her blue-black armor. Her gaze found me immediately, huddled on the bench. She nodded. "Son."

I clenched my jaw. "Did you kill her?" Hopeful, yet dreading the answer.

She blinked, confused, and then finally one of her lips curled up in a slight motion.

"Son," she told me, "whatever I am, whatever command I am under, I am your mother first and always."

"Then Jen's alive?"

A tilt of the head. "Of course."

I let out a deep breath, a breath that came from a furnace burning brightly. The past few hours washed away. The hopelessness. The exhaustion. I pumped my fist and winced at the pain in my arm.

My mother was there in two steps. She reached out and grabbed my hand, placing her other hand against my chest. "Prepare yourself."

A pain—both blazing hot and frigidly cold—swept through me. The nerves in my body lit on fire as if someone had taken a blowtorch to all of them. My forearm cracked once, twice, and then it straightened and the swelling went down.

I was too happy to scream. I felt taller, stronger, better. Healed. I took a deep breath, and then another. Dizziness swept through me as if I stood up too fast, and I sat down. After a moment I squeezed my mother's hand, tightly, and let go. "Thank you."

She seemed to know I wasn't thanking her for healing me. "I cannot always make those decisions, son. But when I can, I will."

Jen *was* alive. I had hoped, but now I knew. She was alive. And I was free of the cell. We could leave this town together.

My mother sat next to me. "We don't have a lot of time," she said.

"Did Dominic order you here?"

She shook her head. "He is half-mad from the drug, and the other half still fights Raphael's last command to him."

Father ... Raphael had said. *You can stop now.*

"I was able to get Dominic away," my mother said. "He isn't lucid and does not know where he is. So I am as free as the geas lets me."

My mother was offering me answers. As much as she could. "Which isn't very free."

She shook her head and smiled. Part of her looked nervous. One hand smoothly drew her blade out again. She placed the tip on the concrete and worked the blade back and forth. As if she needed something to focus her attention on other than our conversation.

My mother wouldn't be able to answer any direct questions. So I tried something else. "How long have we been under the geas?"

"Millennia," she said. "Longer than I know of. My mother had it, her mother before her, and so on ..."

The vampires had had control of us for that long. "How many of us were there?"

"How many through the years?" My mother shrugged. Her hands still worked her blade. "But in the beginning, there were seven."

Seven seemed like an important number. But also a small number, to account for an entire people. I looked at my hands, at my mother's hands, gripping her sword—we looked human. But were we? I still didn't know what had happened to me back at the factory. And both she and I could see and tap into an ethereal plane that seemed not to exist for others.

She continued. "I don't know where you've been. What you've done. What you've seen. But you should know, there is evil in this world. True evil. Not just monsters or vampires or some child molester somewhere. There is a force, and it is driven to overwhelm everything or destroy. There is no middle ground for it."

I had seen the face of that evil. I knew it well.

"But there is good as well, son." My mother took a breath and let it out. Tapped her sword on the concrete. "It has to play by a higher set of rules. It is harder to find. But it exists."

Someone powerful had to have helped Solomon create the Key. Someone powerful had to have helped to capture the demons inside it. And while I could accept that power once existed, I saw no evidence of it being around today. "So you say."

"So I say." My mother smiled. She understood my disbelief.

"It's hard to believe we've been under this geas for thousands of years," I said. "If what you are saying is true, and there is evil, and there is good ... that's a long time for the good side to be losing."

My mother nodded. "It is. But maybe it's time for it to win again."

And then she paused. I felt it too. A rhythm began pounding through the cell, through the walls, through the floor. It felt like someone had turned the bass up to eleven. Everything in the cell vibrated to the call.

Come, come … Come, come … Come, come …

My mother swore. The call from Dominic was so strong I could feel its pulse through her, the panicked rhythm of an erratically beating heart. My mother's eyes glazed over. In a quick moment, she had sheathed her blade and stepped to the hole in the wall.

She turned back to me, slowly. Fighting Dominic's call. "I have to go."

"I understand," I told her.

"You never asked about something." My mother fought the words out through a clenched jaw. "You need to know you have a father."

I had never thought to ask about my father, in much the same way I had never once thought to ask about my mother. I accepted I had one, but it was irrelevant who he was. The person I'd become was the person Parker had shaped, that Miss Tammie had shaped, that Danny and Jen and my friends had all shaped.

My mother had wanted me, though. Enough emotion existed in her to have carved up Parker's face, when I had run away. Enough for her to be here now. I thought she was telling me I had a purpose.

And I should not overlook my father, if he was involved. "Is that important for me to know?"

My mother nodded. "Be careful when you meet him as well." Her eyes flicked to a spot on the floor, where she had sat. "We are all under the geas."

I looked down. My mother hadn't been playing with her sword. She had taken the time to inscribe a picture in the concrete while we were talking. A message to me without words. A message but not a message, because it was just a simple drawing. A feather, a shield, and a staff. One over top of another.

I looked back at my mother. One of her hands pushed against the wall, arm locked, as if that hand alone kept her in the cell.

"Remember, if you see me again," she said, "then I have been sent to kill you." And with those final words, with all the elegance and grace and precision my mother controlled, she let go of the wall and was gone.

It took a long moment for all that to sink in.

I wasn't sure I understood her message. But she had given me something. I burned the picture into my brain. A feather, a staff, and a shield. Were those symbols? What did they represent? Me, my father, and my mother? Who was what?

I had learned a lot. And at the same time nothing. But I would remember it all and remember the symbols. And the number seven. I would take the crumbs she had left and follow the path, and figure it all out.

None of that mattered *right now,* though. What mattered was that my mother had freed me so I could live another day. So I could protect my friends. And possibly—so I could figure out what I was and one day return to save my mother from whatever hell she was locked in.

I didn't know if I was an angel or not. Whether my mother was one or not. But in the past few days, I had done some amazing things. Being around those I cared about had allowed me to become someone different. Maybe a little more like I had been when I was younger. Maybe a little more like the person I should be.

That mattered to me more now.

It was time to stop using the Key as an excuse to run. Protecting the world wouldn't matter if it meant my life, the life of my friends. I needed to protect those I cared about. And to give them a chance to protect me. For us to help each other, and to become greater than the sum of our parts. If I did it right, I had the chance to become greater than who I had been.

Jen was alive.

I stepped through the opening out into the dawn. I could see the round top of the sun over the eastern hill of Grafton. The first thing I did was check out the police cars, but all of them were locked. Somewhere north of me, I could hear the throttled roar of cars racing, and I wondered what was happening. And who. And where.

I ran around to the front of the station and headed toward Main Street. A scent of smoke carried through the air, a scent of the fires of last night. It was faint, but I could taste it in the back of my throat and I coughed at the ash in the air.

I hurried down the sidewalk and got to the crossing at Main Street. The burning shambles of the diner still smoked a bit to my left, and the boarded-up storefronts directly across from me were still standing. The rumbling of car engines grew larger behind me like I was in a race car pit.

To my left was King's Lodge, a couple of miles up the road and almost out of Grafton. The motel stood above the town, in the middle of the northern slope, no smoke or fire around it. The air was still except for the throaty roar of multiple cars racing in concert, the rumbles growing louder and louder behind me.

I turned back and saw Nick's Mustang swerve onto the street, heading my way. Something was wrong with one of the front tires, and sparks flew from the rim as rubber squealed over the blacktop. Nick downshifted. The car surged forward and as it flew by Nick looked over at me, surprised.

I was just as surprised to see Sarah in the car next to him.

Following Nick and cutting across the sidewalk was Raphael's Cadillac. It picked up speed, not surging forward so much as just building momentum. Heavy, thrumming, black with tinted windows, the Cadillac moved with purpose.

I felt for the Key. I felt it to the south now, and more distant than it had been. Nick had found it and made the trade, but Azazel hadn't kept his part of the bargain.

Nick tried to make the turn onto Main Street. The Mustang spun on the tire rim and slid onto the opposing sidewalk before crashing through a couple of parking meters and stopping, the engine dying out. It turned over again and again as Nick attempted to fire the car back up.

The Cadillac ate up the space between it and the coupe. A second later the machine crashed full speed into the driver's side of the Mustang. The impact slammed the red car over the sidewalk and into the boarded-up store next to it. The entire building shook, a window broke apart in a tinkling of glass, the Mustang shuddered, and then everything just stopped.

The door to the Cadillac swung open, and Raphael got out. Faint classical music streamed out of the door speakers, a quartet of violins. Raphael leaped gracefully onto the hood of the Mustang and smiled down at Nick.

I started toward the two cars. Raphael was focused on Nick. The vampire knelt on the hood of the car and punched a fist through the windshield and yanked Nick out. The entire windshield popped out with Nick.

Raph shook Nick briefly and then tossed his body aside with a tinkling crunch of shatterproof glass. The vampire dusted his hands. Nick lay on the ground, arms and legs moving weakly, like a swimmer about to go under the water for the last time.

Raphael reached in again and pulled out Sarah. She struggled against the vampire, punching and kicking him. Raphael took it all, and finally backhanded Sarah. The slap echoed across Grafton. Sarah went limp and hung from his arm.

A cut in Sarah's temple leaked red down the side of her face.

Raphael smiled, leaned forward, and began licking off the blood. He physically grew bigger with each lick. He jumped down in front of Nick and kicked him once, then again. Nick tried to roll away and Raphael followed him, still holding Sarah in one hand.

I ran towards the fight. Nick tried to get away, but the shadows against the building were not big enough to let him escape. He was able to move just enough here and there to keep from taking the brunt of the kicks, but after each kick, Nick moved less and less.

I hadn't known what I was getting into when I came to Grafton. But I knew what I would leave behind me. Raphael had chased me away from this town once. I wouldn't let him do it again. Ghosts or no ghosts, power or no power, I would never run from my friends again. Any of them.

It really had never been the way I was made.

Raphael paused in midkick when I collided with him in a flying tackle. He bounced off the front of the building. Sarah dropped to the ground in a heap. When the vampire turned around I already had a fist headed towards his jaw.

His head snapped back. Then his fist swung back at me. I ended up rolling across the hood of the Mustang and dropping to the street.

Raphael walked around the car. "I'm pretty sure you're out of jail a little early."

"Yeah." I stood there and set my jaw, squared my shoulders. "Out for good behavior."

It seemed like he and I had been fighting since the beginning of time. Since we were kids. Old anger stirred up; old slights jump-started my nerves. As I got up off the ground, my body twitched in anticipation of the upcoming fight. My foot hit something. I looked down and saw the parking meter pole. I grabbed it in both hands.

Raphael cocked his head at me. He was at least a foot taller than he had been just a minute ago. I swung the meter before he grew any taller.

Like I had seen before, he was just faster than anything I had ever seen. Faster than I had ever been, even with the ethereal energy. I missed him with the meter, and he plucked it from my hands and tossed it through the air. He followed that by throwing me into the building. I bounced off the wall and landed on the concrete.

"How long you going to let me beat on you, Grimm?" Raphael asked. "What's this make, three? In as many days? You getting sick of it yet?"

I had walked this street as a kid. I had walked it with Jen and Nick and Johnny and Sarah. And I had walked it with Danny, tossing his baseball back and forth with him. Laughing when he turned his ball cap sideways and showed me his new swing.

The town was dead now. Nothing but burnt building and empty sidewalks. A burned-out diner. Dead friends. Dead family. Grafton had been alive once, but a rot had overtaken it, from a festering wound in the back parking lot of a liquor store. Just a block away.

In the end, we always remember the beginning.

I screamed and jumped up on the back bumper of the Mustang, taking a couple of large steps to the roof before leaping at Raphael. I crashed into him and we both fell to the sidewalk with a loud crack. Raphael grunted. I swung an elbow and felt some of his teeth give a satisfying crack. So I did it again.

Raphael got a hold of me. Both of us rolled around on the ground like we were ten years old, swinging at each other. He landed a lot more than I did. Somehow I kicked him off and stumbled to my feet, holding on to the building as I got up. The sidewalk seesawed in front of me.

Raphael picked himself up next to me. He dusted off his sleeves and snapped his coat straight. One of his lips was turned up in a grin. Down from us, Nick was struggling to get to his feet, Sarah still lay in a heap, and Vivaldi still played from the open door of the Cadillac.

A minute into the fight and I was done. Whatever adrenaline I had had was now drifting below the big red E. I needed time to recover, time we didn't have.

If I could get Raphael away, I might buy some time for Nick and Sarah.

"Hey, Grimm." Raphael grinned. He reached into the broken store window and pulled out a wooden bat. "Look what I found."

He tested the bat and swung it once or twice. It whistled through the air. I backed up and stumbled, caught myself, and slid back some more.

Raphael with a bat brought back the horrible memories. The parking lot down the alley. Danny crying out loud. I took a breath and needed another. Raph stalked me and grinned. His brow was lowered over wide-open, shiny eyes. I kept backing down the street, away from Nick and Sarah.

Get up, I thought to Sarah. *Run,* I willed to Nick.

We passed an older car, parked on the street. Raphael took a test swing, and the side-view mirror went flying. His steps after that were light on the ground, like a cat's. "Where you going, Grimm?"

I took a few more steps. Then a foot hit empty air. I had reached the end of the sidewalk. I stumbled and fell backward onto my ass. Raphael laughed until he had to catch his breath. Then he looked past me.

I turned to look as well. The liquor store sat there at its corner, windows dark, iron bars over the glass. Closed. Dead. Locked.

But still alive, for me.

I turned back to Raphael. He stood there and weighed the bat in his hands.

"You know, Grimm," Raphael said, "these things do end up coming full circle, don't they?"

He grabbed my leg and dragged me down the street. His other hand held the bat. I kicked at him until he turned back and cracked the bat upside my skull.

I went limp. Blood ran down from my temple, and when I felt it, my hand came away sticky.

Raphael walked on, tugging me along behind. I looked for Nick or Sarah, but the motion made me nauseated. I had to fight not to throw up. The back of my head thumped from the sidewalk to the blacktop as Raphael angled us to the back parking lot. It got colder and darker as the high walls of the alley swallowed the two of us.

Memories of back then overwhelmed me. I wish I had stayed and never run. Maybe the ghosts of this town wouldn't be the darkened hulks of burned houses, and the flaming ash of vampires, but ghosts of real people who died normal kinds of deaths.

Maybe if I had stayed I would have stood up to Raphael. Maybe Grafton would have been different, and Miss Tammie and Parker would still be alive. Maybe Sarah wouldn't be the pawn in a vampire plot to overthrow his father. Maybe Nick and Johnny and I would have been hanging out with a beer after a ball game, instead of me watching the business end of a bat wave over Raphael's shoulder in a dark alleyway.

I could see now that I should have spent more time with the people I cared about. Especially if I was going to die here. All those years wasted because I had been scared.

I would miss Jen. And I was scared. If I was going to die, what would happen next?

I'd fought vampires and demons and I'd seen ghosts by the thousands, but I had no idea what came after death. I believed it would be a great darkness. Ghosts disappeared, after all. Things disappeared in the dark.

With all the evil I'd seen, all the ghosts that had made me throw up after living their lies, with Azazel and Raphael and Dominic and all the child molesters or wife beaters or rapists or thieves, I thought I would have seen *something* from the other side. Somewhere a power bright, and honest, and pure should exist.

I had never seen proof of anything from the other side. Not a soul. I had purposefully avoided thinking about that because it frightened me. But I couldn't help thinking about it now, as I was being dragged down that alley.

Chances were, I would get my answer soon. One way or another.

"Today's a great day for me, Grimm." Raphael dragged me to the same spot where I had been held down, on that day he had killed Danny, and sat me there. "I've decided to kill you. And your mother. And my father. Start this whole thing clean. With no one else to worry about. None of this geas bullshit. No one to have to listen to."

"That's where you're wrong," I told him. I was unsteady even sitting there, and put one hand on the ground to stay seated.

He squatted in front of me, the bat resting on one of his legs. "Enlighten me."

"You've got to answer to the guy who gave you the drug."

Raphael cocked an eyebrow. "Browner is dead. You killed him."

"Not him." Nausea racked my stomach. I was pretty sure I had a concussion, if not a cracked skull. "The real guy who brought all this to you and helped you plan it. Helped you get me here. The guy you think is Cole. You got to answer to him, sooner or later."

"So what?" Raphael said. "He can die like anyone else."

"Not this guy," I told him ""He's a little out of your league. You think the drug is something, wait until he gets serious. He's controlled you this whole time just to get what he wants. Wait and see what happens when you're of no use to him."

Raphael puzzled on that a moment. His eyes opened wide, maybe at some memory of a conversation. Then he poked me in the chest with the bat. "Tell me what you know about Cole. You'll still die, but I'll make it quick. Maybe I'll let your friends live."

I grinned. "You're the king of the world. You figure it out."

"Have it your way."

"You mean have it *his* way." I chuckled. "All this work you've done, and you just substituted one father for another."

I wanted to dodge the swing, but I didn't see Raphael's hand move. And when the bat hit, it felt like a boulder had clipped the side of my head.

The world rang like my skull had been a gong and the bat a hammer. The next thing I knew, I was lying on my side on the blacktop. My cheek rested in a large puddle of my own blood.

I glanced up. Raphael had the bat above his head in both hands. His face was twisted in anger. His lips thinned out over his teeth.

Then the shadow behind Raphael *flexed*, and Nick stepped out of the shadow with a tire iron.

Nick swung the iron for all he was worth and connected with Raphael's head. The tire iron clanged at the hit. Raphael stumbled forward a few steps and dropped the bat. He screamed in rage. Nick got in a few more blows before Raphael turned and swung back.

I willed my body to get up, but my arms and legs only moved in random motions, like a newborn. Nothing worked right. The parking lot felt cold against my face, and bubbles of red kept burping out of my mouth.

I could still see the fight. Nick flashing in and out of the alley shadows, Raphael stumbling and swinging and missing. *Nick was a dark fucker.* And Nick was giving Raphael everything he was worth. I watched until blood ran over my eyes and the fight became a blur.

I was no longer cold. My arms and legs stopped moving. I tried to take a breath, but all that happened was a catching motion like I tried to breathe air in but my lungs just wouldn't open up.

Nick must have missed a shadow then, or Raphael guessed a swing right. There was a crack and a blurry Nick fell to the ground. Raphael turned to me, his grin wide enough it looked like a white smear across his face. Feral. A monster that should have been put down a long time ago, had someone had the courage.

The vampire picked up the bat and headed my way.

I lay there and couldn't move. The sliver of the sky was a blue blur above the walls of the alley. It seemed an incredible blue, though, the kind of blue I had seen in pictures of the waters of New Zealand. Such a crystal-clear blue for such a gray day.

That blueness swelled around me, and I thought I could see Danny. Then I realized I was really seeing him. Danny's ghost. Standing here in the middle of the day as though he had been waiting for me all along. The white-and-blue ethereal glow surrounded him, thicker and stronger than other spirits. Like he was a part of something.

I looked at him and cried. Tears mixed with the blood on my face. I tried to reach out to him, but my hand just twitched.

"Hey, buddy," I said. "It's been a while."

Danny knelt down beside me. He looked the same as he had ten years ago. Baseball cap tight on his forehead, a smattering of hair escaping it. He put his hand on my face. His fingers felt so real to me, and a coolness radiated from him across my body. Danny waved between us with his other hand, like he was pulling a rope toward me.

"Oh, Danny ... no." I shook my head. I was dying. And I wasn't going to absorb Danny, live his life, and throw it away in another fight with Raphael. I had seen what I could do with as much ghost as I could pull, and it hadn't been enough.

"You say something, Grimm?" Raphael had paused above me, the bat high over his head.

Danny mimicked the pulling motion again, urgently. He pointed to Nick, who hadn't moved since he fell.

"I'm sorry, Danny," I said. Sorry the world hadn't gotten to see Danny grow older. It could have used him. I could have too.

Danny frowned a bit, sticking his tongue out the corner of his mouth.

I smiled, remembering how many times I had seen that same look when Danny was puzzling something out.

Then Danny smiled again, what we used to call the Danny Special.

Raphael swung the bat downward.

Danny reached down to hug me.

A cool fall day washed over me as he fell into me. Every ethereal particle of Danny sifted through me and settled in, firing up nerves, rebuilding bones, pumping blood. Jolting me like a thousand-amp current. There was no pain, just an overall sense of rightness, of happiness and peace. And power like I had never felt before.

Danny was me, and I was him. Memories fell into my mind, memories of us as a group. Of all of us together, hanging out at the Rock, hanging at Jen's house, at Parker's. Of Danny running the bases, of the two of us walking to school, of him and me eating pie at the diner, of a night when we all had gone up to the water tower and stared at the stars.

His memories swept through me, and I cried at each and every one. Each of them happy, each of them one of the group, each of them a piece of innocence I had been unaware had ever existed in my life. And then a final one ...

"Did you see that?" Danny asked, excited, dropping the bat to the ground. Jen had thrown a soft pitch, and Danny had swung for all he was worth, like he always did, and had finally connected. It was mostly physics, the perfect spot of the bat coming into contact with the baseball at just the right angle and speed. The crack had split the air, and a tiny white ball traveled far over the fence. "D-did you see it?"

"I saw it, buddy." The ball dropped in the air, ending its long, elliptical arc and drifting down over the fence. Disappearing into the field beyond. "It was a great hit, buddy."

"It went forever," Danny said, proud. He still stared far out into the field, one hand over his visor. Trying to see the entire thing for another moment, his perfect hit. Something that even in the majors, even the best only do a fraction of the time. The sweet spot, where everything feels right.

"It sure did, bud," I said. I reached over to him. Jen grinned at the two of us from the mound. I put an arm around Danny's shoulders and tugged him to me, jostling him a bit playfully. It was a good hit to end a

day on. I reached up with my other hand, tugged his ball cap down a bit over his head. "It went forever ..."

Then Danny the ghost was gone.

I blinked. The blue sky was still above me. I lay flat on the ground, still resting a little on my side. Raphael was still in midswing, his face a mix of laughter and rage.

I reached out with one hand and the bat broke over it. The splintered ends skittered across the parking lot.

I stood up. Could feel the power through me, different from the the other ghosts I had tapped into. Different from the liars and the murderers and the thieves. I felt more *right* somehow.

I could see the surprise in Raphael's face. But the surprise changed quickly to anger and the anger to a scream.

I roared back.

This time the fight was different. Where Raphael had been faster and stronger before, now he moved like he was in quicksand. I was faster now, graceful in my movements, elegant in this dance. Powerful in my motions.

Raphael moved as if the air had thickened around him. He swung. I ducked. And then I rocked him with an open palm to the side of his head.

He twisted into the air and slapped against the alley wall. I stepped close to him and saw his eyes still watching for where I had just been. I smiled, reached out, and broke his arm in half.

Raphael screamed and fell to his knees. He swung and swung but missed me every time. At one point his incisors shot out and he tried to bite me, like a feral dog.

I casually punched the top of his mouth and felt the front bridge of his teeth give under the impact.

Raphael fell to the ground, tried to crawl away. Blood poured out of his mouth onto the ground. I flipped him over, held him in place on the parking lot. One of the broken pieces of the bat was next to us. I grabbed the splintered handle of the bat.

"Now let's see," I said. "Do vampires die from a stake through the heart?"

Miss Tammie: if you know what makes people wrong, then you also know how to make it right ...

I took the stake and punched it through his stomach. Raphael screamed and tried to pull away. His good arm pushed at me.

"Sorry, Raph," I said, "I skipped a lot of health class."

"Grimm!" Raphael cursed me, over and over. "You're fucking dead, you hear me? *Dead!*"

He reached out and tried to control me with the geas, and with the drug, but whether it was Danny's ghost, Raphael not being his father, or Raph just being in an incredible amount of pain, I ignored the command. I wiggled the bat out of his stomach with a sticky, sucking sound.

Parker: You got to be strong so they have something to latch on to …

I punched the bat through Raphael once again, feeling ribs crack underneath the bat. Feeling the slight resistance of an organ before it popped like a balloon. Raphael screamed louder.

I stabbed him a couple more times, thinking of Greg and Andy and Danny. All of my friends, but especially Danny. Did vengeance only belong to the pure of heart? Was it okay that I was torturing the man who had ruined so many lives? Probably not. But sometimes you take what you can get.

Raphael tried to pull away. I could feel his body tug on the bat. He was mumbling something about killing me, about killing us all, over and over. I didn't care to listen enough to understand it. I looked around, seeing the parking lot ten years ago, seeing Danny kneeling in front of Raphael and his friends.

I leaned close to Raphael's ear. "I bet ten years ago you never thought you'd be here again. Like this. With me."

Raphael stopped trying to pull away. His eyes were wide-open in fear, and I felt good about it. I pulled the bat out of his side with a sucking sound.

"Who are you?" he finally asked.

"I'm where all this ends, Raph," I told him. And punched the bat through Raphael's skull.

In the end, we always come back to the beginning.

CHAPTER THIRTY-ONE

I stood up, feeling a sense of things being done. Of being complete. I turned back to the alleyway, saw Sarah standing there, leaning against the corner of the liquor store. Her hair was undone, and parts of her face were still covered in blood. She looked at Raphael and smiled, an evil, content smile. A smile for someone who had it coming.

Nick stirred weakly. I went over to him. The side of his face was already swelling from Raphael's blow. The bruise purpled his skin. Sarah was right behind me. He was trying to push himself up, and I pulled him to a sitting position. A moan escaped him.

"He dead?" Nick asked.

"Yeah," I said. Knowing that I would never have had the chance had Nick not come back.

"Good," Nick spat.

"Thanks," I said. Nick knew I was thanking him for coming back and giving me a chance. Our eyes met, and we both understood what we had done for each other. It was a nice feeling. He nodded weakly.

"You okay?" Sarah asked Nick, one hand on his.

"I'll make it," he said. His hand reached out and grabbed my arm. "Grimm, look, I'm sorry."

I knew what he was talking about. Giving Azazel the Key. "Don't worry about it."

"You don't know," he said. "He offered me Sarah for this Key you were supposed to have, and I kept telling him no, but when you went down I just thought—"

"Hey." I stopped Nick. He looked away, but I put my hand on his cheek and brought his face around until our eyes locked. "I'm telling you, I'd have done the same."

Nick smiled, a real smile, and finally nodded.

I stood. Azazel was still out there. And Jen was stuck up at that motel with maybe Father Benjamin and Johnny. I needed to get to her and make sure she was okay.

The Key was something that had taken six years of my life away, and now it was gone. With it, Azazel would bring back his brethren. Seven demon brothers that had been trapped for thousands of years, and would want their revenge on the human race. Real Old Testament stuff.

If Azazel was still around, he might know that I was alive. That I had escaped. That Raphael was dead. And he wanted some new games, and I was worried that part of the game would include my friends. Could include Jen.

That thought crystallized further.

Nick saw something in me change. He grasped my arm, hard. "She's at the hotel. Room one fifteen."

I looked over at Sarah. "Can you take care of him?"

She nodded.

"I've got to go," I said. Nick let go of my arm.

I took off, worry raging through me. I ran to Main Street, saw the Cadillac still sitting there, classical music still singing from the door speakers. I jumped in, shut the door, backed up the Cadillac, and took off.

Vivaldi, I thought again, and for some reason, the name of the particular piece popped into my head. "The Four Seasons."

The car sped off toward the hotel in the distance. Hanging on the hill a little over the town of Grafton. An old sign, rusted and dirty, proclaiming it a place where kings stayed overnight for the low price of twenty-nine dollars and ninety-nine cents a night.

It would be just like Azazel, to let me think that I'd won, only to take away the very thing I had been fighting for. He would consider it a delicious turn of events, a dampening of the spirit. He would delight in knowing that in the moment when I had won, the woman I had fought for was taken from me.

Violins sped up as I punched the gas, a rapid dance of strings, and I could feel their bows saw across my nerves. My hands gripped the steering wheel, knuckles white.

I took the corner into the motel parking lot hard. The back end of the car skidded around until the Cadillac was facing an awkward angle. Instead of maneuvering it around, I jumped out and ran around the back of the lodge, past the large arching columns that held up the second-story balcony.

I slowed as I came across the bodies sprawled in front of the room. Johnny and Father Benjamin. Johnny sat back against the Camaro. Dried blood covered his shirt, and a stained towel hung from his side. He wasn't moving, and I breathed a sigh of relief when I found a pulse. His heartbeat was steady and strong.

Father Benjamin was a different story. He looked much like a mannequin would if it had been tossed off a tall building. Streaks of black ash covered his body and the parking lot around it. The cold feeling in the pit of my stomach swelled into a huge block of ice. I stepped closer and saw one of his eyes wide-open, unblinking.

I don't think I stood there long, but at the same time, I was rooted in that spot. Somewhere I could still hear muted Vivaldi behind me. Azazel had been here. There had been a fight, and the priest had taken the worst of it. The open door to the motel room beckoned. I took a step in that direction and jumped when the priest coughed.

I stopped and knelt by the priest. His eyes were black and burnt as if something had exploded right in front of him. Blood leaked out from between his fingers. His mouth moved in little motions, over and over, the same words again and again. I couldn't make them out, perhaps a prayer.

I touched him, lightly on the shoulder, and whispered, "Father ..."

"Grimm." He sighed, then coughed again. Red liquid streamed out of his mouth. His throat worked hard. *"See."*

"Hold on, Father," I said, looking over him. His chest was so misshapen and broken I didn't know how he was still alive. Whatever time Father Benjamin had left, it wouldn't be much.

"Seeee ..." Father Benjamin repeated. The priest reached out and pawed my face with his hand, fingers brushing my eyes.

I got it. I opened my ethereal sight.

Father Benjamin's body still lay on the blacktop. Next to the priest's body was his ghost, on one knee, in knight's armor. Both of the priest's hands were raised above his head, holding the hilt of a huge sword, which was plunged deep into the concrete before him. The ghost and armor and blade all radiated a golden glow.

I looked down and saw that the ash marks on Father Benjamin's body all lined up with where the sword had been plunged into the pavement. In my ethereal vision, it looked as if a shock wave had exploded out from the tip of the sword, where ash and gold forked outward in all directions.

The priest's armor had a gleaming red cross on it. Father Benjamin himself looked younger, kneeling in a pose of repose, head bowed, and resting against the pommel of the sword. His ghost took a deep breath and let it out in a shudder.

The priest had fought Azazel there, where ash and gold had come together and exploded apart. That explosion had cost the priest his life, but maybe it had saved Johnny's. The ashen streaks ended at the edges of the golden circle. Father Benjamin had kept the worst of the damage to himself.

The ghost shuddered again and faded from view.

I blinked back as Father Benjamin coughed once more, and died.

I rushed to the motel door. There was a smattering of black blood on the floor in front of the door, dark against the faded concrete.

Jen and I had only just gotten back together. And after ten years of being apart, I never wanted to be apart again. I didn't want to be alone anymore. I didn't want to have to face the burden I carried with the Key, with who I was, and what I could do. I didn't want to become so tightly wrapped around myself I became something of a monster myself.

I had been walking that path just a few days ago. I had been running down that path, actually. It was where Azazel wanted me to go, to lose my humanity in a quest to save the world. It was his kind of game, and it was where I was sure he had led many a Keeper of the Key before me.

I didn't know if Azazel really wanted to free his family. Maybe some part of the demon did. But I now thought he enjoyed this game too much to want it to finally be over. All his schemes, and all his corruption, and it was more fun for him to twist, turn, and corrupt me until I couldn't recognize myself.

I swallowed and crossed through the doorway.

It was a normal motel room. The room felt so much like the hotel room I had fought Azazel in, just a few short days ago, that a feeling of déjà vu overwhelmed me. Two twin beds, a table between them. A chair and desk near the big front window of the room. An old television on a dresser in front of the beds. Floral wallpaper layered the walls and matched the faded bedspreads. The old air conditioner still ran, pushing out a cold, musty air that still somehow carried the smell of a lit cigarette.

The bed closest to the door held a body. My heart thudded so hard it hurt. There was a glow from a yellow bulb on the nightstand. Directly inside the lamp's circle of yellow light lay an ashtray with a lit cigarette and a half-full glass of whiskey. The desk lamp made the whiskey look darker, bronzed, and the liquid still waved from side to side in the glass, as if someone had just taken a drink, set the glass down, and left.

I went to the bed. A mass of yellow hair spread wildly about on a pillow. Azazel was nowhere to be seen. With a shaking hand, I reached out and grabbed the edge of the cover and pulled it slowly back.

Jen's legs and arms were tumbled about. Like she was having a bad dream. She didn't have a shirt on, just a bra and panties, and a huge bandage wrapped around the side of her stomach. The bandage was stained with blood. I reached out to touch her and hesitated, scared at what I might find.

Her breasts swelled then, with the inhalation of someone in a deep sleep. I let out a huge breath I didn't know I had been holding.

She breathed again. And again. Jen was alive. I looked at the whiskey, the cigarette, then back to Jen, alive, and Azazel's voice echoed from back in that the jail cell.

A new game, maybe? That would be interesting ...

Azazel had taken the Key and he had left me Jen. Had left me all my friends. And had let me know it. His kind of razor's edge. Damned if I do and damned if I don't. Protect my friends or save the world. He was sure I couldn't do both, and Azazel wanted me balanced on that razor until I slipped and cut my own throat. His favorite kind of game.

I sat on the bed. The thin mattress compressed under my weight. I went to check Jen's bandage and winced at how the blood stuck the wrap to her skin. I wished it didn't look as bad as I thought it did. I pulled back some more, gently, and felt nerves tingle in the tips of my fingers. A static shock of blue light burst from them and flashed over Jen's skin.

Is Danny's ghost still a part of me?

I peeled back the bandage. The skin underneath it was whole, unblemished. Smooth. Like a sword recently hadn't punctured through it. I looked at my fingers. I felt around for any energy I might still have, but I felt depleted now. Empty but also unburdened.

I had never done anything like that before.

Jen's breathing had changed. I found her staring at me. Her lips curved in a lazy, welcoming smile. Her eyes were blue and soft and intimate, and I stopped breathing when we locked gazes.

What I had with her scared me. And thrilled me. Her smile grew wider, my heart raced faster, and she reached out to squeeze my hand.

"Hey," she said. Sleepily. Happily. Her voice was a low, warm murmur. It was rich and molten and poured all through me.

"Hey," I said back.

Some people might have said more at that moment, but those two words had always been enough. For us.

We all left soon after that.

Nick and Sarah had gotten to the lodge not long after I. Between them they roused Johnny. We all witnessed a tearful reunion between the two sisters.

Nick, Johnny, and I went out and buried Father Benjamin in a hastily dug grave. We all felt bad it wasn't something more permanent, but none of us wanted to be in town after dark.

While we dug I told them everything that had happened to Danny and me the day I left. They both listened quietly and said nothing when I was done. Johnny reached out and put his hand on my shoulder, and a little after that Nick did too.

He asked me about the object he had given to Cole and I told them all the truth about that too, at least the truth as far as I had learned it. Nick apologized again after the story. Cole had been working him for days, telling Nick about how I was Raphael's to command. That I would never be able to help Nick rescue Sarah.

He was tense the whole time, telling the story in spurts as we shoveled, but when he was done I just clapped him on the shoulder. Neither of us was guilt-free, and neither of us would ever feel the same again after the past week. What happened to Danny would always haunt me. I would always wonder about what happened to Parker and Miss Tammie and if things might have happened differently, had I just not run.

We would all carry our ghosts from this town.

Nick was the person who said something after the burial, surprisingly enough. It was short and heartfelt and made me think of when we all were kids together. After that, the five of us got in the Camaro and left. Having come in from the north, I decided to drive through town one final time and head south. None of us really knew what the next day would bring.

We were all quiet during the drive through town. Like a slide show, it all passed by us. The burned-down diner, the wrecked Mustang, all the stores and shops we used to run around to as kids, the movie theater.

Twisted gray smokestacks climbed from the smoky remnants of homes and reached into the noonday sun. Here and there lay ashy outlines of vampire bodies. In the rearview mirror, Sarah leaned against Nick, and he had an arm around her, and both seemed content to be near each other, but also maybe tense, an unknowingness of what might be next.

At some point, Jen had reached over and laid her hand on top of mine as we rode through the empty streets. I thought of Danny after his ghost had hugged me. Of how proud he had felt, standing up for me with Raphael. Of him and me and Jen out at the baseball field, smiling and laughing after his perfect hit. I could still hear his voice: *It went on forever ...*

It sure does, buddy, I thought, and squeezed Jen's hand. *It sure does ...*

Finally we left Grafton and headed up the hill out of town. The water tower passed us on the right, still standing, its belly open to the ground. I pressed the gas pedal and the Camaro accelerated smoothly, rumbling away. The cool wind whipped through the open windows of the car. Jen's hair snapped around her face and she laughed, and then Sarah laughed, and then we were all laughing for no reason other than we were alive, at a moment when some of us weren't, where others had fallen, and all of us had scars.

As we topped the hill and headed away from town, I thought about the

Key and what the future held. I could sense it, heading south before us. My mind wandered to my last conversation with Azazel …

"You ever wonder what you would do if we were different … if our roles were reversed?"

"What if I had something, and you desperately wanted it back? What would you do? How far would you take it?"

I pressed the pedal down farther, and the Camaro surged down the hill and picked up speed. The demon would have plans upon plans. Whether I chased him, or ignored him, I would never be sure I wasn't playing out the very action he wanted. So I would pick the one that suited me best.

Jen looked over with one eyebrow raised, curious. I smiled back at her. One thing I could be sure of, something Azazel would never know, was there was power in friendship. In being together. Power in the love and care of my friends, and from my friends. Danny had shown me that. Johnny and Nick and Sarah and Jen had all shown me that what I had been doing alone was exactly what I was doing wrong.

Azazel had a surprise coming for him. One way or another. The demon had made a mistake, bringing me to Grafton. I had lost myself had been as a Keeper, always running. I had been so focused on saving the world I had forgotten what it had meant to be human.

Then here, with my friends, I had found who I always should have been. I would stand up for what was right, I would go down swinging if I had to, and I had friends who cared enough to see the fight through with me. I thought I could play Azazel's game now, and even win it.

So, how far would I take it?

I squeezed Jen's hand tightly. Her fingers twined through mine and pressed back hard in return.

As far as I needed to.

Enjoy *Ghost Town* and looking for more of the Grimm Saga?

Take a step back and find out how Grimm found Solomon's Key in *Recon Team Four*

Also - take a moment and visit chrisjcranford.com, be a part of the Grimm Universe. Discover all the other worlds I'm building. Or just reach out and say hello.

And next, keep on reading about Grimm and his friends with this sneak peak at the next book in the saga …

RECON TEAM FOUR

Master Sergeant Jason Bradley sat on a large flat rock. The mountains of Afghanistan stood tall above him. Scrublike brush dotted the hillsides, leaving splattered spots of brownish green to blot the hard browns of rocky cliffs and tan channels of stone. There was an arid feel to the air, like a desert, except that it was far colder here, even with the sun blazing overhead.

The foothills had been small at first. Like little rows stretched across the land. From the air they would have looked like a large hand lying on the ground, fingertips stretched far apart, as if the hand was trying to palm the earth. Then the fingers had swollen, the knuckles grown into rounded humps, tiny hillsides deepening into sharp ravines. Those ravines had gotten more treacherous, more vertical, until the hills had become true mountains, and then those had grown taller and taller, until they were deep in the Hindu Kush.

Killer of the Hindus, Jason thought. *And I wonder how many others....*

He focused on the small monastery below, the one McNulty had found the night before. Jason was dressed and kitted out in the Ranger camouflage, his rifle kicked up next to him, jacket tightly wrapped around him. The wind, when it gusted, held a sharp, bitter chill. One that cut through the jacket and the layered cloths Jason wore underneath.

He didn't like any of this. It was outside the norm of their usual assignments. Recons, target acquisitions, rescues, assassinations, his team had done them all. But reconning a town that seemed empty, a monastery that looked to have last seen use thousands of years ago, didn't make sense. Doubly so to do this assignment before coming in from the last one.

Their missions always began with a brief. Then the team would practice before hitting the field. Then the execution of the plan. Completing the mission and returning to home base.

The team almost never remained in a field after completion. This time, they had been able to get in a brief resupply as they were ordered to another assignment. And they had rushed out on that mission, without knowing the *whys* and *hows* and *whos* of it.

They just knew the where on this one. And Jason hadn't asked why, when given the assignment. He liked to know, because knowing always improved the success of a mission, but on the times he wasn't given the why, he rarely questioned the order. Answers to those questions were usually far above his pay grade. In those times, with those orders, he fell back to execution. That was his job, and he did that well. Had always done that well.

This time, though, Jason wished he had asked. Some people had showed up in a jeep this morning. Three of them, shortly after Jason's team had gotten there. Jason wasn't sure what they were doing. And the radios had stopped working the night before. Maybe this deep in the Kush, they would. So even if Jason reached out, no one would be listening.

He had a bad feeling about it.

His team was on edge, as well. Sue Franklin lay on the slope above them, rifle trained on the small town below. Her blond hair in a crew cut. Patrick lay next to her, spotting. Lilly Thompson was walking the perimeter with Gus McNulty, their newest member.

Joe Girogilia stood next to Bradley. His second-in-command for a long time. He was a big man, broad in the shoulder, thick in the chest. Normally the man had a five o'clock shadow a few minutes after a shave, but was sporting a brushlike beard now. Joe's machine gun, a compact MK-46, sat on a rock next to him.

"Still not sure?" his second-in-command asked. Joe's accent, Italian, always reminded Jason of New York. With its tall skyscrapers and crazy crowds and the smell of pizza at every corner.

Jason grunted. He and Joe had been together long enough that he knew Joe would take it as an assent. Still, Jason kept watch on the monastery below.

"Not a typical recon," Joe said. Joe, being Italian, was a natural-born talker. But in these moments, both of them knew what was ahead. The large problem in the mission. And so, when the two of them talked, it was something like this. Small sentences. Shorter words.

"No," Jason agreed. Normally they had clearly defined objectives. Someone to rescue. Someone to kill. Something to look at and report on. His eyes were still down the hill. "It is not."

The monastery lay below them, but above the floor of the foothills. Out of the way of where a river might have run, thousands of years ago. It had been cut into the side of the mountain, a square mud-brick thing. It stood multiple levels high, taller than the homes around it, formed from the same brick. Though they hadn't seen anyone, an old jeep was parked between two homes. A four-door vehicle, dusty and white.

The small town, or village, or whatever it was, seemed unobtrusive. Maybe like other towns Jason had seen, not towns in the Kush, but towns he had seen in Nevada. The old Indian homes carved into the red cliff-sides back there.

At the same time, this place seemed far older than those towns. It had been there a long time, the hard corners of the rock worn down by weather. Water erosion in places where there hadn't been water in a long time. The whole place seemed older than it should be. And old places in the Hindu Kush tingled something in Jason's brain. Old places were dangerous here.

"No insurgents," Joe added.

Jason sighed. "I don't know exactly what we're here for, either."

As far as Jason knew, no army regiment was headed this way. There was no reason for his team to be here, scouting this place. But he had a feeling there was a lot riding on this. His subconscious screamed *danger*, and whenever he felt that, the mission *did* get dangerous. Very often people died.

Jason wanted to keep his people from that, as much as he could.

"Call 'em?" Joe said.

Jason shook his head. "Don't think the radios'll work until we're out."

Radio comms had been out awhile. Then the team had gotten lost after the compasses went a little screwy. Jason wondered what else might go wrong. This felt like one of the stories he had read about the Bermuda Triangle. Communication out. Navigation screwy. He was flying blind and didn't know if he was going to land this thing or crash.

At least they had found the objective. What Home Base needed active reconnaissance on. So Jason and Joe sat on the hillside. Looking at the little village, carved out of the rock under the monastery. An old white jeep, topless, by the side of the building. Three people, a large man, a small man, and a thin man, had all at one point left the monastery to go to the jeep.

It was midday.

Jason wondered why he thought it was a monastery. His subconscious had identified it with the name. Maybe because it reminded him of one he had seen in Turkey. Stone. Carved. Thick. Multiple levels, with thick square windows high on each level. The building in Turkey had a dark roof, though. This one was the same color stone, and more square, then arched.

"Doesn't seem right," Joe said.

"No." Jason repeated himself. Which he never minded, if he was working through a thought. "It does not."

"Could be worse," Joe said, nodding to the northeast. "Could be up there."

Up there was the real Hindu Kush. The tall snow-peaked mountains, jagged tops pointing miles high in the air. Dark veins of stone, showing through the white snow here and there. Where Jason's team was now was on the edge, where the hills had become the mountains.

Joe was right; if this place had been up there, they couldn't have made it. Weren't kitted out for it. The bitter cold, the lack of oxygen, all that would have done them in.

Which only increased Jason's worry about this now. To send them here, low on supplies, spoke of critical timing. With what Jason knew about the world, that could be a very bad thing.

Joe grunted this time, patted Jason's shoulder. He was done saying his piece, and Jason was still working through his. Both he and Jason had been around the block a few times. They would get this done, too.

Down the hill from where Jason sat, Thompson and McNulty appeared. Doing their job well. Quiet steps. Smooth movements. Rifles held carefully at the ready. Careful turns of the head, searching the land around them.

McNulty was new. Relatively speaking. He had transferred to their division when they headed out for their turn in the rotation. But they had done enough missions now that he had blended in.

The Ranger was quiet, but intense. Dedicated. Worked with a ruthless efficiency Jason had seen in others. A man who got things done, as soon as they needed doing. Because he lived with a fear that not getting them done would get someone killed. And he was one of the best recon men Jason had been around.

Thompson came up. Her hair was a bit longer than normal, and she had it tied up in a ponytail under her helmet. It was the only thing out of standard with her. She was tall, thin, and athletic. Her shirt tucked neatly into her pants. Her jacket the perfect length. Her rifle at the proper angle, ready in her hands, pointed downhill. Everything just so.

"Nothing, Jason," she said.

Jason nodded. "Take a break."

"Yeah," Lilly snorted. She hadn't been happy at the extended mission. Christmas was coming around, and she was looking forward to getting back to Williamsburg, Virginia. This time of year, she was saying last night, they lit up the town with candles, drank sodas from metals cups. Jason didn't understand the attraction.

She clapped McNulty once on the back and headed back to camp, just a bit uphill. "Maybe I'll catch a movie or something."

Those two had gotten closer since Gus came on. Which Jason found interesting, because Lilly was five-dot-oh, and McNulty was never squared away. His shirt was usually untucked, his jacket open, sometimes even buttoned incorrectly. But he and Lilly were like brother and sister, almost. Closer for their differences.

McNulty still stood by Jason, not moving. The Ranger faced the monastery, below and across the ravine from them. Somewhere over a mile away.

It had been McNulty who found the place, the night before. After a few days of the team searching the hills for it. He had found it in the dead of night, with no moon or moonlight to see by, just the black sky above them holding thousands of pinpricks of stars.

If Jason only talked a little, McNulty might have been a mute. Which wasn't a knock on him. He was good, took the lead in every breach, did things with a silent, manic focus.

"Gus," Jason said quietly.

A few moments later. "Gus."

McNulty stared down at the village as if something there had spooked him. As if he was haunted. Possibly afraid. His rifle was slung around his back. McNulty had taken off his helmet and held it loosely in the crook of an arm. Like he was facing something ahead down there.

"Grimm," Jason finally said. Going to his nickname.

The soldier's head snapped up. Turned to face Bradley. Jason was always surprised at his eyes, an emerald green that at times turned a dark hazel, at times a brilliant sapphire. The change seemed to be mood-dependent. McNulty's hair was a mop of black wavy curls that seemed to grow back quickly after every haircut. His stare was fierce, but quiet. As if ready to challenge whatever Jason was about to ask.

So Jason didn't ask anything. He just nodded at the town. "Tell me, man."

Grimm looked back toward the monastery, then back. His expression became even more guarded. "Tell you what?"

"You found it," Jason said.

"Any of us could have," Grimm said.

"No." Jason shook his head. He traced the air with his finger, pointing out what he was saying. "You see the overhang. How it's tucked into that cliff. Three sides of the mountain around it. No way to see it from above. Even now, midday, it's covered in shadows. This place is as hidden as anything we've seen."

Grimm shrugged. "Luck, then."

Bradley didn't think it was luck. He had been facing Grimm the night before. The whole squad had been huddled in a circle. Talking through their search pattern. Wondering what they had missed.

Then Grimm's eyes had opened wide. Jason had recognized the expression as fear. He had looked west, straight to the monastery, miles away. And reluctantly had led them there. The soldier had wandered left and right a bit, like Grimm was still searching for the place, but Jason knew from the moment he had seen his face that he knew where it was. Jason knew he was hiding something then. And he was more convinced of it now.

"Grimm," Jason said, "I've seen this before."

"What?" he asked.

"People like you," Jason said.

Grimm pursed his lips, maybe to hide a snort. Or a chuckle.

Jason got the feeling Grimm thought there wasn't anyone else like him. So he tried to explain it in a way the man might get. "Look, man, I know the look of a person being chased by a demon. I've been in too many of these battles to not have seen it. Those people throw themselves into a fight. They're first in. Last out. Taking chances. Taking risks. As if daring someone to shoot them."

Jason paused a moment, catching Grimm's eyes. More of a hazel now. "As if daring someone to kill them."

Grimm's gaze flickered back and forth. Away from Jason's eyes, then back. His irises turning a dark hazel. "Are you saying I'm going to get someone killed?"

"That's not what I'm saying," Jason said.

"If you don't like how I operate," Grimm said, hot, "then pass me on. Like the last guy."

Interesting. Jason leaned forward, lowering his voice, but making sure he cut each word with the sharp edge of command. "You don't get the team killed. *I* get the team killed."

Grimm's eyes froze. He blinked, once, twice, maybe fighting something inside him. He set his jaw. "Sorry, Jay." The words came out rusty.

"It's fine, man," Jason told him. "We're all on edge. We all feel it. Something's different here. Something's different with this mission. So I need to figure it out, right? It's why I'm asking."

A few missions ago Patrick had gone down. Clearing a room. A shotgun had boomed as soon as Patrick entered, and the blast had taken him in the side. Even though Patrick had been wearing armor, he still had pebblelike scars along his skin today.

Grimm had hurdled Patrick almost immediately. Firing his rifle in short bursts. He stood over Patrick long enough that Jason could pull him back.

Jason had checked that room later. Each of Grimm's bursts had found a target. Four men, dead, hidden around the room. In places it would have been hard to see, behind furniture, doors. The man seemed to have a supernatural gift. Something not many others had.

"So, what, then, I'm not doing a good job?" Grimm asked.

It was Jason's turn to hold back a chuckle. Grimm was as good as anyone Jason had been around. He was naturally a fighter. He seemed to be born for it.

"That's not what I'm saying," Jason said. "I'm saying someone who lives on the edge of the fight, something happens to them. They work the edge so long they *feel* the battle around them. They *sense* what's coming. Maybe develop a premonition or two."

For a long moment, neither said anything. "I don't know what you're asking," Grimm finally said.

"I'm asking you to take a guess," Jason said. "I've been doing this a lot longer than you. I've ridden that same edge. I get feelings, too. And my gut is telling me that place is dangerous. That if we go down there, we're not coming back out."

"Then we don't go down," Grimm said. Maybe a little relieved.

Jason shook his head. "Right now I don't know what we're doing, other than a little recon. But I have to think of everything, man. Everything." Jason leaned forward, closer to Grimm, just a little, and lowered his voice. "And if you can help me keep our team alive, man, I want to hear what you think."

Grimm's eyes got wet. Which surprised Jason a little. But something inside the man was eating him alive, enough to make him emotional.

"What if it's not just a feeling?" Grimm said.

ABOUT THE AUTHOR

When Chris isn't trying to figure out how to write a bio, he spends time contemplating the fate of the universe. Probably while walking into a door jamb. He's accepted that the two go hand-in-hand.

He currently resides in Florida, though he has some Magellan in him, and loves to wander.

It is his dream to write stories that – through their telling – influence others to live a little better. Stand a little taller. Smile a little wider. Hold someone a little longer. Fiction should be the dream real life aspires to be.

Dogs are his buddies. Football is his hobby. Books are his passion.

Find out more about Chris here:

www.chrisjcranford.com

 facebook.com/chrisjcranford

X x.com/chrisjcranford

 instagram.com/chrisjcranford